D1065019

Bad
& Beautiful

Bad & Beautiful

Inside the Dazzling and Deadly World of Supermodels

IAN HALPERIN

CITADEL PRESS
Kensington Publishing Corp.
www.kensingtonbooks.com

CITADEL PRESS books are published by

Kensington Publishing Corp.
850 Third Avenue
New York, NY 10022

Copyright © 2001 Ian Halperin

All Kensington titles, imprints, and distributed lines are available at special quantity discounts for bulk purchases for sales promotions, premiums, fund-raising, educational, or institutional use. Special book excerpts or customized printings can also be created to fit specific needs. For details, write or phone the office of the Kensington special sales manager: Kensington Publishing Corp., 850 Third Avenue, New York, NY 10022, attn: Special Sales Department, phone 1-800-221-2647.

Citadel Press and the Citadel Logo are trademarks of Kensington Publishing Corp.

First Citadel printing: October 2001

10 9 8 7 6 5 4 3 2 1

Printed in the United States of America

Designed by Leonard Telesca

Library of Congress Control Number: 2001091851

ISBN 0-8065-2310-7

For Elizabeth Tilberis, the British-born editor-in-chief of *Harper's Bazaar* who died in 1999 after a long battle with ovarian cancer. Liz, who began her career as a fashion assistant in 1970 at *British Vogue*, was regarded as one of the most respected people ever in fashion. Her work has always been an inspiration to me during the years I spent researching this book. Liz was "the bright side."

For Princess Diana: your contribution to fashion will never be forgotten.

For Gia: rest in peace.

Contents

Author to Reader

Back in the late eighties, Claudia Schiffer and Cindy Crawford usurped Cheryl Tiegs and Christie Brinkley as the world's most heralded sex symbols. Along with Christy Turlington, Naomi Campbell, Elle MacPherson and Linda Evangelista, they became the legendary Big Six Supermodels. Now, Gisele Bundchen and Laetitia Casta have replaced Schiffer, Crawford, et al as the newest queens of glamour. Where once the career of glamorous supermodels like the Big Six often lasted more than five years, the modern beauty queen is lucky if her reign lasts more than a year. Top covergirls like Frederique and Rebecca Romijn Stamos struggle to stay on top because more girls than ever are lining up to be models. Despite their desire to keep up the semblance of consistency, fashion magazines and designers can't wait to present the next new hottest faces to the fashion public, creating a huge turnover of models.

"The competition has never been stiffer," says well-known Canadian modeling agent Ben Barry. "They [the models] don't last too long today because they can't take the pressure of all the models breathing down their backs. My advice to models is to save their money, no matter how successful they are. You never know when it might end."

As the seismic changes in the world's perception of beauty ripple through catwalks from Milan to New York, the fashion industry has become increasingly obsessed with discovering new faces. Model scouts relentlessly comb the streets of cities around the world, hoping to discover the face that will set the next standard for beauty and glamour. Many of today's top models are discovered in airports, shopping malls, or in a New York restaurant, like Q Model Management model Amy Clark.

Unaware of the ugly underbelly of an industry obsessed with appearances, thousands of teenage girls compete for an opportunity to join the glitzy and glamorous world of modeling, all hoping to build self confidence and handsome bank balances by being the next *Vogue* cover girl.

"I think my best moment was taking the plane when I came to New York," Brazilian supermodel Adriana Lima said in an interview on Supermodel.com. "My family was really poor, and we would never have had the money to take a plane. So that was the most exciting moment. I didn't know anything about fashion. I didn't know anything! If you asked me about *Vogue*, I would have said, 'What is *Vogue*?' "

This book was written for young women: the daughters, sisters, friends, and future trendsetters who are compelled by society and aspire to become models. Because I've witnessed so many disturbing examples of young women who were sacrificed for their fifteen minutes of fame, I wanted to expose this industry that thrives heartlessly on beauty as deception. Through the information I present, I hope to build self-confidence, fuel modeling ambitions, and ensure that any fashion experience, however long it lasts, will be an empowering one.

For those who aren't models or directly involved in the fashion industry, the circumstantial evidence I present should at least reveal how manipulative and seedy modeling can be. You don't have to be Kate Moss or Linda Evangelista to get something out of this book. In imparting these horrifying, occasionally mind-boggling tales about the abuse models are subjected to, I urge you to use this book as a valuable lesson about the outsize egos, greed, and corruption modeling breeds.

Modeling agents have become ludicrously powerful; they not only make mega deals for the girls, they also date them, sleep with them, and sometimes even marry them. When such an agent is no longer sufficiently aroused, however, or when a new look is demanded, a replacement for the girl arrives. Preying upon the models' naivete, vulnerability, dispensability, and low self-esteem, agents occasionally become opportunistic and sexually aggressive, and sometimes even provide drugs—their unconscionable behavior then isolates the girls from the rest of the fashion industry.

Parents of teenage models, many with dollar signs in their eyes, frequently ignore the dangers of an industry focused so intensely on glamour, profit, and fame. They send their daughters to fashion hotbeds like Milan without protection, either unaware or in denial of the potential hazards. Blinded by the promise of profit and fame, many trivialize the problem of sexual abuse and encourage their young daughters to pursue a modeling career without skepticism or hesitation.

Of course, it isn't fair to hold parents and agents solely accountable for the bad things that happen in modeling. The authorities, too, have been laggard in regulating the modeling industry. They react almost as if the models are confabulating stories until the media is forced to publicize avoidable tragedies, such as Kate Moss's long battle with drugs and alcohol, and the gruesome rape of a young model named Maja in the bathroom of a trendy nightclub in Milan.

Don't get me wrong. Modeling is an art form. Great models like Veruschka, Linda Evangelista, and Naomi Campbell are to fashion what Miles Davis, John Lennon, and Prince are to music: they are unique, daring, provocative, and sensitive artists. I must point out that I met many remarkable models, designers, and agents during the course of my investigation. The good people seem to be genuinely in it for the art, while the bad ones are in it for the sex and money.

Fortunately, all kinds of models are getting wise to the reality of the fashion business. Responding to the harsh stories, and recognizing the central role they play in the industry, models are using their influence to reshape the fashion world. Once objectified by the industry, media, and public, the modern model is setting a precedent for female empowerment.

Once upon a time, in the thirties and forties, models were basically just living and breathing hangers. Their sole purpose was to show expensive garb to prospective buyers in the best possible light. Not so today—a model's influence extends far beyond the realm of the few who can afford to wear designer clothes. Millions of teenage girls around the world, representing billions in current and future consumer dollars, aspire to be, or, at least, look like models. Their self-esteem and social status is often reliant upon how close they resemble the current fad or image of beauty.

Twiggy, for example, established an emaciated look in the sixties that spurred a near epidemic of anorexia nervosa, one which has remained to this day. When the curvy Gisele set fire to the fashion world in the nineties with her voluptuous look, breast implants became the rage despite the hazardous consequences. Yet the women who have the most power over how much we eat and where we spend our hard-earned dollars are often subjects of deadly abuse and manipulation at the hands of the men who manage and profit from the trends their victims set.

From the time I began researching this book back in 1997, it was clear to me that modeling is the most glamorous of industries and the most heartbreaking. To get the story-behind-the-story, I spent close to a year posing undercover as a model. I put together a model composite card and portfolio and sent it off to twenty-five modeling agencies. To my surprise, several agencies showed interest. All of a sudden I was doing test shoots for clothing ads.

In the end, my undercover stint was the perfect way to meet the models. By getting invited to many parties and industry functions, I managed to rub shoulders with the world's top supermodels, including Kate Moss, Linda Evangelista, and Laetitia Casta. I also met hundreds of lesser-known women who are working models. Above all, I learned, the modeling industry is filled with sex and drugs. Most people in the industry are not what you would call good role models. Their self-absorbed behavior is a result of fantasy all around them—fast cars, wild parties, and loads of drugs.

Before going on, it's important to differentiate between who is a supermodel and who is a regular model. Many of the women I mention are considered to be legitimate supermodels because they have gained world exposure at major fashion shows and appear regularly in the leading fashion magazines. Only the elite 5 percent of all models ever reach this high level. There are many others who consider themselves to be supermodels, with very little justification. Although they might make good money doing catalogue shoots and cosmetic ads, they haven't yet cracked the international scene. Most models have to pay their dues working their way up to supermodel status. Many of them make it by sleeping their way to the top. Others make it through hard work, like Oklahoma beauty Amber Valetta. Poised on the edge of hitting it big for several years, Valetta finally surged to the top of the supermodel rankings in 1998. Her secret was simple— hard work and power networking. In broad strokes, Valetta became famous, working in ad campaigns for Armani, Versace, and DKNY. She was also the face of Elizabeth Arden's "5th Avenue" fragrance. Magazines lined up to have her appear on the cover, including *Allure, Mademoiselle,* and *Vogue.* To be a supermodel, a model must at least meet the following requirements: she must be ranked in the top 100 models, earn at least a six-figure salary, be a regular in top fashion magazines like *Vogue, Elle,* or *Harper's Bazaar,* and appear in fashion shows all over the world for top designers like Versace, Valentino, and Chlöe.

To be a supermodel, one doesn't necessarily have to achieve celebrity status like Naomi Campbell or Cindy Crawford. In fact, most of the big name supermodels today are not well-known to the general public. A good example is the stunning, leggy supermodel Karolina Kurkova. In 2001, Kurkova appeared on fashion magazine covers six months straight, starting in February with *Vogue*. She's one of the most sought after models in the world today. Still, Kurkova can walk the streets without being noticed. Kurkova places more emphasis on honing her modeling skills than being famous. Today, the same can be said for most other supermodels, including Angela Lindvall, Carmen Kass and Caroline Ribeiro. The days are gone in which a half dozen or so supermodels get all the glory. In other words, your name doesn't have to be Kate Moss or Claudia Schiffer to be considered a supermodel.

During my investigation, I visited Los Angeles, New York, South Beach, and parts of Europe. I periodically enjoyed the perquisites of the modeling world, like fun parties, good food, and way out people. But the sleaze of the industry was disturbingly unpleasant. Specifically, Milan was certainly the sleaziest of all the cities I visited. What I found most unpardonable was the way the fashion industry in Milan imports models as young as twelve years old from all over the world, luring them into a whirlwind of drugs and nightclubs.

To help you understand better what really goes on in the modeling industry, I combine two books in one: my undercover experience as a model is paired with stories of models who have had horrifying experiences. Originally, I was just going to write about going undercover. But in the end I found it impossible to ignore the countless incidents I came across: models being raped; the large number of models addicted to drugs; an astounding number of unethical modeling agents; the many models who suffered acute depression while chasing their dreams and ended up committing suicide. Eating disorders, which I discuss later on in the book, are a big problem. Excessive dieting maims a model's life and career more than it helps them. The last chapter is about a true fashion icon, the great designer Gianni Versace. I included Versace's story because so many of the models I met, even a few years after he was gunned down, still referred to him as the nicest, most honest person ever in fashion.

I hope that by telling many of you all these tales, I can help those

of you who choose to enter the industry avoid the worst of the pitfalls. The world will always be fascinated by beauty and by "beautiful" people. If you can fit into this group in some capacity you'll
become part of an age-old tradition. It's an amazing challenge and
can have amazing benefits. It's an understatement to say that there's
massive room for improvement. And it may be the people like you
who read my account who will make it that much better for their
colleagues and the next generation to follow in their footsteps.

Acknowledgments

I am grateful for the time, the trust, and the indulgence shown me by the subjects of this book, while I do not expect they will ascribe to all my observations or conclusions. Although I don't believe it's possible to be objective, I strive for fairness and accuracy.

Before I thank those who assisted me, I must acknowledge the many brave people who spoke to me on-the-record. Most people agreed to be identified. Several asked to use pseudonyms. I would also like to acknowledge the people who requested anonymity for personal reasons, but who were nevertheless committed to the truth. Some were too frightened of reprisals from people in the modeling industry and law enforcement. These people include models, those involved in the fashion industry, friends and relatives of models, the former New York drug dealer who sold heroin to several models, and an ex-wife of one of the world's leading model agents.

Most of all I thank Bruce Bender for his unwavering support. Bruce is the only person who believed in this book from day one. This book would not have been possible without his valuable insight and direction. Bruce, it's been both a pleasure and honor to work with you.

Without Bob Shuman, this book would not be the same. "Editor" is too limiting a term to describe his contribution. Bob has been a remarkable inspiration and friend.

Esmond Choueke, the well-known journalist, was invaluable—he provided unflagging help in every phase of the book.

Deborah Jaschik has been fun to work with. Her editing, good humor, and stylistic and factual insights were much appreciated.

Thanks to Jacquie Charlton, the great Montreal writer-journalist whose work inspires me to strive for excellence.

Finally, I acknowledge the valuable contribution of my wonderful wife Jennifer Walker, the writer-photographer who contributed time, advice, and excellent research throughout the project. Her passionate commitment helped get the project off the ground.

My thanks to Lyde Moynier, Jay Sangiacomo, Shelly Canzeri, Al Newman, Ron Carrigan at Brehon, Albert Forelli, Andy Nulman, Dan and Deb Hartal, Brenda, Marv, Erin, Ryan, Daniel, and Alyssa, The Los Angeles Times library, Benny Amalfatano, Chaim Rothman, Sydney Goring, Mark Fleming, Jamie Roskies, Nick Chursinoff, Susan Varga, Arlene Bynon, Alastair Sutherland "Media Circus," Elle, Noah Lukeman, Tony Garafolo, Anthony Haden-Guest, Neil Strauss, Charlie Parker (for musical inspiration), Madonna, Matt Radz, Elliot Finkelstein, Jack Rabinovitch, Cheryl Tiegs, Dino Savano, Kate Moss, Michael Blutman, Barry Shrier, Veruschka, Tina Evans, Connie Jerome, Mike Burke-Gaffney, Bernadette Mora, Jennifer Fowler, Paula Potvin, Mark and Steve Baylin, Pierre Turgeon, Mario Tauchi, Alicia DeAngelis, Daniel Sanger, Patrick Glemaud, the British Broadcasting Corporation, Enrique Garcia, the Tate family, Martin Smith, Martin Siberok, Martin Racette, "Falcone" Salerno, Paul Taylor, Simon Anderson, Edith Harvey, Frances Rothstein, Tomaso Valente, Palo Macagnano, David Gunther, Franco Morchino, Hanz Fritz Freuberg, Lars Christensen, Alfredo Viggiano, Muriel Hagman, Yitzhak Dorfman, Alan Reed, Lou Corbett, Pino Fiorio, Dexter Low, Alain Leduc, Carl Holinger, Roberto DiSipio, Roxy Lewis, Eileen Warden, Jason Brackman, Paul Morin, Mersy, Terry Lake, Allan Katz, Robert Katz, Colleen and Dan, Timothy Boville, Rhonda Hoffman, Michelle Bisares, Richard Hartman, Lady Di, Jason Katz, Grant King, Vice Magazine, Stuart Nulman, Cordelia Jones, Brian Newman, Marcus Jeffers, Freddie Travanti, Anne Walcott, the Schaeffer Brothers, Wanda Stone, Tom Grant, Tim Perlich, Vonda Barnes, Jean-Pierre Ouesset, Arthur Cooke, Julius Grey, Alan McLean, Chris Yurkiw, Joel and Dione, John and Mara, Tony Sherman, Beverly Young, Russ Weston, Erica Pace, Joel Risberg, Gerry Wagschal, Peter Svenson, Barry, Ondine and Tasha, and Kevin Sheehan. I'd also like to thank my family, for always being there.

It is also important to acknowledge many sources for background information, including Elle, Vogue, and Vanity Fair magazines; Model: the Ugly Business of Beautiful Women by Michael Gross; the New York Post; 60 Minutes; The Learning Channel; Giant Robot Magazine; and the Washington Post.

Jennifer Walker and Hollywood Photo Agency took the photos of me going undercover as a model. The other photos were provided by Keystone Agence De Presse and Getty Images.

PART ONE

• • •

Posing Undercover

CHAPTER 1

•   •   •

L.A. Confidential

March 1999, 11:00 A.M. I arrived in Los Angeles from Montreal tired and numb, mumbling the same cheesy Bryan Adams, Shania Twain, and Faith Hill tunes I'd been listening to over and over again on my portable headset. I staggered off the jumbo jet feeling like I could have kissed the L.A.X. tarmac if I thought I'd be able to get up again afterwards. L.A is a rough place if you're not a millionaire, so I had to shore up my strength.

I came up with the idea for this book after my seventeen-year-old relative complained that he had been sexually abused by the male agent who'd recruited him to be a model while in Milan. My relative wisely cut his experience short after only two weeks. When he arrived back in Montreal, he told me that the Milan agent had been more interested in trying to get him into bed than in helping his modeling career. The agent took him to parties, plied him with alcohol, and offered him drugs so he could try to take advantage of him.

After hearing my relative's story, I made several phone calls to friends in the entertainment business and started digging up information about the modeling industry. "It's a terrible world," a friend who works at Warner Brothers Music told me. "If you think the music business is corrupt, it's nothing compared to the modeling business. Every day models are drugged, raped, and sometimes killed. It's a very shady business."

My memories of previous trips to L.A. are not of beach parties, sumptuous Hollywood suites, and fancy restaurants, but of the seedy hotels where I stayed while doing research for a book about the late grunge icon Kurt Cobain. This time, however, I wouldn't be roughing it. Thanks to Susan Varga, an L.A. television journalist who wanted to interview me for her new show *VH1 Confidential*, I had a decent pied-à-terre reserved at the legendary Sportsman's Lodge Hotel, home to many a Beverly Hills 90210 location shoot.

As I left the L.A.X terminal to pick up my rented car, I noticed that the scenery was pretty much the same as the last time. Big limousines with smoked glass windows purred into the parking lot to pick up the privileged. Several feet away, a few not so privileged were trying to bum money off travelers who'd just arrived.

It was hot and muggy in L.A. and "avoid" was the operative word. Avoid traffic, avoid the heat, avoid panhandlers, avoid being mugged, avoid reality. Yet avoiding was impossible. Traffic on the 105 Freeway was bumper to bumper. In L.A., morning, noon, or night, it's the usual—heavy traffic, thirty- to forty-minute delays. The radio in my white, economy class Cavalier—rented from Enterprise at L.A.X for $149 a week, sans air conditioner—blared the chorus of Tupac Shakur's "Changes."

Within a few minutes, I was trying to make up for time lost to traffic delays like a native Angelino. In L.A., there are hazards; during my last visit, I read a story in the *Los Angeles Times* about a man shooting another driver in the back of the head after he cut him off on the freeway. I always think back to that incident when I get frustrated in an L.A. traffic jam, and wonder if my windows would protect me from being the next tourist-victim of California road rage.

From the moment I arrived, I knew this trip would be different. I had brought some photos previously taken of me in Montreal and New York, a model's composite card, and designer clothes. I had spent about $1,000 to prepare for this assignment. I was going undercover as a model.

Oddly, when I began my research on the industry as a journalist, doors formerly open to me were mysteriously slammed shut. I decided that the best way to get the real story behind the modeling industry was to go undercover and pose as a model. Los Angeles was my third stop undercover. I had already submitted my portfolio in New York and Miami. So far, I had not received any concrete offers. Most model agents had rejected me, telling me that I was too short at 5"11', or that I didn't have "the right look"—whatever that is. One agent said I was wasting my time because I didn't have the look of a Tyson Beckford or a Marcus Schenkenberg, while another had refused me because I looked "too Jewish." Once I arrived in L.A., however, my luck changed. I was signed by several agents, and by the time I left town a few weeks later I was booked to do some test shoots wearing FUBU, a New York clothing company very popular in America's black community.

I wondered if the California health and fitness craze had impacted on the partying attitudes of L.A. models. As I cruised down Sunset Boulevard on my way from L.A.X. to my first appointment at the Look Modeling Agency, I passed several of L.A.'s hottest rock clubs: the House of Blues, the Viper Room, and the Whisky A Go-Go, whose marquee advertised a special performance by Nancy Sinatra. I was reminded of how one night in a club in New York's East Village, I watched as three supermodels rolled a joint with a one hundred dollar bill not five feet away from me. The three models, who had been drinking champagne all night, snorted several lines of cocaine in full view of anyone who was looking their way. "Scenes like this happen all the time," the club's bartender told me. "A lot of models hang out here. I've seen them take ecstasy, shoot up smack, and have sex in the bathroom. Models are party animals. They live like there's no tomorrow."

Many of the models I met confided that they had been born with silver spoons in their mouths and had never known financial struggle. "That's why they party so hard during their careers," says New York sociologist and pop culture critic Earle Weston. "They don't care about saving money because their daddies will support them when their careers are over. So they blow all their earnings on drugs and alcohol. It's a disease. They don't realize that they're destroying their bodies. No amount of money can fix the damage they do to themselves."

Arriving at the Look Model Agency at 8490 West Sunset Boulevard, I found the waiting room walls plastered with photographs of models all smiling down at me. I smiled back self-consciously. Dozens of composite cards, listing the models' specific measurements, were on a tray next to me. I tried to look casual as I perused the intimate details of the same women most men only get to fantasize about. I noticed that one model, Greta Corey, stated that she modeled for *Esquire* and for the 1998 *Sports Illustrated* swimsuit issue. Another model, Jennifer Howard, appeared in a recent Hole video and was a regular on the *Dr. Gene Scott* show.

After a few minutes, a tall, elegant woman with a thick foreign accent greeted me. She introduced herself as Susanne Lundin, a former model who now works as a modeling agent. Susanne had gained a few pounds since modeling, but her well-preserved beauty was still

apparent. Our meeting didn't get off to a roaring start. After I introduced myself, Lundin abruptly informed me that she could spare
only five minutes for me before her next appointment. "Make it
fast," Lundin said, sounding for all the world like Eva Gabor. "I'm
very busy today. What can I do for you?" I explained that I was
looking for work as a model and that I needed an agent. "You look
more like a singer than a model," Lundin said, as she examined my
resume. "But I never discard anybody. I've seen many people succeed
in this business who you'd think would be the least likely to, because
they don't look like your average model. I'll represent you. You seem
like you're willing to work hard." Lundin handed me an application
and asked me to fill it out.

I had long ago decided that my undercover alias would be "Alfred
E. Newman," the name of the *MAD Magazine* character. Incredibly,
not one agent realized whose name I was using; perhaps they'd seen
it all and just didn't care anymore.

"Alfred, leave me your photos and I will call you if anything
comes up." Lundin said. "There might be some work for you doing
commercials. I'll check into it." On my way out I noticed a tall,
brown-haired model coming toward the Look office. I stopped to
ask if she'd mind telling me a bit about Look, as I was new to modeling and needed an agent. "Not at all," the model replied.

"They're not bad, but it's difficult to find a good agent in this
town. No matter who represents you, you'll always run into problems. My last agent said he would only get me work if I agreed to
sleep with him. I told him where to go. Look is a good agency because they have women running it. For a female model, it helps eliminate the risk of being sexually abused. The key to finding a good
agent is to make sure that the agent doesn't have dozens of other
clients. If they do, it's likely they won't have enough time to devote to
your career."

Mulling over those pearls of wisdom, I cruised along Ventura
Drive until my next stop at the World Modeling Agency on Van
Nuys Boulevard. I was shocked by what I saw going on inside. It was
as if you had to have breast implants and dyed blond hair to feel
comfortable there. When I entered, I thought maybe I had mistaken
this agency for a strip club. Sleaze filled the room. The World
Modeling Agency advertises for models in local papers, but when I
walked into the office, it reminded me of central casting for a porno
flick. Pictures of naked women and men adorned the walls, floor to

ceiling. The room was filled with women who looked more like strippers and prostitutes than models.

As I waited for my turn, a blonde model seated next to me confided that she did hardcore porno films and poses nude in magazines. "I used to be a serious model," she said, "but it doesn't pay nearly as much. I've managed to support two children, own a house and sports car by doing this." I was understandably nervous by the time the woman behind the front desk shouted, "Alfred E. Newman, you're next."

The interview barely lasted two minutes. The first question the World Modeling agent asked me was how much experience I'd had posing nude. "None," I replied. "Are you willing to pose nude?" she asked. When I told her no she told me that she would not be able to represent me.

As I made a hasty exit, I couldn't help but feel sorry for all the young models I passed in the waiting room, all so willing to sacrifice their bodies to make a buck. "It's subtle prostitution," model Nancy Jackson told me outside. "But it's a job. At least agencies like this are honest with their models. You know what you're getting into. The so-called legitimate agencies pretend to be concerned about fashion. But they're just as bad or worse. I was once with one. Like so many other models I had a bad experience. My agent beat me up, raped me, and stole all my money. It may sound strange, but I feel safer here."

I got news of my first paid modeling contract when I arrived back at my hotel, the Sportsman's Lodge, that afternoon. A photo editor for a Canadian Magazine called *Between the Cracks* had called to request that I pose in an outdoorsy, cold weather shot the next day. One thing led to another and within a week, I was posing in shoots for FUBU and Willie Esco. What had started as an investigative technique had blurred into a very real and very lucrative job.

I was nervous at first, but by the end of my first shoot, I was into the whole scene and looking forward to the next. I was a few dollars richer and my ego had been stroked more than I care to admit.

CHAPTER 2

• • •

Photog Prolix

Four days after I arrived in Los Angeles, I saw an ad for new models placed by a photographer who was said to have photographed many of the world's top models, including Elle MacPherson and Gisele Bundchen. I promptly called and left a message, explaining that I wanted to get some photos done for my portfolio. Several hours later I received a call back, and was told the shoot would cost $350 an hour. Although it was a bit more expensive than the going rate, I booked the shoot for that Friday afternoon. I was determined to hook up with people who had direct contact with the key players in the modeling business.

Carl Shea began his professional life at the age of sixteen, when he freelanced as a photographer for several fashion magazines. At thirty-two, Shea's success is evidenced by his home-studio, a large, art deco loft with shiny wood floors and an antique sink in the heart of Hollywood. On the walls, the smiling faces of Gisele, Kate Hudson, and Jodie Kidd share space with many undiscovered beauties.

When I arrived at his studio, the overtly gay Shea was capped in an orange beret. He greeted me with his sweetly brutal charm and an irritating nasal voice that would take a bit of getting used to. Looking me over with incandescent blue eyes, he asked, "Boy, do you want to be an actor or a model?" When I replied that I wanted to be a model, he mulled it over for a bit before commenting that I was far from the worst material that'd showed up at his door with modeling ambitions. "You're not runway material," he said, as he lit up a joint. "But I can see your face being used somewhere. Maybe in some magazines. You'll have fun working with me today. Let's get started."

As Shea got me accustomed to his studio, he offered me some of his joint. His weed was powerful. After a couple of tokes I was completely buzzed. He really warmed up to me after I told him I was from Canada. "How does a nice Canadian boy like you end up in the grungy model life of L.A.?" he asked. I played dumb and asked him to elaborate. "This business is not for everyone," he said. "I've seen so many people like you, coming here for the big dream. Let me tell you, no matter how good you look, this business can eat you alive. A model I've been shooting for years recently got arrested for smuggling heroin from China in condoms pushed up her rectum. Nothing that happens in this business shocks me any-more."

At the beginning of our session, Shea advised me to ignore the camera and pretend that I was at some way-out party. He told me not to feel intimidated and to express myself freely. Coupled with his weed, his words put me completely at ease. In fact, I found posing for Shea to be a truly artistic, erotic, and spiritual experience. I appreciated his candor and offbeat humor. While taking my headshots, he told me to imagine watching the Queen Mother and her twenty-one-year-old boy toy having sex. I burst into laughter at the thought, while his fancy Nikon camera clicked away.

After more than an hour of posing, Shea called it a wrap. He said that he would contact me in a couple of days to see the proofs. "You were better than I thought you'd be," he said. "Good job." I was re-lieved.

As I was leaving, Shea asked if I'd be interested in joining him for dinner that night. "Do you usually take your clients out for dinner after you photograph them the first time?" I asked. "No, not really," he replied. "But since you're new in town I wouldn't mind pointing out some of the do's and don'ts of being a model in this town."

Although I wasn't sure what his real motive was, I accepted Shea's invitation. Since he'd already spoken very openly about his business and all the famous models he'd worked with, I knew I could get some great leads from him.

Later that night we dined at a cozy French restaurant around the corner from the Troubadour Club on Santa Monica Boulevard. Shea was in fine form. He ordered expensive white wine and hors d'oeuvres.

At one point he started speaking French to the waiter, unaware that, being from Montreal, I understood every word he said. "My friend comes from Canada. Don't you think he's cute?" he asked the waiter in French. It became frightfully clear to me that Shea's hidden agenda involved getting a piece of my ass before the evening ended. I played along with him anyway, hoping to get some good information. It worked splendidly. Twenty minutes into our date, Shea started opening up.

When I asked Shea what his long-term goal was, I hit a sour note. He explained that he was tired of being in a business that he thought was extremely seedy. No matter the occasion, no matter the circumstance, Shea said that there always seemed to be an underlying dark side to the modeling industry. He blamed the grisly style of the fashion industry for his bouts with severe depression. "It is just too likely that if you stay in this business as long as I have, you might end up trying to commit suicide."

I pressed Shea to elaborate, but he said he preferred to skip the gory details. Yet as soon as I moved on to another subject, he returned to his thoughts on modeling. "If you stay in this business as long as I have, you'll end up feeling pretty negative," he said. "So many of the people I've worked with over the years are now dead because of drugs, suicide, or murder. I always wonder why anyone would want to be in this business in the first place. When guys like you call me to do their photos, I often feel sorry for them. They have no idea what they're getting themselves into."

Shea told alarming stories about some of the people he'd met during his career as a fashion photographer. One of his favorite models to photograph, a sixteen-year-old brunette from Tacoma, Washington, bought methadone that other addicts spit into bottles and eventually died of AIDS. "She came to L.A. with such an innocent look," Shea recalled. "But as the weeks passed I noticed a drastic change in her. She began to look pale, almost as if she hadn't slept in weeks. I tried to confront her but it was already too late. The creeps who run this business had already gotten to her. Her agent, a man in his early forties, was having sex with her and supplying her with drugs. There was nothing I could do. She was already on her way to becoming the next victim."

Shea knew his cold-eyed rationality would satisfy neither the moralists nor the media who report the sordid, junkie glamour to armchair fashionistas. He said that he deals with it by taking care of himself first. "If I'd spent all my time trying to protect models, I wouldn't have any time to make a living as a photographer," he said. "I feel helpless when I see how some of the models get sucked into the sex and drugs. But if I don't mind my own business, I won't get work. It's that easy to get blacklisted."

CHAPTER 3

• • •

The Ruby

After dinner, I asked Carl Shea to take me to a club where the models hang out. I told him I was eager to meet more people in the business. Shea took me to a trendy club called The Ruby, located in the heart of Hollywood at La Brea Avenue and Hollywood Boulevard. Inside, there were party animals slinking in and out of different doorways. It was just past 11:30 P.M., and the three large dance floors were jam-packed.

As we walked around the club, Shea was recognized and greeted warmly by several people. Carmen, a teenage model with a thick Southern drawl, gave Shea a big hug and planted a kiss on both of my cheeks after introducing herself. "Where you from?" she asked. "Montreal," I answered. "That's in Canada. I love Canadians," she said. Carmen, who seemed to be in a party mood, was wearing a revealing white see-through blouse and a short skirt. Her nipples stood out like sore thumbs.

Carmen joined us for a drink in a side lounge where we found a comfortable red-velvet bench seat to plunk down on. Shea ordered a round of martinis. As the conversation evolved, Carmen confirmed my worst fears about modeling. Though I had found her witty and intelligent, it quickly became clear that since her recent arrival in L.A., Carmen had developed nightmarish drug habits. Several minutes into the conversation she asked if we wanted to join her in a line of coke. I politely declined while Carmen withdrew some cocaine from a small makeup kit in her purse.

Carmen and Shea each did a line. Shea seemed a bit bored, like he had done this many times before, and more lines of coke certainly wouldn't aid in his escape from disenchantment and self-contempt. "You Canadians are too innocent," Carmen said to me. "This is L.A. You've got to have fun here."

Fueled by cocaine, Carmen regaled us with tales of her L.A. modeling experience, stories as frightening and heartless as any made-for-TV horror movie. Only two months after she arrived in L.A., Carmen found herself living happily in Santa Monica with her agent (by whom she had become pregnant a month later). At first she considered having the baby, but changed her mind after she found out her agent was having affairs with several other young models.

"I moved out and got an abortion because he was a total sleaze," Carmen said. "He became possessive and violent when other guys looked at me. He treated me as a possession, trying to keep me home all day to spread my legs for him whenever he was horny. I knew he was cheating on me because he'd call and say he had to work late. When he came home he'd reek of booze and sex. He was a complete squirrel!"

Carmen said that after the relationship ended, she vowed never to fall in love again, especially with someone in the industry. "I've seen how so many of the young girls who come here wind up getting screwed," she said. "Before I came here, I just wanted to be a model like Cindy Crawford and Kate Moss. There's so much that goes along with the package. This business is filled with creeps who are only in it to fuck as many girls as possible."

Bobbing her head to the beat of The Ruby's house music, Carmen reached into her purse for more coke. This time Shea declined. "This is what keeps me going," she said. "Without escape your mind can go crazy here. This makes me feel so good. Sure you don't want some?" Again, I said no.

Shea started poking fun at the people in the club. He called them intolerant, reactionary, and stupid. "They're a bit of a joke," he said. "I'm sure most of them have no idea why they're really here. They all think they're important but really they're just ignorant pieces of shit."

Another model soon approached Shea and started making small talk. It was now very clear that Shea was indeed a dandy, a well-entrenched man about town. Everybody who looked like a model recognized him. "Carl is the man," Carmen said. "Everybody knows him. He's a real player. He's one of the very few nice guys in the business. He's one of the only people I've met in L.A. who I feel comfortable being around."

Carmen said Shea's greatest talent is making models feel at ease, which brings out the most in them at photo shoots. She said she knew of models with the slightest bit of talent who managed to get work because of Shea's ability to make them look good. "I recommended a model friend to Carl who was having trouble getting jobs," Carmen said. "As soon as she did a shoot with Carl, things started happening for her. Within a month she landed an ad in *Harper's Bazaar*. If not for Carl, she would have had to go home because she was running out of cash."

Although Carmen was as high as a kite, she was quite comfortable pouring out her heart and soul to me. She confided that she cared for no one, as her heart now belonged to cocaine and heroin. Calling it a "Catch 22," Carmen said she now needed to work in order to buy heroin, and she needed heroin in order to work. As sad as her story is, Carmen didn't appear to be unhealthy and was one of the nicest models I met during my undercover adventures. At the end of the evening she gave me her number and made me promise to keep in touch.

"If there's anything I can do for you, please call," she said as she got into a cab outside of The Ruby. "Ciao."

Meanwhile, Shea tried to get me to go back to his apartment for a nightcap. When I told him that I was straight, Shea told me not to worry. "I think you're cute but it's pretty obvious that you're straight," he said. I told him that I was too tired to keep the party going. He told me to call him in the morning, and we went our separate ways.

CHAPTER 4

• • •

Party to Hell

A few days later I received a voice message from Carmen inviting me to a party at her apartment. She said that many of her model friends would be there.

I remember it as a scene right out of the Peter Sellers movie *The Party*. People dressed in sixties-style flowery clothes were sitting around drinking and smoking joints. Beck's "Mutations" album was playing in the background. Carmen, her breath reeking of Johnnie Walker, greeted me with a big hug and kiss. She took me around the room, introducing me to each one of her friends as "My buddy from Canada."

I sat down next to Amanda Reilly, a tall, lanky seventeen-year-old from Boston who had been in L.A. for the past four months doing test shoots. Articulate and strong-minded, she described her L.A. experience as "wild." "It has changed my life completely," she said. "One day it can be the most fun and you feel like you're on top of the world. The next is a heartbreak and you're hanging on by a thread."

Amanda told me that within a few months, she had gone through at least $35,000 chasing the dream. She ran up thousands of dollars of credit card debt and had yet to land a solid contract. She did develop a fascination for partying and drugs. While smoking a joint, Amanda admitted that she'd experimented with ecstasy and other designer drugs. "I love getting completely wasted," she said. "If I didn't, I don't think I'd be able to last out here. Everyone I meet in this business seems to depend on drugs. I got into it because I didn't want to feel like the oddball, or like I'm missing out on something."

Like many other models, Amanda's new lifestyle is a contradiction to her upbringing. Most of the models I met were from solid middle to upper income families. However, once they got out on their own, they were easily drawn into the low life.

"I'm fascinated by the wild and crazy elements of this business," Amanda said. "It's so different from the life I led before. In Boston, I played everything by the book. I practically lived to please my family. I got good grades and played life straight. Here I feel as if I don't have any responsibilities. I'm not being watched or held accountable to anyone but myself. I go through life here living day by day, not knowing what awaits me. For now, I prefer living life on the edge."

Another model, Mira, soon joined our conversation. She spoke about some of the hottest parties she'd attended in town where she'd mingled with the likes of Kate Moss and Naomi Campbell. "Naomi's a party animal," Mira confided. "I've been to a couple of penthouse parties that she attended and her glass was never empty. She's very nice, and she loves to have a good time. I once was alone in a bathroom with her and couldn't help but tell her how gorgeous she is. I actually got turned on. It was so embarrassing. I felt like kissing her all over. But I was too shy. It's too bad because if I ever get the chance to be alone with her again, I'd probably start kissing her madly and lick her all over. She turns me on more than anyone or anything in the world."

Mira, who is 5 feet 11 inches, weighs around 115 pounds, and has wavy, dirty blonde hair, was clearly an insatiable partier. A self-described Hollywood junkie, she was sweet and funny, and spoke openly about her experiences. She attributed part of her success to pandering to corrupt agents. "Let's say that I've been forced to do some things that I didn't want to do," Mira said. "No matter what an agent says and how innocent he looks, when he meets a model, he wants to fuck her. Any man who goes into this business wants to fuck lots of women, unless he's gay." Mira emphatically credited the majority of her success to fashion's ugly networking rituals: doing lots of drugs with the right people, sleeping with people who know the right people, and partying seven nights a week with her colleagues. "This business is not for prudes," she said. "Most of the successful models have fucked their way to the top."

Mira boasted about having a photo shoot the next morning for a magazine ad. "I'll probably show up completely wrecked," she said. "I always do. But they don't care. As long as I look pretty and keep to myself, I'll be fine. Many times other people on the crew are high.

I'll probably smoke a joint with the photographer before we start shooting."

Mira admitted that she tried to clean up her act six months ago, but had a major relapse after a friend of hers, another model, had died from injecting contaminated heroin. "I thought I could manage one drug binge and stop in memory of him. But the day after, I was doing coke and smoking pot, and couldn't stop again."

Mira believed that her extraordinary experiences as a model in L.A. had led to emotional paralysis—and to her addiction. Emotional duress had caused her to suffer from several skin disorders, including dryness and hyper-pigmentation. She'd tried several stress reduction methods to no avail. In the past month she claimed to have lost at least three jobs due to her skin irritations. "I take drugs to escape," she said. "My body has been falling apart. I look so awful compared to when I first arrived here. It's not an easy life. I need drugs to feel the way I want to feel. This business can be pretty shitty. You need to escape."

Mira practically drowned out her industry analysis with dense accounts of insignificant events that not even the most dedicated modeling aficionado would want to hear. Practically dropping a name with each breath, she described how she'd once bummed a cigarette off of Kate Moss outside a pizza parlor, and how she had seen Claudia Schiffer making out with a strange man near the bathroom of a trendy Beverly Hills restaurant. She accused the authorities of being in the dark about what really goes on in the modeling industry, and the extent to which drugs and sex are abused. "If they knew, we'd all be behind bars," Mira said.

In the fashion industry, there are many opportunities for self-destruction, the most popular being drugs. Like Carmen and Mira, Rose was brought up in a respectable and loving family. She made no excuses for her sinister involvement with hard drugs. She claimed that before she came to L.A., she never thought that drugs would touch her life, let alone control it. But in the world of fashion it can and does happen to almost everyone. Rose, sitting on a yellow pillow on the floor, told me that she was a straight A student when she was discovered by an L.A. model scout while waiting for a bus. She had never before considered modeling.

"He convinced me to come to L.A. to do some test shooting," Rose said. "My parents were skeptical, but I couldn't refuse. I felt like I'd be living the life that every teenage girl in the world only dreams about."

While reflecting on her experiences as a model, Rose made an important distinction between "work" and "play." She told me that work is the primary focus, the only way one can last more than a couple of months. Play, she said, is the key ingredient to getting the work.

"If you don't play you won't meet the right people," said Rose. "Most of the important contacts I made, I made at parties. I smoked joints and got wasted with some important people, people I never imagined I'd party with. It's the best way to network. A lot of the men want sex. I flirt a lot to get them interested in me and I've gone on a few dates with men old enough to be my dad, but that's it. It stops there. I don't go home with them. I know many models who sleep around. They try to fuck their way to the top. I don't mind playing the game and I love to party, but it completely grosses me out to even think about sleeping with most of the men in the business. They're all older, bald, fat, and disgusting. Most of them are married and just want to cheat on their wives."

Something of value emerged from Carmen's party. Before the night was over, I'd met a middle-aged man who told me he was once one of the biggest model scouts in the world. He claimed to have been blacklisted because he refused to cover up for a powerful agent friend who'd been accused of sexually abusing a teenage model. "He asked me to lie for him and I wouldn't do it," the man told me. "My phone stopped ringing. The agent vowed to put me out of business. And he did. He was close to all the key players in the business. I haven't had work in more than eight months. If you don't do whatever the power brokers say, you will not work no matter how talented you are."

He knew all the big names—Naomi, Cindy, Claudia, Elle, et al—and I told him I was interested in hearing his story in more detail. Eager to find out how this stocky, middle-aged man, who looked like a nine-to-five businessman, had become a top model scout, we agreed to meet for lunch the next day.

CHAPTER 5

• • •

Confessions of a Model Scout

The Beverly Hill Cafe on La Cienega Boulevard was jam-packed. Above the din, you could hear hamburgers sizzling on the grill in the kitchen. I was lucky enough to get the last table available, and managed to avoid a twenty minute wait. I must confess that I had a pounding hangover from the party the night before. I really didn't feel like getting out of bed, and wondered how the models did it. Yet there was no way in hell I'd have missed this opportunity. If the model scout's story was credible, I would at the very least be able to get all kinds of new leads.

He was a half hour late. Meanwhile, I had struck up a conversation with a waitress. She told me that all kinds of famous people frequented the cafe, including Tom Cruise, Dustin Hoffman, Farrah Fawcett, and Jay Leno. I asked her if she had ever served any supermodels. "Yeah, the tall blonde who used to be married to Mick Jagger has been in here a couple of times," she replied. "She's awesome. She's been in here with her kids and she's always polite and fun." I asked the waitress if Jerry Hall is as pretty in real life. "Not really," she replied. "I've seen her on some of her very bad days. If not for her height, you might not even think she's a model. A lot of these beautiful actresses in person look nothing like they do on TV."

When my source finally arrived, he greeted me with the familiar L.A. "sorry I'm late" mantra. He said that another meeting had run late. "Finally, things might be opening up again for me," he said, "I've just interviewed for a job at another agency. It would be stupid to rock the boat now." Insisting that I wouldn't use his real name in publication, we agreed that he'd be referred to as "Tony."

19

Tony painted a portrait of the modeling industry that was sad, dramatic, and sordid at best. He said that during his years working for several top agencies, including Elite, he'd heard countless stories of models being deceived and sexually abused. He elaborated on the psychological price models pay for their ambitions in the end, stressing that modeling-related crimes are not motivated by money, as there's plenty of money associated with the industry. Crime in modeling, Tony stressed, is motivated by the pleasures of drugs and sex with the women who are renowned objects of desire.

"No matter how much money they make, by the time their careers are over, most of them have put it all up their nose," he said. "Today they're on top of the world and tomorrow nobody wants to talk to them. It's cruel shit. Nobody prepares them for what happens at the end."

I asked Tony to give specific examples. He told me about an incident involving a fifteen-year-old German model whom he'd discovered on the streets of Hamburg in early 1999. She came to America searching for fame and fortune but ended up a big heroin junkie. The day after she was found dead in her Studio City apartment, Tony went to church and confessed.

"In a way I felt responsible for bringing her here and for letting her fall into the wrong hands," he said. "I couldn't prevent what went on because my job was limited to discovering new talent. But I felt guilty anyway, because if not for me, she'd be alive and with her parents in Hamburg today. When I first met her, she was just an innocent kid from a very good family. I never thought she would get messed up. She seemed to have her feet planted firmly on the ground. But I've seen it happen so many times, all the time! Innocent, young kids come here and get messed up faster than the hair grows on your head."

Tony said that despite all the horror stories of sexual abuse, greed, and deadly addiction, people still find the modeling industry alluring. "Many people down the line profit if a model is successful," he said. "The profits are so huge that they boggle the mind. To make matters worse, the civil rights of models are ignored while sleazy agents avoid due process. I know several people in law enforcement in L.A. and New York who have admitted that they turn a blind eye to what goes on in fashion because they just don't have the time. They're too busy chasing hookers and drug dealers. Yet when you think about it carefully, there are plenty of hookers and drug dealers infiltrating the modeling business. Don't be as naive to think that none of these girls sleep around for extra cash. I've known many models who end up desperate for cash and have no choice but to turn tricks."

Tony then started to tell me some pretty wild stories about many of the top supermodels. He recalled getting drunk one night with Cheryl Tiegs at a friend's Manhattan loft. He said that Tiegs was too tipsy to go home on her own, so he offered her a ride. On the way, he got caught for speeding. "The cop recognized her and asked her for an autograph," Tony said. "Luckily he didn't give me a breathalyzer or we both would have spent the night in jail. The cop was so impressed to meet her that he let us go with a warning."

Tony also was close to Kate Moss. He aptly labeled Moss as "fashion's wild child." "Kate lives every second as if it's going to be her last," he said. "I've never met anyone in my life who lives so on the edge. She's had her share of problems over the years. It's too bad, because Kate is one of the best in the business. But like so many others, she was led astray by the many undesirables who run the business."

Tony is fascinated by the extent to which the agonies of models can be attributed to drugs. "It was rare for me to meet a model who would stay a Miss Goody Two Shoes," he said. "Once they arrive here, they almost feel an obligation to party. Otherwise, people will look at them as if they're strange."

According to Tony, very little can be done about it as long as modeling agents like Jean-Luc Brunel and Claude Haddad remain at the forefront of the modeling business. For years, Brunel and Haddad have directed or been associated with some of the biggest agencies in the world, including Karins and Elite. Both men have had several allegations of sexual abuse levied at them by disgruntled models. Tony says that unless the industry is run by new people, parents should hide their daughters.

To give more substance to his pessimistic outlook, Tony told me that almost all model agents he's worked with have admitted to having sexually abused their models. "I know these guys better than I know my father," he said. "They all want to fuck lots of girls. They brag about how many girls they sleep with. A friend of mine at Elite once told me that he slept with more than two dozen young models during a one week casting call in Paris. And that's far from being the worst story I've heard."

Tony vehemently expressed the need for an independent watchdog body or government intervention program to regulate the industry. "Until someone holds these gross abusers accountable, the nightmare will continue," Tony said. "The models experience the devastating effects of these experiences long after they've left the scene. It's not easy to tell your parents that you were raped while being away. Many models keep the horror stories to themselves and try to go on like normal. It's not an easy situation. You can fall apart so easily."

CHAPTER 6

• • •

Wanted—A Big Schnoz

Carl Shea left a message that he had a lead for a magazine ad for me. "They need someone who's a cross between Ben Stiller and Dustin Hoffman," Shea said. "It's for a men's cologne ad." In other words, what Shea really needed was a middle-aged Jewish male with black hair and a big schnoz. When I called Shea back, he told me he had already booked an audition for me. He gave me the time and address and told me to ask for Diane Weston, a close personal friend of his. "In this business it's all about who you know and being in the right place at the right time," Shea said.

When I arrived at Weston's office, a sunny top-floor office across the street from Fox Studios, there were seven other candidates in the waiting room. I couldn't help but notice how alike we all looked. While we waited our turn, I struck up a conversation with another model who introduced himself as Al Kates. Kates told me that it had been more than two years since he'd left Detroit to pursue fame and fortune in L.A. He told me that he'd had to work as a waiter on the side to make ends meet. "I've been in a few ads here and there but I just can't seem to get the big break," Kates told me. "This business is ruthless. If you make it, you make it big. If you don't make it, you're going to eat tuna out of a can for the rest of your life. That's just how it is in this business."

I was the sixth person to be called. Weston was dressed casually, donning a designer T-shirt, jeans, and a hip pair of sneakers. She was holding a couple of photos of me that Shea had sent her. "Not bad," she said. She wanted me to play up the fact that I was Canadian and was new in town. "When you're new it usually works to your advantage," she said. "People in the business are always looking to discover someone new."

Weston was the only agent who caught on to my modeling pseudonym. "Alfred E. Newman—is that your real name?" she asked with a loud giggle. "You have the same name as the *Mad* character. What a riot."

Weston seemed to have a keen eye for finding new, raw talent. Her walls were plastered with composite cards of the models she represented. She told me that several of her clients had been discovered while doing ads. "Some of my models ended up in Hollywood films and TV shows," she said. "I try to provide a good launching pad."

Weston told me straight out that I wasn't exactly what she was looking for. "You're too thin," she said. "We need someone a bit more rugged. Someone who all men can relate to, from doctors and lawyers to construction workers."

On my way out I noticed a tall woman coming out of a modeling agency across the hall. She was definitely a model. In the elevator, I started talking to her. In a thick French accent, she introduced herself as Corine Porte from the South of France. She told me that she had been in L.A. for only three weeks. It turned out that she was a well-known model in France who'd decided to try working in L.A. to advance her career. "I've done everything I can in my own country. I'm now twenty years old, which is already old for a model. If I don't try now, in a year it will be too late. I want to put France on the modeling map the same way Claudia Schiffer did for Germany."

I asked Porte if she had time to go for a coffee. She said that her next appointment was in two hours so she had some time to kill. At a Starbuck's coffee shop, I told Porte that I'd come to L.A. hoping to get some work as a model or actor. I asked her for advice, telling her that I was new to the business. "You look more like an actor," she said. "But I'll be glad to tell you a few things."

Porte made explicit the stark reality of the modeling business. She admitted to me that her longtime agent tried to blackmail her the day before she left. It was his last desperate attempt to prevent her from ending their six-year relationship. "He told me that if I left he was going to tell my parents that I was sleeping around and doing drugs," Porte said. "He also told me that he would make sure that I would never work again if I came back to France."

"He tried to possess me. During our years together, I partied with him regularly but never slept with him. I always knew he was bad, but I kept quiet because I needed to get jobs. Whenever I would talk to another guy he'd get jealous. Even though there never was anything between us, he treated me as if I was his girlfriend. He gave me lots of gifts and extra money. I'm not saying that I'm completely innocent myself, because I certainly flirted with him to get the best assignments from him. I'm not stupid. I treated him like a king but my plan was to make sure I never slept with him. If I'd have slept with him, he would have moved on to the next pretty girl. That's how all the agents are in this business. They don't stop until they get what they want. No matter how high the price is."

Porte described the modeling business as a "legalized form of crime." She admitted that for almost every model she's ever met that the pursuit of happiness and the escape from misery is as much a part of the business as anything else. The popularity of modeling may still be growing, but the popularity of leaving the business is growing faster, Porte said. "If I would have known it would be this crazy, I would have stayed in school," she confided. "Now it's too late. I have no choice but to continue. It's the only thing I know how to do to make a decent living. Most models I've worked with only last in the business a year or two. They give up because they see how crazy it all is."

Porte's analysis is not launched in the abstract, but is based on her own experiences over the years. To a far greater extent than in America, she said, modeling in Europe is more of an art form. "In France, you have to be good to break into the business," she said. "Here in America it's so different. At every party I go to, all the models are doing a lot of hard drugs. They sleep with their agents and all of a sudden they've become nothing more than glorified prostitutes. Back home, some of the same things go on, but at least we show some class. The other night at a rehearsal for a fashion show, I saw a young model, who was clearly drunk, vomiting backstage. Nobody said anything or tried to help her. It was as if nobody cared, as if it was common for this to go on. In France, this would have caused a major scene."

Before leaving, Porte made it clear that her bleak observations did not mean to imply that everyone in the modeling business is screwed up. She gave me an example of an agent in Milan she knew who condemned his colleagues' nefarious deeds. She said that when he'd hear about a girl being mistreated or sexually abused, he would call the police. "The problem is that the police are not always too interested," Porte said. "A lot of the top fashion people are close to the police, and the police understand it's expected to look the other way. I don't know why nobody is interested in doing anything to clean up this business. It's very strange."

Porte, a pragmatist, argued that modeling is here to stay, no matter how corrupt the business is. "Do you think that someone will just come in and shut down what's going on?" she asked. "This is a big business and people want to protect their interests. There's a lot of money to be made and until people put their greed aside, there's nothing anyone can do. It's the same in the tobacco and alcohol industry—people know it's corrupt and not good for you, but they continue to support it anyway."

CHAPTER 7

• • •

Venice Ho House

As I scrambled to get the inside scoop on the L.A. fashion scene, I ran into a series of bad luck. Then, my investigation came to a standstill. I'd wrangled an invitation to a private party on a Saturday night that was billed to have about a dozen of the world's top supermodels present, including Claudia Schiffer and Naomi Campbell. At the last minute, however, the party was canceled because the organizer's mother was killed in a car accident.

To make matters worse, an interesting woman I had arranged to meet canceled our appointment. Kara Charles worked for a cosmetic skincare company that catered to many of the top models, including Cheryl Tiegs and Iman. A friend of mine, fashion designer Drew Young, knew Kara and had arranged the meeting. Drew told me that Kara had all kinds of wild model stories. An hour before we were supposed to meet, Kara left me a message explaining that she had just received an offer to go to Europe for a couple of weeks to work on a major Paris fashion show. I decided it was a good time to move on to Milan.

The day before I left L.A., I witnessed a scene that made me realize just how seedy the modeling industry actually is. I'd received a call from Freddie Lowry, a photographer I had met a couple of days before, inviting me to go to a crazy modeling party that night. Lowry explained to me that once a month there's a wild party held in a loft in Venice Beach for men to hook up with some of L.A.'s finest models. He said the organizer, a former model in her late twenties, procured the services of models-turned-prostitutes for wealthy men. There was an exorbitant $200 entrance fee to fraternize with these beautiful women. The possibility of paying the models for extra services was emphasized by a money-back guarantee.

"It's like something right out of Heidi Fleiss," Lowry said. "I went a couple of months ago and ended up fucking the most beautiful thing on two feet you've ever seen."

When we arrived at the loft, a burly, black doorman, who looked like a reject from the World Wrestling Federation, screened us carefully before letting us in. He asked us how we found out about the party and if we had been there before. When he seemed convinced by Lowry's explanation, he had us put our arms in the air and frisked us for weapons. He then took a couple hundred bucks from each of us and let us in.

Inside, the dark room was clean and elegant. Candles were lit everywhere and incense was burning. There were about two dozen scantily clad young women milling about. They were all wearing high heels and loads of makeup, and looked like they were trying to become the next *Vogue* cover girl. An equal number of men rounded out the room. Most of the men looked very rich and were over forty. I didn't notice any men who looked younger than me.

Lowry introduced me to our hostess, a heavily scented auburn-haired woman named Tisha. Tisha invited me to make myself at home and offered me a shot of vodka, while Lowry started mingling with the girls. After downing our shots, I told Tisha that I had never been to a party like this before. She admitted that the parties had proven to be both a lucrative and satisfying venture, but were the cause of some worry. "I just want everyone to have fun," she said. "But it's not easy. I try to make sure that everybody who comes in is respectable. I have to protect my girls, you know."

After I bought another round of shots, I started pumping Tisha for the details of her past. At first, she was hesitant to discuss herself or her work. But after various reassurances—I told her she was one of the most fascinating people I'd ever met and that I wanted to hear her incredible story—Tisha was in full, eloquent form. We sat down at a table and I listened to Tisha talk about her wild past. She told me that she had been a successful model in the early nineties. Six years later, she decided to try something new. While barely keeping a half step ahead of her younger model sister and the police, Tisha managed to make more money than ever by throwing her outrageous parties. She'd built a reputation for being one of Hollywood's foremost madams, albeit an elegant one. "My sister knows what I do and she's dead set against it," Tisha said. "But she understands that I have to earn a living somehow. She's more worried that the cops'll bust me. If I get busted, then so be it. In life you take risks to succeed."

Tisha took me by the hand and introduced me to Daisy, a tall, beautiful blonde. "Daisy will take good care of you," Tisha said. "Have fun!" Over drinks, Daisy revealed that she had taken this job because her career as a model appeared to be stalled. She told me that she'd appeared in *Vogue* and *Elle* and had once worked alongside the likes of Cindy Crawford. "I know her well," Daisy said. "She's a class act. Cindy's one of the nicest people you will ever meet."

Since switching careers, Daisy said she's made very good money. She bought a new apartment and a Mercedes sports utility vehicle. "When I worked as a model, I couldn't buy those things," she said. "Now I'm finally able to get whatever I want. I don't have to worry about money anymore."

With a twinkle in her eye, Daisy suddenly started running her thin, smooth fingers through my hair. I ordered a bottle of champagne that cost $600.00. The hefty price was a sign of things to come. Halfway through the bottle, Daisy started caressing my thighs. She suggested that we go upstairs to one of the private rooms. "It costs $2,000 for a full hour service," she said. I told her I was going to pass because I had a wife. "Every man in here is married," she replied. "It's really not a big deal."

Soon after, Daisy left me to find someone else in the room who'd be willing pay her price. I then met Tara, a pleasant, eloquent woman who claimed that she'd once been a top runway model in New York. Although I wasn't prepared to entrust my life story to her—to avoid blowing my cover, I never felt comfortable telling models much about myself—I couldn't help but enjoy Tara's company. We talked about everything from Bill Clinton to Evian water. "It's the only water that I trust," Tara said. "It really does taste like spring water. Some of the other bottled waters taste recycled."

Tara confided that although working these parties was a bit embarrassing, it had been well worth it. "Many models like myself get screwed over by the powers that be and have to come up with new ways of making cash," she said. "It's not as glamorous as working as a fashion model, but it's certainly better than sitting on your ass at home."

At around 2:00 A.M., Lowry materialized at the bottom of the stairs with a smile on his face. He told me he was ready to leave. On the way home, he bragged that he had had sex with a busty brunette who reminded him of Pam Anderson. "If not for the different hair color, you would think they were twins," he said. Lowry asked me how my night went. When I told him that I didn't go upstairs with any of the girls he began berating me. "You're an idiot," he said. "It's not everyday that you get a chance like this." Lowry said that he would come to every party Tisha throws. "Even if I have to save up a couple of months in advance, it's not everyday that I get the chance to meet such beautiful girls."

CHAPTER 8

• • •

From Hearst to Ford

The modeling industry has been plagued by drug and alcohol abuse from its earliest days. Rose Gordon, who was a stunning brunette model in the 1920s, recalls how many of her colleagues were strung out on opium and cocaine. Gordon says that like many modern models, she was also usually drunk on the catwalk and at photo shoots. "It was unbelievable," said the ninety-three-year-old Gordon, "If you think it's bad today, it was just as bad back then, but in a more subtle way. We would always be plied with alcohol and drugs before shows. The men in charge knew what they were doing because they wanted to make sure that we were in the mood to go back to their beds with them after the show. Many girls I knew had to earn extra money by sleeping with guys. We had to just to survive. We didn't earn anywhere near the kind of money top models get today. The big difference with the drugs is that we weren't injecting needles into our arms the way girls do today. I still go to fashion shows when I can, and it scares me to know that there's bound to be several models who are totally strung out on heroin."

Much as in the fashion industry today, many models and fashion moguls of years gone by have their own horror stories of death, drug abuse, and suicide. The models of yesteryear suffered from the same insecurities and vulnerabilities that ruin the careers of so many models today. Thirties Russian model Ludmilla had trouble coping with the chauvinistic attitudes that dominated the industry. Ludmilla got hooked on alcohol and drugs, and went into a deep depression before finally deciding to give up her career to become a devoted housewife.

The extravagance of today's modeling industry has its roots in the grandiose design of publishing baron William Randolph Hearst. The industry's luxuriant character was born at the turn of the century, when a Chicago photographer named Beatrice Tonneson started using female models in ads. Soon after, in 1913, the world's first full-time fashion photographer, Baron de Meyer, was hired by *Vogue* in New York. He earned more than $100 a week, the equivalent of $10,000 in today's market. That same year, William Randolph Hearst bought *Bazar* (the third "a" in "Bazaar" was added fifteen years later) and immediately hired de Meyer away from *Vogue*, doubling his salary and promising him work in Paris and abroad. De Meyer, the first known fashion photographer, became addicted to cocaine after he was fired from *Bazaar* in 1932. He was a junkie for the rest of his life, living like a pauper on the streets of New York and then Los Angeles before his death in 1949. At one point, Hearst liked de Meyer's work so much that he hung a couple of his photos above the low-flush cistern in the marble bathroom of his office suite. But Baron de Meyer quickly went from Hearst's penthouse to the outhouse because of his drug use. He hadn't bothered to save a penny of his earnings—he had spent it all on drugs and alcohol. At one point, Baron de Meyer was so broke that he had to sell his last two cameras for a dollar, enough money to buy a hot meal.

Meanwhile, Hearst started cashing in. From the first day he decided to buy *Bazaar*, Hearst said he could smell success. "Everybody wants to see beautiful women and men model clothes," Hearst said. "There's room for every fashion magazine because the public wants more and more. But my goal is for *Bazaar* to be number one and to get the best looking models on our pages. And I'm willing to pay whatever it takes to accomplish that." Hearst wasn't kidding. Nobody was able to compete with the huge salaries he offered to models. Hearst firmly believed that spending money was the key ingredient in making money. The stage was set for the bitter rivalry between *Vogue* and *Bazaar* that has lasted to this day.

Anita Miller was an aspiring New York model in the thirties. She had appeared in *Bazaar* several times and was widely recognized as one of the top models of the day. A tragic incident ended her life in 1939. A man named Joey Galluci paid Miller's agent the hefty sum of $300 to arrange a date for him with Miller. Galluci promised Miller's agent that through his connections, he could help advance Miller's career. However, Galluci neglected to mention that he was involved with underworld figures and had spent time in prison.

One night, Miller met Galluci for dinner at an expensive Italian restaurant. Everything went well until Galluci pressured Miller to go back to his apartment with him. When she refused his invitation, Galluci plied Miller with alcohol hoping to change her answer. As the evening wore on, Galluci steadily drank himself into a stupor, and, by around 2:30 A.M., had convinced a now inebriated Miller to go home with him. On their way to his Upper West Side apartment, Galluci's Ford crashed into an oncoming truck, instantly killing both of them. The career and life of the twenty-year-old model was over. Had she not been coaxed into accepting a date with the seedy Galluci, Miller probably would have went on to become one of the most successful models of her era.

"Ever since I can remember, models have been forced to make money on the side, but many times it's dodgy and dangerous," said former model Rose Gordon. "What seems like an opportunity can easily backfire and turn into a major tragedy."

One of the world's most well-known fashion journalists is Michael Gross. Gross has covered fashion for more than fifteen years for *Vanity Fair, The New York Times* and *New York* magazine. In 1995, Gross penned the New York Times bestseller *Model: The Ugly Business of Beautiful Women*. In his book, Gross said the first recorded instance of models walking down a fashion runway was at Chicago's fashion exhibition in 1914. Gross said it was the first time that a catwalk stretching into the audience had been built to give people a closer look at the models.

"Back in those days a dollar went a long way," said eighty-nine-year-old Eli Anderson, whose father Max owned a clothing store in New York.

Beautiful girls would be plucked off the street and offered jobs to model. It was a new industry and there was plenty of work to go around. Sure there were a lot of perverts who were more interested in getting fresh with the girls than in having them model, but in those days it was a much more distinguished and honest job. It's changed much for the worse. Many people in the fashion industry today are crooks and they don't really care about the product they put out. They just want to make loads of money while skimping on the amount they spend on the product. The models today are spoiled and stuck up. Back in the good old days much more work and effort was put into making new outfits. And the girls who wore them were down to earth. They didn't have the arrogant attitude of some of the models today, like Naomi Campbell. It was a much more pleasant atmosphere.

As the Great Depression approached, the modeling business showed no signs of slowing down. Although the garment industry was hit hard, the fashion magazines were doing better than ever. People wanted to see gorgeous men and women in magazines to help them escape from the harsh reality of their lives. People soon became obsessed with beauty.

"Most businesses have been hit hard," John Powers said back in the Depression. "But the fashion business continues to live on. The demand for models has never been stronger. It's a business that will survive forever."

Perhaps the only models who suffered during the Great Depression were those who refused to perform sexual favors for their agents. "There was definitely a period in the late twenties and thirties when it was considered taboo not to cooperate with what the girls' agents demanded," said pop culture historian Jack Norman. "The agents wanted their girls to go out with famous actors and athletes because it was good publicity. And the girls were instructed not to hold back when advances were made at them. It was a P.R. dream for an agent to have one of his girls going out with somebody famous, because it guaranteed them press, and the more press they received, the higher their stock rose."

Prospective employers often blacklisted girls who refused to play the game. As a result, modeling jobs became scarce, ruining careers. "It was a tight circle of people who ran the modeling business back then," Jack Norman said. "If a girl didn't cooperate with her employer, word spread quickly and she was looked upon as being untouchable. . . . The models who played the game did well. Men were willing to spend big money to be cheered up during the Depression. They wanted to party and be with beautiful girls to help them forget their problems."

John Powers opened the very first modeling agency on Park Avenue in New York. He is considered to be the godfather of modeling agents. His flamboyant personality was legendary. A man of prodigious appetites, Powers was known to be the Hugh Hefner of his day, often dating more than a dozen models at a time. He boasted about his priapic prowess and called his girls "long-stemmed American beauties" instead of models (The cigar chomping Powers thought this moniker gave his models a more unique identity than that of screen and theater starlets.)

"Every man who was somebody wanted to go out with a Powers model," recalled longtime entertainment writer Jacob Hamlich. "By far they were the most glamorous and beautiful women in the world. The models you see today are nothing compared to the models Powers had. They were all classic American beauties who had class and lots of pizzazz. They looked sparkling and glamorous, unlike the models now who all look like they're strung out on heroin."

Powers's models became known as the most beautiful women in show business. The world's most eligible bachelors would carefully scan the Powers catalog for the girl they wanted to meet, just like actors and rock stars peruse the catalogs of Elite and Storm today. Marshall Hemingway, Frank Sinatra, and Howard Hughes all married Powers models. According to Paul Stern, a former Powers employee, Hughes once slipped John Powers $50,000 cash in a briefcase for a date with Rosalind Russell. "Hughes was so desperate to get a date with her," Stern said. "He offered Powers a wad of cash to arrange the date and Powers graciously obliged."

To this day, many people accuse Powers of stealing the idea of starting a modeling agency from a notorious Harlem street hustler known as Big George. Big George, whose real name was George Wilson, spent his days roaming the streets of Harlem looking for sexy, young black women who were interested in making a few extra bucks modeling. He'd invite them to be photographed at his studio in an unmarked concrete blockhouse in the middle of Harlem. With its broken windows and filthy, neglected walls, it could have passed for an abandoned warehouse. After developing the photos, Big George brought them to local clothing businesses, trying to get his girls work as models. Many of Big George's girls made a decent living doing ads and promotional appearances.

Powers, who enjoyed Harlem's nightclubs, once noticed a photograph of a girl advertising a flimsy summer dress in a storefront. He asked the storeowner who the stunning girl was. "She's a beauty," the store owner growled. "She's one of Big George's girls." The storekeeper explained to Powers that Big George made decent money promoting his models through ads. Powers's business instinct took over. The very next morning, Powers, resplendent in a black suit with brass buttons, went looking for office space in Manhattan. He decided that he would open up the first legitimate modeling agency.

"Big George was a small-time entrepreneur whose idea inspired Powers to take it to a higher level," said former thirties Harlem model Doris Brown. "I don't think it's fair to accuse Powers of stealing Big George's idea. Powers saw a good opportunity and took advantage of it."

At the youthful age of twenty-eight, Powers had become one of the most powerful people in the entertainment business in America. He frequented the top nightclubs in New York, meeting gorgeous women and signing them to contracts; his roster included such beauties as Ava Gardner, Rosalind Russell, and Lauren Bacall. Legend has it that the very straightforward Powers approached Gardner at a jazz concert in New York, told her how sexy he thought she was, and offered her a contract on the spot, asking "how much are your tits worth?"

Powers also represented several big male models, including Henry Fonda and Tyrone Power, who would later become stars on the silver screen. But it was his female models who changed the face of fashion.

"If not for John Powers, there might not be the supermodel phenomenon as we know it today," said former thirties model Rhona Bonder. "He opened the door for everyone. Soon after he started his agency, other people copied him and opened up their own agencies. Young girls dreamed of getting signed by an agency. All the big magazines started using models on the covers. Girls who would have been making $40 a week in any other job were earning more than $100 a week. That was big money back then."

The birth of new modeling agencies across North America and Europe was good news for fashion photographers. *Vogue* and *Harper's Bazaar* branched out into European markets. Lisa Fonssagrives, a ballet dancer from Uddevalla, Sweden, was discovered while riding in an elevator. Famous *Vogue* photographer Horst P. Horst said Fonssagrives was the best model he'd ever photographed. Fonssagrives is remembered most for being one of the most intrepid models ever, using her ballet and athletic skills to do daring poses that had never before been attempted. She once posed lying down in the middle of the street wearing only panties and a pair of black socks. An Erwin Blumenfeld photo of Fonssagrives hanging from the Eiffel Tower is one of the most renowned photos ever taken in Paris. It remains a popular image on postcards and T-shirts sold to tourists visiting Paris from all over the world.

Renowned French photographer Jean Moral shot Fonssagrives parachuting from an airplane several thousand feet in the air. Moral wanted to shoot the beauty in midair because Fonssagrives's friends often called her "the beautiful bird." Clearly, Fonssagrives was the darling of the fashion and entertainment industries. It seemes that no other model was more of a photographer's delight to work with.

"She was the top model in the world," recalls Alice Robert, a former model in the thirties who knew Fonssagrives. "She was really the first person to treat modeling like an art. She had a different perspective from everybody else. Nobody since has even come close to doing what Lisa did. The models today are all boring. If someone would model the way Lisa did, they would make a fortune. How many people have the courage to pose hanging from the Eiffel Tower?"

Perhaps Fonssagrives rose to superstar status when she posed nude for legendary photographer Horst P. Horst. Those nudes are widely regarded as some of the best model shots ever. "They were so artistic," Alice Robert said. "Lisa was a real renaissance woman. Her photos were like a classic painting. Every young model should study her career. They'll understand how Lisa made everybody realize that being a model is an art. . . . Having a good-looking appearance is just the first step. Lisa showed everybody how important it is to know what to do with it during a photo shoot."

By the forties, copycat model agencies had sprung up everywhere and began vying with the Powers Agency for the number one spot. The Ford Agency was launched right in the home of Eileen and Jerry Ford in New York in 1946. Eileen Ford became known as the godmother of modeling. She formulated her policy on ethics and power schmoozing. The erudite, suave, charming socialite knew all the important people in the fashion industry. She wined and dined them, winning their support. Her first goal upon starting the Ford Agency was to make sure that all the models she represented got steady work. Ford worked around the clock, soliciting magazines, newspapers, and potential advertisers to hire her models. And it was easy to sign the top female models because many had heard the horror stories about sleazy male agents and preferred Ford's honest, humane, and motherly approach. Lauren Hutton, Christie Brinkley, and Jerry Hall are only some of Ford's long list of successful models.

Dorian Leigh, who had been a top model herself, founded the Fashion Bureau, France's first model agency. Leigh, an intellectual raised in a family of artists, promised the big French and European fashion magazines top American models instead of the mediocre models they had learned to expect from rival agencies.

"Before Dorian Leigh you didn't see the top American models working in Europe," explained Alice Robert. "She really opened things up. At the beginning she got into a lot of trouble with the police because she ran it in a very clandestine way. The police thought she was using her agency as a front for prostitutes. Eventually the police gave in, allowing Dorian to make her mark on the fashion industry."

Meanwhile, by the early fifties modeling agent John Powers had had enough. Heavy competition had forced him to close his agency's doors. In 1952, he relocated to Beverly Hills in order to lead a quiet life. He stopped going to major fashion events, even though his name remained on Hollywood's A-list for years. The only modeling-related work he did was the occasional stint as a consultant. At one point, Powers tried to break into Hollywood as a director but had no success. Nobody took him seriously. Powers was unable to switch careers because everyone still thought of him as a model agent. Even his close pal Frank Sinatra couldn't help him break into the Hollywood scene. Sinatra tried to convince a good pal at Warner Brothers to hire Powers, but the deal fell through when the friend demanded that Powers work freelance.

"He wouldn't even consider it," a friend of Powers said. "Sinatra stepped up to bat for John, but it all collapsed because of John's big ego. His motto was 'all or nothing.' There's no way he was going to settle for anything less than a big position."

Before he died in 1977, Powers told an interviewer how much he resented new agents stealing his formula for success. "I worked very hard to set up the groundwork and when I finally got it done, dozens of people came along and stole my idea," Powers said. "When I first started working in the business it was fun and everybody made a bit of money. But after so many new agencies sprang up, the business got out of control and it became a slimy game. That's when I decided to leave. It wasn't fun anymore. It became a war, a dog-eat-dog world."

The Fords and Dorian Leigh succeeded Powers as the biggest agents in the world. They worked closely together and became partners in Europe. As a result, many models' gross earnings skyrocketed. By 1958 the average top model earned between $3,000 and $5,000 a week. A modeling boom erupted, and models now rivaled film stars as the hottest celebrities.

"They really created opportunities on an international level," Alice Robert said of Leigh and the Fords. "Before the Fords came along, it was rare for a model to work overseas. They made it standard practice. Some of the models I knew who were with them weren't too happy, because they were being overworked. But the bottom line is that if you were with Ford, you were guaranteed lots of work. Some models thought they were being underpaid in proportion to the amount of work they were doing, but that's the reality of the business. Agents always find ways to increase their own fees."

One benefit of being a Ford model was being acquainted with Eileen Ford. Ford enjoyed playing matchmaker for her models. She was like a mother to them, and made a habit of trying to fix her models up with eligible bachelors. Many models married rich men as a result of Ford playing cupid. "That's how Ford kept her models loyal to her," said an ex-Ford model. "You might not have been paid as well as at some of the other top agencies, but if you stuck around long enough, you probably would end up marrying a millionaire."

Heading into the flower power era of the sixties, the fashion industry exploded. Because it was generating more revenue than ever before, involvement in the modeling business was the envy of everyone interested in glitz and glamour. It seemed that every young woman dreamt of being a model, while every man dreamt of being an agent in order to meet beautiful women. Millions of dollars were spent on marketing every year. New designers kept popping up. Everybody wanted to be involved in the industry in some capacity. Even John Lennon described the sixties fashion craze as more momentous than the music of the times.

"Music reaches lots of people, but the fashion business dictates the trends our society follows," Lennon said. "Musicians wear the latest clothes to make a statement. Some of the new clothes are unbelievable. If you compare music to fashion, I would have to say that fashion is more progressive, because new designs and trends evolve each day. Most of pop music stays and sounds the same. It gets boring. Fashion never gets boring."

The person who revolutionized the fashion industry in the sixties was a petite, ninety-pound model, the daughter of a carpenter from the tiny London suburb Neasden. Lesley Hornby, who became known the world over as Twiggy, wore her blonde hair short and her body ultra-thin, sparking the skinny look that continues to shape the fashion figure to this day. Young girls everywhere cropped their hair and went on crash diets in an attempt to emulate fashion's newest sensation.

"Twiggy created a whole new look," said British journalist Martin Smith. "Up until she came along, most of the models shared the same classic look. Twiggy became to modeling what the Beatles were to popular music. She began a whole new trend and everybody started copying her unique look and style. The first time I saw her on

TV, I said to myself, 'You've got to be kidding.' She looked so skinny—practically anorexic. It looked like she hadn't eaten a meal in a long time."

Twiggy's agent and longtime lover Justin de Velleneuve introduced the waif to America with a fanfare rivaling the Beatles arrival in 1964. De Velleneuve arranged a big cross-country publicity tour, inviting hordes of media to swarm everywhere Twiggy appeared. His plan worked brilliantly. In each city, Twiggy received the adulation normally reserved for rock stars. The American public went wild for her. People stopped her on the street for autographs. Her public appearances were jam-packed with curious fans. And, Twiggy was a hit with the press. In 1967, *Newsweek* ran a cover story about Twiggy—the rest of the media quickly followed suit. The *New Yorker* ran a 100-page story on Twiggy's trip to the U.S. Indeed, America had gone Twiggy crazy.

"The fashion industry had never seen anything remotely like Twiggy's popularity," said entertainment author Esmond Choueke. "It was wild. Anybody who thinks that the heroin-chic phenomenon of the 1990s was something new is completely wrong. Twiggy pioneered that whole look. Sure, there have been big-name models over the years, but nobody has had the drawing power of Twiggy. People went completely nuts over her. She became a cultural icon."

Twiggy's rise to the top didn't last long. By the time she was twenty, she decided to retire because she felt burned out. She had lost faith in the modeling business because of the way women were mistreated. She also didn't like the way De Villeneuve treated her. De Villeneuve, who claims he first had sex with Twiggy when she was just fifteen, reaped the benefits of fame-by-association, enjoying fine wine, food, and women. He cheated on Twiggy many times during their tumultuous five year relationship. De Villeneuve had earned a reputation as a playboy, using his connection with Twiggy to pick up gorgeous young models behind Twiggy's back.

"Justin's behavior crushed Twiggy and ruined her career," said a British fashion designer who knew the model during the sixties. "Twiggy was very much in love with Justin and tried to dispel the rumors that he was cheating on her. But on a couple of occasions, she caught him red-handed, making out with other women. It really hurt her and it left her with a bad taste for the business. That's why she quit at such a young age."

Another model who emerged in the sixties was the tall and lanky German-born model Veruschka. Veruschka was the fashion industry's most interesting and provocative model by far. Although she has been forgotten somewhat in the U.S., Veruschka remains a legend in Europe.

The young Swedish model Dite Vorn says that whenever she needs inspiration she pulls out an old Veruschka photo. "I collect her old clippings and photos," Vorn says. "She's my role model. There has been no model remotely close to having an impact like Veruschka. She was completely cutting edge."

Veruschka's collaboration with German visual artist Holger Trulzsch is legendary: Trulzsch painted all kinds of crazy designs on the tall blond's body. Veruschka became what many consider to be the most radically unique model ever. Her appeal to the young artistic and intellectual crowd was unprecedented. She's one of the most photographed women ever, having appeared on the cover of fashion magazines around the world more than any model before her. By the time she left the modeling business in the early seventies, Veruschka had been on the cover of *Vogue* eleven times.

"Veruschka had more of an alternative look than any model I've ever seen," said former Paris model Estelle Bergeron. "Her presence was mesmerizing. She was totally into expressing herself artistically. And if people didn't like what she was doing, she didn't care. She wanted to be different from everybody else."

Veruschka herself says that if she hadn't been allowed to be creative and emotive, she wouldn't have lasted as a model. "For me, modeling was just an extension of the theater," she said. "I liked being on stage dressed up in costume. I like expressing myself. If I would have had to be a model who just got up there in pretty outfits, I would have gotten bored quickly. I was always fascinated by the endless amount of possibilities a model could explore. For me it was much deeper than just making money. I did it for the artistic and spiritual benefits."

Many fashion insiders are outraged that the industry has not done anything to honor Veruschka. Since retiring, Veruschka has all but disappeared from the fashion spotlight.

"Veruschka is a legend and legends should be honored and paid respect," says fashion critic Tom Weiss. "I'm surprised that not more has been done to keep her fashion legacy alive. Without Veruschka there would be no Naomi, no Gisele. That's how powerful she was. She was to fashion what Elvis was to rock and roll. It would be fitting to call Veruschka the queen of the catwalk."

The seventies saw even more growth in the modeling business.

John Casablancas's Elite Agency quickly became, and remains to this day, one of the two biggest and most powerful agencies in the world. Several other agencies sprung up during the seventies, including Wilhelmina, which was founded by the cover girl of the same name. Still, Elite was the flagship. Casablancas, who grew up the son of wealthy Spanish refugees, was inspired to start his own agency after dating several models. Although he loved being around beautiful women, he claims it wasn't his first motivation. "I didn't get into the business to pick up girls. I got into it because, after being with several models, I realized that most of them were miserable and that there was a huge void in the industry for good agents," Casablancas said. "I did a lot of research before I opened up shop. My goal was to find beautiful girls and market them to the maximum. You can have the most beautiful model in your agency, but if you can't market her properly, there's no use going further. Marketing is everything. You've got to get the message out clearly as to what's out there."

Before he opened Elite, Casablancas faced several challenges. A compulsive gambler, he owed lots of money to his second wife, Danish model Jeanette Christjansen. Christjansen pressured him to pay her back—or else. At one point the slim, mustached playboy was so broke that he couldn't even afford the down payment on his office space. He had to borrow the money from a friend. Cash flow wasn't Casablancas only problem. His reputation took a beating with the stories of womanizing that were bandied about the fashion industry. Boasting that his sexual appetites could only be satisfied by dozens of women, Casablancas always seemed to be seeking a new woman. Countless stories floated around about how some of the models he recruited were steered into a life of drugs, alcohol, and sex. Scandal rocked Casablancas wherever he went. Two of his models were dead before Elite was barely a year old. Casablancas was in hot water deep.

The first to die was Paula Brenken. One night, after a party, Brenken mysteriously dove out of a window in a drunken state. Details of Brenken's death are still murky. Casablancas to this day rarely talks about what happened. He firmly denies any involvement. Yet, according to several people who knew her well, Brenken had become addicted to drugs and alcohol, and became chronically depressed after Casablancas recruited her to join Elite. Several days before Brenken died, she was spotted partying in a nightclub with Casablancas. A friend of Casablancas introduced her to a photographer who took Brenken home later that night. The next day, Brenken told a friend that she had been raped. She claimed that she had refused the photographer's advances, but he wouldn't take no for an answer and threatened to beat her up if she didn't comply.

"Nobody's ever gotten to the bottom of how she really died," said the friend. "It was covered up quickly. The cops obviously got paid off by somebody to shut up. There's no other explanation."

The second death was that of Emanuelle Dano. Casablancas found Dano dead in her apartment one morning when he knocked on her door to confirm a booking. When Dano didn't answer, Casablancas called security to break down the door.

Dano had a reputation for being a party animal. She did drugs and drank heavily. She enjoyed flirting with the wild side, regularly sleeping with several men a week. She was addicted to cocaine and champagne.

One night, Dano had been out partying with a group of male friends. On the way back to her apartment, things got out of hand, and the men tried to have sex with Dano in their car. One of the men put his hand under her dress and between her legs, while another fondled her breasts. The men told Dano how much they wanted to fuck her. According to Casablancas, Dano was roughed up in the car and fell out while she was trying to fight off her attackers. Dano died instantly and her body was brought back to her apartment and laid to rest on her bed. Casablancas insists that Dano's death was an accident, not attempted murder. He claims to know who was with Dano in the car, but refuses to reveal their names.

According to one of Casablancas former Elite models, Dano's death was not properly investigated. The model, who prefers to remain anonymous because she fears retribution by Casablancas, said that the police didn't conduct a thorough investigation and that Casablancas's role was suspect. "I couldn't believe it when I found out that it was Casablancas who discovered the body," the model said. "I know for a fact that he wanted to cover it up quickly because he feared the bad publicity. I'm not saying by any stretch that he was involved, but it was obvious that there was foul play and that charges should have been made. Emanuelle Dano was a very nice and caring girl. I met her when she first started modeling and there's no doubt in my mind that if she hadn't become a model, she would still be alive today. She got mixed up with a lot of seedy people, like a lot of other models who wind up dead at such a young age."

Casablancas, a marketing genius, was able to turn these tragedies into good publicity. A certain glamour and mystique that no other agency had started to surround Elite. People in the fashion industry, the media, and the public became obsessed with every detail of the Casablancas model agency. Casablancas made headlines wherever he went, and was spotted with gorgeous young models in discos from Paris to New York. Many of the models claimed to have slept with him, which generated more publicity for his fast and furious playboy image.

"Casablancas turned the modeling business upside down during the seventies," recalls Eric Hetu, a French fashion scout. "He got more publicity than any agent ever. He had a crazy lifestyle and the press ate it up. Wherever he went and whatever he did made news. Companies spent millions of dollars and didn't get anywhere near the same amount of publicity he got."

Casablancas's success triggered what was called a "model war" between Elite and Ford. With the huge success of the film *Saturday Night Fever*, the fashion industry capitalized on the disco look. In May 1977, Eileen Ford launched a $7.5 million lawsuit against Casablancas for violating the "fiduciary trust" to which she claimed Casablancas had committed. Apparently, Casablancas and Ford had verbally agreed that Elite would remain in Paris and not interfere with Ford's turf in New York. But in May 1977, Casablancas opened up shop in Manhattan and recruited former top Wilhelmina model Maarit Halinen to be Elite New York's first model.

The model war became one of the hottest news items in New York that summer. In July, *New York Magazine* journalist and social butterfly Anthony Haden-Guest wrote a controversial story about the modeling business entitled "Model Wars." In a May 1998 interview, Haden-Guest recalled the mood that summer. "It was a volatile situation," he said. "Casablancas and Ford were at each other's throats. They both wanted to be number one, and the only way to do it was to take out the other person."

In his article, Haden-Guest exposed the lasciviousness of the modeling business and the wild day-to-day operations at Elite. Several models admitted that they spent as much time in bed with their agents as in the office. Many of these dalliances were extramarital affairs.

Cover girl Janice Dickenson admitted to Haden-Guest that she had had to run nude around the Elite office; she also revealed other unsavory antics that took place in the Casablancas work environment. Haden-Guest quoted several people who had negative things to say about Casablancas, portraying Casablancas as a sleazy hustler. Unfazed, Casablancas reveled in the publicity.

"He didn't care what the media said about him, just as long as they spelled his name right," said entertainment critic Thomas Mann. "He knew how to play the media to a tee and was a master at turning any publicity he got into dollars. The craziest thing is that he didn't have to spend a dime marketing himself. The press followed him wherever he went and became obsessed with every detail of his life. The only people who received that kind of treatment were big Hollywood movie stars."

Modeling agent Wilhelmina despised Casablancas because of his chauvinistic attitudes, and, like Ford, launched a multi-million dollar lawsuit against him. Wilhelmina and Ford conspired to put Casablancas out of business. They used their lawsuits to bad-mouth him in the press and threatened to get other people in the fashion industry to launch similar lawsuits. But the scheme backfired. The press became even more infatuated with the Casablancas story and upped the publicity ante, overshadowing everyone else in the fashion industry. Casablancas became a legend and every young model worldwide dreamt of working for Elite.

"Eileen Ford was Casablancas's best publicist," said a longtime *Vogue* editor. "By saying nasty things about him, she gave Casablancas even more publicity than he ever dreamed he could get. If she had backed off, Elite probably would never have become so big. But because she and Wilhelmina were on his back in the press, everybody became familiar with him and he became a celebrity."

In the eighties, the fashion industry changed dramatically. Elite and Ford opened offices all over the world. Many large independent agencies also emerged and the competition became fierce, increasing opportunity along with it. Cosmetic and clothing companies vied for the hottest new faces to advertise their products on billboards and in magazines. The emergence of people like Cindy Crawford, Naomi Campbell, and Linda Evangelista, marked the birth of the supermodel era.

"Up until the mid-eighties, the biggest models didn't receive anywhere near the kind of publicity that the new supermodels enjoy," said French fashion critic Jules Bisson. "Models like Christie Brinkley and Cheryl Tiegs were big during the seventies, but they didn't receive the kind of exposure the top supermodels of the eighties and nineties got. Some of the supermodels like Kate Moss, Stephanie Seymour, and Linda Evangelista became more popular than actors and rock stars. They made headlines not only in the fashion magazines, but in all the newspapers and tabloids. The whole supermodel fad exploded worldwide."

CHAPTER 9

● ● ●

Wrong Turn

A rainy day in Milan in mid-January. It's noon and I'm sitting in a cafe in the heart of the fashion district. Outside, it's drizzling; inside, there is constant chitchat among fashion designers, buyers, and models who are taking a break for lunch. Everybody seems to be in a good mood. I ask a woman sitting within earshot if there's an event going on because the cafe is so packed, and people are now lining up outside to get in.

"Everyday here is an event," the woman responds in a thick Italian accent. "It never stops. Morning or night in Milan, something is always going on. The men are always busy making deals or chasing beautiful girls and the women are busy shopping and trying to look sexy. That's pretty much what goes on here every day of the year."

Clearly the hotbed of the fashion world, Milan is legendary for its stories of model abuse. During my ten-day stay there, I heard far too many tales of models being raped, drugged, and beaten. Some of it I witnessed firsthand. Late one night in a disco, I saw a group of men in their forties ply three young models, all around fourteen or fifteen years old, with champagne. Within a half hour the men were slow dancing with the girls, rubbing up against them on the dance floor. One of the men had his hand under a model's skirt while French kissing her. Ten minutes later I spotted the pair in the men's bathroom. They didn't even notice that I was standing just feet away. The gray haired, burly man was demanding that the girl have sex with him. He kept snarling aggressively, "I want to fuck you baby, I want to fuck you now." The teenage model was in tears, and repeatedly asked the man to stop. I decided to intervene, and tapped the man on the shoulder.

"Hey, you, mind your own fucking business," he said in a thick French accent. "Mind your own fucking business or I'll have you fucked up." Luckily, one of the bouncers had just entered the washroom. He got between us and told the man to back off. The man returned to the club. The girl, sobbing hysterically, stayed. The bouncer calmed her down and promised to put her in a taxi.

"This goes on here all the time," the bouncer told me. "These girls should know better than to be out so late with creeps like that. It's so clear that all these guys want to do is fuck young girls."

What sets modeling apart from other performance industries is not the quantity of related crime, but the quality. The modeling profession is plagued by crimes that are even more violent, frequent, and shocking than those we've come to expect from the high profile music and acting milieus.

Take, for example, the music industry. Since hip-hop first surfaced on the mean streets of New York some twenty-odd years ago, there have been a number of highly publicized shootings that involved big name stars like Puff Daddy and Snoop Doggy Dog. Yet despite the murders of music legends Tupac Shakur and the Notorious B.I.G., among others, the violence associated with the music industry pales in comparison to that which marks the modeling industry. Simply put, stabbings, rapes, murders, and overdoses are more likely to involve models than musicians or actors. The rate of criminal homicide in modeling is at least twice as great as that found in other entertainment fields, according to reputable Louisiana University sociologist George Carter.

"In the music industry you only come across instances of the big name stars being murdered," says Carter, who over the years has advised various troubled artists, including members of the Beach Boys and the late John Denver. Carter has written extensively on violence in the entertainment industry. "You rarely hear about unknown musicians getting abused. Only if you become a big star do you really have to worry. In modeling, the situation is completely different. Every day you hear about young, unknown models being raped, beaten, drugged, and even murdered. And despite all the horror stories that do surface, the modeling industry remains a magnet for young women. It's really unbelievable how the people running the business have managed to brush it off or cover it all up."

Carter is not surprised by how enthusiastically young girls pursue modeling, even though it's no secret that it can be a very dangerous business. His rationale is that they are completely overtaken by the hype in fashion magazines and on TV, and dream of becoming rich and famous like Cindy Crawford and Claudia Schiffer. Carter says that parents are just as naive—they get dollar signs in their eyes and choose to ignore the harsh realities of the business.

Those who believe that human behavior is governed by rational principles are hard-pressed to explain much of the crime that plagues the world of high fashion. In Carter's view, the particular motivations of these crimes are not materialistic. What makes crime attractive here is its association with pleasure—the criminal mind in these people of power is enticed by the passion of adultery or the freedom of drug use. Meanwhile, the fashion media stands united in its mutual admiration of these criminal rogues.

"Fashion journalists are smitten with the Jean-Luc Brunels-and John Casablancas-types [important male agents] of the fashion industry. It's all greed," Carter says. "The men running the fashion industry are fascinated with two vices, sex and drugs. Money is third. They're drawn to this lifestyle because many of them grew up in oppressive social backgrounds, or they were unpopular in school. Now, they're pretty much able to get any woman they want. It brings them closure, and reward per se for past failures. Women fashion executives are almost immune. Rarely do you hear about a woman agent or designer getting into trouble. It's almost always the thrill-seeking men, who pretty much run the industry."

Carter gives an example of a well-known supermodel he consulted for in early 2000. Due to client confidentiality, he cannot reveal her name. He does, however, describe the abuse this model endured during her six-year career as "horrifying." To the public, the model was a symbol of success, but she became addicted to hard drugs and could no longer cope with the daily grind of the modeling industry. The last straw was when her agent pulled a gun on her after she confronted him about the tens of thousands of dollars he had cheated her out of. Apparently, he had used the cash to feed his coke habit, and to buy her drugs over the years as well. After the gun incident, the supermodel quit the business and decided to get professional help.

Most models are neither street smart nor fortunate enough to learn from such raw human tragedies. More and more, however, models are starting to wake up and seek revenge. In 1998, nineteen-year-old Israeli beauty queen Linor Abergil was raped at knifepoint while in Italy to test shoot for modeling jobs. Abergil had turned to an Israeli travel agent to help her get to Rome from Milan. The travel agent told Abergil that he couldn't find her a seat on a plane or train to Rome, and offered to drive her there himself. During the eight-hour drive from Milan to Rome, the travel agent stopped the car, tied Abergil up, and gagged her mouth with adhesive tape. He tried to choke her with a rope and a plastic bag. After he raped her, he threatened to kill her if she revealed what had happened to anyone. Abergil said that if she had put up a fight she would have been murdered.

The travel agent brought Abergil back to Milan. She took a train to Rome, where she reported the incident to Italian police and then to the Israeli police when she returned home. The Italians arrested the travel agent, but released him after accepting his story that he had had sex with Abergil with her consent. The Milan police are notorious for turning a blind eye to the atrocities that plague the modeling industry. "Literally, they let people in the modeling industry get away with murder," George Carter says. "Many of them are paid off by the sleazebag agents who run the modeling business."

Israeli police arrested the forty-three-year-old travel agent, Shlomo Noor, at Israel's Ben Gurion airport when he returned to visit his wife and children. Seven weeks later, Abergil won the Miss World crown on the Seychelles Islands in the Indian Ocean. During and after the pageant, rumors began swirling about the alleged rape, with much speculation that a pageant judge, rather than a travel agent, had been involved.

Abergil came forward with her story and made headlines all over the world. She begged the authorities not to be lenient on her attacker Noor, who had already been acquitted of rape twice in the past—once by the Jerusalem District Court and once in Milan. She said that it was important that the matter be made public, to serve justice and prevent her attacker from ever raping again. Noor's defense was that Abergil consented to the physical contact between them. "Incidents of rape and sexual abuse are not only restricted to the exclusive territory of model agents and scouts," George Carter says. "The girls can be attacked by almost anyone they deal with."

In this case, as noted, it was the model's travel agent. Noor was already well known to the authorities for being accused of rape. He had managed to walk away in the past either because his victims were too scared to come forward, or the charges had been dropped. And the police seemed to do everything they could to help him get off. Documents were hidden and key evidence was not permitted to enter the court.

This time, however, Noor's victim decided to take matters into her own hands. Abergil went to the media with her story and got a lot of publicity, causing a major international incident. The Tel Aviv District Court tried to slap a publication ban but eventually was forced to remove it because of Noor's dark past. The police could no longer do much to protect Noor. They had to pursue the case to appease a huge public outcry.

Tall, with an innocent schoolgirl look, sixteen-year-old Teri James went to Milan during the summer of 1999 seeking fame and fortune as a model. According to eyewitness accounts, her Milan agent sexually abused her and holed her up in her apartment for days, cutting her off from the outside world. "He was a total monster," recalled Sharon Barr, a model who became close friends with James that summer. "One night I heard him force Teri to have sex. I was in the next room. I tried to intervene but he yelled at me to fuck off. Teri was yelling and screaming but she told me she didn't want me to get help. She was afraid of the man. The next morning we went to the police but they refused to listen to us. It seemed as if they were in cahoots with the agent."

James bought a plane ticket and fled to the airport to fly back home while her agent went to his apartment to take care of a few errands. Once safe at home, James had to undergo several months of psychiatric counseling to help her deal with the terrible ordeal. "If I wouldn't have escaped on my own, he might have ended up killing me," James said. "It's a time in my life that I must try to completely forget. I wish that I would have the courage to talk about it in more detail, but it's too painful. I need more time to let the wounds heal."

Today, Teri James works as a waitress at Denny's. She decided not to pursue her former agent because she believed the authorities wouldn't have done a thing. "There was nothing I could do," she said. "I'm not the first girl he abused, and unless someone does something fast, he'll keeping on raping the young models in his care. It seems like the media turns these rapists into heroes by exaggerating their status, wealth, and power. In the meantime, young, innocent girls are being abused and nobody seems to want to do anything about it. It's outrageous."

CHAPTER 10

•   •   •

Milan Marauders

Size and spectacle count for a lot in determining whether a modeling industry crime can qualify as newsworthy. Murder itself stands a better chance of making headlines when it is grand in scale, bizarre in design, or uncommonly morbid in execution. Likewise, the media and public usually turn a blind eye to model's tales of sexual abuse because they aren't considered juicy, major crimes.

In March 2001, however, the case of a young model being badly abused made headlines around the world. It happened during the middle of Italy's biggest fashion event of the year, Milan Fashion Week. While the fashion industry's biggest names congregated in the Fiera, Milan's exposition center, to watch 112 shows of the year's coolest new designs, rumors about the sexual abuse of a teenage model ran rampant through the crowd. Police were pursuing two executives of the well-known Flash Model Management—renowned for representing tennis beauties Anna Kournikova and Martina Hingis—in connection with the rape of an underage model from Slovenia.

The model, a long-legged, blond, fifteen-year-old named Maja, drifted into a whirlwind of parties and drugs during her one-week stay in Milan. She was forced to take hard drugs, raped numerous times—once in the bathroom of one of Milan's trendy nightclubs—and ended up in a psychiatric hospital.

Maja's Milan nightmare actually began when she was discovered in Slovenia during a modeling casting call. Massimo Mandelli, one of the two Flash executives accused in the case, believed Maja had the right look to become a successful cover girl.

"She was dressed like a schoolgirl: blue suit, white stockings, no heels," Mandelli told Italian journalist Alessandra Rizzo. "I thought she had what it takes."

When she arrived in Milan, Maja posed for pictures with the best photographers in the business to build a strong portfolio. She shared an apartment with a model from California, and was given some spending money and a cellular phone. Maja's father, who had accompanied her to Milan, left to go back to work after a couple of days. It was then that the trouble started. Older men repeatedly hit on her, taking her out to Milan's notorious drug-infested discos until the wee hours of the morning. Maja was introduced to booze and cocaine.

"I knew she was in for serious trouble because she was hanging around with men who clearly wanted one thing—to get in her pants," says Mira Germaine, an eighteen-year-old model from France who met Maja at a photo shoot. "She was abroad for the first time and had no idea what to expect. She trusted everyone she met. She was so naive. When you come to Milan, you have to be very careful. Every man in the discos wants to fuck a model. That's all they care about. That's why I never go out when I'm there. I just go about my business and then go home."

According to eyewitnesses, Maja was treated like a piece of meat. One night at a disco, she was seated with four Italian playboys who plied her with vodka and took turns fondling her. "They were all over her, putting their hands under her dress and touching her breasts," recalled Filio Dipili, a fashion photographer who was in the club that night. "It was so disgusting. These men, old enough to be her father, were taking total advantage of her. But it's not the first time I've seen it happen. And I've seen much worse. I've seen girls thirteen and fourteen having sex with forty-year-old men in the club bathrooms."

Only when Maja developed a vaginal infection did she come forward. She went to a Milan hospital accompanied by Silvia Ranzi, her booking agent at Flash. The doctor who treated Maja immediately noticed that she had been sexually abused and called the police.

Milan prosecutor Marco Ghezzi sought the indictment of two Flash executives, Massimo Mandelli and Alberto Righini, for abandonment of minors, a charge usually applied in the case of children under the age of fourteen. But the law applies to anyone else who can be proven unable to care for themselves. Ghezzi made a case that Maja fit into that category.

The Flash executives shifted the blame onto Maja's father for leaving his daughter alone with friends of her roommate who took advantage of her. "It happens everywhere—in Paris, New York and London—where models and other fashion professionals work together," said Mandelli, who serves as chief executive officer of Flash. "But along with the professionals come these parasites, playboys with money in their pockets who promise the girls the world and deliver violence and drugs instead."

Maja's case was the first in Milan in many years to capture the attention of the media. Journalists called upon the Italian government to come up with stricter regulations. "The girl was steered in the wrong direction by her roommate and her shady group of male friends," said Thomas Ageni, a Milan-based freelance fashion journalist. "The Italian government is very aware that the many young girls like Maja, who come to Italy alone to work, don't speak the language and need to be protected. I think it was a bit out of Flash's control. But maybe we need to clamp down on a big agency like Flash to set an example. Incidents like this have gone on in Milan for far too long. It's time for someone to take the blame."

One of fashion's biggest names, respected designer Giorgio Armani, supported Ghezzi's prosecution of the Flash executives. For years Armani has been one of the few well-known people in fashion to speak out against model abuse. Armani says that there should be a minimum age of sixteen for models everywhere. "I agree with those who say that the agencies should be legally responsible for the young models in their care. These kids are minors, and parents entrust the agencies to take care of them in their absence."

The public seems not nearly so concerned about a model agent's guilt or innocence as it seems determined to have the agents judged. Guilt or innocence aside, a big trial ensures that everyone involved in a celebrity crime suffers equally in full public view. A good example is the Maja case. Nobody emerged unscathed. Many fashion and media insiders tried to discredit Maja, accusing her of being an opportunist who fabricated the whole thing. On the other hand, people focused on how and why fashion moguls like the accused Flash executives might be drawn to such negligent and immoral behavior. Still, amidst the clamor there was little discussion of the need for prevention and retribution.

"There have been many unreported rapes and murders in the fashion business," says L.A. freelance fashion writer Joel Sayers. "It's appalling. Unless it's really gory and involves well-known models, the media usually ignores the story. I'm just as guilty as any other fashion journalist. Several times during my eight years covering the modeling scene, I received calls from models feeding me leads about violent crimes. Usually, I'd tell them that I'm not the police and they'd be better off contacting the authorities. I'm not a policeman. I got into the business to cover fashion shows, not model abuse."

Retired Florida State psychology professor Al Ford, who has acted as a consultant to several models over the years, says the public is obsessed with hearing about the dirty details of high-profile crime in the fashion industry. "Meanwhile," Ford says, "the media ignores the real issues—like why the people running the modeling industry can get away with such acts of violence. If it were any other occupation, the perpetrators of the crimes would be put in jail. Rarely in the modeling industry does this happen. And the saddest part of all is that the young models are left severely scarred for the rest of their lives."

CHAPTER 11

• • •

Gunned Down in Milan

The modeling metropolis is preoccupied with violence. As a result, personal alienation is not merely routine but respectable. The Maja case brought back memories of a scandal that rocked the fashion world back in 1984. An American model, Terry Broome, murdered the notorious Italian playboy Francesco D'Allessio for breaking up her engagement to wealthy jeweler Gorgio Rotti.

After Terry Broome refused his sexual advances, D'Alessio, the wealthy son of a thoroughbred horse breeder, bragged to Rotti that Broome had the "wettest pussy in Milan." When D'Allessio's malicious gossip about Broome's past promiscuity and participation in numerous orgies caused Rotti to demand his engagement ring back, Broome took matters into her own hands. Using a gun she had taken from Rotti's apartment while he slept, Broome, high on cocaine and alcohol, broke into D'Alessio's apartment at five in the morning. Finding him in bed with model Laura Royko, the two stoned on cocaine, Terry forced D'Alessio to beg for his life at gunpoint. Then she started shooting like a madwoman, hitting D'Alessio several times in the head and the chest while Royko, who barricaded herself in another room, screamed for help.

A hysterical Broome rushed back to Rotti's apartment. Rotti, scared that he would be charged because Broome had used his gun, took Broome to the airport and put her on a plane to Zurich. Several hours later, Broome was arrested in Zurich's Bahnpost Hotel.

The story made headlines around the world, and forced the Italian government to impose some legislation to appease an incensed public. Underage models were given an early curfew and club owners were warned that they would be heavily fined if they were caught admitting people under the age of twenty-one. Police soon roamed the streets of Milan checking models' I.D. cards and sending home those whose visas had expired. Meanwhile, Broome was handed a fourteen-year prison sentence for voluntary homicide.

"Milan was under the microscope of the world," recalls Jorge Vincent, a photojournalist who covered the Broome scandal. "This was not the first time that a murder was linked to a model in Milan. But it was the first time that the press got wind of it. The police were ordered by the government to do whatever they could to convince the world that it would never happen again. For a while, it looked like things would get better. But after a few weeks, when the paparazzi returned home, it was the same old story. I would go to the nightclubs and see young female models partying their brains out with much older men. And I'd see young models doing cocaine and having sex with the men in the bathrooms. Nothing had changed."

According to a friend, the innocent looking Broome had cavorted with many of Milan's richest playboys. The teenage model would accompany them to the city's trendiest discos, like La Penta, Roma, and Amnesia, where all the models hung out. Broome had a reputation with the playboys for lots of drinking and cocaine. She was also known to sleep around. Model Donna Broome (best known as the live-in lover of Fashion Model's Agency owner Giorgio Sant'Ambrogio), to this day does not deny the charges brought against her younger sister Terry.

"She was a wild child," explained Barbra Cox, a former model. "There were rumors circulating about how she'd sleep with three or four different guys in the same night. Terry completely lost herself. She was taken in by the glitz and glamour of Milan. She would be out every night partying till the wee hours. The men she surrounded herself with were total sleazebags. I'm not sure if she was sleeping around, but she certainly made it look like she was looking to have fun. When she went out she dressed very provocatively. It's amazing, but I can't recall her staying in one night. She pretty much partied twenty-four-seven."

Although Terry Broome accomplished very little as a model, many models credit her for educating the world about the dark side of the industry. While some argue that Broome should be remembered solely as the murderess she was, others say that her crime serves as a deterrent to potential model abusers.

"What she did was show these men that we can only be pushed so far," said Dana Wilson, a model from New York who worked in Milan in the mid-nineties. "Every model starting out today in Milan should thank Terry Broome. The modeling industry is still filled with horror stories, but Broome at least made a lot of creeps aware that there could be a big price to pay for their abuse. Terry Broome was not an evil person. She was a victim of the industry who decided to take justice into her own hands because nobody else wanted to listen. I don't condone what she did. But I'm sure it would have never gone so far if the men in Milan . . . treated her properly."

Broome's case generated much debate of freedom of choice, social responsibility, and the impartiality of the justice system. Questions were raised about how much influence the industry itself had on Broome's choices, such as her entanglement in a web of sexual excess, and their consequences, as well as the social systems designed to keep such abuse in check. Observers questioned why Broome felt so socially alienated that she could not seek or find redress through established channels. What prevented this helpless teenager from filing charges against D'Alessio and the group of playboys who continually abused her, and what motivated her sister Donna to look the other way until it was too late?

"Simple," says Jorge Vincent. "Broome lost trust in everyone. She knew that the police would probably do nothing. She feared that if she sought their protection, the police might opt to send her home instead as in the case of other models who had complained before her. Broome was desperate and angry. Her life had become a complete mess. The only way to get even was by taking matters into her own hands."

During a merciful week-long break in her trial, from within her steel cage, Terry Broome told her sister Donna that she regretted seeking revenge. Soon after, Donna demanded a large cash payout from the media for the full story, allegedly to cover her sister's legal expenses. "She wants to tell her side of things, but it's going to be for a big price," Donna said. Although Terry Broome's story was sold for a reported six figures, the money wasn't enough to cover all her legal bills, leaving her deeply in debt.

Released from prison in 1992, Terri Broome is now living in the United States. She has tried hard to stay out of the public eye, even though she receives dozens of media requests for interviews each year.

CHAPTER 12

• • •

Livin' la Vida Loca

It was a chilly January evening in 1999, one day before a fashion show in Milan. A fashion scout known for throwing parties reserved the penthouse suite of a big hotel for a champagne dinner for two dozen models. The partygoers didn't want any of the dozens of photographers who were in Milan for the fashion show to get wind of it.

The scene was reminiscent of something out of a Hollywood movie. As the models arrived they were greeted by topless waitresses who carried big silver trays of hors d'oeuvres that included smoked salmon, caviar, and lobster tails. Everyone took advantage of the open bar, and the champagne flowed. Joints were passed around all night and lines of cocaine were served by the waitresses on small silver trays. In one corner of the room, two female models were sipping champagne and French kissing. In another corner, an agent in his early forties was touching the breasts of a blond American model. His hand was underneath her blouse caressing her nipples. Everyone in the room seemed to be whacked on something. By the middle of the night most of the people in the room had already found a partner to have sex with, and every bed, couch, and even the large old-fashioned bathtub had been used for sex. A teenaged Spanish model had a threesome with an Italian agent and his male lover on the floor of the large balcony that overlooked the heart of downtown Milan. Nobody seemed to care at all about contracting sexual diseases or AIDS, a big killer for so many years in the fashion industry. I couldn't believe what I was witnessing.

"I've been to so many parties like this," says Bronwyn Pace, a seventeen-year-old model. "I've gotten used to it. There's parties like this all the time the night before a major fashion show. It's frightening because the next day the models have to try to look their best to the people of the fashion world. I've seen people shoot up heroin, make love in the middle of the floor, and have sex with several partners only twenty-four hours before a big fashion show. I've done it myself. Somehow, we manage to recover."

Pace says that models know every trick in the book about hiding traces of drug injections from the night before. She explains that most models shoot up heroin under their toenails, under their tongue, or between toes to hide any track marks. Pace herself has often covered up needle marks with body foundation she borrowed from the on-site makeup artist. "The fashion show's organizers all know that a lot of the girls were out partying the night before," Pace says. "A lot of the organizers were out themselves doing drugs and having sex with the models. They do everything they can the next day to help the models cover it all up. The makeup artists are instructed to look for track marks on their bodies and if they find any they give them a good pancake makeup to cover it up. By the time the show starts, the models look good. A lot of them do cocaine and drink champagne shortly before the show starts to help calm their nerves."

Vanalina Spanier was a makeup artist for seventeen years before finally quitting the business in 1996. She quit because she became too disgusted with what was going on behind the scenes. Spanier has worked with dozens of the world's top models, including Kate Moss and Naomi Campbell. Spanier admitted that she has covered up hundreds of the models' track marks over the years because she was ordered to do so by the people paying her salary. The models are wearing the most expensive clothes on earth, and soon will be walking down the runway stoned out of their minds. "I've seen the models shoot up in all kinds of crazy places," Spanier says. "I've often been instructed to cover up their track marks. If I didn't, I would probably be out of a job. I've worked with models who were so strung out they looked more like they should be in the intensive care unit of a hospital than working a fashion show. I've seen them puke backstage before a show and I've also seen them shoot up right on my makeup chair. It's a disgusting business. The public has no idea what really goes on behind the scenes."

Harriet Connors, forty-seven, is still blond, and still wears her hair long, falling in soft waves below her shoulders. During the 1960s, Connors was regarded as one of the top models in California before she became addicted to alcohol and LSD. By the time she was just nineteen, Connors was committed to a private psychiatric hospital.

It has been many years since Connors looked like the all-American cover girl she once was. In her hayday Connors dated several of Hollywood's leading men, including Elvis Presley and Peter Lawford. Her once soft, sultry voice has become harsher with time and tobacco. But with her slanting blue eyes and carefully tended face, she still looks and acts very much the supermodel. Today, Connors is still bitter that her modeling career went astray. She says that she was introduced to drugs by her agent, who she claims also sexually abused her on at least two dozen occasions. Connors says that the phony and superficial people who ran the modeling world drove her over the edge. "My agent was only interested in using me as a sex object," she says.

He got me into drugs when I was sixteen, and he spent more time fixing me up with Hollywood celebrities than he did getting me photo shoots. He instructed me to have sex with the men he fixed me up with. He said that if I didn't, it would hurt my career. It was the most awful period of my life because I felt more like a high-class hooker than I did a model. I became addicted to drugs and had several nervous breakdowns. One time my agent was trying to cut a deal with some rich Japanese businessmen. He sent me to their hotel to have drinks with them. They got me very drunk. They were giving me screwdrivers that had about 95 percent vodka and 5 percent orange juice. By the end of the night they had put me in the bedroom and started taking turns on me. One by one they came in and had sex with me while I was too drunk to realize what was happening. The next day I woke up naked in the room and realized what had happened. I had a complete nervous breakdown and wound up spending the next eleven months in a psychiatric hospital. That was the end of my modeling career.

Connors now lives alone in a quiet apartment building in southern California. She works part-time for a telephone company and is barely able to make ends meet. "There was a time when I was making a couple thousand dollars a day," Connors recalls.

I never thought that I would ever have financial problems. I was always being driven around in a limo and eating at the most expensive restaurants. After my nervous breakdown, I was left virtually penniless and without a home. A relative of mine footed my hospital bills and was kind enough to let me live for a year in the basement of his house when I got out of the hospital. Today, when I read about models like Kate Moss going through almost the exact same thing I went through, my heart goes out to [them]. I guess nothing has changed. The people who run modeling are still up to the same old tricks. They supply the models with loads of drugs and treat them like prostitutes. When is it finally going to stop? People should realize what kind of business it actually is and they should find something else to do with their lives. I know that so many young [girls] will wind up like me— have their lives ruined before they're even 20.

Most executives in the fashion world deny that there is so much drug abuse. The head of one well-known American agency discredits the tales of sex and drugs in the modeling industry. "People tend to overexaggerate things because it makes good headlines," he says. "This is a regular business. Everybody goes through job interviews, and if they have big drug problems, their chances of getting hired are nil. If the use of drugs are as bad as some people say they are, then why haven't people been arrested? It's all a bad lie. This is a very respectable business."

Most of the models interviewed for this book agree that there's a simple reason why arrests are relatively few: it's a combination of money, power, and connections. "The models and their agents are a closed world and they don't create a nuisance for the general public," says well-known entertainment author Esmond Choueke, who has covered the fashion industry both as a journalist and photographer since the early seventies. "As long as people don't draw attention to themselves, they won't draw the attention of the police and authorities. People in power don't want to be seen persecuting our cultural icons. These are our heroes and we don't want the wind knocked out of their sails by mean-spirited government officials. Whenever they've gone after musicians—like when they busted John Lennon and Keith Richards for drugs—they ended up getting a black eye. There have been many reports that beautiful women are often used to get officials to turn a blind eye if they come sniffing around too closely. Also, they know so much about security that they're able to lock themselves away where no one outside of their own inner circles can see what really goes on," says Choueke.

Ex-model Rosa Frias accuses the agents and designers of trying to cover things up. Frias was a victim herself in 1989 when her London agent slipped a sleeping pill into her drink, dragged her to his South Kensington apartment, and raped her. "I've been there, and let me tell you the agents who deny foul play sound like complete idiots," Frias says. "How can anybody deny what really goes on in this business? Everybody who has ever worked in this industry knows what really goes on. It's no mystery. Each year there are models all over the world who are raped, drugged, and even murdered. Anybody who denies it is just trying to cover their own ass."

Frias says she wanted to report her agent to the police but was threatened and then paid off. "He knew that I could have put him away on rape charges," she explains. "But before I had a chance to call the police, he showed up at my door . . . with an associate and offered me $25,000 to shut up. I took it because I was afraid. I knew if I didn't cooperate, something bad would happen to me. Since then, I've never worked again as a model." Depressed by the traumatic incident, Frias spent all her money in less than a year and ended up on welfare. She became addicted to cocaine and tried to commit suicide twice. "I didn't know what to do," Frias says. "I was afraid that if I ever spoke up, I would be killed. I've seen it happen before in this business. All that you're supposed to do is shut up and smile. And if you don't, you're asking for a whole lot of trouble."

Finally, in 1997, Frias sought help and decided to go public with her harrowing story. She cooperated in a documentary study about the modeling business, and told all about the night she was drugged and raped. Ultimately, she gave up drugs and married a British stockbroker. "I'm one of the lucky ones to have survived and to have gotten back on the right path," Frias says. "Most people with stories similar to mine don't live to tell them. I have nothing to fear now. I'm not afraid to tell people what happened to me. If I can prevent a young girl from being raped by telling my story, that will make it worthwhile."

According to a former top Elite model, the personalities of people who run the modeling business are too intimidating for the models to handle. "They're all mean, unscrupulous, and treacherous," the model says. "I've rarely met a person in the industry who doesn't resort to dirty tactics. My first agent raped me on several occasions and beat me up at least ten times. Usually I would cover the bruises with lots of makeup. One time I was so bruised I had to cancel a shoot that was going to pay me $12,000. When my agent found out he beat me up again because I didn't do the gig. He was pissed because I had lost such a big contract. He told me if I ever didn't show up to a shoot again, he wouldn't hesitate to kill me."

One powerful agent's standard procedure is to call in three girls to his office at once. He then tells all three that he has only one shoot to choose a model for. Then he asks each girl to perform a sexual act on him in competition for the job. "I left when I heard him explain his sick little game," says one of the man's former models. "The very next day I went to another agent and now I warn other girls about him. But I worry about those girls who are caught up with this guy and stay." The model refused to be identified in this book and did not report the agent. She fears being blacklisted. "He's one sick puppy alright, but he's also very powerful and anyone who goes up against him would lose," she adds. "He saw me at a party months later, and he winked at me as if to say, 'We both know my secret and we both know you can't do anything about it.' And he's right, he's a sick power freak, but he's right—I can't do anything to stop him."

CHAPTER 13

• • •

Illegal Runway

After making a final round of Milan's nightclubs, my last night in Milan was spent talking to a French model about how dangerous the modeling industry has become. I had met the six-foot, twenty-six-year-old brunette Helene Rio at a cocktail party the previous night. She had lots of fascinating stories about her nine-year modeling career. I told her I wanted to talk to her privately. She told me the best time to talk was late that night, after she finished her shift as a waitress at the restaurant where she works part-time to help make ends meet.

At her tiny apartment, Rio welcomed me with wine and cigars, enough to turn most stomachs at two o'clock in the morning. After a couple of glasses of wine, Rio provided intimate revelations. She told me how she had once ended up in a hospital held down in a strait jacket after her agent tried to drug her. "He slipped something in my drink to knock me out so he could rape me," Rio said. "The drug didn't put me to sleep. It had a bad effect on me and I completely freaked out. I leapt to my feet and lost control of myself, hitting my agent over the head with a beer bottle before roaming out into the street naked. I started yelling and screaming for several minutes before a cop picked me up and rushed me to the hospital."

It had taken every penny Rio had, and a piece of her father's savings, to straighten her out. "My father helped me bounce back," Rio said. "He made me get professional help. I stayed in Milan because modeling is all that I've ever wanted to do. My father supported my decision as long as I switched agents and got a part-time job waitressing to help support me."

Rio spent the next four hours convincing me how dangerous modeling has become. She admitted that she had been beaten, held at gunpoint by a jealous boyfriend, and raped at least six times. Rio, who had proven herself to me to be a top model by showing me a magazine with her picture on the cover told me one horror story after another. In May 1996, her former agent came to her apartment uninvited. He barged in, threatening to beat her up for firing him. "Get out, get your hands off of me," Rio yelled. She tried to stand her ground, but the agent's voice contained a fury she had never seen before—he appeared extremely disoriented. The agent then pulled a gun on Rio and held her hostage for the next two hours. Finally, she persuaded him to put the gun down.

"I didn't think he would pull the trigger," Rio recalled. "He was just pissed off because I switched agents. When I convinced him to stop, he literally broke down in tears. He begged me not to call the police. I agreed, so long as he promised to never come within walking distance of me ever again. I felt bad for him because he was so emotionally unstable. I never thought he would hurt me. He just needed attention and some serious professional help."

I probably could have spent another day listening to Rio, but I had a plane to catch at noon. Before I left, she gave me the names of several agencies to contact for work in New York. She said these agencies consider model's headshots without any fees up front. I thanked her and hopped into a cab to the airport.

Not so long ago, in the seventies and early eighties, being a supermodel was reasonably safe; models went out without fearing for their safety. Hollywood actresses had a long history of having their rights violated and being sexually abused. There are many stories legendary of models and actresses—beauties like Marilyn Monroe, Ava Gardner, and Jane Russell—having to fend off sexual advances right on their agent's casting couch. Because of the drugs and undesirables connected to the fashion industry, today's modeling scene has become more dangerous. Egregious crimes, including murder, rape, and stalking, plague the industry.

In one month in early 1999, a seventeen-year-old model was stabbed to death by a stranger who was stalking her, another was kidnapped and held hostage for five days by a former boyfriend, and a fifteen-year-old model's older boyfriend was arrested for selling cocaine in a trendy nightclub in New York's East Village. Conscientious agents caution their model clients about the rising crime rates. "They're walking targets," says model agent Jeremy Teiman. "Everywhere they go people try to get a piece of them and get them involved in some crazy scheme. A model might not even know when to expect something bad to happen. There are so many sexual predators out there who follow the girls and do something like pulling a knife on them or following them back to their apartments and raping them."

And along the way, many of the models get sucked into the immorality and illegality that pervades the system. The business is full of models who plot against each other, a reality that leaves many others in a state of panic, fearing violent attack. Some models use their beauty as a commodity in organized crime. These crimes are then covered up by agents and designers who fear the backlash of negative publicity. Only a tiny fraction of the perpetrators are ever punished.

"This business is notorious for being filled with so many criminals," said Robert Hartman, who has worked as a fashion photographer and consultant for eighteen years. "So much illegal stuff goes on. You only hear about the incidents when a model is unjustly abused or commits suicide. You don't hear the other side, like when a model steals clothes from a department store or threatens to beat up another model she's jealous of. The percentage of models who get involved in these schemes has drastically increased over the years. It's gotten completely out of control."

Each year, dozens of models participate in criminal activity. Models are lured into committing crimes by the entourage of undesirable people—agents, managers, jealous boyfriends—who surround them. Some see it as a lucrative opportunity to make extra cash. Others do it out of desperation or on a dare.

"In practical terms, most of the time the public doesn't hear about what really goes on," says private investigator Peter O'Grady, who has worked on several cases involving well-known models. O'Grady claims the authorities are usually bought off to keep it quiet. "The people who run the modeling business have a lot of money to throw around and they'll do anything to avoid a scandal. It's frightening because a lot of the models should be put in jail and forced to do time like anybody else. But they're let off without even a slap on the wrist."

Just where does all the money come from? Simple—ads and more ads. According to New York advertising executive Ronald Harris, who, over the years, has placed ads for big companies like the Gap and Johnson & Johnson, fashion advertisements bring in the most revenue, more than those for cars and food. Harris says that as long as magazines like *Vogue* and *Elle* are around, the public will never get tired of looking at or spending money on expensive clothes. Harris says these magazines put pressure on people to keep up with the latest styles. "When you see a sports car ad on TV, not everybody pays full attention, the main reason being that they're not in the market to buy. When you see Naomi Campbell wearing a slinky dress in *Vogue*, millions of young women rush out to buy the dress so they can feel like they're wearing the hippest and latest fashion trend."

This financial excess helps to shield everyone in the industry from the law. O'Grady says that the perpetration and disguising of crime touches everyone in the fashion world—models, agents, designers, photographers, and even the media. The countless stories of corruption and crime within the business is sobering. While there is no precise record, and fear of police and scandal keeps many victims from reporting crimes, O'Grady says that fashion industry crime levels increased substantially in the nineties. O'Grady estimates that people in the fashion business who are involved in unrelated crimes like robbery, rape, and drug dealing have multiplied tenfold in ten years. He claims that at least 200 models a year participate in these crimes. "There's a clear association between the fashion business and crime," O'Grady says. "A lot of shady characters work at all ends of this business. Until somebody steps in and does something to try to clean it up, the situation will continue to worsen. Never before in the history of this business has crime grown so rapidly. It's become a lower form of organized crime."

Antonio Mortina used to work in Milan as an undercover cop. He says that the authorities have not only lost control of crime in the fashion industry, but that some members of the police force are now collaborating with the criminals. According to Mortina, since the late eighties the police force has begun to allow underage models into nightclubs, and hasn't tried to stop the flagrant drug dealing and money laundering that is common among the fashion industry's upper echelon. Mortina says that the Milan authorities practically give the fashion industry a license to commit crime.

"That's why we see so much crime in the modeling industry here," Mortina says. "The police know what's going on but they don't want to stop it. Too much money is on the line. A lot of cops are bought off and bring home triple the amount of money they normally would . . . in a single year. If you're in this business in Milan, you can deal drugs, kidnap, shoplift, rob banks, and most likely you'll walk away totally unscathed. It's outrageous."

One top model said that it's common for agents to get their clients off the hook for the crimes they commit. But a hefty price tag is attached. "You can get away with murder in this business and avoid going to jail," she said. "Usually a model's agent gets them out of a sticky situation. They have connections with the cops. You get off the charges, but you pay a huge price in dollars or in other ways, like sexual favors. A female model friend of mine was caught dealing drugs last year and her agent got her off after she promised to have sex with him. It was her only way out. The agent told her if she didn't cooperate, he would make sure she spent time in jail."

The crime surge in the modeling business doesn't seem to make sense. Why would rich, young, beautiful people want to risk everything? Some people believe that growing inequality and favoritism is the cause. "There's only an elite few who are getting the big break," says London-based sociologist Alan Gorman. "It's a fierce business and careers don't last very long. Statistics show that only one in every 12,000 models get the big break. The rest are thrown to the wayside. They become bitter, disoriented and prone to drugs, prostitution, and crime." Gorman says that both the crimes and investigations are treated so lightly that it becomes almost impossible for the models to be punished.

The case of well-known designer Danny Wise, who was stalking NYPD Blue actress Andrea Thompson, is one example. Wise and Thompson were lovers and were planning a future together before their relationship went sour. Thompson dumped Wise because she thought he was too agressive and dishonest. Then, for the next several months, Thompson's life became a nightmare. Wise, an Italian national who made his mark as a top fashion designer in Milan before coming to the U.S., followed Thompson almost everywhere she went. He repeatedly showed up at her apartment uninvited and threatened her on several occasions. Wise had appeared in Vogue and had designed clothes for many of Hollywood's elite, including actress Salma Hayek. But ultimately he was charged with a felony for stalking Thompson. Although initially he denied the charge, Wise finally entered a "no contest" plea to one count of felony stalking. He was given a two-year sentence in state prison and was ordered deported back to Italy upon his release.

"He got away with it," says entertainment journalist Robert Warwick. "He refused to leave the poor girl alone. That's how fashion people are. They have big egos and they can't take being rejected. They go to any extreme to try to get what they want. Oftentimes it gets out of hand and people get hurt. Wise should have been given a stiffer sentence but I'm sure that a lot of his influential friends helped play a role in getting him off easy. If it was a regular person instead of a fashion mogul who stalked a Hollywood celebrity, the penalty would have been much stiffer."

For months the Wise case received almost no publicity, until the television tabloid talk show *Inside Edition* aired a piece about the case on June 23, 1999. "That's how it works in the fashion business, the powers-that-be have a lot of connections with the media and are able to suppress the negative stories," says Robert Warwick. "If it was an athlete or an actor who was stalking someone, there's no way it would have gone unreported. It would have been reported all over the world. For some reason the fashion business exudes more power with the media than anybody else."

Again, many people link advertising to the fashion moguls' ability to control the media. The fashion industry is one of print and electronic media's biggest advertisers, and thus a tremendous source of revenue. "Like in any other business, you don't cut off the hand that feeds you," Robert Warwick says. "It would be suicide. So much advertising money comes in from major designers like Calvin Klein and [Tommy] Hilfiger, it's easy to understand why reporters are often instructed not to report some of the dark moments in the fashion business. It could cost millions of dollars in the long run." Several fashion editors interviewed for this book admit that they are often paid off for favorable press. "I've received many free things over the years, including trips around the world and a Harley Davidson motorcycle," admits one editor. "The people in the fashion business have big money and they aren't afraid to throw it around, especially if it guarantees them good press."

As the Danny Wise case dragged on, many people in the business were perplexed. There was almost no publicity. Even a colleague who worked with Wise couldn't believe what was happening. "Usually something like this the media goes wild over," he says. "It sounds like something that's perfect for a TV movie. I was shocked how Danny avoided publicity and how he got off lightly. Danny's a real charmer and was a powerful player in the business. Many important people in the industry stuck by him and used their clout to help reduce his sentence. In a short time he'll be back in Milan designing clothes, making lots of money, and getting some of the world's top models to work for him. People in this business tend to have a short memory."

The Danny Wise case is a stark reminder of how crime has infiltrated the modeling industry. Many of the most glamorous models become involved with crime when they move from small towns to the big cities where the head offices of the world's top model agencies are. Young and naive, the innocent girls are easy prey.

Amanda McCullen is a striking, flaxen-haired supermodel who was represented by the DNA agency. She's been linked romantically to several well-known models and actors, including Matt Dillon. In 1999, McCullen was accused of shoplifting by the storeowner of a downtown New York boutique. The owner, Greg Gumo, claimed that McCullen came to his Fiend boutique-art gallery on Orchard Street on June 17 with two female friends named Sage and Graph. Gumo said that McCullen walked out with about $1,500 worth of the latest imported Japanese fashions. McCullen and Sage, who is the former girlfriend of rap star Q-Tip, used to work for Gumo in a postcard business in Miami. McCullen asked Gumo to reimburse her money that she felt he owed her, but Gumo responded that he didn't owe her a dime. Gumo claims that McCullen brought her pit bull into the shop to threaten him. After McCullen refused to leave the shop, Gumo called the police. At that point, Gumo said, McCullen took shirts, pants, and skirts right off the racks and made a quick exit. When an officer from the Seventh Precinct arrived about twenty minutes later, he and Gumo drove around looking for McCullen but were unable to find her.

Later, McCullen was tracked down by reporter Jared Paul Stern of the *New York Post*, and offered a completely different explanation. "He's just insane," McCullen told Stern. "I'm not the type of person to steal anything. He [Gumo] owes me about $2,000 from Miami, so I went by there and told him he should give me clothes—not that I'd ever wear any of that stuff anyway. But I've lived in this neighborhood for eleven years, and he must be crazy if he thinks I'd steal like that. And besides, my dog is the biggest baby in the world."

Gumo said that he intended to pursue the case. He told the *New York Post* that McCullen had a very cocky attitude. "She thinks she's above everything, that it's all a joke, but she's in trouble now," Gumo said.

A Seventh Precinct detective who worked on the case was hesitant to put the blame on McCullen. "This is an ongoing investigation," he said. "All parties involved are going to have to come down to the station for questioning. There's always two sides to everything."

A source close to both Gumo and McCullen reveals that the model was trying to get back at Gumo for not paying her. The source, who requested anonymity, said that Gumo had indeed reneged on several payments he owed McCullen.

Designer Miriam Gordon says that it's common for disgruntled models to steal clothes and harass their former bosses. "They become very angry and resort to unorderly conduct," Gordon says. "The models don't give back the clothes they're supposed to and they start becoming a nuisance when they don't get jobs. I've been harassed by several models over the years whose careers slowed down. They started calling me and threatening me over the phone, promising that they would ruin me if I didn't start using them more. It's unfortunate because they should realize that this is a very competitive field and that not everybody gets a big break. It's very disheartening when bad incidents happen. I stand up for all of my models and try to encourage them as much as possible. If they want to blame me for their failures that's their problem. It's hard to please everybody."

In the fashion industry it is a very common occurence for disgruntled ex-lovers and -employees to seek revenge. Money is usually at the center of such actions. One of the most horrid incidents took place in late 1998 when the multibillionaire fashion mogul John Badum, forty-six, was stabbed to death by his gay lover over a squabble about a green card. Badum died after a bloody battle with twenty-three-year-old Hamid Ouhda at the mansion of Badum's sister Theresa in Batavia, New York. Theresa, forty, was also stabbed but managed to flee. An hour later, Ouhda, hysterical, threw himself in front of an oncoming van and was killed instantly.

John Badum, who created the highly successful line of washable silk clothes with Jerry Hirsch called Go Silk, was one of the most likeable figures in the fashion industry. His death stunned his many celebrity close friends, including Elton John, Iggy Pop, fashion photographer David LaChapelle, and designers Todd Oldham and Thierry Mugler. "I can't believe this has happened," Elton John remarked. "He was such a caring and nice individual. Why would anybody want to do this? It's incomprehensible."

Badum originally met Ouhda on a trip through Europe, Asia, India, and North Africa that Badum took shortly after he sold his stock in Go Silk in 1995. He fell in love with Ouhda and arranged for Ouhda to marry his younger sister to get a green card. But after a huge falling out between the two a year later, Badum reported Ouhda to the Immigration and Naturalization Service in an attempt to start deportation proceedings. The relationship between the men went sour when Ouhda told Badum that he only wanted to be friends and that he wanted to date women. Ouhda was enraged when Badum squealed on him to the INS. He vowed revenge. He told a model friend that he was going to get Badum if it was the last thing he ever did. "I can't let him get away with this," Ouhda said. "He's ruined my life by shutting me out of his circle. He used me. The only thing I can do is to get even."

For years, Badum had a reputation for having affairs with men young enough to be his son. He'd call them his "toy boys." In the early nineties, he was lovers with an eighteen-year-old male model from France, who he met at a party in New York thrown by Elton John. A few months later, things came to a boil when the parents of the boy flew in from France for a visit. One night the boy broke down and told his parents what was going on. They had no idea that their son was involved in a gay affair with a much older man. The boy admitted that he was scared of Badum, that Badum had become too possessive. The parents booked their son on the next available flight to Paris. They phoned Badum and threatened to call the police. In the end, they did not.

Many of Badum's close friends constantly warned him to be more careful with his carefree lifestyle. They were worried that his penchant for young boys might backfire. A soaring romantic among groundling realists, Badum loved his flamboyant image and burnished it constantly. The more attention people gave to his sexual exploits, the more inspired Badum was to live up to his wild reputation. Still, many of his close friends recall only fond memories. Photographer David LaChapelle says that Badum died the way he lived life. "He literally died for love," LaChapelle says. He had a very colorful, romantic life and it had this dramatic Tennessee Williams-Puccini ending."

Brian Redmond, a former colleague of John Badum, says Badum's posh and massive East Village apartment was always filled with well-known industry figures. "His parties [were] legendary," Redmond says. "It was quite an atmosphere. He had this massive bed with a disco ball above it in the bedroom and there was always lots of activity there. Never a dull moment. Lots of gorgeous young men and women, lots of booze and drugs. Nobody I ever met had such incredible style."

Milan-based model scout Jean Lorraine says Badum should never have gotten involved with a younger man. Lorraine says it is common, especially among gay male designers, to recruit gorgeous young men from exotic parts of the world. "I've heard so many bad stories about this practice," Lorraine says. "The designers want to have the best looking young boyfriends with them at parties and clubs. They have huge egos and want to impress. Badum is not the first one to be murdered by a disgruntled ex-boyfriend. It's unfortunate that the same old story has been written so many times before."

Badum's death did not seem to deter crime in the fashion industry. Many models who turn to crime use guns. Melanie Pavicic, a twenty-one-year-old model from Vancouver who also acted on the *X-Files*, wore a different sort of outfit on March 29, 1997. She dressed up in a black catburglar's uniform—a balaclava and tight black stockings—when she and her twenty-three-year-old boyfriend, Vahid Mahanian, broke into the home of Robert and Glennis McArthur and held them up at gunpoint. The McArthurs, a quiet, well-respected family, begged for their lives. Mr. McArthur, forty-two, had been relaxing in his hot tub while his wife and two children, aged four and six, were upstairs sleeping in bed. Pavicic and Mahanian planned the robbery after watching the famous bank robber film *Bonnie and Clyde*. They burst in with machine guns, tied McArthur and his wife up with rope, and taped their mouths. They stole a diamond ring and a VCR, and obtained the PIN numbers of the McArthurs' bank cards and withdrew cash. After the robbers fled, police recovered a sawed-off shotgun and a semi-automatic .22 calibre pistol. A couple of weeks later Pavicic and Mahanian were arrested and charged with breaking and entering, using a firearm to commit a robbery, and unlawful confinement. The couple pleaded guilty to all three counts.

British Columbia Supreme Court Justice Alexander Henderson said in handing down his sentence that "no explanation was given as to why a young woman succeeding in her pursuit of a career would suddenly turn to a serious act of crime."

Pavicic was the last person one would expect to commit such a crime. She was an honor roll student at her high school in the Vancouver suburb of Coquitlam and was very well-liked by her classmates. She seemed destined to become rich and famous. Many of the top modeling agencies and TV directors showed interest in her.

"She was so quiet and sweet," says one of her former classmates. "She was the person who everybody thought was the most likely to succeed. She was good at everything—sports, art and academics. When I heard what she did I just kept shaking my head in disbelief. She just didn't seem like the type to do it."

Pavicic and Mahanian received a four-year, three-month sentence, which Judge Henderson said was the equivalent of six years because the accused spent slightly more than ten months in custody before the trial, which was worth double time. News of the sentence stunned the modeling world. "Melanie had such a good career ahead of her on the catwalk," says model Beverly Fagan. "I can't believe she would throw it all away. It's a shame because she had the potential to make so much money. By the time she gets out of prison she'll be considered too old to model. So many times in this business, models do crazy things and don't realize what the consequences will be. One bad move can ruin your entire career."

A Vancouver artist and longtime friend of Pavicic claims that he saw her a few days before the crime. According to the artist, Pavicic was acting very weird. She kept saying how bored she had become of show business and was looking for a new challenge. She was stumbling on her words and appeared to be stoned. For her part, Pavicic has said publicly that she regrets what she did. She said that the high pressure of show business stressed her out and that she lost control of herself completely. Although she has refused to elaborate on her motive, she intimated that she might consider revealing the rest of the story if she got a book deal.

Jennifer Carleton, a promising young model from North Carolina who had remained clean despite the pressure to do drugs, became a victim of her modeling agency's retrenchment in 1997. She should have had no difficulty getting another contract, but for some reason no one wanted her anymore. A former lover and advisor of Carleton's called all his contacts and spread the word that she was a troublemaker. He was trying to get revenge against Carleton for dumping him some months earlier. Carleton had dumped the lover because of a nasty cocaine habit for which he refused to seek treatment.

Before long, Carleton was feeling suicidal. She couldn't get any contracts and by the age of twenty-two was feeling washed-up. At the same time, she witnessed models with nowhere near her talent and looks earning enormous sums of money. Because she couldn't afford to keep living the lavish lifestyle to which she had become accustomed, Carleton became more and more desperate. Her chronic depression eventually turned her toward drugs. Ironically, Carleton developed her own cocaine habit. She was abusing it several times a day, and spending to the tune of $700 a week on it.

Carleton needed to find work to support her drug habit. In September 1997, she found something through an old model friend that brought her all the money she needed. She became a high class hooker in New York City under a new name—Jenna Peters. Carleton made up to $7,000 a day cavorting with wealthy businessmen, athletes, and entertainers. The owner of the Manhattan escort agency that hired Carleton says she was his number one girl. "Her clients would all come back for more," says Albert Maurice. "She was by far the most beautiful girl we had. Whoever wanted her had to pay big bucks. She was the most high-class call girl I've ever seen. Many famous people were her clients, including a famous politician and a former heavyweight boxing champion." Maurice reveals that the most lucrative offer Jenna received was $80,000 to accompany an English billionaire on a week-long cruise in North Africa. "She would always get all kinds of crazy offers," Maurice says. "She was so successful. She's what I call the first millionaire hooker."

One of her former clients exclaims that Jenna was worth the exorbitant $1000/hour fee. "She's one of the most beautiful women on the planet," he says. "To get to sleep with her is worth any price she wants. It's like sleeping with royalty. She really knows how to please her clients"

But Carleton still recalls her painful initiation into the world of prostitution. "It was a Saturday afternoon when I got the call, the date was for eight o'clock that night," she says. "I was so nervous and so scared. I washed my hair, I put lotion on all over my body, I didn't know how to get ready for a client. I'd never done this before." Carleton was so intent on her preparations that she got completely made up and dressed by 6:30 that evening. "Then I changed my mind, washed my hair again and re-set it a different way just for something to do. The agency sent a car for me. I was afraid the driver could see my knees shaking on the way there."

Carleton was to meet the client, a sportswear importer from Chicago, at his luxury hotel. "When he opened the door, I took one look at him and I thought, hey, I could do this! I had been expecting a much older man, but he was mid-forties, had dark, shiny, curly hair, and a nice, fit body. He told me to call him Saber and I introduced myself as "Irene" and we took it from there. He had thought to have champagne sent up, as well as a dozen roses for me. I'm thankful he made my first experience in this business so pleasant."

Carleton recalls that Saber was a good lover, who cared about her being pleased as well. "And he didn't stop, he asked me to stay the night, and he made love to me four times. I left his room exhausted, but thousands of dollars richer."

Carleton says that Saber remained a regular customer as long as she was in the business, and once gave her the use of his yacht in the Bahamas for two weeks. "He wasn't even there, he just let me go down for a few weeks to relax. Saber was a real gentleman." When asked how Saber got his name, Carleton laughs, "I found that out, too, but I'm not telling. You figure it out."

One year later, in July 1998, Carleton had more than $900,000 saved up in her bank account. She didn't feel suicidal anymore and she had stopped using drugs. She had become a successful businessperson. She sought the advice of a top New York investment broker because she wanted to ensure that she could hold on to her cash and live off it for a long time. Carleton told the agent that she wanted to put the money into setting up her own business in another part of the world. Within four months Carleton had relocated to the sunny Algarve coast in Portugal, where she set up a bed-and-breakfast. Today, Carleton lives like a millionaire in Portugal, largely due to the increased value of the American dollar in comparison to the weak Portuguese escudo. Carleton says that she's better off now than ever before. "Even when I was making good money modeling, I never lived nearly as well as I do now," she says. "I don't regret doing what I did because I felt like I was blacklisted as a model and I had no other alternative. At first I was strung out and didn't really know what I was doing. But when the money started to roll in I became a businesswoman with a game plan. I wanted to work hard for a couple of years to make enough money to set up a legitimate business. I don't miss the phony fashion world at all. I've fallen in love with the man of my dreams and we're planning to start a family together soon. I've never been happier."

PART TWO

Beautiful Women, Bad World

CHAPTER 14

● ● ●

The Big Six

During the course of my investigation, I was constantly amazed by the amount of personal turmoil some of these big models had gone through. It's difficult to imagine how unhappy some of the top supermodels are when you see them smiling every month in the fashion magazines. Most of them, however, seem to have had an equal share of ups and downs.

Despite achieving fame and fortune, many of the world's most recognized supermodels seem to create more of a stir off the catwalk than on it. The so-called "Big Six"—Naomi Campbell, Cindy Crawford, Claudia Schiffer, Christy Turlington, Linda Evangelista, and Elle MacPherson—have all, at one point or another, made news for the wrong reasons. It seemed as though the top beauties of the nineties have become unglued in the new millennium.

Naomi Campbell enrolled in a anger management program after a series of blowups with her colleagues and family. Campbell's fiery temper had cost her many friendships and even more money. Former personal assistant Georgina Galanis sued Campbell for $2 million for allegedly clubbing her over the head with a telephone and threatening to throw her out of a moving car during a trip to Toronto. Campbell vehemently denied the charges and challenged Galanis in court. Galanis said that she had been abused by Campbell and had launched her suit to get justice. "Nobody has the right to treat a person that way and expect to get away with it," she said.

Eventually, Campbell settled out of court with Galanis, paying her a reported six-figure sum to drop the civil suit. Galanis, who now works in New York, was ecstatic that justice had been served. "I was mistreated and abused," she said. "I tried my darndest to be the best worker for Naomi but it just didn't work out. She's not easy to work for."

Another Campbell outburst made headlines in April 2001, when the temperamental supermodel screamed obscenities at Tiziano Mazzilli, owner of the elegant U.K. boutique Voyage. The feud with Mazzilli began in December 2000, when Campbell was rude to Voyage's salesclerks, and as a result was banned by Mazzilli from the store. Mazzilli, whose clients include Nicole Kidman, Gwyneth Paltrow, and Madonna, was disgusted with Campbell's behavior and promised to have her ejected if she ever tried to shop at Voyage again. "She needs to learn to show respect," he said.

Then, on a Sunday in April 2001, Campbell spotted Mazzilli and his girlfriend coming out of the Harvey Nichols department store in London. The couple had just gone on one of their regular shopping sprees. According to eyewitnesses, Campbell jumped out of her Range Rover and started hurling verbal darts.

Canadian tourist Shane Williams was at the scene. In his opinion, Campbell was completely out of control. "I was walking down the street and all of a sudden I see Naomi Campbell throwing a shit fit in the middle of the street," he said. "At first I thought it was some sort of wacky publicity stunt, but then I realized that it was for real. I guess celebrities aren't above the rest of us after all. They get mad just like everyday people do."

The bad blood between Campbell and Mazzilli has created animosity between members of their respective entourages. Mazzilli was refused entrance into a nightclub owned by Campbell's wealthy Italian lover, Flavio Briatore, the fifty-one-year-old managing director of Benetton Formula One. Mazzilli's son Rocky has remarked that Campbell has no class. He told the London paper the *Mirror,* "Her attitude is appalling. She ought to keep her mouth shut. I want to teach her how to behave properly." And so the war continues.

Campbell's history of striking the fear of God into people began back in the early nineties, when she became one of the most recognizable faces on earth. During her twenty-second birthday celebration in New York, Campbell threw punches at actress Troy Beyer after an argument they'd had in a club spilled out onto the street. Beyer incensed Campbell by poking fun at Robert De Niro, Campbell's lover at the time. Campbell's handlers tried to restrain her, but she insisted on settling things her own way.

"She doesn't take shit from anybody," says journalist Martin Smith. "Naomi is one of the most feared people in showbiz. If you get in her way, watch out. She'll make sure you'll regret ever meeting her."

Even Campbell's longtime fashion mentor, her mother Valerie, has had viscous confrontations with her daughter. In December 2000, Valerie Campbell, forty-eight, was admitted to a mental hospital after suffering from a depression following a blowup with Naomi in Milan. The pair had a falling out after Valerie demanded that Naomi clean up her act. Valerie was displeased with the toll Naomi's jet set life was taking on her. News of Valerie's condition broke after she failed to show up for a World AIDS Day charity event in Spain. Campbell's camp denied the report. Valerie, a big supporter of AIDS awareness, was in no state to make a public appearance. "As far as we know, Valerie is in Milan preparing her collection and she's fine," a spokesperson for Naomi Campbell said.

According to a source close to Campbell, however, mother and daughter had indeed had an argument. "Valerie confronted Naomi with several of her concerns and Naomi simply hit the ceiling," a friend of the family said. "It's disgusting that Naomi can be disrespectful to even her own mother."

Campbell claims that she's been victimized by people who are trying to take advantage of her wealth and fame. Campbell says it's important for celebrities to stand up for their rights. "People look at us and see dollar signs," she told the London Daily Telegraph. "I hate people who, because you are in the public eye, try to take advantage of you, blackmail you. Unfortunately, lawyers quickly become your best friends."

In March of 1999, another tumultuous period in Campbell's career came to a head—She announced that she was severing ties with the house of Versace, the very fashion dynasty that had catapulted her to the top. Ever since the death of founder Gianni Versace, Campbell's relationship with those managing the fashion empire had become strained. She had fallen out with Versace's sister Donatella, and his brother Santo, after they refused to pay Campbell the $100,000 appearance fee she demanded just to walk down a runway. "Nothing is more important to me than Gianni Versace," Campbell said. "I loved him and I loved working for him. I have worked for the house for twelve and a half years. But things change. The situation is not the same as it was when Gianni was alive."

The tragic death of Gianni Versace, a shooting victim of serial killer Andrew Cunanan, shook the fashion empire to its very core. Versace's siblings struggled to hold on to the business and to put the world famous fashion house back in order. Some insiders claim the cash they needed to bridge the transition came from cutting Naomi Campbell's huge fees.

At a ceremony organized by the city of Milan to honor Campbell for her local charity work, the teary-eyed model spoke of the changes at Versace since Gianni's death. "They say I am treated like a member of the family. Well, I used to be. But I certainly have not felt like a member of the family in the past six months. I am not just like any other model. They have been treating me like a stranger for months."

At a press conference, it seemed like Campbell was trying to get revenge on the Versace house by wearing a stunning Armani suit. Both Donatella and Santo Versace were fuming. "Naomi's acting up," Donatella Versace said. Santo Versace, who was present at the ceremony honoring Campbell in his capacity as chairman of the Italian Fashion Chamber, went into greater detail. "It is just that, at times, suddenly and without reason, people start to speak different languages, and then they don't understand each other any longer."

Campbell told reporters that her agent had faxed the Versaces on February 25 and March 3, 1999, to inform them that she would not be available to work at either the Versus (Versace's younger line) or Versace show. "I was not dropped," Campbell insisted. "It had nothing to do with the money and there was no fight. I was the one who was unavailable."

Campbell was discovered by Gianni Versace in the mid-eighties, and helped him to revolutionize the fashion industry with his colorful, provocative designs. She became Versace's most famous model, and was known as the "goddess of the catwalk." When Gianni Versace was gunned down outside his Miami mansion in July of 1997, Campbell was deeply affected. At a memorial fashion show in Rome, she wept uncontrollably as she walked down the Spanish Steps in a splendid Versace gown. "I can't even describe what Gianni meant to me," she later said. "It's a loss that will never be replaced. He was the kindest and most charismatic person you'd ever want to meet."

After Gianni's death, Campbell had difficulty adjusting to the new direction the Versace team was taking. She simply did not always agree with the way Donatella Versace was steering the empire.

"Naomi and Donatella had difficulty meeting eye-to-eye," said a model and good friend of Campbell's. "I don't think it was anything personal, because Naomi used to speak highly of Donatella and the rest of the Versace family. I think that after Gianni's death, Naomi's heart just wasn't in it anymore. Without Gianni calling the shots, things just couldn't be what they used to be. After his death, Naomi became very depressed and self-destructive. Her career was on the slide. She desperately wanted to revive it. And the best way for her to do so was to make a fresh start."

But the Versace fiasco wasn't the first time Campbell had had a falling out with an employer. In 1993, she was fired from the Elite Model Agency after a dispute. Her boss said that Campbell was the most difficult person he had ever worked with. "Naomi's a manipulative, scheming, rude, and impossible little madam," he said. "She has treated us and our clients like dirt." Campbell and Elite eventually reconciled, but the whole incident left a dark cloud hanging over Campbell and her handlers.

Many industry insiders view Campbell's conflict with Elite, among others, as her own fault. Over the years, Campbell has acquired a reputation as a primadonna. One rumor had Naomi refusing to leave her dressing room at a photo shoot until someone delivered her favorite brand of mineral water. The wrong brand of mineral water was originally provided and allegedly she had hurled the bottle and glass against a wall.

"Let's face it, Naomi has always been one of the hardest people to work with in this business," said longtime fashion consultant Irene Brown. "She marches only to the beat of her own drum. If someone pisses her off or offends her, watch out. She'll throw a tantrum and embarrass the hell out of you. But you must sympathize with Naomi. She's endured so much bullshit in her career. I can't blame her for taking the offensive. If she doesn't, people will walk all over her. Anybody can say anything they want about Naomi, but nobody can deny that she's one of the best models ever to step onto the catwalk. Not many models even come close to her. She did so much to change the face of the fashion world for blacks and other visible minorities. In a hundred years, people will still remember her for that. They won't remember the arguments and her temperamental attitude. She'll be remembered as a great artist, like Mozart or Martha Graham were to music and dance."

Cindy Crawford was upset that her much publicized ABC TV special *Sex with Cindy Crawford* was the top flop of the year, coming in last in the ratings for its time slot. Crawford, who lives with hunky, nightclub-owner husband Rande Gerber, and their son, Dylan, unwittingly revealed that her talent as an on-air personality was a far cry from her talent as a model.

"Cindy became the laughing stock of the television industry," said TV critic Don Thompson. "She practically made a fool of herself. Shortly after, she got pregnant. Maybe it was a way of taking her mind off how badly her show turned out. I think that she should have done more consultation and research before delving into the project. Just because she was one of the prettiest women in the world in no way guarantees that people would want to watch her show. I've seen television producers make that mistake so often over the years. They take a well-known beauty and put her on the tube, thinking that everybody is going to want to watch. It usually backfires."

If there's one supermodel who could have been Miss America, it's Cindy. Her gleaming smile and all-American look captured the hearts of the fashion public more than any other American model ever. An excellent athlete and straight-A student in high school, Crawford's goal was to become the first female President. Eventually, she settled for life on the catwalk. Her modeling career took off in 1986, when she was selected as a finalist in Elite's Model Look contest. She immediately transferred from Elite Chicago to Elite New York, where, as the official face of Revlon, her image was emblazoned in the world's mind. The biggest boost to her career came when she took off her clothes for *Playboy*, and catapulted her face and her body to the top.

"Many people were mad at Cindy, because there's always been an unwritten law in the modeling business among the top models not to pose nude," said fashion writer Deidre Brown. "When Cindy posed nude, a lot of people were upset because they thought she was trying to steal the limelight from the other models. Many worried that it would set an ugly precedent. But Cindy is one of the smartest models ever. She knew exactly what she was doing. The *Playboy* spread not only gave her a lot of attention, it also placed a spotlight on the entire fashion industry. Everybody cashed in. Models became bigger than ever before, and Cindy had as much to do about it as anybody."

Shortly after Crawford's *Playboy* centerfold, offers started pouring in from every direction. An MTV producer, impressed with the *Playboy* shoot, signed Crawford to host the popular *House of Style* show. For years, *House of Style* has been regarded as the hippest fashion show on TV, one which introduces the latest trends to America's youth. In addition to on-screen success, Crawford put out the most successful exercise video since Jane Fonda and launched her own swimwear calendar, from which she donated more than half the money to the Children's Leukemia Foundation.

Indeed, Cindy Crawford became such an icon that most Hollywood insiders agree her short-lived marriage to heartthrob Richard Gere did more to boost his career than it did hers. When the couple posed for a *Vogue* cover shot by famed fashion photographer Herb Ritts, a lot of people felt Gere was trying desperately to increase his profile. "Richard's films weren't as popular as they once were," said a close friend of Crawford. "He went about it in a very discreet way, but I honestly think that he used Cindy to help his career. He loved having the most gorgeous young star in the world draped around his arm whenever he appeared at film premieres, concerts, and entertainment-industry functions."

Deborah Winger had repeatedly stated that Gere was impossible to work with. While shooting the Academy Award winning An Officer and A Gentleman, Winger claimed that Gere's personality made the work a living hell. She particularly hated the sex scenes with him, and said so publicly to Barbara Walters in a televised interview. She told Walters that Gere's big ego was too much for her to handle, making it difficult for her to be convincing in bed with him.

When Crawford and Gere finally divorced in 1994, many speculated that the breakup was due to the fact that they were both gay. Crawford and Gere never denied the rumors and even heightened them by hinting to the press that it was true. Gere wouldn't answer an interviewer who asked him what his sexual orientation was, and Crawford made headlines when she appeared with the singer k.d. Lang, who is openly gay, on a magazine cover. "Cindy is a marketing genius," said a close friend. "Everybody knows that Cindy is not gay. She was just trying to make some sort of statement. With all the rumors about her and Richard being bisexual, she decided to pose with k.d. to play it up and make people wonder even more. It worked. That photo of her and k.d. is one of the most memorable in fashion history."

Several gay models applauded Crawford for her efforts. "I'm gay and I've had to hide it for years because my agency was worried that it would hurt my career," said Fiona, a five-foot, ten-inch, red-headed beauty from California.

I always thought it wasn't right to hide from the public what I really am. Everybody knows that at least 50 percent of this industry is gay or bisexual. It's sick to think that my career would suffer if people found out that I'm a lesbian. When Cindy posed with k.d. Lang, I thought it was brilliant. I know of at least a dozen other models who felt as relieved as I did. The days of just appealing to men who lust over beautiful women were long over. Sure, many men still pick up fashion mags to stare at the women, but fashion has become more of an art today. There are a lot of men and women who want to see gay models. People are much more open about sexuality today. It's puzzling why the fashion industry still tries to sweep it under the rug when the fact is, in nine years in the business, I don't think I've worked with one male designer who is not gay."

Crawford is a natural celebrity—she's in no way camera shy—and her work on MTV acclimated her to being in front of a TV camera as well. Yet she was by no stretch of the imagination a natural on television. "Cindy is one of the brightest models I've ever come across," said television producer Allan Crawley. "But being on TV, coming down the runway, and hosting a show are completely different things. People go to school for years to learn the art of TV. I don't think it's Cindy's fault that her ABC show did so bad. It's the fault of the bonehead producers who go in with the attitude that looks are more important than the craft. Never judge a book by its cover."

Claudia Schiffer stunned the modeling world by announcing that she was quitting the business after a Giorgio Ferrari show in Milan. "I'm never going to model again," she was quoted as saying. She later denied that statement, but has since spent more time making Hollywood films than walking down the runway.

Schiffer grew up in Rheinburg, Germany. The two top executives of the well-known Metropolitan Model Agency of Paris discovered Schiffer in a Dusseldorf discotheque. They knew immediately that Schiffer would be a star. Schiffer was offered a contract on the spot.

Over the years, Schiffer became known for defying convention. In the mid-nineties, she appeared on the covers of a variety of non-fashion magazines, including Rolling Stone. Schiffer's Paris agent, Arline Souliers, said that if Schiffer hadn't branched out, she might have been bored, and retired. "She's different from the other models," Souliers said. "Claudia doesn't like to do the same thing over and over. She's very creative and likes to try new ventures. That's what she lives for."

Schiffer's penchant for the daring has hurt her career on many occasions. She has taken a lot of heat for appearing in several sexually
provocative television ads, most notably a 1998 Citroen Xsara commercial that featured the sultry blond stripping off her dress and
underwear. Outrage from feminist activists poured in from all over
the world, claiming that the ad was in poor taste and used a woman's
body gratuitously. The outcry sparked a review of all car advertisements that too often use sex to sell product.

"On one hand it was good, because the key is to get publicity,"
said New York advertising executive Al Tanner. "On the other hand,
I think it hurt Claudia's career, especially in the long run. People
were incensed because it was clear that she was willing to sacrifice
her body and morals to make a buck. I'm sure she knew the outrage
the ad would cause, but maybe she didn't care because she knew the
attention would be priceless."

Needless to say, Schiffer ranks as one of the most successful models ever. She has decreased her modeling forays to pursue an acting
career, and has landed medium-sized roles in several Hollywood
films. Although her films have bombed at the box office, some re-
viewers have praised Claudia's competent performances. Schiffer is
determined to make it as an actress.

"I've always wanted to try acting," she said. "And now is the
right time. At this point, I don't feel the same motivation and positive
energy in the modeling business the way I used to. I needed a new
challenge."

Christy Turlington decided to take a respite from modeling after
declaring that she was bored and burned out. She enrolled as a liberal arts student at New York University, and, in May of 1999, grad-
uated. She was the star attraction at a cap and gown ceremony where
Bill Cosby delivered a moving commencement speech. Cosby received a standing ovation for telling the class of '99 to choose a direction and to pursue it without sacrificing one's morals and
integrity—Turlington hung on to each of Cosby's powerful words.
After the graduation ceremony, Turlington addressed the persistent
rumors that she had retired from modeling. "I wanted to distance
myself, just be myself again," she said. "Of course, people were
bored with us [supermodels]; we were bored with each other. The
whole supermodel thing was just a moment in time; it wasn't anything worth hanging on to."

Turlington, who started modeling at the age of thirteen and was awarded The Face of the 20th Century Award by New York's Metropolitan Museum of Art, is one of the most outspoken models in the business. In a 1994 documentary about her life and career, *Christy Turlington Backstage*, she shared some of the pros and cons of being a supermodel. She discussed the importance of education and awareness. Teenage models, she said, should not give up their education, since there are no guarantees in modeling and it's important to have an education to fall back on. A model's career, she urged, can be very short lived.

Turlington's modeling history is unusual in that she put off becoming a Ford model until she was eighteen—five years after she was discovered—in order to finish high school. She's also one of the most verbal celebrities about animal rights, and is a favorite spokesperson of PETA, an animal rights organization that supports positive action. She has always refused to model fur in shows—even garments trimmed with fur—and has set a precedent for other animal-loving models. Turlington created a sensation when she posed nude for a billboard-sized photograph in an anti-fur campaign. Ever the activist, Turlington even shot her own calendar in El Salvador, her mother's native country, and donated hundreds of thousands of dollars from the proceeds to the El Salvadoran Foundation.

"Christy's a real gem," said photographer William Rue. "She doesn't take herself so seriously, like most of the other models do, and she is very socially conscious. She's made a lot of money and has used a good chunk of it to help people who are less fortunate than her."

Turlington, for her part, is amazed at how big a deal the press and public have made of her social activism. Sometimes, she says, it's embarassing. "I'm just one person out there trying to do my small part. I enjoy working with people who are committed to changing injustice."

Linda Evangelista made international headlines for allegedly being drunk and overweight at a Portugal fashion show in the Fall of 1999. The show's organizer tried to recoup Evangelista's $100,000 appearance fee, but had to settle for a fraction of it. The media reported that Evangelista was pregnant with her boyfriend Kyle McLachlan's child. The rumor proved to be false, but it ended up hurting Evangelista's image. The consensus was that Evangelista had been abusing alcohol while pregnant.

"People started to wonder if Linda was being an irresponsible mum-to-be. Once word got out that Linda had gained a few pounds and was not pregnant, a lot of people lost interest in her," said fashion journalist Karen Porter. "She did appear to have put on a few pounds, but I think too much of a big deal was made of it. According to several of my contacts in Portugal at the time, she might have been drunk as was reported. But that's nothing new in this business. I've seen so many of the models over the years appear on the runway way more drunk than Evangelista was. Apparently, the organizers of the Portuguese show were more concerned about the big fee they had to pay her. They might have been looking for a way out of paying her the full amount. Her handlers didn't go for it, and wound up pulling her out of the show."

Evangelista has long been regarded as one of the best models to ever strut the catwalk because of her easygoing manner while being photographed. She's a photographer's dream, able to pose and look good at all camera angles. Ever since she hooked up with well-known fashion photographer Peter Lindbergh in 1989, she has become one of the top-earning supermodels of all-time. It was Lindbergh who convinced her to crop her long hair, a style choice that became her trademark—the Evangelista look. Until her negative experience in Portugal, Evangelista consistently headed the modeling A-list.

"I think that Linda was caught off guard in Portugal," said one designer. "I can't believe what happened. Everybody knows that Linda can be flamboyant at times, but the way the media portrayed her was unjust. They said she looked pregnant. I saw the photos, and maybe she had gained a pound or two, but she looked more tired than anything else. What happened is unfortunate, because it hurt Linda's career. Ever since Portugal some designers have been reluctant to work with her. That's the sad part about this business. Once it's in print, people want to believe it regardless of whether or not it's true. And the person who suffers in the end is the one who was the victim of lies."

Evangelista has learned that to get anywhere in her battles with the male-dominated circle of fashion world moguls, she has to prove herself equal to the fight. And she knows the only way to do that, is to stand her ground, to resist flinching. She refuses to suck up to them, win them over with feminine charm, or sleep with them. "Linda has been through so much during her career," says London fashion reporter Milos Gurvin. "When she was still a young model trying to make it in Paris, she married one of the biggest agents in the business [Gerald Marie], a man old enough to be her father. In the process, she became one of the greatest models ever. Today, she puts up with no bullshit. The fiasco in Portugal was not good for her career, because the media were against her. It was almost as if they were desperate to write something bad about her. But being the pro she is, she managed to bounce back right away and put it behind her."

After Portugal, Evangelista longed more than ever to settle down with the right man. She pined after French World Cup goalie Fabien Barthez. Barthez was a dedicated companion to Evangelista, standing by her side during a year filled with emotional turmoil. In July 1999, Barthez and Evangelista wed. They honeymooned on St. Martin several weeks before the wedding to avoid conflicting with the start of the new soccer season. Less than a month after exchanging vows, the couple's apartment was burglarized while they slept. More than $150,000 worth of jewelry and valuables was stolen. "Linda didn't get too upset," said a close friend. "The thieves could have taken everything from her and she wouldn't have cared, because she still had her most valuable jewel—Barthez."

CHAPTER 15

● ● ●

Cigarettes, Alcohol, Heroin . . .

After the Big Six sensation started to die in the mid-nineties, British supermodel Kate Moss created a sensation with heroin chic. Heroin chic was fashion's version of grunge music. When Nirvana's lead singer Kurt Cobain became the father of the heroin-inspired grunge music movement in the early nineties, Moss's waiflike, drugged-out look was changing the face of the fashion world. Suddenly, young models felt the urge to emulate the lead singer of a grunge band rather than a member of the pampered elite. For the first time, fashion magazines embraced the idea of having models appear on the cover with small breasts, dark eye makeup, and pale skin, painting a gaunt, strung-out look. The fashion industry embraced grunge as being "cool."

"If you didn't look like you were on drugs, you didn't have a chance of being in the big magazines," said Paris-based fashion writer Stephane Pilote. "The world went grunge crazy. Nobody at this time was interested in seeing the traditional-style models like Claudia Schiffer. People wanted to see something alternative, something that reflected the alternative grunge music invasion of that time."

Heroin chic was typified by a notorious mid-nineties Calvin Klein ad campaign that used models who looked like drug addicts. Kate Moss was the featured model. It was this alternative heroin-chic lifestyle that would eventually almost ruin Moss's life and career. Most people thought that Moss was simply playing a junkie role, but like Kurt Cobain, she was living what she played.

It was Kate Moss's custom to return home to London between photo shoots. In late October of 1998, Moss spent most of her time being whisked through the streets of London in plush limousines. On the surface, she appeared to be living a charmed life. In truth, she was on the verge of an emotional breakdown that would put her in the hospital for the next two months.

A couple of weeks before her breakdown, on one of her usual visits home, Moss dyed her hair orange, creating a stir during a European fashion show where she modeled Versace's latest fall designs. A week later the waiflike Moss was seen surrounded by the British paparazzi at the opening of a west end nightclub. Britain's sweetheart was also spotted at a Halloween party and at a fashion show singing "Happy Birthday" to one of the Backstreet Boys. "She looked terrible," remarked Andre Ducharme, a freelance photographer who snapped photos of Moss a few days before her collapse. "Kate has always been someone who plays up to the cameras. She's usually smiling and cheerful. She's always had a reputation as being a party animal, but it never affected how she dealt with people. She's one of the most polite models I'd ever come across. But on this occasion, she looked like a wreck. I had never seen Kate look more distressed. When I found out a few days later that she checked herself into a hospital, I wasn't surprised at all. I felt relieved. Too many models realize they have a problem when it's too late. Many of them wind up dead. I'm glad Kate came to her senses. I would have hated for her to be the next casualty. She's a person who has done so many positive things, both for models and the whole fashion industry."

Moss had always balked at the incessant frenzy of performing on catwalks in city after city. She found catharsis in partying wildly every night. But ultimately the euphoria and pressure of fame proved too much to handle. Despite all indications that Moss needed help, none of her handlers tried to help her. Her band of managers, agents, and fashion designers seemed to be more interested in making money off her. If anything, they continued to stoke her reckless lifestyle, booking her into more shoots than ever and encouraging her to attend industry parties. Moss's life, meanwhile, became punctuated by emotional upheavals that she tried to soothe with booze and drugs. Moss was typically able to recuperate from a night of intense debauchery in time for the next day's shoot. But this time she fell apart.

After her breakdown Moss—who began taking drugs regularly when she was only twelve years old—admitted that she hadn't been sober on the catwalk in more than a decade. And perhaps she might have been spared a lot of grief if she hadn't been at the vanguard of the heroin chic movement—a movement that also required her to stay ultra thin. In fact, the need to remain slim was a major reason for her drug use. To maintain her waiflike look, Moss often replaced food with drugs.

Moss said she usually started her days by sharing some champagne and marijuana with several of her close model friends. Often, she would sneak a joint or flask of whisky to photo shoots. "Kate found it difficult to cope with the twelve- to fifteen-hour photo shoots," said Peter Sorensen, who once worked with Moss at a fashion show in Milan. "To everybody on the set it was often obvious that Kate was stoned. But her handlers didn't seem to be bothered. If anything, they encouraged her to do more. All they wanted was for her to pose and look good on the runway and on the magazine covers."

Clearly Moss isn't the only person in fashion to have abused drugs. Photographers, designers, and many models consume drugs and alcohol regularly. But Moss's problem was more serious. She had become an addict. It's unfortunate, because Moss was a consummate professional, and never really needed stimulants to help her perform. What she did need, however, was more guidance to help her cope with the daily rigors of fame. She had trouble being followed by photographers wherever she went. She didn't like having her privacy invaded. She wanted to lead a more normal life.

When I first met Moss at a party in London's Soho district back in 1998, she appeared to be a beautiful, intelligent, and complex woman possessed of a smoldering sensuality. Sensitive, friendly, aloof but extremely vulnerable, she has a history of being careless and erratic at times. At the party, she was dancing with a champagne glass in her left hand. A few seconds later, I noticed she had put the glass on the floor while she continued to dance. Shortly thereafter, a tall, twentyish man stepped on the glass with his bare foot, shattering the glass and hopping up and down in pain as blood poured from a deep gash. Several people crowded around, trying to help him. Moss didn't seem to notice what had happened, and instead continued to dance.

After a few more days spent with pals in London, Moss hit rock bottom. She appeared to be emotionally drained and depressed. Her rollercoaster love life, marked by a four-year, on-again-off-again relationship with actor Johnny Depp, was marred by violence, booze, and drugs.

In 1997 Moss was with Depp when he was arrested for trashing a New York City hotel room in a drunken state. The couple broke up that summer, but were reunited a year later at the Cannes Film Festival. There, Moss made a gross spectacle of herself by spending thousands of dollars entertaining friends at the posh, $4,000 a night Hotel du Cap. At 5:00 A.M., Moss was thrown out of the hotel and barred from setting foot on the premises again. "Her whole gang was extremely rude and drunk," said Jerome Robert, who served drinks to Moss that night. "She looked like a mess and the whole thing got entirely out of hand."

The hotel maids spent hours cleaning Moss's suite after the drunken melee. Jars of cream and cosmetics had been hurled at the walls, ruining a silk wall treatment that was worth thousands of dollars.

After the end of her relationship with Depp, Moss's lifestyle spun further out of control. She was seen or linked with a different man every few days. First, Moss was spotted cuddling with Lemonhead singer Evan Dando both at the opening of a Louis Vuitton store and at a Yoko Ono benefit. Then, in short order, came record producer Nellee Hooper, British millionaire Dan Macmillan, and singer Bjork's ex-flame Goldie. "After her relationship with Johnny Depp ended, Kate would always show up at clubs holding hands with a different bloke," said Carmella Edwards, a London nightclub regular who had met Moss several times. "I really felt bad for her because it seemed she was living in self-denial of her bad habits. Even though she led a glamorous lifestyle, she didn't seem to be happy. I think she became famous at too young an age and has no sense of who she really is."

In a short time, Moss had certainly come a long way from her middle class upbringing in a London suburb. Her story is of the many young girls who catapult to fame and fortune after being picked off the street by a modeling scout. In 1988 Moss was discovered at the tender age of fourteen by Storm Model agency founder Sarah Doukas. Doukas found Moss at New York's JFK airport as she was boarding a flight to London after a family vacation in the Bahamas. Doukas offered Moss a contract on the spot. "I knew then and there that I had found a superstar," Doukas said. "There are thousands and thousands of models out there, but you only come across models like Kate once in a lifetime."

Doukas put Moss to work right away, sending her to a series of shoots for teen magazines. Within months, Moss was in great demand, and quickly became one of the highest paid supermodels in the world. A *Harper's Bazaar* cover brought instant international fame, and fashion editors and photographers lined up to hire her. In a matter of weeks, Moss's face graced the covers of *Vogue* and *Elle*, two of the world's top fashion magazines.

In 1992, photographer Patrick Demarchelier introduced his long-time friend Moss to famed fashion designer Calvin Klein. Klein said that Moss impressed him like no model had ever before. He offered her a $1.2 million contract and Moss became the face of Calvin Klein. She promoted all of the designer's signature products, including his Obsession perfume and his clothing line. Posing beside rap star and heartthrob Marky Mark, Kate modeled Calvin Klein underwear in what would become one of the most controversial television ads in history.

The underwear ad with Marky Mark was too explicit for some people to handle. But because it got so much publicity, nobody questioned its effect. The people who put it together knew exactly what they were doing. "There's nothing that I'd rather be doing now, because I like to go out and have a good time with my friends after work. I'm young, so I might as well enjoy it, 'cause I know it won't last forever."

And party she did. During a transcontinental flight to India for a photo shoot in September 1998, Moss and her model pals turned the plane into a mess, partying non-stop the entire way. "It was then that I realized that I needed to get help," Moss later explained. "My life was getting totally out of control. I couldn't stop abusing my body. I had become very self-destructive. All the years of heavy partying had caught up with me. If I didn't do something about it, something bad was going to happen to me."

On November 4, 1998, Moss's flamboyant lifestyle did finally catch up with her. She collapsed physically and plummeted into an emotional abyss. She decided to check herself into the Priory Clinic, a southwest London psychiatric center that specializes in treating depression, drug abuse, and other psychological illnesses.

Built in 1811 as a private residence, The Priory became a psychiatric hospital in the 1870s. Today, it is Britain's most exclusive private hospital. The parking lot is filled with Rolls-Royces and Mercedes. Many famous people, including Eric Clapton, Sinead O'Connor, Paul Merson, and Paula Yates have checked in seeking psychological help. The 105 private rooms are decorated with soothing colors and tones. Patients there enjoy the best food and service. The hospital claims a 70 percent cure rate for drug addicts and alcoholics.

Friends close to Kate Moss say that the rail-thin model might have wound up dead if she hadn't sought assistance. "I'd been working too hard and partying too much," Moss told London's *Daily Mirror*. "I wasn't happy with the way my life was going. So I decided to step back and assess my life and future."

Nobody seemed at all surprised when Moss checked herself into Priory. Many of her close friends and relatives were relieved that Moss finally got the help she had avoided for so many years. "She'd burned herself out and was living too fast," said Geoff Collman, Moss's stepfather. "I had hoped that the rumors in the press were not true. Kate is really a good, kind person who would do nobody harm. I hoped that she would come around . . . but it was obvious that she'd been over-indulging. It has finally taken its toll, and she just needs a good, long break."

Moss spent two months at the $500-a-day clinic undergoing extensive counseling and psychological treatment. She didn't watch television or read newspapers. She was virtually cut off from the outside world. "I went in to assess my life and future," Moss explained. "I reached a point in my life where the only solution for me was to face reality and get help."

Although she kept a low profile after her discharge from Priory on January 5, 1999, it didn't take long for Moss to make more headlines. Upon her return home, Kate found a brand new $100,000 BMW in her driveway, a "get well" gift from ex-boyfriend Johnny Depp. She decided to take the new car for a spin, forgetting to extinguish the meditation candles she'd left burning next to a scarf her mother had given her. The smoldering fire in Moss's bedroom exploded into flames, and everyone in Moss's building was evacuated. Fortunately, no one was injured. Shortly thereafter, Kate was spotted riding with Depp through the English countryside on the back of his motorcycle.

A month after she got out of the Priory clinic, Moss gave an exclusive interview to *The Face*, the British magazine that had given her the first major photo shoot of her career. Moss blamed both herself and the people who ran the fashion industry. "I kind of lost the plot there a little bit," Moss told *The Face*. "In France and London we're allowed to smoke pot all day . . . I'm changing. But I've always liked that lifestyle. . . . Things got out of control. I don't want to go back to how I was . . . I'm sober. I'm single. I have great friends. I like my job. I'm not stupid."

For the next several months, Moss attended meetings of Alcoholics Anonymous and Narcotics Anonymous. "Kate definitely had a different outlook on life when she got out of the hospital," said one of her Sloane Street girlfriends. "She was much more mellow and did everything she could to avoid the party atmosphere she had become so accustomed to."

But her new outlook was short-lived. Reports surfaced about Kate's return to the late-night party scene, where she had been spotted doing drugs again. Although Moss denied the rumors, the publicity had done its damage. Calvin Klein opted not to contract her as his main model anymore.

Klein hadn't been pleased with Kate's behavior for a long time. Her recent depression was a timely excuse for him to break the multimillion dollar contract she had signed with him. On February 20, 1999, it emerged that Klein had chosen an unknown eighteen-year-old Moscow beauty, Colette Pecheckhonova, over Moss to open and close his biggest show of the year at New York Fashion Week. After eight years, Klein and Moss had severed ties. Although Moss's agency, Storm, was quick to issue a statement to the contrary, the media reported that Moss had been fired. Storm countered with the claim that Moss's contract had been ended by mutual agreement. "She wants new challenges, and that is why she decided not to renew," the statement said.

For his part, Calvin Klein didn't refute Storm's statement. In fact, Klein was reported as saying, "No one can replace Kate." But if that's the case, why did Klein replace her? If he liked Moss so much, why didn't he wait for her to complete her rehab program? According to one of Klein's close associates, the designer was tired of dealing with Moss's erratic behavior. He needed to find a new model who was more stable than Moss. In the U.K., he signed another brunette, nineteen-year-old dental assistant Lisa Ratliffe, to replace Moss as his top British model. Klein hoped the move would generate new positive energy and much media attention. It worked splendidly. The British media descended on Ratliffe, who had only started her career as a model toward the end of 1998. She had been spotted by a scout for Select Model Agency while shopping with friends in London. Ratliffe appeared in Klein's renowned autumn collection, shot by famed photographer Steven Meisel. "Calvin's infatuation with Kate had long since worn off," a Klein associate said. "He was tired of all the excess baggage that Kate brought along with her. Everybody from her agency to her friends—who always hung around the photo shoots—had started to annoy Calvin. He wasn't too happy that reports of her drug abuse frequently surfaced in the media. Calvin paid Moss millions of dollars more than any other model earned, and he wasn't satisfied with the return he was getting on his investment."

Moss was crushed when Klein chose Colette Pecheckhonova over her for the New York show. She couldn't believe that a virtual unknown was replacing her. For Calvin Klein, it was more of a business decision. He didn't have to pay Pecheckhonova the fat fee that Moss commanded, nor did he have to worry about the Russian being stoned out of her mind on the catwalk.

Moss returned to the runway in early February 1999, only a month after being discharged from the Priory Clinic. She modeled at the Versace show in Milan, and at the French Fashion Show in Paris. On the Paris catwalks, Moss appeared slightly different, but still defiant. Her brown hair was slicked back and braided at the crown with silk ribbon. Moss admitted that it was the first time she had strolled down a catwalk sober in more than a decade.

"It was deeply touching to see Kate try to come back sober," said fashion designer Guy Mournier.

Nobody in the modeling business captured the hearts of the public more than Kate. When her drug problems got the best of her, many people were disappointed. It was almost as if their sweetheart had betrayed their trust. When she returned, everybody in Paris was wondering how long she would be able to survive the grind of this business sober. A lot of people wondered if she might be a walking time bomb. Over the years so many models have tried and failed to come back after going through drug rehab programs. It's daunting to leave behind all the psychological scars they've accumulated. Most of them are unable to do it, and they wind up fading into oblivion, making way for the next young beautiful face to replace them.

Moss admitted that her psychological problems were still far from being resolved and that she would continue to see a psychiatrist at least once a week. She described her stay at Priory as being a real eye opener. "Kind of like being at boarding school," Moss told *The Face.* "At The Priory, they believe that either you are an addict or you have an addictive personality. There are patterns, and all addicts have patterns. Being in there with other alcoholics and drug addicts, you start to see the patterns . . . I don't really want to go back to how I was drinking. It wasn't a healthy drinking pattern. I was in denial for a long time, I think. I could have carried on drinking, but I was beginning to be very unhappy. It stops working after a while. A bit messy."

Moss's attempt to clean herself up hit a snag at the 1999 Cannes Film Festival. She was spotted at her old haunts, drinking champagne till the wee hours of the morning with a rowdy group of friends. Having been banned from the exclusive Hotel du Cap after the ruckus she caused there the previous year, Moss rented a house with several freewheeling friends, including Oasis star Noel Gallagher and his wife, Meg Matthews.

Moss was at Cannes that year to shoot a fashion story for *W Magazine* with photographer Juergen Teller and fellow supermodels Claudia Schiffer and Gisele Bundchen. She managed to get as far as the Hotel du Cap's terrace bar, where she partied with the likes of Daryl Hannah, Mel Gibson, and "It Girl" Tamara Beckwith. According to a bartender at the hotel, Moss got tipsy and made a spectacle of herself. "She was drinking quite a lot," the bartender said. "I was quite surprised because I had heard that she was trying to give up alcohol."

One of the things that drove Moss back to the bottle was Johnny Depp's relationship with French singer Vanessa Paradis. Paradis became pregnant with Depp's child and told people that she and Depp were planning to settle down together. "Kate was jealous because she wanted to be the one to settle down with Johnny Depp," a close friend revealed. "When she found out that Vanessa Paradis was pregnant with Depp's child, Kate was heartbroken. She couldn't believe what had happened. She still had hopes of reuniting with Depp."

Moss's heartbreak over Depp triggered more bouts with booze and men. MSNBC's Jeanette Walls reported that Moss had been seen partying excessively with her new lover, Massive Attack's Robert Del Naja. Moss was shocked when Del Naja later dumped her to return to his old girlfriend. "Kate was stunned because all of a sudden she was being taken for a fool again," confided a close friend. "She was trying desperately to clean herself up, but returned to booze briefly, after enduring a few bad experiences. Kate went for counseling again, and, from what I know, she seems to be trying to kick her bad habits again. I think it's only a matter of time before Kate is cured. She's a strong woman and the more bad experiences she has, the easier it is for her to see through all the bullshit."

CHAPTER 16

• • •

The Great Gisele

Many models are bitter because their careers got steered in the wrong direction by unscrupulous agents. Some of the current and former models I met told me that they would like to seek revenge against the people who mismanaged their careers. Maria Santos is a good example. She once had a shot at being Brazil's answer to Cindy Crawford. Today, Santos believes that model agents are not merely sick—they are evil. She says that if she ever sees her former agent, she might try to hurt him.

Santos, the youngest of nine children raised in extreme poverty in a small town outside of Rio, spoke of the fashion scout from London who'd discovered her on a bus in 1996. The scout offered Santos, then sixteen, $1000 plus expenses to go to London for some test shoots. Realizing that this could be a once-in-a-lifetime opportunity, Santos packed her bags. She had never modeled before. When she arrived in London a week later, Santos, who didn't speak a word of English at the time, was in for a shock. The fashion scout who'd discovered her told her that she would have to stay with him for a few days because all the hotels were full.

That first night, shortly after Santos had fallen asleep, the fashion scout barged into her room wielding a big knife. He grabbed her from behind, and Santos screamed for help, but to no avail. The scout raped and sodomized her. He then tried to strangle her with a nylon stocking that she had placed on a nearby dresser. Santos, realizing that her best hope of survival lay in submission to the man's demands, was left stunned and shocked. Sealed off from the world for the next two months, she virtually became the man's sex slave. Santos didn't seek retribution because she says she feared for her life.

During her four years as a model in London and New York in the late nineties, Santos underwent what she described as the most hellish experience of her life. The Brazilian-born teenager says that the most powerful agents in the business often ally themselves with pimps, thieves, drug dealers, junkies, and murderers. She provided chilling evidence from her own experiences.

"Looking back, it might seem ridiculous, but I can find something positive from an experience that I don't wish on any human being," Santos said. "It made me grow up quickly. As bad as the experience was, from then on, I knew what to expect from the modeling business. I should have known better than to accept an offer without doing more research on the man. In Brazil, he showed me an impressive portfolio of some of his models. He convinced me that he was legit. Alone in a foreign country, I was so scared that I never even thought of pressing charges against him."

After a few months in London, the scout finally delivered on his promise and hooked Santos up with several top agencies. She was invited to audition for Elite, but accepted an offer with a smaller agency based in New York. It was there that her life began to change drastically. The elegant, 5-foot 11-inch brunette became a respected runway model and began making lots of money. Along the way, however, she developed a bad drug habit that almost killed her. The once-innocent teenage girl got hooked on heroin. On one occasion she was found stretched out and unconscious in a dressing room minutes before she was supposed to go on stage. The show's organizers called an ambulance. Santos spent the next week in a Manhattan hospital.

"I tried to keep a low profile but I always got caught up with evil people," Santos recalled. "The pressure of trying to make it got to me. I turned to heroin. It was my most trusted friend. I knew what it would do for me. I got hooked because, in my desperation, it was the only thing that I could trust. Every person I worked with in this business seemed to have an ulterior motive. In New York I became more successful, but it was rare to go through a day when I didn't have an agent or photographer trying to get me into bed."

As the glow of the Cindy Crawford-Claudia Schiffer Big Six-era began to fade, Santos had a shot at becoming the new model of the moment. Due to her bad habits, however, she missed the opportunity to become Brazil's best-known export. Meanwhile, a leggy, big-bosomed sixteen-year-old German-Brazilian became the new queen of the catwalk, breathing new glamour into modeling.

Gisele Bundchen had been modeling since the age of fourteen, when she was discovered by an Elite fashion scout during a school field trip to a São Paulo shopping mall. Bundchen, the daughter of a bank clerk and a business consultant, had never before visited a city larger than Horizontina, Brazil, the small, rural town where she was raised. She is the middle of six sisters, including her fraternal twin, Patricia. In June 2001, the gorgeous sisters shared the cover of *Harper's Bazaar*. Patricia told *Harper's* that growing up in the shadow of her famous sister had had its tough moments. "Growing up, we argued about everything," Patricia said. "Now we have conversations instead. That's probably because we live so far apart."

Despite her humble beginnings, Gisele is currently the world's most famous supermodel. She received the Model of the Year Award at the VH1 Fashion Awards in 1999, and was voted as one of the faces of the Twentieth Century. Sought after by the likes of Dolce and Gabbana, Dior, Ralph Lauren, and Victoria's Secret, her face has graced the covers of *Marie Claire, Elle,* and *Vogue.*

Gisele's on-again-off-again relationship with Hollywood sex symbol Leonardo DiCaprio has been worth untold millions in free publicity. When she revealed to Brazil's *Veja Magazine* in February, 2001 that DiCaprio had proposed with a diamond and platinum engagement ring at his Malibu home a few weeks earlier, it became the biggest story in Hollywood in months.

"Not since Priscilla and Elvis Presley did a celebrity couple receive so much attention," said entertainment writer Martin Smith. "It was clearly going to be Hollywood's version of the royal wedding. The publicity that Gisele received was priceless. Her stock rose a million percent."

Maria Santos claims that Gisele would not have become as well known if she hadn't been associated with a star like DiCaprio. "Gisele's a good example of someone who was coached well," Santos says. "She's beautiful and smart, but so are thousands of other models from Brazil. She connected with the right people and didn't let herself get pushed around. It also helped that she was dating the sexiest man in Hollywood."

Gisele's career, however, has had its controversial moments. In September 1999, Anne Nelson, Gisele's booking agent at Elite, left to join one of its major competitors, IMG. Soon afterwards, Gisele stunned the fashion world by announcing that she, too, was defecting. Elite's chairman John Casablancas hit the ceiling when he found out. He had envisioned making Gisele the world's number one model. He had poured lots of time and energy into making her happy at Elite. Casablancas promised Gisele that his staff would work round the clock to get covers on all the big magazines. Instead, he was left with nothing. He mouthed off to the media, calling Gisele a "monster of selfishness," and condemning her "thanklessness, pushiness, and greed." The media took Gisele's side, interpreting Casablancas venom as sour grapes. They remembered that this was the same man who had fired Naomi Campbell a while back, calling her the most "odious of all the mean and ungrateful" models he had steered to the big time.

According to fashion critic Jane Reed, "Casablancas was upset because he wanted to get credit for Gisele. I think that Gisele lost trust in Elite because some of the men at Elite had ugly track records. She didn't want to become their new possession."

Casablancas filed a multimillion-dollar lawsuit against IMG and Anne Nelson for stealing his prize model. The case is still pending. According to a close friend of Gisele, the supermodel is hardly worried. "Casablancas has no case," the friend said. "It's a free market and Gisele is free to have whoever she wants to represent her. Casablancas has a reputation for being a worm. I know that I wouldn't want my daughter to go near him or his people. Would you?"

Maria Santos says that she's happy for Gisele, but can't help feel sorry for her at the same time. "You think it's going to be easy being married to Leonardo Di Caprio?" she asks. "It's going to be a nightmare. As big as Gisele is, Leonardo's bigger, and she'll have to play second fiddle to him. I don't know if she'll be able to accept that. I'd be surprised if their marriage lasts more than a year or two."

Meanwhile, Santos continues to live in New York with her American boyfriend of three years. She's also managed to clean herself up. "If I had to do it all over again, I would definitely think twice," she says. "I'm lucky that I found a nice man who convinced me that drugs are not the answer. I'm lucky to be alive. I really messed myself up. Today, I stay as far away from the fashion scene as possible. I don't read the magazines, and I don't go to the shows. I'm just trying to be a more simple person, appreciating each day that I'm alive."

CHAPTER 17

● ● ●

Fading Away

All the stories of drugs and rape in fashion have made both the public and the media increasingly skeptical about the future of the supermodel industry. Behind the carefully staged facade of the supermodel scene lie the heartbreaking stories of naive young beauties who shoot to the top of the fashion world only to wind up wrung out by sex and drugs within a few years. Fashion is a world in which tragedy shares the stage with beauty. And although fashion's key players still hold a captive audience, many people in the industry admit that supermodels no longer have the seismic effect on the fashion world that they used to. In November 1998, *Time Magazine* reported that the influence of the world's top supermodels is giving way to that of actresses and gangly teens. Before, magazines like *Vogue* and *Harper's Bazaar* limited themselves to using well-known models. Now the playing field and its players are becoming more diverse. It's good to shake things up and throw in the occasional cover story featuring somebody other than a supermodel.

"Nine years ago, you couldn't get more glamorous than going backstage at a Versace show," *Time* quoted Alisa Bellettini, the executive producer of MTV's *House of Style*. "Now you see Amber Valetta at a Beastie Boys concert with no makeup on and her hair back. They're not like goddesses anymore. They're real people, working really hard."

Many people accuse the models' haughty attitude as the reason for their decline. Linda Evangelista enraged both the public and the industry when she was quoted as saying, "Christy and I don't get out of bed for less than $10,000 a day." More recently, Brazilian sexpot

Gisele Bundchen has demanded $50,000 for an appearance. Many fashion industry insiders agree that outrageous appearance fees make it tougher for the next generation of supermodels, who will probably never have the same power as the Big Six.

"By 1995, several of the girls had acted up so much, there was a building resentment against them," said Michael Gross, author of *Model: The Ugly Business of Beautiful Women.* "They'd sit in the back of limos and kick the driver in the neck with their high heels when they weren't happy with the way he was driving. Editors who had to deal with these girls probably weren't sad to see them go." Gilles Bensimon, former husband of Elle Macpherson and the creative director for *Elle,* told *Time,* "Claudia Schiffer is the best example of the rise and fall of a model. For me, we don't need her. She doesn't represent anyone alive. After some point, you become a Barbie doll. If you have one more interview with Claudia Schiffer, people say, 'Again?' It's like hearing more about Monica Lewinsky and the President."

Many fashion professionals believe that the public is bored of seeing the same old faces grace magazine covers and that a fresh crop of beauties is waiting in the wings. "No doubt that we've seen a bit too much of the same models," said Elite Models founding chairman John Casablancas, whose agency scouts 350,000 potential models from seventy-five countries each year. "But things are changing rapidly. The public loves fashion and beauty, and they're just waiting to see who will be the next Claudia Schiffer or Linda Evangelista."

Casablancas compared the supermodel industry to other businesses. He said that the fashion industry is undergoing a metamorphosis since Big Six models like Cindy Crawford and Naomi Campbell decided to reduce their modeling activities in the late nineties. "Like any other industry, we have the good years and the bad ones. There's no doubt that, recently, there have been lots of changes in the business, but I think that most of it is positive."

Stephen Irskine was hired by a New York modeling agency to bring in beautiful young women. He quit after a short time because of the way the models were treated. "It's no wonder that this industry is in turmoil," Irskine says. "They're treated like dogs. I wasn't surprised when I heard that Kate Moss had an emotional breakdown. I'm only surprised that it wasn't sooner. Until the people running this business wake up and decide to treat the models like human beings, there will always be horror stories and the industry will suffer. I disagree with people when they say that it's the girls' fault. It's the people running the business." Irskine says that he quit because his boss was more interested in getting the young girls into bed than onto the runway. "My boss would make advances at the girls and make them false promises," he says. "That's why I had to quit. There are no morals in the modeling business. I love fashion and really believe that there's a great future for supermodels, but first the people running the business have got to learn how to treat their employees right."

Irskine does not believe that the supermodel phenomenon will ever die. In sum, Irskine would like to see supermodels—the Crawfords, Campbells, Bundchens, and others who appear regularly in the big magazines and on the catwalks, and who earn at least $100,000 a year—form a union to protect themselves. "There's usually some dry years when you're in the entertainment business," Irskine says. "You have to protect your rights so that you don't starve during those dry periods."

Others in the industry echo his opinion. "Supermodels were created as a response to a need for glamour, fantasy, and escapism, rather like the movie goddesses and Miss Worlds of the past," says Jonathan Phang, of London's renowned IMG model agency. "They have reigned over the world's catwalks for well over a decade and—love them or hate them—have become a part of all our lives. But the supermodels, as we have come to know them, have started to move into other lucrative areas such as television, advertising, and film. Nowadays, models' careers don't seem to last as long as they used to—girls can be in one season and out the next."

Some supermodels behave like adolescents everywhere they go. They dress ratty, act obnoxious, and act as if they're the center of the universe. The industry is littered with deceit, snobbery, and plastic personalities. But most critics of this business agree that supermodels are a genuine paradigm shift and not a fad. At the top of the show-business Everest for the last few decades, supermodels are, quite simply, the most glamorized women and men in the world today. They are the very apotheosis of unabashed self-promotion, of overexposure to the hilt. Yet the public always seems to crave more. So the fashion industry shamelessly packages and repackages the supermodels as we wait eagerly for each new incarnation. "Despite all the bad points, men and women will always seek jobs as models," Kate Moss has said. "I'm not going to retire. If people are still willing to pay me money to model, then I'll keep doing it."

The obvious oddity in the supermodel world is that it may be the only work where women are paid so much more than men. While the top female models regularly fetch $10,000 a day, the best male models, like Tyrese, or Tyson Beckford, can hope to earn only a fraction of that at best. "Up until recently, the men didn't come close to earning what the average female model got," says fashion journalist Peter Barbera. "But with the emergence of several big name male models in recent years, things have started to change. But still, the men have a long way to go to catch up to the women. And I don't think it will ever be even, because society has been infatuated with beautiful women for thousands of years."

Supermodels face an uncertain future on the designer front as well. As the era of the high-profile supermodels, like Claudia Schiffer and Cindy Crawford, draws to an end, well-known entertainment personalities are slowly replacing lesser-known models. There is a lingering debate among many of the fashion industry's top designers over whether or not the days of celebrity supermodels are over.

One designer who firmly believes the era of the supermodel is over is Calvin Klein. Klein says that he has branched out and hired actors and musicians as models instead of curvaceous beauties. Recently, Klein hired rap star Foxy Brown, teen film star Julia Stiles, and alternative songstress Liz Phair to model his latest designs. "I don't think people are that interested in models anymore," Klein said in a June 1999 interview. "It's not a great moment for the modeling industry. It says a lot about our society, and I think that's good . . . just a pretty face isn't enough. It's an indication of how lots of people are thinking."

A lot of people in the fashion industry have followed Klein's lead. In June 1999, *Friends* star Courtney Cox was featured in *Harper's Bazaar*. The illustrious fashion magazine had set a new trend for replacing models with TV stars late in 1998, when it put *Ally McBeal's* Calista Flockhart on its cover.

"It's incredible to think that *Harper's Bazaar* featured both of these waiflike stars over the likes of Claudia Schiffer and Kate Moss," said entertainment critic Jane Strachan. "It clearly sends a message that the industry is fed up with all the old faces we're used to seeing. There's a trend now in television to use skinny actors in the lead roles who look like they almost have eating disorders. Just look at people like Jenna Elfman and Calista Flockhart. These are people who have pizzazz and are more marketable than your average supermodel because of the fact that they're always in the public eye. The average person watching television at home is more likely to buy a magazine with their face on the cover. That's the way it was done in the seventies when Farrah Fawcett was TV's top beauty. She must have appeared on every magazine cover at least five times. The industry is reverting back to this trend. Economically, it makes way more sense."

The new trend to replace models with celebrities in top fashion magazines created a window of opportunity for record companies to promote their artists to a larger audience. Music magazines such as *Rolling Stone* and *Spin*, which have smaller and predominantly male readerships, began to face stiff competition from fashion and beauty magazines whose audience demographics were much wider. "For the record labels it was the greatest thing to happen in years," said a Sony Music executive. "A lot of these magazines refused to cover the careers of many of the artists unless their record label was willing to buy ads. We were long at the mercy of these magazines. There's so many more options now that magazines like *Vogue* and *Cosmopolitan* have started using musicians."

The trend to put musicians on the covers of fashion magazines is also attributed to a significant change in the demographic music buyers. In 1998, the Recording Industry Association revealed that, for the second straight year, more women spent money on music than men. According to music journalist Martin Smith, this demographic shift is mainly due to the emergence of so many female pop stars, like Shania Twain, Lauryn Hill, and Celine Dion, in the latter part of the nineties.

"Who would have thought that you'd see the day when there were more women stars than men?" Smith says. "Pop music was always dominated by men. Male stars, like Elton John, Sting, and Prince, had always been at the forefront of the music industry. Today it's all women. Male artists' popularity pales in comparison to the Spice Girls, Madonna, and Jewel."

In recent years the leading female pop stars have been appearing on the magazine covers that were once the exclusive domain of supermodels. Country music diva Shania Twain was dressed in pink on a cover of *Cosmopolitan*, Madonna graced the cover of *Harper's Bazaar*, Celine Dion appeared on the cover of *People*, while both Jewel and the Spice Girls got covers of *Vogue*. In August 1999, Hole's lead singer Courtney Love, who had previously appeared on the cover of *Vanity Fair*, showed up on the cover of *Jane Magazine* to discuss "celebrity dating, threesomes, and why fatter is sexier."

Entertainment critic Rosalind Tobin explains, "Today's generation wants to see their rock heroes glamorized. It's not that they would rather see Shania Twain over Claudia Schiffer. They want to see them both." There are many benefits for musicians who are featured in women's magazines. It offers them and their record labels an escape from the scrutiny and traditionally critical reviews of most music magazines. "If a fashion magazine wants to do a cover story about a famous singer, it's guaranteed that the story will be very positive," says music publicist Earle Farmer. "If *Rolling Stone* wants to do a story, there's no guarantee. Sometimes it could be a negative story that could ruin an artist's career. That's why the music industry is so excited about being in publications like *Vogue*. It's guaranteed to be positive publicity."

According to an advertising executive at *Elle Magazine*, the fashion magazines are banking that the latest trend of putting pop stars on its covers will translate into mega dollars in advertising revenue. "The music industry has the biggest advertising budgets," he says. "We're not putting these rock stars on the cover just for the fun of it. Everything is dollars and cents. Music's a powerful market, and we're hoping that the big labels like Sony and MCA will throw some advertising dollars our way."

Alan Light, longtime editor-in-chief of *Spin* and former editor of *Vibe*, both owned by Miller Publishing Group, admits that the major labels can't lose by branching out into new markets. Light says that music magazine coverage has always had "a collecting-baseball-cards attitude to it, a boy's club insider feel . . . whereas a publication such as *Vogue* has an enormous reach. It's not the easiest time in the world to put out a magazine like *Spin*." Light points out that *Vogue's* circulation is 1.1 million, in contrast to *Spin's* 525,000. "It's like comparing apples and oranges," says a *Rolling Stone* magazine editor. "But in the end, music lovers will stay loyal to the music magazines because they're guaranteed a more objective view. The fashion magazines cover music almost as if they're paid publicists [of] the record labels. People will get tired of it very quickly."

Yet there is no denying how much a cover shot of a pop superstar can boost magazine sales. Since Time Warner started *Teen People* in January 1998, the biggest-selling issues, except for one featuring Leonardo DiCaprio, have featured musicians on the cover. Another good example is Conde Nast's *Allure*. When the magazine put departed Spice Girl Geri Haliwell on the cover, she outsold Cindy Crawford by more than 21,000 copies. "Figures like this tell the whole story," says fashion consultant Liz Darwin. "Fashion editors have

Women of the club:
Flynow C. at London
Fashion Week,
Tracy Bingham in L.A.,
model at the Fire Fliss
fashion show in
Hollywood.
(Courtesy Keystone Agence
De Presse and Getty Images
News Services)

• • •

The next face: Designer Giorgio Armani poses with his models in Milan. *(Getty Images)*

• • •

Nikki Taylor before her accident in May 2001; her sister Krissy tragically died on July 2, 1995.
(Courtesy Keystone Agence De Presse)

• • •

Elle MacPherson (left) and Linda Evangelista. Who's hot?
(Courtesy Keystone Agence De Presse)

• • •

In Versace: Madonna rules.
*(Courtesy Keystone
Agence De Presse)*

•　•　•

The late Gianni Versace in the
mid-nineties with his favorite
model, Naomi Campbell.
*(Courtesy Keystone
Agence De Presse)*

•　•　•

Veruschka was one
of the top models of the
sixties and seventies.
*(Courtesy Keystone
Agence De Presse)*

•   •   •

Tennis star Vitas Gueralitas
dancing with supermodel
Cheryl Tiegs at Studio 54
in the seventies.
*(Courtesy Keystone
Agence De Presse)*

•   •   •

Jerry Hall and Mick
Jagger in happier times.
*(Courtesy Keystone
Agence De Presse)*

● ● ●

Claudia Schiffer with
her longtime close friend
designer Karl Lagerfeld.
*(Courtesy Keystone
Agence De Presse)*

● ● ●

Cindy Crawford's glamorous look changed the face of modeling in the late eighties.
(Courtesy Keystone Agence De Presse)

Just between us girls: Linda Evangelista, Naomi Campbell, and Kate Moss.
(Courtesy Keystone Agence De Presse)

Kate Moss and Johnny Depp
before their split in 1998.
*(Courtesy Keystone
Agence De Presse)*

• • •

Claudia Schiffer and
David Copperfield.
*(Courtesy Keystone
Agence De Presse)*

• • •

Helena Christenson
with late INXS singer
Michael Hutchence.
*(Courtesy Keystone
Agence De Presse)*

• • •

woken up and are becoming open to new things. In any business if there's a way that your sales will increase, you've got to be open to it and not be afraid to offend your market. At the beginning a lot of people thought that the women who buy *Vogue* would be offended by having somebody like Courtney Love on the cover. But the exact opposite has been proven true. They'd rather stare at Courtney than Cindy."

Jann Wenner, founder and publisher of *Rolling Stone* magazine, isn't at all worried about the new competition. Wenner says that music fans prefer reading well-balanced articles and not the fluff some of the fashion magazines put out. "I think music fans understand that what they get from a fashion magazine is superficial treatment, or stuff they've read before," he says. "Any core fan will go to *Rolling Stone* first. Plus, I think we are talking about primarily pretty, women stars."

In the early nineties, the music and fashion industry regularly collaborated on music videos and fashion shows. RuPaul's "Supermodel" hit the top of the pop charts, and artists like Prince and George Michael used some of the top supermodels in their videos, including Linda Evangelista and Naomi Campbell. Now things have changed. Both industries see the other as competition for the advertising dollars of major record labels. Conor Kennedy, an agent at Company Models, is worried that the use of celebrity models might eliminate a whole new generation of supermodels. "It's very frustrating right now," Kennedy says. "If magazines are making such an effort to feature Gwyneth Paltrow over and over again, well, what happens to the next generation of Linda Evangelistas?" One editor at a Conde Nast magazine told journalist Alex Kuczynski that she didn't have any sympathy for the supermodels because she was "fed up" with their behavior. She described models as spoiled brats, and said that movie stars were much less difficult to work with, mainly because their studios relish the free publicity.

"When we deal with a movie star or pop star, it's much easier," says an editor at *Vogue*. "Usually they do the shoot at little or no charge because they want the free publicity to support their latest project. When it's a supermodel, it's often just one big pain in the ass. Their fee is very high, they often want to be treated as if they're the Queen of England, and half the time they're stoned out of their minds."

While fashion magazine publishers report that, between 1997 and 1999, celebrity covers were among their best-sellers, the Audit Bureau of Circulation's figures paint a somewhat different story. The Audit Bureau of Circulation is the independent body that tracks magazine and newspaper distribution and sales. *Allure*'s newsstand sales had fallen during that period, and its celebrity covers had produced mediocre sales. A March 1998 cover featuring Jennifer Aniston sold 257,047 copies, slightly more than the magazine's six-month average of 242,244. *Vogue*, conversely, was one magazine that clearly profited from the use of celebrities. *Vogue* editor Anna Wintour has said that featuring celebrities like Oprah Winfrey and Hilary Clinton instead of gorgeous supermodels has paid off big time. According to Wintour, today's supermodels don't have the appeal to the public and media as they did ten years ago. "They were celebrities. The paparazzi were chasing them. Everyone cared what they were having for breakfast and who they were having affairs with." Indeed, *Vogue*'s newsstand sales jumped as high as 500,000 for its coverage of celebrities like the Spice Girls, Sandra Bullock, and Renee Zellweger, while sales of issues with blond models like Carolyn Murphy on the cover lagged behind.

"The problem is not that the celebrities have become more appealing to fashion, it's just that there are no new models emerging with the pizzazz of a Naomi Campbell or Claudia Schiffer," said entertainment journalist Keith Brown. "The fashion industry has become quite boring. Until some new, hot faces come along, you'll see celebrity faces on the covers. Frankly, I find it quite boring, because let's face it, there's no way someone like Calista Flockhart has the same appeal and exotic look as someone like Kate Moss or Karen Mulder."

Linda Evangelista blames the media for the current state of the modeling industry. She claims that the press has placed too much pressure and too many high expectations on today's models by labeling them supermodels. "The term supermodel is a press-induced word," Evangelista says. "We have never called ourselves supermodels." However, Evangelista is far from worried about being replaced by a celebrity. She says that this is only a trend in American magazines, while in European, Australian, and Asian magazines they still prefer using real models. Evangelista herself, for example, graced the covers of the German and British *Vogue* in January 1999. "She's right," says European fashion journalist Etienne Dury. "The Americans always come up with new fads and then they die out. Replacing models with celebrities is like replacing elite football players with celebrities. It just doesn't make sense. They don't have the same skills."

It is very easy to tell the difference between the skills of celebrities and models in front of the camera. Their routines are completely different. When a model goes in front of the camera she must be able to be comfortable at all angles. A photographer's dream is a model who is able to recognize the importance of being able to make love to the camera while staying cool and relaxed. Models are used to twelve- to fifteen-hour shoots. Musicians and actors usually do a couple of hours worth of publicity shots for their projects. There's little similarity in the work. Model shoots are more specific, detailed, and elaborate—more makeup, hair, and body concept. Shania Twain might look stunning on the cover of her new CD, but it does not mean that she should be put on the cover of *Elle;* Cindy Crawford might look good on the cover of *Vogue,* but it does not mean that she would be good in a role opposite Tom Cruise on the silver screen.

Many industry people, however, are taking the celebrity threat seriously. Wilhelmina International Modeling Agency grosses about $40 million annually. Because of the recent trend to use actors and rock stars on magazine covers, Wilhelmina formed an alliance in 1998 with Atlantic Records, the major record label owned by Time Warner, Inc. Dieter Esch, the owner of Wilhelmina, said it was a necessary business move. Teenage pop music sensation Brandy was signed to a multimillion-dollar contract to become the new spokesperson for Cover Girl cosmetics. "We're just creating new opportunities," Esch said. "Celebrities have always been an integral part of the fashion industry. The public likes to see the latest styles of their favorite celebrities."

The well-known fashion photographer Sante D'Orazio says that shooting celebrities has revived his business. He says that by the late 1990s the supermodel craze had died down. "I had a rough five years there," D'Orazio says. "Glamour was out. And I wasn't willing to shoot that way, that not-beautiful way. Depressed girls who looked like they were high. And so I started photographing celebrities, because they wanted to look glamorous. So I made those movie stars look like the supermodels once did."

Fashion consultant Eve Beaulieu doesn't believe that the era of supermodels is over. Her excitement grows as she predicts the status of supermodels in the new millennium. "Anybody who says that supermodels are a thing of the past has no idea what they're talking about. If you look back at the history of models, there has always been a little grace period when the models fade out for a while. There was a time in the late sixties, after Twiggy had long made her mark, when the industry slowed down and models weren't getting as many jobs as they once did. Several years later, things picked up again with a whole new crop of faces led by Cheryl Tiegs. The supermodel industry is at a bit of a standstill now, but there's no doubt in my mind that, in a few years, Claudia and Naomi will be long forgotten and a whole new generation of beauties will have emerged."

Male model Marc Brennan says it's only a matter of time before all the fuss about the demise of the supermodel era dies down. It will happen, Brennan insists, when an agent discovers the next great face roaming the streets in some austere part of the world. "It could happen anywhere," he insists. "You could be walking in St. Louis or St. Lucia and if you catch an agent's eye, chances are good that you'll get offered a contract. Right now the modeling world is in need of new faces. Nobody has stepped up yet to replace the elite class of the Cindy Crawfords and Naomi Campbells. But it takes time. And when it happens, the whole supermodel business will be revived. Models have their low periods, just like actors and musicians. But eventually the dry period ends and business starts to boom again. The people in society who buy fashion magazines are sitting back and eagerly waiting for the next era of the supermodel to emerge."

British sociologist Alvin Bailey blames the designers themselves for the recent slide of the supermodel. He believes that by hiring actors and musicians instead of models, the designers are reacting too hastily. "It's ridiculous," Bailey says.

When Calvin Klein comes out and makes the kind of statements about the era of the supermodel being over, maybe he's talking about his own plight. This man has been in the business for many years and maybe he's a bit burned out. The society we live in today is obsessed with glamour. We buy fashion magazines and designer clothes more than ever. And before we buy them, we love to see beautiful people wear them because we want to believe that we'll wind up looking like them when we slip into the clothes. I've counseled many young teenagers, both male and female, who are distraught because they're not happy with the way they look. About 75 to 80 percent of the time they say that they want to look as beautiful as a famous model like Claudia Schiffer or Tyson [Beckford]. It's sad, because young people are too obsessed with looking like other people instead of establishing their own identity. Who should we blame? That's a good question, because things have become more and more out of hand. The people who run the fashion industry don't care. Just because a couple of important people in the industry claim that the era of supermodels is over has not slowed things down. If anything, it's opened things up more. Now, not only do you have the models agents vying to get their clients work, but you also have agents for actors, musicians, and other famous types. I don't think it has left the good models scrounging around for work. I think it's just opened up a whole new block of opportunity, and, in the end, the fashion designers and people who run the industry will increase their business at least twofold.

CHAPTER 18

• • •

Lesbian Chic

As the era of heroin chic fades away, the fashion world eagerly awaits a new breed of models to strut the catwalks and appear in *Vogue* and *Elle*. In Hollywood, where models are as glamorous as movie stars, and today's new pretty face is tomorrow's throw-away, preoccupation with the latest trends surpasses most other leisure activities. Innovation, which has led to much-admired and often-copied creations, is unfortunately often practiced for its own sake. Major designers like Versace and Valentino have been raked over the coals in the past by fashion critics for unveiling new designs that, more than anything, seemed to exist solely to elicit shock.

Originality is the cornerstone of new fashion trends, the style of the movement that is dubbed "in vogue." Experimentation in fashion takes many forms. One new spin has affected the modeling industry itself—lesbian chic. In 2001, fashion designers have started to replace waiflike models with plainer, tougher, butchier looking women. Many of these models have multiple body piercings, shaved hair, and tattoos. This pervasive freewheeling, almost rock 'n' roll spirit seems to have resulted from a desperate attempt to create a new fad. But it may very well be a rebellion against the misogynistic exploitation of past years. Marked by an irreverence for convention and a backlash against the male moguls who have long objectified models, lesbian chic may set a new standard for beauty, one based on strength, health and independence. Indeed, it's a far cry from the overly thin addict image of years gone by.

The movement toward lesbian chic may stem from the fashion industry's attempt to reintroduce models instead of celebrities as trend-

setters. London fashion critic Jo Ross predicts the campaign to replace models with well-known actors and singers will fail. "The industry is desperate to create something new," Ross said. "People are
tired of seeing the anorexic look. Maybe the plain, tough, masculine
look will last for a while. Until something catches fire, the designers
must keep trying to create a sensation to surpass the heroin chic of
the nineties."

Like their male-model counterparts, who can be found pumping
iron at the gym every day, butch models must opt out of starvation
and drugs to develop their strong, muscular physique. Los Angeles
model Avery Jones described lesbian chic as a satisfying change.
"Finally, we don't have to look like we haven't had a meal in weeks,"
she said. "The name lesbian chic defines it all. A lot of models I
know, including myself, are tired of men. We're tired of the shit men
who only want to get us into bed. I've been a model for six years and
I live with my lover, who is also a female model. So many models are
lesbians. It really defines who we are. I hope that the term lesbian
chic sticks around for a long time."

Judging by some recent fashion ads, lesbian chic is gaining mo-
mentum. Top model Eleonora Bose, with a Beatles-like hairdo and
"Tony" tattooed above her left breast, has become a primary chal-
lenger of voluptuous Brazilian model Gisele Bundchen. In 2001,
Bose became Gucci's number one model. "Bose is capable of doing
everything against the norm, and the public loves it," says New York
designer George Freed. "The fashion public always wants to see
something fresh, something that has an edge. Gisele was more of a
throwback to the beautiful models of yesteryear. Bose has a look that
is different, a look that is completely outrageous and crazy. She's way
more interesting to look at than Gisele."

Even more radical is the eye grabbing Omahyra Mota, a sixteen-
year-old Dominican featured in *Italian Vogue* with Bose. The tall,
rugged, butch Mota, with her short, dark, punk hairdo, looks like a
cross between rock stars Joan Jett and Prince. Mota has claimed that
she did not get into modeling to be just another pretty face. She
wanted to make a statement. "I think you can look sexy without
having to look too feminine," Mota said at a Milan fashion show. "I
want people to pay careful attention to everything going on around
me. And I want them to believe that what I'm about is something
they haven't seen before, something unique and different."

By mid-2001, the advertising campaigns of most top fashion
houses, including Versace and Dior, had featured lesbian themes.

According to a number of experts, the fashion public is tired of models who have either the traditional Claudia Schiffer or Cindy Crawford look or the skinny Kate Moss look. They believe the only way to revive mega interest in modeling is by using models who are more cutting edge. "For so many years it's been the same old boring theme," says respected New York stylist Celine Granger. "Beautiful, skinny girls who look like they're made of porcelain glass. You've got to remember, this is showbiz and you've got to put on a show and entertain the public, otherwise, they're going to get bored. That's what happened with models. Nothing exciting had happened for so long. The shift away from the feminine look takes away the sterility. For the first time since the mid-nineties, I look forward to attending the fashion shows."

Ivan Bart, vice-president of IMG Models, which represents such new butch models as Eleonora Bose, Anouck, and Erin Wasson, thinks the new look has allowed models to create more distinct identities. Bart, whose company also represents Gisele Bundchen, Alek Wek, and Shalom Harlow, said that the old look made models seem too much alike—it was difficult to tell them apart.

"We represent a new breed of models that may or may not transcend this moment," Bart told *Montreal Gazette* fashion editor Eva Friede. "Eleonora, too, will not be typecast. There's a lot of interest about her. I think she's even going to transcend this moment, because she's very versatile, very eclectic, and has a lot of fabric to her life."

Despite all the publicity surrounding lesbian chic, there appears to be a major downside regarding the well-being of the models. Many fashion critics are skeptical. Valerie Deskin, a longtime New York freelance fashion writer, is concerned that lesbian chic will encourage teenage girls to restrict their love relationships to include only other women. She envisions more than 50 percent of female models having affairs with other women before 2003. Deskin, a fierce guardian of the privacy of young models, claims that many thirteen- and fourteen-year-old models are now indulging in lesbian affairs.

"It's disgusting," Deskin says. "I'm not against homogenous affairs, but not at such a young age. Again, the people running the industry are playing with fire. I'm one who tends to shrug off gossip, but ever since this lesbian chic look has taken off, there've been lots of stories circulating about some of the girls. I saw it firsthand at London Fashion Week this year. I was in a bar where many of the models were hanging out. In the bathroom I saw a well-known designer in her early thirties making out with a model who couldn't have been a day over fifteen. They were really going at it, licking each other's breasts and grabbing their thighs. I wonder what the girls parents would do if they knew what was going on."

Peer pressure is a game best played by young models. When these new kids in town arrive in big cities like New York and Milan, they desperately want to be accepted. They follow the patterns of their peers, and end up getting involved in sex, drugs, or whatever the flavor of the week might be. Lily St. Claire was a convent girl born to a distinguished Texas oil family. New York model scout Robert Luft spotted her at a Dallas Maverick basketball game in January 2001. The masculine looking seventeen-year-old St. Claire accepted an invitation to do some test shooting. During her two-week stay in New York, St. Claire was aware that the other models staying in her dorm sought sex of every variety without reservation. She says that one twenty-two-year-old model, Karina, pursued her relentlessly. St. Claire claims that more than half of the models in her dorm were bisexual, lesbian, or just experimenting. They would meet late at night in each other's rooms for drinks, drugs, conversation, and possibilities.

"I couldn't believe what was going on," St. Claire says. "When I went to New York I was warned about being hit on by the men. But it turned out that the women were more aggressive. A couple of the models asked me to have a threesome with them. They tried so hard to convince me. Lots of the girls did coke, got drunk, and, later on in the night, ended up in bed together. Everyone wanted to seem cool, to make it seem that lesbianism was the only way to go."

Jessica Brewer, a model from Boston who took her portfolio to New York to find work in November 2000, was shocked by what was going on around her. She has numerous anecdotes about lesbian models whose prospects, she believes, would have been bleak if not for the current fad. "Most of them looked horrible, horrible beyond belief," Brewer says. "If the clock would have been turned back a couple of years, they would never have gotten any attention. I met one girl who looked like anything but a model, but because she was openly gay, she was able to get the attention of the top agents."

Modeling was once a vicious exchange of heterosexual favors for recognition. But Brewer stressed that lesbian chic has altered the tone of the industry. "It used to be that if you were a model, you were expected to sleep with key people in the industry," she says. "Now, it's not such a certainty. You don't know who's gay and who's not." Still, Brewer adds, female models will always have to fend off male sexual predators, no matter the new trend. "I guess that even if you're gay, the men in this business will always be trying to get a pretty model between the sheets."

Perhaps models have opted to change their sexual habits and adopt a lesbian lifestyle in order to protect themselves against the frightening pattern of sexual abuse that has plagued the industry for so long. This logic, however, is not persuasive to feminists and sociologists who theorize about the reasons that women freely choose to love other women in a male-dominated industry. According to these people, it's far more likely that lesbianism is replacing past submission to sexual abuse as a tactic to build both a career and self-esteem.

"The young girls aren't doing it just to avoid being hit on by men," says California feminist activist Kia Torn. "They're doing it to pretend that they're cool. They have no idea how it really is to love another woman. They're doing it more for recreation and fun. It's sad that the fashion industry condones this. They just want to create a stir, get a lot of publicity, and make money at the expense of innocent teenage girls."

Surprisingly, the aggressive men who run the industry have been more or less tolerant of the explosion of lesbian romance. According to one New York model agent, these men find it easy to trivialize. "We get a real kick out of it," he says. "After getting so much bad publicity in the past for abusing young models—and most of it was well warranted—now we're able to sit back, relax, and go about our business. Several models I work with go out of their way to brag about their lesbian affairs so that the men know not to hit on them."

There are some men, however, who are eager to say good bye to the lesbian chic era, and soon. Los Angeles agent Barry Roth promulgates the notion that lesbian chic is like an illness that should be cured. Walker says that if the modeling industry promotes lesbianism for too long, it's likely that men will get turned off. "Men love models because [they] stimulate the construction of sexual fantasy," he says. "When men watch Claudia Schiffer, Gisele [Bundchen], and Tyra Banks on TV, their notion of the fashion industry is eroticized. Plain and simple, sex sells!"

The sudden popularity of lesbian chic is puzzling to some industry veterans. Older models say that lesbianism has been part of the fashion world for years. "When I was a model, at least half of the girls I worked with were bisexual," recalls former seventies model Julia Bell. "The only difference today is that they're making the girls look more masculine. And they're putting a big spin on the girls' sexuality to try to stir up lots of hype. But the reality is that lesbianism is not new to modeling. Some of the biggest models ever, like Gia Carangi, were openly gay."

Bell, a California native, remains active in fashion by working as a beauty consultant. She admittedly pays close attention to the industry's growing pains. "I have a sneaking suspicion that the current look won't last too long," she says. "I don't think that it's doing any justice to the industry. The butch look is interesting at first glance, but people will tire of it quickly. The mainstay of this industry has always been a very feminine look. Nothing will ever change that. Over the years, I've seen many alternative looks come into style, but they go away just as fast as they came. People want to see models who have beauty and grace, regardless of their sexual preference."

CHAPTER 19

● ● ●

Online Ecstasy

The supermodels of the nineties became a generation's most sought after figure. They were some of the planet's most intriguing celebrity figures, perhaps since Elvis and The Beatles. As one Hollywood critic notes, "The public can't get enough of today's supermodels. They've become bigger than Frank Sinatra, baseball, and apple pie." The nineties supermodels' messianic status can be attributed, in part, to the proliferation of websites that feature models' faces and bodies on their model homepages. Since the nineties, thousands of sites about models have popped up on the Internet. Many of these include fully or partially nude photos of well-known models, including Kate Moss, Naomi Campbell, Cindy Crawford, and Veronica Webb. According to New York Internet analyst Brad Chapman, many such sites are in the top 5 percent of popular sites on the Web. Chapman says that model sites receive far more hits than other celebrity sites, including those of rock stars and actors.

"No comparison," Chapman asserts. "People surfing the net would rather stare at Claudia Schiffer's boobs than download a new song by Sheryl Crow. Models are probably the most exploited group of people on the net. Hundreds of . . . sites are posted every week with new revealing photos. Many of the sites charge a registration fee and the people in charge of the sites are laughing all the way to the bank. I know of one guy in California who charges a few bucks per month to visit his model site and he has over 50,000 people who have registered. Just do the math and it's easy to figure out why so many people are posting these sites. They're making a killing."

Chapman is concerned that some of the site owners are going too far to get exclusive photos for their site. He says that many website designers hire top photographers to act like paparazzi, staking out models and taking their pictures. Chapman worries that the trend is getting out of control. "Some website designers are sending photographers . . . where the models vacation [in order] to snap photos of them naked on the beach," Chapman says.

It's an invasion of privacy. We live in such a big world, yet it's becoming more and more difficult to find any privacy. When Naomi Campbell was vacationing in southern Europe last year, a photographer who was hired by a website was camped on the roof of her villa. He planted a highly sensitive microphone on the part of the roof above her bedroom and was able to record some erotic noises Campbell and her male friend were making in the early hours of the morning after they had been out clubbing all night. They then downloaded the noises onto the Internet and people were able to pay a small fee to hear [them]. People will go to any extreme today to get what the other person doesn't have. Until Internet rules and regulations are set down, it'll be open season. Celebrities will find it impossible to find any privacy. And the Internet paparazzi will just keep cashing in at their expense.

Los Angeles based website designer Rob Garo has set up more than 100 sites on the net that display model photos. Garo, who started his business in 1994, gets more than 100,000 hits a day on his various sites. He says that many people in the fashion industry have taken notice of his work and are lining up to pay him. "Agents want me to post photos of their models, and designers want me to post models wearing their clothes," Garo says. "It's better publicity than being in any fashion magazine because people really take time to study the models on the net. In magazines they just quickly browse through the pages. In a way, I'm being bribed. I used to not do it, but the money has become too big to pass up. Aside from making a lot on the site fees I charge, the money I get on the side for using certain models can increase my income by at least 40 percent. You'd have to be crazy to turn that kind of money down."

Garo estimates that in 1997 alone he earned nearly half a million dollars from his model sites. He has hired twelve full-time employees to assist him. "It's gotten completely out of hand," he says. "I could work twenty-four hours a day and still not be able to finish all the work that has to be done." Garo's plan is to keep posting beautiful faces on his sites for the next three years and then sell his business at a high price. "I'll be able to convince prospective buyers that this is more lucrative than almost any other enterprise in the entertainment business," he says. "The numbers are phenomenal. The public can't get enough of staring at gorgeous, naked models. And the overhead is almost nil. The price I'll ask when I sell will be in the millions. Just the catalogue of model photos that I own is worth a lot, and that's before you take into account all the users I have registered who pay the monthly fee. This is the way of the future and I was lucky to get in at the ground level. There's room for everybody, but it would be much more difficult to start something like this today because so many people are doing it."

Finding new talent, Garo says, is the easiest part of the job. When he placed an ad for hot young models on a fashion newsgroup, he received more than 5,000 resumes in the first week. Garo believes it's easy to find new models because the world is overly obsessed with celebrities. "People want attention, and what better way is there than seeing their picture on a magazine cover or an Internet site?" Garo says. "They're so desperate to get their fifteen minutes of fame. They would probably pay me—if I asked—to appear on my site."

What Garo enjoys the most is the opportunity to hobnob with some of the world's most beautiful women. Before he started designing web pages, Garo worked as a pharmaceutical assistant. "My life was completely boring," he says. "I was surrounded by all these pretentious medical people. Today I get to go to parties and meet people like Claudia Schiffer and Tyra Banks. It has made my life become so exciting. I've learned so much about the fashion industry. It's exciting because there's so many crazy things that go on day in and day out. Sometimes I feel like I'm living in a dream and I pinch myself to see if I'll wake up."

Garo has many outrageous stories about his experience with models. He recalls one September night at a private loft party in New York. He was sitting alone in a corner with a martini when he noticed two male supermodels making out. "I was shocked," Garo says.

These two guys would be the last people on this planet who you would think were gay. They came across as being super masculine. But you should have seen them, they were all over each other. They were french kissing and feeling each other's crotch. Not many people noticed them because the room was very dark. It was a crazy party. A couple of hours later I found myself doing lines of coke with a Euro-

pean fashion designer and three of his female models. They didn't
know who I was and they started offering me coke because I was sitting right beside them. One of the models sat on my lap while she
sniffed some coke. I got an erection. It was embarrassing, but I couldn't
help myself. I really got turned on. Afterwards I started getting her
drunk on champagne and then we hit the dance floor. By the end of
the night she had fallen all over me and we were making out. I took
her back to my apartment and had one of the best nights of sex I've
ever had. Not bad for a guy who used to hang around with a bunch of
boring doctors.

Brian Donnelly is a sex therapist who says that model sites on the
Internet have created a lot of tension within married couples. He believes that sites with revealing photos are responsible for the demise
of many marriages. "These sites are very dangerous for married couples," Donnelly says. "I had one woman in here recently who was in
tears because she caught her husband on the net at four in the morning staring at nude photos of Cindy Crawford and Bridget Hall. Her
husband claimed that he came across the photos by accident. That's
the explanation most men use." Donnelly claims that more than 30
percent of marriages end in divorce because of the Internet. "It's a
disease," he says. "Thousands of provocative photos are available at
just the click of a mouse. Both men and women can't control themselves. One man I know left his wife because she spent more time
staring at Brad Pitt photos on the net than she did being a wife to
him."

Another client of Donnelly's caught her husband staring at completely naked young male models at the steamy site www.sugar
boys.com. Their six-month marriage dissolved soon after, when the
husband came out of the closet and admitted his homosexuality.
"That was one of the most bizarre cases I've come across," Donnelly
says. "Everything was fine in their marriage until the husband
bought a computer and started spending hours on end downloading
photos of young male models. It became an obsession. At first the
wife didn't think anything of it. She thought her husband was just
having a good laugh. But one day she walked into his office at home
and found him completely naked on his computer chair staring at a
photo of a young boy who couldn't have been a day over sixteen. He
was masturbating over the hot photo. That was the end of that marriage."

Donnelly advises newlyweds to avoid spending lots of time on the computer during the first couple years of marriage. He says it's important to limit the time spent in front of the computer screen in order to free up more time for the bedroom. "The only way a young couple's relationship has a chance to succeed today is if they realize that less time should be spent worrying about computers and careers," he says. "That's why the divorce rate has become so alarming. The couples don't spend enough time with each other. After a few months they wake up and wonder if their spouse married them or a computer terminal. Back in the old days marriages worked because the partners knew each other better. There were less distractions. It was almost unheard of for a spouse to walk in a room and find their partner staring at a nude photo of someone else. We've got to go back to the basics and avoid the distractions that are out there that are known to ruin marriages."

In June of 1998, Ellen Worrell of Michigan answered an Internet ad for photos of young models. Worrell, then a nineteen-year-old aspiring model, sent photos of herself to a Chicago-based website designer. After numerous e-mails, Worrell was offered a free trip to the Windy City and a chance to model. But from the moment she arrived at Chicago's O'Hare Airport, she was subjected to treatment she never anticipated. She was met at the airport by the website designer who escorted her to his beat-up 1979 Camaro. In the car she was offered marijuana and scotch. She smoked some of the joint because she wanted to "pretend to be cool." When they arrived at a seedy hotel near Chicago's South Side, the designer sweet-talked his way into Worrell's room. Once inside, he took off his shirt. He opened another bottle of scotch and a bag of cocaine. Worrell was afraid that if she refused anything, the man might get violent. She started drinking and doing drugs with him. After an hour, the man jumped on Worrell and tore off her dress. He then raped her several times and sodomized her. Worrell passed out. When she woke up hours later, the so-called designer was gone. She never heard from him again. She tried to track him down through e-mail, but he had changed his address and seemed to have disappeared. Worrell tried the site where she was first lured into her nightmare, but found it closed down. She didn't report the incident to the police because she feared that her parents would disown her for going to Chicago despite their objections.

"I was naive and stupid," she says. "I should have listened to my family and stayed home. I'm lucky to be alive. Ambition got in the way. I felt that it was a good opportunity for exposure and to make some money doing what I love. He had promised me in the e-mails that the photo session would not involve any nudity. I was so dumb to believe him. When I got home I didn't tell anybody for weeks. Finally, after several months, I told my family the entire story. But there was nothing anybody could do because so much time had passed. Hopefully when people read my story they'll think twice about being conned like I was. We're such easy victims over the net. People can set up false web pages and e-mail accounts and pretend to be a legitimate business."

Worrell has since quit being a model and has enrolled in nursing school. She will never return to modeling because she fears it will dredge up bad memories. "I made one silly mistake and now I have to pay for it," she says. "It's too bad, because when I was growing up I always wanted to be in *Vogue* like Cindy Crawford and Linda Evangelista. But now it will never happen. If I could put it behind me, I'd be out there in a second putting a portfolio together and trying to get some work. But it's too late. I'd always be afraid that somebody would try to pull something like this again. I still pick up *Vogue* and *Elle* and dream about how it might have been if I hadn't been conned over the Internet."

The tech-savvy people in the fashion industry have set up successful websites and online promotions to spur Internet-based sales. One of the first, and most infamous, online promotions was part of a Victoria's Secret ad campaign that debuted during the 1999 Super Bowl. More than a million people logged on to the website within an hour of the TV ad.

"It was a brilliant idea," says web analyst Ian Harmon. "The response they got was record breaking. Millions of people who were exposed to the ads during the Super Bowl logged on in the next few days after the commercial to check it out. Whoever thought of that idea deserves a huge raise."

The draw was a chance to win tickets to an exclusive online lingerie fashion show that, live, normally costs $10,000 a ticket. To spotlight their Internet site and boost online sales, they placed the advertisements during the Super Bowl—it worked better than they expected. "The Web is an additional way to reach different and new customers, such as men in particular," said Cynthia Fields, president and chief executive of Victoria's Secret. According to Field, research showed that men who buy from the Internet greatly outnumber those who buy from catalogue. "It's a lot more stress-free for a man to buy lingerie online than in a shop," said Evie Black Dykema, an analyst at Forrester Research, a firm that monitors online technology issues. "You can complete a transaction without talking to one person."

The fashion show, which began at 7 P.M. Eastern time, featured many of the top supermodels, including Heidi Klum, Laetitia Casta, Tyra Banks, and Stephanie Seymour. The show was being hyped as the biggest Internet event ever. Close to one million people logged on for the netcast. The Victoria's Secret website was so busy that many surfers couldn't connect, or once they did encountered Web congestion that slowed the video feed to a halt or, worse, disconnected them. "This event will go down in history, it will be remembered for years," said Mark Cuban, the president of Broadcast.com, the webcaster who produced the online fashion show and delivered the live feed. "I'm not here to tell you that this is going to look like television. It's not. But it's about access—getting access to things that you might otherwise not get."

The event took place at Cipriani's, a restaurant on Wall Street. Rich businessmen and celebrities were packed into the invitation-only show. Supermodel Stephanie Seymour turned heads wearing a very conservative blue suit when she rang the closing bell at the stock exchange. Victoria's Secret banked on the hope that hundreds of thousands of men would log on to the website to buy Valentine's Day presents for their wives or girlfriends. The company's market research showed that the Internet would be an ideal place for men to buy lingerie, since most men are simply shy and embarassed to shop for lingerie in person.

But a grainy online picture turned many people off. "I accessed it for a few minutes before I logged off because the quality of the video was terrible," says Frank Bertucci, a viewer from Maine. "I was far from impressed. It was a good publicity gimmick with the Super Bowl ads and all the advance hype. But the end result was a disaster. I think it did the company more harm than good. I don't think many people will fall for it again next year unless they increase the quality."

According to veteran TV technician Bruce Sandworth, the greatest problem was that there was only one camera, positioned at the end of the catwalk, that transmitted the images of the scantily clad models to the Internet. "I think they have to beef up their equipment and do dozens of test runs before the show," Sandworth says. "I was very surprised with the end result, because you would think that a company of that stature would make sure that everything ran smoothly.

They weren't prepared for the huge amount of people that logged on. I read one story where a representative of the company said she anticipated about 250,000 people to log on. Had they done more research, they would have found out that model sites have become the most popular on the net, and they could have avoided this disaster. I don't think they were very pleased with the end result."

Only two items from Victoria's Secret spring line were sold online after the webcast ended. The Victoria's Secret V-String set, which was marketed as a great Valentine's gift, and the Dream Angel bra were available. Shoppers were also able to buy items from previous catalogues.

Victoria's Secret's biggest disappointment, however, was that the Webcast didn't impress investors—share prices in both Intimate Brands and Broadcast.com dropped quickly the day after the show. Intimate Brands, which had seen its shares double in four months, slipped 5.2 percent. Similarly, Broadcast.com shares fell 4.9 percent the day after the show. In the previous four months their shares had more than quadrupled. Still, the companies will probably land on their feet. "I don't think they're going to lose too much sleep, because Internet stocks are known to go up and down quickly," said Wall Street financial analyst Mark Fleming. "Look at Amazon.com. If you had bought its stock two years ago, you could have retired a millionaire. The same goes for stocks like Ebay.com and Priceline.com."

In the end, Victoria's Secret maintained that the viewers who logged onto the webcast were pleased with what they saw. But many people disagreed and hoped that things would improve in the future. "Anybody who loves beautiful women would have to be crazy to pass up the chance to see Heidi Klum and the rest of the models walk down the catwalk in their underwear," said fashion photographer Allan Klein. "This event will become the Super Bowl of the fashion industry. But they clearly need to take time to work out the kinks on the technical side of things."

Victoria's Secret spent more than five million dollars marketing and producing the show. A spokesperson for the company said that they were not deterred by the technicalities or the drop in stock. "We'll do it again next year, and you can expect it to be done on a much bigger scale," she said. "We treated this as a sort of test run. You can be sure that everything will work well next year."

CHAPTER 20

● ● ●

New Blood

In recent years, unless a model is able to fit into the new celebrity or lesbian chic trends, graduating from model to supermodel has been as difficult as winning the lottery. Because the market has become so oversaturated, models often work on hundreds of small shoots before they are considered for a major magazine spread or fashion show. And they have much less job security than their predecessors.

A few years ago, appearing in *Vogue* or *Elle* usually meant fame and fortune. Today, there are no guarantees. Although one month a model may appear in a big magazine, the next she may have trouble finding a gig. According to many of the models interviewed for this book, today caution is the norm. "It's a rollercoaster ride," one model said. "You're here today, gone tomorrow. There's too much competition out there. A couple of months ago I did a major fashion show in Milan. All the media and key people were there. I thought I would get lots of quality work out of it. I'm surprised, because nobody's called since. Today, you're only as good as your last shoot."

Frustration finding major magazine and runway jobs has forced models to increase their number of minor jobs, such as store catologues and local TV commercials. To make ends meet, models are working harder than ever. Though some models own houses throughout the world, they often spend fewer than fifty nights a year in them. They are forced to live in tiny apartments in big cities like New York and Paris while working to become the next famous covergirl. "It's grueling," says fashion assistant Deidre Stober. "It's not as if you could go to work and drive two hours to a suburban area of

New York to relax in your home. A model has got to live right in the big city and be on call twenty-four hours a day. They work harder than most people can imagine. They have to grab opportunities as they occur."

As the age of the Big Six drew to a close, the new faces on magazine covers, billboards, and bus shelters had to work twice as hard to keep the supermodel phenomenon alive. "They have extremely big shoes to fill," says journalist Esmond Choueke. "It's almost unbearable pressure. And the models who aren't strong mentally will drop off quickly. The only way to survive this pressure is by working doubly hard, and to carefully study how models like Claudia Schiffer and Kate Moss managed to become so big."

Whether or not it's fun, there are more models in the market today than ever before. As the fashion industry entrenches itself in its greatest period of sustained growth, tens of thousands of young men and women beat down the doors of modeling agencies all over the world hoping to find work. Their self-confidence remains rooted in the notion that their good looks will help get them through the door, instead of the reality that their chances of becoming successful are slim to none. According to model scout Kris Weber, fewer than one of 20,000 wannabe models ever get work.

The new models who attract serious attention must find unique ways to stay connected to the enduring power network that includes the world's top agents and designers, like Elite and Calvin Klein. According to many of the industry's key players, besides lesbian chic, the trend for the new millenium, is to use models from different parts of the world, lending fashion a more diverse exotic flavor. As a result, more jobs will become available for model scouts, who comb the streets of remote cities throughout the world searching for interesting new faces.

When model Adriana Sklenarikova's career took off in North America, she was already a superstar in Europe, thanks mainly to her role as the principal model for Wonderbra. Sklenarikova, who was raised in Brezno, Slovakia, was in medical school studying to be a doctor when she turned to modeling. She is by no means an overnight sensation—she has done many small modeling jobs and appeared in small roles in several films, including Robert Altman's *Prêt-à-Porter*. But Sklenarikova's biggest claim to fame is that she's listed in the *Guinness Book of Records* for having the world's longest female legs at just over four feet. Like Brazilian beauty

Gisele, Sklenarikova's every move is followed closely by the paparazzi. Her big boobs and healthy body differ from the heroin-chic look of the nineties, and she likes to flaunt them.

"Adriana will be the biggest supermodel for many years to come," says fashion historian Adam Druker. "She is more marketable than any model I can remember. Aside from her stunning looks, she's very smart. People are tired of seeing bimbos pose in the magazines. Society's more sophisticated today. Parents don't want some dumb blonde who's on drugs being a role model to their children. They want somebody intelligent like Adriana. The day of the blonde bombshell or skinny, heroin-addict looking model is gone."

Bidding wars erupted between fashion designers worldwide for Sklenarikova's services in early 2000. Many predict that Sklenarikova will set the standard for supermodels for the next two decades. "The way Naomi and Kate changed things in the ninety's will be nothing compared to what Sklenarikova and her generation of models will do for the fashion industry," says one well-known designer. "People are tired of the way a lot of the supermodels have abused their privileges and have ruined their lives with drugs and alcohol. Models like Sklenarikova are the exact opposite. They have proven that models can be intelligent and not have to sniff some cocaine before they get up on the catwalk."

Devon Aoki, a stunning schoolgirl who is part Japanese, part German, and part British, is challenging Adriana Sklenarikova as queen of the catwalk. Aoki's china-doll face became famous worldwide after supermodel Kate Moss saw a photo of her in *Interview Magazine* in 1998. Moss's instincts took over. She had never been so impressed by another model. She immediately contacted Sarah Doukas, the head of Storm, who decided to offer Aoki a contract after one glance at her photo. "I had never seen a face like hers," Doukas told journalist Catherine Wilson. "She almost looks unreal, as if someone has painted her."

Aoki, the daughter of millionaire Japanese restaurateur Rocky Aoki and American artist Pamela Price, was introduced to the world of fashion at the tender age of five by her godmother's best friend, celebrity hairdresser Sam McKnight. McKnight, who became famous for doing the hair of the late Princess Diana, loved dressing up little Aoki in different wigs and putting makeup on her. "She's going to be a knockout," McKnight once said. "She's got the most unique and stunning features I've ever seen."

Since Moss discovered her at age fifteen, Aoki has signed with

Chanel and has become the company's hottest model. She has also been photographed by legendary photographer Steven Meisel for *Vogue.* "Aoki personifies the new type of supermodel," said a Chanel representative. "She combines an incredible combination of beauty and intelligence. She's a straight-A student in school and she has the most exotic and natural look ever seen on the catwalk."

Aoki's parents are protective. During the first couple of years, they chaperoned her to photo shoots, making sure that their daughter was in good hands. When they were unable to make it, they'd arrange for a chaperone for their daughter. "That's smart parenting," said model agent Dick Warren. "At the beginning it's good to make sure your daughter is watched over. It's the best way to protect [her] from drugs and sexual predators. Eventually, agencies will have to make this mandatory, or risk losing people from signing up because of all the horror stories that have been going around."

Aoki realizes that a model's career is not long. An avid reader, she has other career aspirations aside from modeling. "I write a lot of poetry," she says. "That is what I would really like to do after college." Aoki's mom Pam, a tiny, blond ex-mannequin herself, was concerned when her daughter became a model at age twelve. Aoki appeared in a Duran Duran video after photographer Ellen von Unwerth discovered her at a party for the legendary fifties pinup Betty Page. "I warned her about all the pitfalls of being a model," Pam Price says. "You hear so many bad stories in the press that it makes you feel scared to have your daughter in the business. . . . I think you need to start very young in this business if you are going to have any kind of longevity. What can you do? You just have to hope she can maintain her career like Madonna, and not have a very rocky time like Drew Barrymore."

Similarly, Israeli model Maya Shoa has had a couple of remarkable years. Shoa, who grew up in Tel Aviv and spent time as a soldier in the Israeli Army, is a stunning five-foot, ten-inch brunette who, like Adriana Sklenarikova, believes that education comes first. Although she has earned big money doing major fashion shows across the world, Shoa plans to get a degree in alternative medicine while modeling. "I want to have a broad background," Shoa says. "Modeling is fun, but it's important to have something to fall back on."

In 1999, Shoa climbed to the top of the supermodeling charts. She was featured in several fashion magazines and became one of the most sought after models. "Whoever says that supermodels are dead really means that models without brains are dead," says fashion critic Emma Canning. "Today, agents and designers are looking for models who are smart. The industry is tired of its terrible reputation for sexual abuse and drugs. The new generation is desperately trying to clean it up. And it's people like Maya Shoa who are helping it become a reality."

Sara O'Hare's rise to modeling fame has also been fast. The Wonderbra spokesmodel is the most famous and respected model in her native Australia. She hosts Fashion Week every year and has become Australia's spokesperson for breast cancer research. "I believe that I'm fortunate to have gone as far as I have and I feel an obligation to help people who are less fortunate than me," O'Hare says. "My modeling schedule is very hectic, but in the free time that I have I feel a need to work for worthwhile, charitable causes. Models are in a position to have an impact and to help people. It's important that we take advantage of this opportunity."

Argentinian model Yamila Diaz-Rahi is known for her intelligence and poise. She says she would prefer being on the beach in Buenos Aires, the city in which she grew up, than mingling with the fashion cocktail crowd in Paris or New York. She has lent her presence and name to numerous benefits and cultural events for worthwhile causes. Her wisdom and savvy played a big part in landing her a job as a model with Victoria's Secret. These attributes speak to the new unofficial motto and rallying cry of the supermodel industry. "She's the full package—gorgeous looks and high intelligence," says one model agent. "She will help set the standard for the new generation of models. Girls like Yamila are making sure that new models must be well-educated and business-oriented as well as being beautiful. It's a new standard that will help erase all the abuse and finally clean up the industry."

The most promising young American supermodel is Texas-born Bridget Hall. Hall, who started modeling at age nine, is a favorite of Gucci designer Tom Ford, who once said that Hall is as talented as anybody he's ever seen on the catwalk. The tall, freckled Hall has drawn praise from every corner of the industry for how comfortable she is in front of the camera. "I've never seen anybody appear so at ease," says one fashion photographer. "Bridget is a natural. And she's not your stereotypical, empty-headed model. She's been in this business for years and it's very hard to pull something over on her. She's a natural beauty whose I.Q. probably is double that of most other models I've worked with."

According to fashion critic Emma Canning, some other new models to watch for in the early part of the millennium include twins Heather and Melissa Lloyd from Virginia, Botswana-born Karen Ferrari, and, of course, Gisele Bundchen. "These models are much more different than the supermodels like Cindy Crawford who have ruled the fashion world for so long," Canning says. "There's been so much talk about the end of supermodels, but models like these are proof that the supermodel business is alive and well. It's frustrating when people keep saying that they're waiting for the next Linda Evangelista or Naomi Campbell to come along. Those models were one era and the new models are another. It's not fair to compare them. The new models will offer things that the old ones didn't. That's how modeling has always been, one big progression. Anybody who thinks that the best times are over is blind. The new generation of models is more interesting than ever before, because, for the first time, we're starting to see models emerge who have college degrees and who are more than just a pretty face."

CHAPTER 21

• • •

Proverbial Opportunity

Many current models sympathize with the harsh experiences their predecessors were forced to endure. Drugs and alcohol have been a staple of the fashion industry ever since a struggling, handsome young actor named John Powers opened the first modeling agency on Park Avenue in 1925. There has always been an unwritten rule in the industry to keep the secret. Models constantly worry about their own plight. Intent on doing whatever it takes to amass enough money to support a lavish lifestyle, models lust for their personal safety. There have been too many reports of models who mysteriously disappear or have to jump out a fourth-story window to avoid being raped by a drugged-out agent.

One of the few reported cases is that of seventeen-year-old Danish model Elizabeth Sorensen. During the mid-nineties, Sorenson was a young model who disappeared on a "shoot" with a nonexistent Moroccan fashion magazine. One of her close friends, Elizabeth Dankov, believes Sorenson was drugged, raped, and kidnapped when she arrived for a shoot in Tangiers. Her whereabouts are still unknown. Rumor has it that she is still alive and is being used as a sex slave in the southern part of Morocco. "If it was another industry, people would be combing the streets of Morocco trying to find her," says her former boyfriend Lars Christensen. "It's just that in this industry people like to sweep things under the rug. They're afraid if the truth comes out, it might destroy the public's perception of the industry. The fashion industry is supposed to be filled with beauty, but that's totally untrue. Instead it's filled with beasts."

Sorensen's nightmarish story is one of hundreds that have gone virtually unreported in the modeling world.

Antonio Luciano, who worked as a model in London and Milan in the late eighties, feels that the number of murders and suicides in the modeling business has drastically increased. Luciano attributes this to the fact that the authorities tend to ignore what's really going on. "My cousin is a cop in Milan and he's told me that a lot of the cops are paid off to keep silent," Luciano says. "I've heard from other people that this is also common in other cities as well. They could [split] things wide open by investigating some of the cases of abuse, but they'd rather ignore it. They're afraid that tourism will drop. Lots of people come to places like Milan to hang out with the models and the fashion crowd. If rumors of violence start to circulate, people won't come. The fashion industry is worth millions of dollars a year in business to places like Milan. The authorities care more about preserving the business instead of solving a murder or drug case. It's totally backwards."

Milan is not the only cosmopolitan center where crime is at the core of the fashion industry. In January 1998, Tina Vazquez was recruited off the poverty-stricken streets of her hometown in the Dominican Republic by an agent who operates out of Miami's South Beach area. Vazquez, who looked like a cross between Sophia Loren and Raquel Welch, had spent her entire life living with her family in a tiny one-room apartment that had no running water. Within thirty-six hours Vazquez was on a plane to Miami with no return ticket and just the twenty dollars that the agent had given her. Over the next few weeks Vazquez's life became a walking nightmare. She was raped several times by the agent who recruited her and was too terrified to go to the police. "He said that if I went to the police that he would have me killed," Vazquez said. "I didn't know what to do. I only went to Miami because I thought it was a chance to make some money to help out my family. My father didn't have a job and we lived in the most terrible conditions you could imagine. When I arrived the experience was not at all similar to what was promised to me. I was forced to have sex with my agent, and if I didn't want to, he would get violent with me and would rape me. He once ripped off my clothes, tied me up to his bed, and forced me to have sex with him for over four hours. I spoke to a lot of the other girls who were recruited to go to South Beach and they have similar stories to tell. They say the people who run the business in Miami have been up to the same old tricks for many years."

Vazquez cut off ties with her sleazy agent after a couple of months. But finding another agent was not easy. She claims she was blacklisted in the Miami fashion scene for leaving her agent. "I went door to door to try to get work with other agencies but they all refused me," Vazquez recalls. "It was like a terrible nightmare. I didn't have a penny on me and no return plane ticket. I felt like I was going to die, that's how bad it was."

Fortunately, a female model who Vazquez met through her old agent was kind enough to let her crash on her couch until she found some work. A month later Vazquez finally landed a job in a well-known topless nightclub. The young, innocent girl from the Dominican Republic was now taking off her clothes for a living under the stage name "Angel." Two years later Vazquez still works the evening shift at the same club. She says that she hopes to work there for three more years and then return to the Dominican Republic with enough money to ensure that her family is comfortable for the rest of their lives.

"Sometimes I make two thousand dollars a night, cash," Vazquez says. "It's better than what the average model makes. I would have liked to have a better shot in the modeling business but it's so corrupt. You would think the business I'm in now would be more corrupt but it's not. There's people who look after me here. If a customer gets out of hand, the bouncer will throw him out of the club. The worst experience I've had here was one night when a well-known member of the Florida Marlins baseball team came in and made me dance for him privately for several hours. He kept touching my breasts and kept trying to put his fingers down my pants. He was very drunk and he was paying me about a thousand dollars an hour. I played the game with him because I knew it was good money, but I kept having to throw him off me. Suddenly, he jumped on top of me and tried to have sex with me. I yelled out loud and the bouncers came in and a fight broke out. He was a big guy so he wasn't easy to handle. But the bouncers threw him out of the club onto the street. I went in the bathroom and cried for a long time because I felt so abused and ashamed of what I was doing. It's not an easy life. Man, I thought I was going to America to lead a glamorous and amazing life. It was going to be a dream come true. My folks back home would see me on the pages of the beautiful magazines and I thought I would be one of the beautiful models that everybody would want to look at. But now, after these few months, here I am in a darkened little corner of a strip joint with a big, drunken, American athlete pawing me. But if I don't do it, I would be back home on the streets without a cent. I'm here just to take care of business so I can help my family."

British psychologist Rebecca Holmes has counseled many female models over the years. Holmes says that she has met hundreds of women over the years who have stories exactly like Vazquez. "Sometimes I get ten new girls a week coming in with horror stories," Holmes says.

They reach the point where they have become so disgusted with themselves that they want to commit suicide. And the ones who aren't fortunate enough to get counseling often do. The problem is that the agents take advantage of the girls naïveté. They lie to them and promise them things that they never live up to. The girls don't see through it until they get on a plane and go to Paris or South Beach. When they get there they realize that they've been duped and have no other recourse but to cooperate with the people who brought them there. It's horrifying. Girls think that they'll be the next Cindy Crawford or Naomi Campbell when they're recruited. But that rarely happens. In most cases, the girls are in for a very heartbreaking time. The modeling business is rampant with fraud artists and cons. Until we get rid of these guys by either putting them in jail or having their businesses shut down, it will continue to go on. I had one girl in the other day who was beaten up by her agent because she didn't want to have sex with him. I told her to go to the police, but she didn't want to because she was too afraid. She said that the agent had several guns in his house, and she feared that he would kill her if she ratted on him. It's attitudes like these that have got to change. Until somebody steps up and blows the whistle on these people, it's going to be hard to change the way things have been for so many years.

According to British supermodel Iris Palmer, the life of a supermodel seems to be a charmed one—Hollywood parties, lots of money, the finest clothes. But once the reality of the business sets in, it is a much different scenario. Palmer, the daughter of Sir Mark and Lady Palmer, started doing fashion shoots in New York when she was sixteen. She had become well known by the time she turned eighteen, after being discovered in fishnet tights and a revealing miniskirt by Storm agency owner Sarah Doukas. "She is the look of the moment," Doukas says. "Beautiful, off-beat, and with a huge personality." Reaching the top was not like anything Palmer had envisioned. "I can't stand all the empty bullshit," she says. "There is such a myth about how wonderful it is. The people who run it have no understanding of all the young girls they have. . . . Drugs are everywhere. Models can get into them very early now."

The sudden death of a close supermodel friend left Palmer disillusioned and angry with the people who run the modeling industry. "It could have been avoided if the people who handled her career were more concerned about her well-being than making money," Palmer laments.

> She was so naive, she didn't know what she was doing. She would come home tired and instead of just having a cup of tea, she would order loads of coke because she totally thought that was what everyone did. When I came back to New York I arrived at her apartment and she was like, "Hi!" Then she jumped into a huge white limo that was waiting outside. Inside was a video camera and lines of coke all racked up. I was like, "Excuse me!" Anyway, we drove around the block for a while and I was thinking, this is quite funny. But then she started doing the drugs and videoing herself and I realized she really had lost it. I was a totally shocked, uptight English person, but she didn't understand and started to get wound up. She was from a small town in Florida and suddenly she was a model living on her own in New York. What do you think goes on in a girl's head when her life changes overnight?

Palmer qualifies as a supermodel because she has been ranked in the top 100 models and earns a salary in the mid-six-figure range. She has also been featured in all the major fashion magazines and on Fashion TV. Palmer, like every other supermodel interviewed for this book, confirmed that drugs, alcohol, and sexual abuse are the plagues of the modeling world.

But the problem is more shocking now than ever—some of the models being abused are as young as eleven and twelve years old. Chicago housewife Connie Drucker's daughter Roberta was recruited to model for a Chicago-based agency at age eleven. By the time she turned thirteen, Roberta had been committed to a drug rehabilitation center after almost overdosing on heroin. "I should have never encouraged Roberta to model," Mrs. Drucker said. "She was too young. She was only eleven years old and she was dressing up in fancy dresses and putting on loads of makeup, going to discos with men three times her age. They would tell me it was for business, but it turned out that these bastards were taking her dancing and giving her cocaine and lots of champagne. At first I had no idea what was going on. But after a while I caught on and tried to get my daughter help. I made her quit the modeling agency she was with. But it was too late. I got a call from the hospital one night and they told me that my daughter had almost died of a heroin overdose. Luckily a friend of hers called 911 to get help. I can never forgive myself because as a parent I should have not agreed to let her model at such a young age. I strongly advise other parents not to let their children model until they're in their twenties and are old enough to make educated decisions about what to do with their lives."

Roberta Drucker's story struck a chord with other teenage model victims. It also affected models' parents. As a result, many parents have become more reluctant to let their teenage children be recruited, even by the bigger and more well-known agencies. "My daughter Mary has had at least a dozen offers to model since the age of thirteen," says Molly Hunter of Florida. "She's tall and slim and has a smile to kill for. But I've read about some of the horror stories in the modeling business and I won't let her do anything until she's at least eighteen or nineteen, when she's finished high school and has something to fall back on. There's just too many young girls who have been sucked in and have ended up being used. I might be making a mistake because Mary could be making lots of money. But as a parent it's my duty to protect her. If she were to model, I can't go and be with her every second, and that's how long it takes for something really bad to happen to a girl that age. I intend to make damn sure that nobody takes advantage of my daughter. Good looks eventually fade, but a high school education doesn't. That's the way I look at it."

Not all parents are against their child becoming a model, and not all models are against the jet set lifestyle of the fashion industry. Many bask in it for years before waking up to reality. At a recent casting for a fashion show in Paris one of the organizers admitted that every model in the room was under the age of seventeen. One of the girls who auditioned, fifteen-year-old Elise Robert of Lyons, France, said that she would go to any lengths to make sure she got the job. "I don't care if I have to take off my clothes or sleep my way to the top," Robert said. "I want to work and make money. And if you get involved in this business, you better be prepared to make sacrifices. I'm young and I've already been through a lot. But what the hell, you only live once. When I was twelve I slept with my first agent, who was forty-one at the time. My friends think I'm nuts. My family thinks that I need psychiatric help. But ever since I was five years old the only thing I wanted in my life was to be famous in France the way Madonna is famous in America. And like Madonna, who made a lot of sacrifices to get to the top, I will do whatever it takes to make my dream come true."

Although Robert is not afraid of sleeping her way to the top, she won't be persuaded to do hard drugs. "I always have men offering me cocaine and trying to get me drunk. I tell them to stuff it. Sure, I admit I've slept with a lot of guys for somebody so young, but that's because I love the human body and I find sex to be beautiful. But I don't want to fuck up my body and destroy myself with drugs. I love life and I intend to be around for a long time. I've seen too many people in this business die young because of drugs."

During the nineties there were countless fatalities in the modeling business due to drug abuse. Most industry insiders attribute the high rate of tragedy to the fact that most models start out in the business without any other experience in life. "Girls are getting started in the industry really young," says American model James King. "They're not spiritually or emotionally evolved. They're not even women yet."

Supermodel-turned-*Pearl Harbor* film star, King was only eighteen when her twenty-year-old fashion photographer boyfriend, Davide Sorrenti, died on February 3, 1997, from complications caused by heroin use. Sorrenti had been surrounded by the fashion industry ever since he was a little boy. He was the son of legendary fashion photographer Francesca Sorrenti. He was also the brother of Mario Sorrenti, the former Levi's jeans model who was romantically involved with Kate Moss for several years. David grew up around models, and often accompanied his mother to shoots. When he was fourteen, he had an affair with a well-known model who was eleven years his senior. At only nineteen years of age, he was featured in *Interview Magazine's* "One to Watch" column. In the column Davide listed his Beauty Top Ten, which included Carolyn Murphy (the Prada model), Levi's jeans, the Leica M5 camera, and the thirteen-year-old model Filippa. But Davide could not cope with his success and turned to heroin. "He was very into the nineties ecstasy crowd," said Daryl Wilke, a close friend of Sorrenti's. "Davide had lots of success but it meant nothing to him. He saw through it all and he often said that it was all just a load of bullshit. If anything, being involved in the fashion business made Davide depressed and suicidal. He completely lost control of himself and needed to take drugs to escape from it all."

James King, who has been through drug rehab herself, was not surprised by her boyfriend's death even though she believed that he was off drugs. Since she started out in the modeling business at age fourteen, King has seen many close model friends die from drugs. When she met Sorrenti he seemed just as desperate and distraught as a lot of the people she had worked with in the modeling business. "When girls start making lots of money, there's so much pressure, they might start getting a little stoned to take the edge off," says King, who admits she was offered drugs on modeling assignments when she was a teenager. Throughout the years, King has seen fashion people take drugs and alcohol at photo shoots. She has witnessed people doing drugs in the bathroom at fashion shows. King says not many other industries would tolerate the constant drug abuse in the fashion industry. King blames the people running the fashion industry for steering the models in the wrong direction. "I don't care what anybody says, but the reality is that the people in charge of things encourage the models to destroy themselves. . . . If a girl becomes a star and she starts to do drugs, no one does anything to stop it. As long as she keeps making money, it's fine. It's New York—they don't care."

If Francesca Sorrenti could turn back time, she wouldn't have encouraged her son Davide to work in the fashion business at such a young age. While she approved of her son's relationship with King, Sorrenti still can't forgive herself for her son's death. "They were very much in love," she says.

But it was sort of sick, because they were both heroin addicts. James has come out of rehab and looks amazing, but she is so ripped to pieces. She loved him dearly, you know. At the ripe old age of nineteen she has to cope with the fact that she has had four years of heroin addiction and a dead boyfriend. Is that right, that we as adults exposed her? The photographer's assistant turned her on to heroin. He offered it to her. She got hooked. We, as adults, did it. . . . In a million years, as a parent you don't think because your child is entering the business, they are going to be harmed in any way. You [say to yourself], "Oh, wow! This is a beautiful, glamorous business with lots of money and my son or daughter is going to do really well." And then the bomb falls, and people say, "How did this happen?"

Since her son's death, Francesca Sorrenti has become an activist who works to help protect models. She is pressing for tough legislation similar to that which governs the film industry. Sorrenti hopes that, in the foreseeable future, laws will require random drug testing, parental supervision for underage models, and an agreement between agencies not to hire models with known addictions. "Editors watch as children cover their track marks with body makeup," she says. "Bags of cocaine are given as Christmas gifts. Children are lured to other agencies because they are drug-friendlier." So far, Sorrenti's efforts have fallen on deaf ears or met with harsh words.

Most politicians claim that cleaning up the fashion industry is not high on their priority list. "There are so many problems we have to deal with first," said a Republican senator (who did not want his identity revealed). "Just because Sorrenti's son died doesn't mean that we have to push the panic button. If we would call an inquiry into this particular case, we would be setting a scary precedent. Every time someone tragically dies we would have to spend millions of dollars investigating the death. Davide Sorrenti died because he was doing illegal drugs. He shouldn't have been hanging around that scene in the first place. Everybody knows how common heroin use is in the fashion industry. His mother shouldn't be surprised by what happened."

Many politicians blame the models' parents for allowing them to walk down the runway. "The parents are more guilty than the children," said the senator. "They should concentrate on keeping their kids in school instead of trying to make a quick buck off them. Any parent who lets their kid model when they're only twelve or thirteen should really think twice. It's not like they're letting their kid join the school choir. They're throwing their kid into the hands of sexual predators and drug pushers."

Sorrenti says the support she's received so far has been very weak. "Models are not considered an empathy group," was the reply she received from one well-known politician. But Sorrenti does not intend to give up her fight easily. "There is a dislike factor," she says. "They are young and beautiful, and have money. But they have a whole set of problems that come with the runway. What makes them a specialized group in need of special care are the conditions which make them particularly vulnerable to the use of drugs: isolation and a need to escape. . . . Look at movie sets, which are a bit like fashion shoots. There are strict rules about the hours a minor can work, teachers are present, and you sure don't see tables full of alcohol put out for the crew."

Only a few politicians have started to take notice of Sorrenti's pleas for reform. Former President Bill Clinton, a longtime admirer of the fashion industry, has become one of its harshest critics. Clinton blasted fashion executives for glamorizing heroin addiction in order to sell clothing. Before leaving the Oval Office, Clinton beseeched the fashion industry to adhere to a new code of ethics.

"There are too many young, innocent girls and boys who would not be addicted to drugs if they didn't become models," Clinton said. "We've got to look carefully into this business and change things now before it's too late. Young models should not have to resort to heroin to lose weight. The fashion industry has got to readjust its criteria for models. If they don't, they should be held liable and face the consequences."

Clinton blamed the world's leading fashion designers for glamorizing heroin chic by putting pale, anorexic-looking models on billboards and magazine covers. He was sickened by the overwhelming majority of magazine covers that were featuring models who looked emaciated and strung out. "You do not need to glamorize addiction to sell clothes," he exclaimed. "Some fashion leaders are admitting flat out [that] images projected in fashion photos in the last few years have made heroin addiction seem glamorous and sexy and cool. And as some of the people in those images start to die now, it's become obvious that it is not true. The glorification of heroin is not creative, it's destructive. It's not beautiful, it is ugly. And this is not about art, it's about life and death. And glorifying death is not good for any society."

Dr. Herbert Kleber of the National Center on Addiction at New York's Columbia University says that the number of heroin addicts in America rose by more than 200,000 in the 1990s. According to Kleber, there are now more than 700,000 heroin addicts in America, compared to 500,000 a decade ago. He added that another 100,000 more were recreational users. The National Household Survey on Drug Abuse has reported that the number of people using heroin is six times greater than it was five years ago. Dr. Kleber is one of many U.S. researchers who blame the prevalence of heroin on the fashion industry.

"If the fashion industry was more responsible, lives would be saved," agrees Dr. Harvey Gelman of Toronto. "When you see models posing looking like they're on heroin, it has a very unfortunate effect. People think it's cool and they go out and get addicted to dope. If we were to see healthier looking models on the covers of magazines, perhaps a good percentage of our nation's heroin users wouldn't have become addicted."

In the nineties, heroin became cheaper than ever before, making it more accessible to youngsters from all social backgrounds. "It used to be a drug that only certain people took," Dr. Gelman says. "But now it's as easy to buy as a candy bar. And it's available in a purer form, so the kids don't have to worry about injecting it. It can be sniffed through one's nose or smoked. Recently I met with a colleague friend in Atlanta who did a study about heroin use today. He told me that in one high school he visited, more than 40 percent of the students he interviewed admitted to having used heroin. This is not an isolated incident. Everywhere in America the same thing is going on. We must stop it now before half of our next generation winds up addicted. People in the fashion and entertainment industry have got to wake up and stop trying to make a quick buck by promoting the heroin-chic look. They have to realize that the consequences are devastating."

President Clinton's attempt to shake up the fashion industry was not received very well by some of the industry's top players. Fern Mallis, executive director of the Council of Fashion Designers of America, disagreed with the President's statements. "It is unfair that the whole industry should be blamed for heroin abuses. However, we understand the responsibility of being more responsible."

American designer Marc Jacobs called Clinton's remarks unfounded and ridiculous. Jacobs urged Clinton to rethink his stance. He felt Clinton was simply trying to gain political points without understanding the reality of the situation. "Fashion isn't healthcare," Jacobs said. "What do you want to see? A cover of *Vogue* with someone sipping orange juice?"

But those who have been stricken with tragedy insist that people like Jacobs are just trying to protect their security. "Of course it hurts when a person like Marc Jacobs refuses to admit the severity of the problem," says Arlene Dyson, whose sixteen-year-old model daughter Frederique died in 1995 of a heroin overdose. "Until people step up and admit what's really going on, there's no hope in hell that things are going to change. People who are successful in the fashion business live in denial, because if they speak up, they might hurt their own business. They're hypocrites. They know what really goes on. In fact, many of the people who deny it are the same people who are supplying the models with drugs."

Strolling backstage at a recent fashion show in New York, it appeared to me that the fashion industry was far from cleaning up its act. Empty liquor bottles were everywhere and ashtrays were filled with roach clips. I even spotted a used syringe on the floor beside the models' dressing room. When asked to explain why there were so many traces of drugs backstage, one well-known model replied, "This is normal. Most of the time it's worse. It's a tough business. It takes everything out of you. It's almost impossible to get by in this business sober. It will only change when somebody has the courage to step up and rat on the people who have turned this industry into a sleazy industry. I think everybody keeps silent because we're afraid of the people who run [it]. Some of them are quite scary."

Andrew Tyler was a model agent in the mid-nineties. He says he quit the business because he couldn't bear so many innocent, young girls being misled. Tyler says that young models are coaxed into doing hard drugs by older men and women with severely mercurial temperaments. "It gets worse and worse because the people running the business have become scarier," he contends. "At first everything seems alright. The models are lavished with new cars, lots of cash, and new clothes. Once the agents start making money they have to try to keep the models in their stable. The easiest way to control them is with drugs. When I was in this business I couldn't believe what was going on. So much of the activity was illegal and not a thing was being done about it. If the authorities ever decide to step in, a lot of people will go to jail. Maybe that's the only way the business can be saved. If it keeps going the way it has been going during the past ten years, there won't be anybody left to walk down the runway. Everybody will be dead."

CHAPTER 22

● ● ●

Catwalk Overkill

It seems that often the toughest challenge for a model is handling success. Every model I interviewed agreed that reaching the top is not as difficult as staying there. Just ask British supermodel Debbie Linden.

As 1990 approached, Debbie Linden's career was building in an ever-increasing crescendo. She seemed to be the happiest girl in the world. Linden, then a twenty-nine-year-old veteran model, had become one of Britain's most well-known faces after years of paying her dues since her debut at age seventeen. She first achieved notoriety and fame as one of the voluptuous girls on the *Benny Hill Show*. Hill considered Linden to be one of the most interesting girls he had ever worked with. "I've worked with so many beauties over the years, but Debbie is probably the most sexy and naturally beautiful of the lot," Hill told journalist Iain Clarkson just before his death. "She's not only stunning, but she also has a good head on her shoulders. She's not afraid to add her creative input and she's a natural at working in front of the camera. She's going to go places in life."

Benny Hill's foresight proved to be true. Linden became one of Britain's most popular tabloid page three pinup girls and started appearing in countless TV and magazine ads. By 1993, Linden had become one of the most recognizable British models ever. But as fame and fortune set in, her personal problems mounted in direct proportion to her triumphs. At age thirty-four in 1995, she started having difficulty keeping up with younger models who nipped at her heels for the higher paying jobs. Linden gained fifteen pounds, finding it excruciating to try to compete with models who weighed less than

100 pounds. She turned to hard drugs in an attempt to control her weight. Linden went regularly without eating. In an attempt to keep her weight down, she endured excruciating hunger pains and limited herself to only one bite of bread and a teaspoon of orange juice a day for days at a time. Her new diet included daily doses of heroin, cocaine, and alcohol. "Debbie had finally reached what she had strived so hard for and as soon as she got there her entire world fell apart," commented Evan Baker, a model friend. "It's a very sad story because she had so much talent and desire. But the modeling industry is so demanding and it wears you down and makes you depressed, regardless of how much money you're making."

Linden had hoped that her problems would somehow go away, but instead they became bigger. She heard whispers from her agent that she was getting too old to model, but she refused to quit. She often said that she would have liked to stop but she didn't know what else to do with her life. Many girls who, like Debbie, start modeling at a young age eventually face the same dilemma. They don't know what to do with their lives after their stint on the catwalk ends. And for many, it literally drives them over the edge. Linden spent the next fifteen months in a whirlwind of drugs, sex, and booze. She spent every penny she had on partying hard. It was common for her to spend thousands of dollars a week on drugs. In this relatively brief period, she consumed a mind boggling amount of drugs. Linden could have died of a drug overdose on dozens of occasions. But fate stayed on her side—until one rainy October night in 1997.

On that night, Linden and her boyfriend Russell Ainsworth, twenty-seven, had stayed up partying till the wee hours of the morning. Several of Ainsworth's friends were present at his home in Kingston, England. Champagne was quaffed and heroin was injected. Ainsworth's home looked like a scene right out of a sixties movie. It was another one of Ainsworth's typical drugfests.

This time, however, Linden went too far. Ainsworth, who had a long history of drug addiction, didn't seem to care that his gorgeous girlfriend was about to shoot up a massive dose. He seemed out of it himself. Soon after the heroin was injected into her arm, Linden fell down and her lips turned blue. Amid the screams and chaos, Ainsworth and his friends tried desperately to resuscitate Linden. One of Linden's girlfriends tugged on her arm and started to cry because Linden was not responding. It was too late. Linden would never regain consciousness. When the ambulance arrived, Linden was brain dead. Soon after, her life support systems were turned off. In one of the most publicized cases of a model's death, Ainsworth was later charged with manslaughter. He was accused of injecting the fatal dose into Linden's arm. Ainsworth insisted that he hadn't done it.

"Russell is one of the wildest men I've ever met," says a close female friend of Ainsworth. "He's dated a lot of beautiful women and he's done every expensive drug you can think of. I wouldn't put anything past him. We once got high at his house together and wound up spending the next three days experimenting with drugs naked in his bed. He's capable of anything."

Eleven months after Linden's death, Ainsworth told a London judge and jury that he was innocent. Ainsworth said that Linden had encouraged him to buy heroin and had injected it by herself. When the verdict was rendered, Ainsworth was cleared on the manslaughter charge but was sentenced to two and a half years for supplying the heroin. Judge Gerald Gordon said that Ainsworth and his friends weren't responsible because they didn't realize that they were "dabbling in death." "I only wish attempts by so many people to stop others from taking drugs had more effect," Judge Gordon said. "I hope the sentence that has been handed down will be a deterrent to others. Miss Linden's death is a strong reminder that people who are addicted to drugs live in a sad and unhappy world."

Models all over the world spoke out angrily against what they viewed as too light a sentence. "Debbie Linden is another model who became a victim of her own success," said Swedish model Karin Bromberg, who once worked at a fashion show with Linden.

In this business there have been so many tragedies and people get away with murder. Debbie Linden would not have got involved in heavy drugs if she [hadn't] been forced to. Can you name any other business that makes its workers feel washed up and useless by the time they turn thirty? Maybe Russell Ainsworth wasn't the only person who should have been charged with manslaughter. What about all those dirty men who run this business who kept encouraging Debbie to take drugs? They're the ones who should go to jail. I've seen it happen so many times. When the girls become successful they become targets of abuse. People start buying them drugs and booze and try to take full advantage of them for their own personal gain. Debbie Linden would still be alive today if the modeling business had someone who looked after the welfare of the girls. We need a policeman. Somebody who will eliminate all of the crap we put up with. Until something like that happens, sadly, there will be many more girls who wind up like Debbie.

Jack Dolman became friends with Linden when he worked at London's trendy Wag Club on Wardour Street, where Linden partied regularly. Dolman says Linden was the nicest model he ever met. He struck up a relationship with Linden and remained friends with her for years. Dolman believes that Linden was a victim of her own good fortune. He was furious at the way she was treated during the last year of her life, and blames her handlers for ruining her career. "She worked her way to the top and then everybody clung to her like leeches," Dolman says. "She was the sweetest girl you would ever want to meet. The people around her took advantage of her nice personality. If she would have been able to resist the evil forces that surrounded her, she would still be up on the catwalk making loads of money. Ever since Debbie died I have lost all respect for the modeling and entertainment industry. Nobody who worked with her tried to save her. All that they wanted to do was exploit her and make as much money off her until she went to her grave."

PART THREE

Model Agents: Princes or Pimps?

CHAPTER 23

• • •

Modeling Schools?

Three angry mothers strode toward Rob Starr's office in Queens, New York, with one thing in mind—getting a refund. After learning that Starr was a convicted pedophile—once jailed for sexually assaulting a thirteen-year-old girl—they removed their daughters from his so-called modeling school. They had filed a complaint with the police a few days earlier about Starr's attempt to recruit young models for his school through an ad in a local newspaper. But their complaints seemed futile—Starr was still in business.

Months earlier, the three women had all enrolled their young daughters in Starr's modeling school. After persuading them to pay nearly $1500 to transform their daughters into the next Cindy Crawford, Starr reneged on his promise to engage several top-name models as guest instructors. Despite his pledge to provide the girls with respectable portfolios, they had received only low-quality videotapes of themselves walking down a mock runway, a couple of black-and-white photo negatives, and a graduation certificate. Although Starr's brochure had promised leads for modeling work, the girls were given nothing of the sort, and had only attended a few introductory classes at Starr's cramped Queen's studio.

In the minds of the girls' mothers, who were concerned for their teenage daughters' well-being, Starr was nothing but a scam artist. Starr had been convicted several times in the past for taking people's money and failing to deliver on his promises. The mothers, whose gentle appearances belied their ability to act with impassioned fury, besieged Starr's office when news of his history of child molestation emerged. One of the women thumped on Starr's office door shouting obscenities. The others heckled, chanting, "Give us our money back you pervert." From within the office, the abuse was hurled back. Starr's secretary branded the women "a bunch of troublemakers." Incensed, one mother hurled a rock at Starr's window, the shattered glass triggering another round of vitriolic insults.

"We wanted to get him out to face the music," says Roxanne Koffman, recalling the incident. "I wanted to let him know that if he didn't pay us back, he'd be in for some serious trouble. I felt like killing him."

The taunting continued even as the police arrived and broke things up. Within a month, Starr closed the doors to his modeling school. He never refunded the money, and left thousands of dollars of debt in his wake. His former secretary estimated that Starr made off with at least $200,000. His whereabouts are unknown to this day.

"He knows how to beat the system better than anybody," the secretary says. "He played on people's emotions. After parents would flip out about his high registration fees, he would make them feel guilty and tell them that they owed it to their daughters to pay that much. When you walked into the office there would be pictures of famous models on the wall, like Christy Turlington and Cindy Crawford. Starr told the youngsters that they would be just like them if they joined the modeling school. He told them complete nonsense. He was only interested in their checkbooks. He didn't really have any contacts in the modeling world."

From the classified sections of newspapers to side panels on buses, the public is bombarded with modeling-agent and school ads that claim stardom is just a call away, regardless of one's looks or previous experience. Prospective models are wooed by the prospect of fame, and are led to believe that they will effortlessly become the next Claudia Schiffer. Unfortunately it seems like 99.9 percent of these supermodel-wannabes never make a dime, and usually end up being taken for thousands of dollars by unscrupulous modeling agents. Although it's one of the oldest scams in the book, for some reason there never seems to be a shortage of suckers to feed the agents' pockets.

Essentially, an agent's job is to get models booked for jobs by submitting their headshots and composite sheets to photographers, magazine editors, and casting directors. An agent negotiates the deals and collects all monies when they are due. The agent can only recommend a model for jobs, he does not participate in the final casting decision. Agents usually charge a 15 to 20 percent commission, excluding extra expenses such as phone bills, photocopying, and courier services.

Many so-called model agents make more money ripping models off than booking them. Joel Wilkenfeld, who runs Next Model Management, is not a member of this group. Founded in 1989, Next has become the third largest modeling agency in the world. Next's stable boasts such supermodels as Yasmeen Ghauri, Adriana Sklenarikova, and Irina Pantaeva. Next's success and prestige can be attributed to a well-established code of business ethics. Wilkenfeld won't settle for anything less. "We treat our models with respect and take pride in protecting their rights," Wilkenfeld says. "If you are 5 feet 4 inches and going to modeling school, you're in the business for fun. We don't believe in being paid for something you think you have or don't have. Nobody can turn you into a professional model. You either have it or don't have it."

Unlike most other agents, who are masters at spewing out false statements, Wilkenfeld doesn't mince words. After watching him interview three prospective Next models, it's clear that he doesn't tolerate any monkey business. "At Next I've always been treated in a most professional manner," says eighteen-year-old Renee Lacombe, a top model from Quebec City who made waves on the fashion runway in 2000 and has appeared in several *Vogue* ads. "They never made me pay any start-up fees, and made sure that I only got good jobs. I've heard some terrible stories about this business, but thanks to Next, I haven't seen anything bad."

Over the years, Next has expanded from managing just a handful of girls to handling more than 200 male and female models. It has offices all over the world, in cities such as New York, Paris, Miami, and Rio. Many fashion experts predict that within the next two to three years, Next will become the largest modeling agency in the world. "With all the bad publicity at Elite, parents have become wary of allowing their children to model," says entertainment journalist Esmond Choueke, who has contributed to the *New York Times*. "Next is the only agency that is 100 percent credible. Their people don't carry a hidden agenda. If I was the parent of a young daughter with modeling potential, I would only send her to Next."

A recent Canadian Broadcasting Corporation (CBC) exposé on the Barbizon Modeling School raised salient questions about deceptive advertising. Although it began as a charm school in the 1930s, Barbizon is now one of North America's biggest modeling schools and boasts offices in Toronto and Miami. The promotional videos, brochures, and personal letters suggest that anyone of any age and size can become a model. Former Barbizon teacher Patricia Boone admitted that she felt uncomfortable deceiving the public when she worked there. Boone said that Barbizon is not up front about how slim a model's chances are of finding work after going through the school's program. According to Boone, Barbizon's first concern is making lots of money. "For sure, I had concerns," she said. "It started to play on my own sense of morality."

Setting up a system of accreditation akin to those for other educational institutions would deter organizations like Barbizon from opening and conducting shopping mall expeditions to recruit innocent, young models. Many parents are infuriated about the deception and lack of accountability that seem the norm among modeling agencies and so-called modeling schools. In Ottawa Canada, for example, hundreds of model wannabes flocked to a hotel in response to a Barbizon ad in a local paper. While the winter winds raged outside, it was standing-room only in the hotel's conference center, where many waited hours to be assessed by a Barbizon representative. Ironically, not one of the girls present seemed to have the right physical criteria to become a model. There were few tall girls, many of them were overweight, and some looked like they didn't even know why they were there in the first place.

"I came because I'd like to be in magazines," said one fifteen-year-old girl who, at 5 feet 2 inches and 124 pounds, was clearly not model material. After she did her test walk down the mock runway, a Barbizon agent told her that she'd probably be accepted into their school. "They told me that I have good potential," she said. "They said with a little work I'd have a good chance to become a model."

The CBC's Barbizon exposé illustrated just how greedy modeling schools can be. Barbizon owner Dominic Camposeo was filmed telling his staff to accept anybody who showed the slightest interest. "You accept everybody," he said. "Play with them a bit and they'll want to become part of this group even more."

Attitudes like Camposeo's have plagued the modeling industry for years. While the entertainment industry and related artist associations such as ACTRA and Actors Equity support an industry-wide code of ethics called EIC, which clearly outlines how an agent should treat an artist, there is no equivalent set of standards for the fashion industry. Even if such a system did exist, most modeling agencies and

Naomi Campbell, alone.
(Courtesy Keystone
Agence De Presse)

• • •

Back to work:
Donatella Versace.
(Courtesy Keystone
Agence De Presse)

• • •

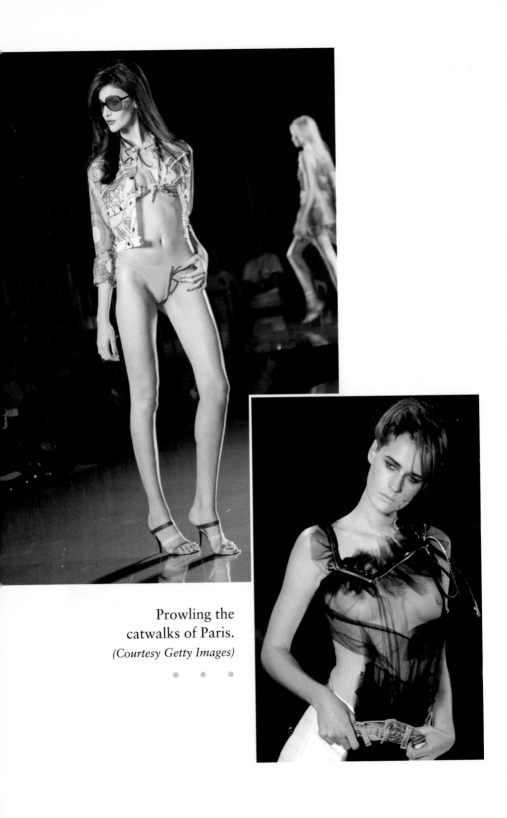

Prowling the
catwalks of Paris.
(Courtesy Getty Images)

Naomi Campbell strolling with supermodel friend Karen Mulder.
(Courtesy Keystone Agence De Presse)

Christy Turlington at the much criticized fashion café.
(Courtesy Keystone Agence De Presse)

•   •   •

Kate Moss demonstrates her special affection for the paparazzi.
(Courtesy Keystone Agence De Presse)

•   •   •

Laetitia Casta
is one of today's
biggest models.
*(Courtesy Keystone
Agence De Presse)*

• • •

Bursting on the scene:
Amber Valetta in
the late nineties.
*(Courtesy Keystone
Agence De Presse)*

• • •

Tyra Banks. *(Courtesy of Getty Images News Services)*

Gisele Bundchen. *(Courtesy of Getty Images News Services)*

Ian Halperin undercover as a
model for Fubu sportswear.
(Courtesy of Hollywood
Photo Agency)

schools would refuse to adhere to it. "Very few agents would agree to a code of ethics," remarks entertainment journalist Martin Smith, who has written for the *London Evening Standard* and *Time Out* magazine. "It would cramp their style. They want to be able to go out every night and have fun with the beautiful models."

A former Barbizon model described how she'd spent thousands of dollars on her training and got absolutely nothing in return. After finishing a modeling program in Toronto, the Barbizon staff convinced her to go to an International Modeling and Talent Association (IMTA) convention, a popular gathering for graduates from schools like Barbizon. At the convention, IMTA showcases models to talent scouts from all over the world. Just as with the modeling schools, there's a huge fee to participate in the IMTA convention. "It's nothing but one big money-grab after another," said the former model during the CBC exposé. "After I went through the whole thing and spent thousands of dollars, I only got one audition and no job."

The Barbizon exposé was produced by award-winning CBC documentary producer Gerry Wagschal. Wagschal said he uncovered many serious credibility problems with modeling schools in general. "The conventions can be very expensive," he said. "You have to get photos, your hair done, everything else to make your appearance look good. I met a guy who is still paying off a $20,000 debt from this. All that you really need is a Polaroid and a stamp. You send it off and find out if any agencies are interested in you. Frankly, you don't need to join a modeling school to be successful. Either you have it or you don't."

What modeling schools conveniently neglect to tell youngsters is that only a handful of the world's top models ever went through such training. Most were discovered by scouts or agents attracted by a "look" that they deemed worthy of the covers of *Vogue* and *Elle*. The likes of Kate Moss, Gisele Bundchen, Christy Turlington, Claudia Schiffer, and Naomi Campbell never had to pay money to learn their craft. In fact, it's difficult to find a supermodel who attended a modeling school before hitting the big time.

Empty promises seem to be the biggest part of the ruse. "I'm 5 foot 4 inches and Jewish," explained Wagschal. "There's nothing wrong with me going to basketball school, as long as they tell me the reality of my chances. The [modeling] schools aren't truthful about the girls' opportunities. They mislead them. Parents shouldn't play along with the fantasy. Eventually, these kids will get their hearts broken and then Mom and Dad will have to mop up the mess. These schools rarely deal with the real world of modeling at all."

The late supermodel Gia Carangi, a Philadelphia native, often criticized modeling schools for preying on the vulnerability of children and glorifying models as cultural icons.

"There's no way a modeling school can help you become a model," Carangi once told New York fashion journalist Bev Sayles. "I would never spend a penny on a modeling school. Most of them are scams. You can't teach someone how to become a model. That's ridiculous. The only way to learn is by firsthand experience. And the only way to get that experience is by having an interesting look that appeals to legitimate agents who have the right connections to make things happen for you. In all my years of modeling, I've never met a top model who came through a modeling school. If the modeling schools are as good as they advertise, why aren't their girls in the big magazines or on the runway at the big shows? To me, it's all a scam to get money out of innocent, young girls."

Carangi advised neophyte models to avoid paying out of pocket. "Start from scratch and fill your portfolio with tear sheets," she said. "Your first job will lead to your second, which will lead to your third. There's no reason to spend your money. Do you think Marilyn Monroe or Greta Garbo ever paid a modeling or acting school? In fact, an agent friend of mine once told me that the real players in the fashion and entertainment business purposely avoid recruiting talent from these schools because they recognize them for being scams."

Laurie Gordon was the undercover camera operator for the CBC exposé of Barbizon. She applied for a job at Barbizon as a sales representative, and then, for the next ten weeks, filmed Camposeo and the Barbizon staff in action. Gordon used a wide-angle lens inserted into a cell phone attached to her purse. She got more than 400 hours of shocking footage, including a clip of a Barbizon sales rep admitting that deceit was part of the game. "You have to lie sometimes," the sales rep said. "If the model or her mother wants to give me a Visa card, let her give me a Visa card. You can't refuse a Visa card."

Gordon, also the lead singer for a Montreal pop group called Chiwawa, wrote an exclusive letter about her Barbizon experience for this book:

> First of all, it is my impression that Barbizon is purposefully misleading people and misrepresenting itself. They also had a more "legit"

modeling school, so they must have known the way things really work in the modeling business. In the CBC piece "Skin Deep," an official from New York's Next modeling agency said that all they really needed was a Polaroid of the "wannabe" au naturel, without makeup or special photography. This is such common knowledge that there is no way that Barbizon or any other school/agency could not know this.

I was once a fifteen-year-old wannabe model who spent money on pro shots and whatnot, but I never attended any modeling school. I got some work as a movie extra, but as far as modeling was concerned, I never got further than a couple of catalogues and department store ads. I never had to pay for "training." Being just under 5 feet 7 inches, there is no way I could have made it in the high fashion modeling world, with or without "it." Yet, my hopes and aspirations of making it overshadowed the deeper knowledge that I didn't have "it." I thought I was going to be the "exception." Every teenager thinks they've got "it," or that they're special and will live forever. Modeling schools profit by playing on the teenage ego.

In my opinion, modeling schools are not essential to succeed at modeling. If ever some success story comes out of one, it's really only a stroke of luck for that school. Barbizon was lucky that someone like Christina Thes (now a well-known model) set foot in their school before she was recruited by a legit agency. Barbizon needed her more than she needed them, and they used her as a mascot in order to lure more students to the school.

I believe that the salespeople or student advisors at Barbizon were well aware of the facts, although some of them did seemed to believe the lies they were telling potential students. Hey, some of these so called "student advisors" have been at Barbizon for twelve years!

CHAPTER 24

●　　●　　●

Wakeup Call

What could be more flattering? You're in the local mall looking for a bargain on Kotex and out of the blue, a modeling scout approaches you and tells you that you have "it," the right look for a fashion model. Blind to your bloat and the big zit about to erupt on your nose, the agent gives you a fancy business card and begs you to call for an appointment. Visions of fame, glamour, and wealth obliterate the cramps, and show you a way to escape from your boring teenage life.

Although it's true that some successful models have literally been plucked off the street, the great majority of wannabe models have to knock on a lot of agency doors before they finally get any work. If and when you actually get that follow-up appointment, you'll end up in an office full of other model and actor hopefuls waiting for a chance to hear an aggressive sales pitch for modeling classes or "photo shoots" that can cost as much as several thousand dollars. You'll be told that you need a costly portfolio or training program to get a break, and you'll be promised fame and fortune. The fashion business is all about glamour and image, and those involved, no doubt, are masters at the art of deception. They are talent image-sellers who profit by creating the illusion, invoking your desire, in-flating your ego, and taking your money.

A person's appearance usually makes no difference to bogus model and talent agents, while legitimate agents turn many hopefuls away. Legitimate agents take a percentage of the work they get for a model; corrupt agents demand cash up front for registration fees, headshots, and modeling classes. These fees can range in the thou-sands of dollars. The only thing that these agents are after is money—and they'll say whatever is necessary to get it. Usually, what they say is the furthest thing from what they mean, and further still from reality. A good way to find out if a model agency is legit is by checking with the Better Business Bureau or the Models Guild. They have records of any complaints that have been filed against the agency.

Several independent organizations, including the New York Department of Consumer Affairs, have conducted probing, well-balanced, and lively analyses of the modeling schools and agencies at the heart of this controversy. Akin to the findings of the Canadian Broadcasting exposé, these reports uncovered that modeling schools share a consistent and unremitting routine when it comes to doing business: They rarely vacillate when it comes to making money—their method of conducting business is invariable. Finding out why they charge such exorbitant registration fees is difficult. They usually generalize, demanding a fixed sum that they claim is for classes, photos, and portfolios.

The New York Department of Consumer Affairs posted a website to warn the public about modeling schools that are under the unfettered control of sleazy entrepreneurs. The department warns that the dream is so pervasive and the industry so alluring that modeling schools are undaunted by public scrutiny or complaint.

In its report, Consumer Affairs outlined the following tactics used by unscrupulous modeling agencies to snare new talent:

- Making inflated promises of securing jobs
- Pressuring prospective clients to make and buy expensive sets of composite cards and/or portfolios made by a photographer on the premises or secretly affiliated with the agency
- Failing to disclose the full costs of photos and other services beforehand
- Pressuring clients to pay with a credit card
- Not disclosing the financial connection between the agents and the photographers
- Mailing out "You have been selected" letters falsely claiming special treatment
- Making false claims about the success of the agency's "Print Books," publications that contain listings and photos of models and actors
- Saying that the "real people" look is the "in" thing now and that "you have that look"

Consumer Affairs urges people to be wary of any modeling agent or school that demands fees up front for photo shoots or any other type of service. "The best defense against scam artists who prey on models and actors is an educated consumer who keeps his or her feet on the ground while they reach for the stars."

Another website that offers modeling tips and scam advice is www.supermodelguide.com. This site has become a popular information mecca for the parents of young models. Several fashion veterans offer advice here, including Claudia Schiffer and photographer Stephen Aubuchon. The website urges up-and-coming models to avoid taking training courses, since reputable agencies will instruct models for free. "If you have extra money to spend and want to learn about makeup and walking, etc., then go ahead and sign up for modeling classes" the site recommends. "Otherwise, makeup counters like Lancôme, MAC, and Estee Lauder will often give free makeup lessons."

Rigorously documenting the bad experiences many models have endured, the site www.modelingadvice.com calls for both caution and courage on the part of young models. The site makes it clear that few have become models without being harassed. To avoid harassment, Modelingadvice.com suggests that parents should always accompany a young model on go-sees. In addition, schools, agencies, searches, conventions, and competitions that charge up-front signing fees should be avoided. The website issues a stern warning to wannabe models: "These enterprises pray upon an individual's desire to be a star and their lack of knowledge about how the modeling industry really works. And this leech industry seems to be getting bigger everyday."

Modelingadvice.com presents a frustrating example of how corrupt some pseudo-agencies can be. A Los Angeles operation ran ads in small town newspapers in Oregon to recruit models for TV commercials. People were urged to send in some personal information and snapshots. All the respondents were signed up to do test shoots before the actual TV commercial, with the agency promising to pay for everything except the makeup artist. The agency sent contracts, airline vouchers, and official-looking contracts to each model. The catch was that the models had to pay a $500 initiation fee in advance to cover makeup costs. The innocent, small town girls sent their money. Once the checks were cashed, the scam artist disappeared. The contracts, airline tickets, and guarantees of TV commercial work turned out to be part of a big hoax.

"This sort of thing happens time and again," says respected New York entertainment consultant Mark Fleming. "I've seen it happen not only in the modeling business, but also in acting and music. My advice to any artist is never to pay sign up fees. There's no need for it. Only take an agent seriously if he has a proven track record. It's important to check out his history and call some of his clients to ask serious questions. If everything checks out, then it might be worth considering."

Fleming responds coolly to the idea of regulating the industry. "In any entertainment industry, you'll always have scam artists," he says. "The only way to get rid of them is by boycotting them. It's easy to find out who the bad apples are. All that is required is a bit of research. That's the problem. The scam artists are pros and know how to put stars in a person's eyes. They take their money so easily. The key is to never give money at the first meeting. Go home and do your homework on the person you're dealing with first."

Fleming is a realist. He knows that his recommendations will not be universally endorsed. Some will argue that parents should be more careful and that agents and schools are entitled to make a buck if people are willing to pay. Given the fact that so few girls who sign up for courses actually get work, Fleming says it is difficult to understand why the corruption endures. "If the Better Business Bureau or the federal government would start a more aggressive national campaign to educate people about modeling scams, [they] would probably be eradicated," he asserts. "There's no need for a set of rules. All that we need is to raise awareness. Once the models and their parents are properly informed, it will be very difficult for these pseudo-agents to take [the models'] hard-earned money."

The Federal Trade Commission (FTC) is active in the fight against modeling scams and abuse. In 1999, the commission published a brochure detailing how to spot illegitimate agencies. The FTC report warned the public to steer clear of agencies or schools that attach fees to their services. The report says you should hightail it when "what you thought was a job interview with a talent agency turns into a high-pressure sales pitch for modeling or acting classes, or for 'screen tests' or 'photos shoots' that can range in price from several hundred to several thousand dollars. Often, these scouts are after one thing—your money—and will say just about anything to get it."

The FTC also issued a stern warning to parents of infants and toddlers. During the past decade, many agencies have targeted this age group due to the growing presence of small children in TV and magazine ads. Yet, the reality of finding legitimate work is the same as it is in the adult modeling realm. Jobs are few and far between. "Bogus talent scouts will gladly set up a professional photo shoot to allegedly help you get modeling and acting jobs for your tyke," the FTC reported. "Of course, they don't tell you that the market for infant models and actors is very small."

Despite the many websites now ringing out warnings against a plethora of modeling scams, many people are still lured into the trap. Increasing cooperation between so-called modeling schools and conventions like the IMTA lend an aura of legitimacy that makes it even easier to convince young hopefuls that the professional network they'll need will be available. IMTA is the biggest association of modeling and talent schools and training centers in the world. Its modeling school members are located in the United States, Canada, Scandinavia, the Carribean, and Latin America. Their convention is held twice a year, once in Los Angeles and once in New York. According to former model agent Lloyd Coutts, attending an IMTA convention does not guarantee access to the pages of *Vogue*. "The concept of IMTA or any other event that showcases new faces is good," Coutts says. "But the problem is that you usually still have to pay to participate. And there's no guarantee. It can add up to a lot of money."

Citing facts, figures, and examples of con games that he's gathered from his experience as an agent, Coutts argues that the survival of modeling schools will eventually be jeopardized. Coutts has yet to come across anything resembling an honest and effective modeling school. He claims that collusion between the schools constitutes either a plot to fool the public, or a set of backward business arrangements. "They're all in this together. Face it, some of these outfits have received such bad publicity that it is amazing they still exist." Coutts believes these charlatans work together because it is the only logical way for them to keep the scam going. The grifters avoid cannibalizing their business with an unwritten rule that prevents them from stepping on each other's toes.

Although conning agents and fraudulent agencies and schools come from a wide variety of backgrounds, they share similar methodologies, goals, and values. Exaggeration to the point of outright deception as a means of profit is a central theme. Lloyd Coutts claims that during his twelve years as a talent agent, he never met a colleague who didn't have a professional interest in deception. As part of the evidence he's gathered against these dissemblers, Coutts cites the story of a New York agent who'd boasted about making millions of dollars without ever having a client hit it big. "My friend was only concerned with his monthly figures," Coutts reveals. "He had no interest in helping his talent get work. Over the years I've met many people like that. Remember, it's a business and the first thing that everyone's concerned with is making money." It seems that as long as enough hopefuls are willing to pay through the nose for the dream, agents need not actually promote them in order to make a profit. In fact, the only real guarantee is that the agent, not the model, will be successful.

In 1999, New York Department of Consumer Affairs Commissioner Jules Polonetsky charged three New York City model agencies with making false promises about potential jobs. Polonetsky discovered that the agencies had been charging prospective models exorbitant fees to purchase portfolios, and this was in addition to high commissions paid by those for whom they found work. The Yes Modeling agency, located on Lexington Avenue in Manhattan, faced fines of more than $50,000. Plus Models and Next Stop Ideals were both charged with operating without a proper license.

Polonetsky explained his decision, saying, "Home to the world's most famous modeling agencies, New York City is the place to be for models hoping to get their big break. But the modeling agencies we've investigated had promised to make stars out of clients, and failed to deliver even fifteen minutes of fame. After seeing the ads and hearing the sales pitches, prospective models were convinced that these agencies could make them stars. Yet customers never received the promised jobs, and after Yes Models took hundreds of dollars for photographs, they would refuse to even take [the customers'] calls. The few who actually got work were charged excessive fees."

After receiving fourteen complaints from the victims of Yes Models, Jules Polonetsky ordered an undercover investigation of the agency. A Department of Consumer Affairs inspector went undercover, posing as a wannabe model. She called the agency in response to a Yes Models newspaper ad promising an earning potential of "$1500 a day, with no experience." After an agency representative told the undercover inspector that she could earn $200 a day as a model shortly after she signed up, Yes demanded that she pay their company photographer $490 for photographs and composite cards.

A couple of weeks later, the inspector made her final payment for the portfolio package. A Yes agent told her that more than 500 of her photos were being sent to bookers. Two months later, Yes Models had not secured her a single interview. Yes then refused to refund the inspector's money and stopped taking her phone calls. The whole thing smelled fishy.

Aspiring model Barbara Kulpa of Queens responded to a Yes Models newspaper ad. She was told that she had a good chance of getting work at several upcoming fashion shows. Yes then asked Kulpa to pay nearly $700 for a portfolio of photographs. After paying for the photos, Kulpa never heard from them again. When she went to Yes's office to pick up her portfolio, they refused to let her in.

"Despite their assurances, Yes Models meant no jobs for prospective models," Commissioner Polonetsky said. "After being directed to a company photographer, clients paid $195 to Yes for the photos, but only received contact sheets. Clients were then forced to pay an additional $295 to have their composites sent out to booking agents, but Yes Models refused to tell modeling hopefuls where exactly these photos were sent. Yes Models is nothing more than a photography service. Aspiring models should understand that if a legitimate agent believes a model shows promise, they would likely invest money in him or her—not charge hundreds of dollars for photos."

Ford Models Chief Operating Officer Jack Maiden collaborated with Commissioner Polonetsky to compile tips to help prevent aspiring models from being conned. Like other major reputable agencies, Ford Models does not charge extra fees. Ford's founders, Eileen and Jerry Ford, have taken a strong and very public stance against agencies like Yes Models.

"There's a lot of abuse in this industry by people trying to make a quick buck," Eileen Ford once told fashion editor Liz Tilberis. "Those people unfortunately give everyone else a bad name. I'm all for taking whatever action is necessary to make this industry safer. It upsets me so much every time I hear about a model getting taken in."

Even the much-maligned John Casablancas of Elite criticizes agencies for profiting from model sign-up fees. Casablancas maintains that Elite only signs the models that meet certain qualifications, such as height, weight, and a unique look. He cautions models to be wary of agencies that make inflated promises. Up-front fees for photo shoots or other services are not appropriate. Legitimate agencies will invest money in models who show potential. "We never go after a model knowing that they don't have what it takes to be successful," Casablancas says. "I don't know how an agent can look a girl in the eye and convince her that she can be a model when she isn't the right height or is overweight."

Ottawa, Canada, modeling agent Ben Barry is similarly disturbed by the growth and success of modeling agencies and schools like Yes and Barbizon. As Barry points out, the proliferation of modeling schools that charge sign-up fees presents parents with a classic dilemma. How far should parents go in allowing their children to get involved in modeling? Barry urges parents to encourage their kids to stay in school and to be wary of modeling at an early age.

"Some of the parents get too caught up in it themselves," Barry says. "The key is to do research on the modeling schools. I don't think anybody should have to pay fees to become a model. The parents should try to remain more level-headed than their kids. It's easy to get taken in. But there are some realities about this business. If you're not the proper height and don't have a certain look, then there's no real chance of you finding modeling work. Unfortunately, the modeling schools often conveniently forget to point this out."

Barry hopes his views will not be seen as another piece of unsolicited advice on the fashion world. To help curb the rampant fraud, he has contacted several people in the Canadian government to further explore the possibility of regulating the modeling industry. "It's got to be done, and I won't rest until the public becomes more aware about some of the dangers of the industry," Barry says. "I've met far too many girls who have been burned. This has got to stop. Not everybody does this, but it still gives the whole industry a bad name."

Barry offers a few tips to help detect con artists. He advises model hopefuls to steer clear of agencies that require use of a specific photographer. Instead, he encourages models to shop around, comparing the fees, credentials, and work quality of several photographers. He says models should walk away from any agency that requires a down payment for their services, and should be wary of any modeling school that has a special relationship with an agency—the two could be splitting fees, and one or the other may not be suited to a particular model's needs. "If the modeling school brings in any of these elements, it would probably be wise to look for another company," Barry says. "It's essential to be leery of any company that brings up money. In most cases, they're just trying to make a quick buck."

Barry asks that models contact their local consumer protection agency or Better Business Bureau if they've been the victim of a scam or an attempted scam. "The only way to stop this is to make some noise," he says. "Too many of the scam artists have gotten away with murder in the past. It's important to let the authorities know if you've been scammed so that they can take the appropriate action to make sure it doesn't happen again."

CHAPTER 25

* * *

MacIntyre Undercover

Shortly after I began my undercover investigation, a major scandal erupted in the modeling industry. British Broadcasting Corporation (BBC) documentary filmmaker Donald MacIntyre had captured several Elite Model Agency executives making shocking sexist and racist remarks on film. Simultaneously outraged and intrigued, the modeling world lapped up MacIntyre's exposé. Sleazy agents feared that the BBC piece was only the tip of the iceberg, and that more executions were on the way. For every Elite executive stupid enough to be filmed making disgusting comments and gestures, there are thousands of faceless agents just as unscrupulous. "The BBC documentary scared everyone," said a Karins agent. "Elite was singled out, but everyone in the industry knew that there were far worse things going on. I know several people who started saying their prayers because they feared they would be the next to be exposed."

Elite sued the BBC, claiming MacIntyre used his footage selectively to defame them. In June 2001, Elite and the BBC announced that they had settled the case out of court. As part of the settlement, the BBC issued a public apology. Several Elite executives boasted that they had been vindicated and the BBC was wrong in alleging sex and drug abuse. No damages were paid to Elite but the BBC had to pay legal costs, estimated at more than two million dollars. Elite had demanded 1.7 million pounds (more than 2.5 million dollars) in compensation from BBC. In a joint statement, the BBC said that "Elite, as an organization, warns and seeks to protect its young teenage models, whether from sexual exploitation or other potential dangers to them (such as from illegal drugs) and that this was not reflected in the program." The BBC also admitted that MacIntyre's report failed to reveal sexual abuse by Elite executives of its models or Elite Model Look contestants. The BBC termed MacIntyre's investigation "inappropriate." As a result of the MacIntyre expose, Elite chairman John Casablancas announced his retirement a couple of months later, while two key executives at Elite were suspended. Both are now back at work. Suddenly, the men who had made an art form of profiting from an immoral abuse of power were being taken to task.

The most explosive statements in the MacIntyre story came from Elite Europe President Gerald Marie, and Elite Model Look Contest President Xavier Moreau. Marie, the Svengali ex-husband of supermodel Linda Evangelista, was caught on a hidden camera asking for sex from an undercover reporter posing as a fifteen-year-old model. Marie offered the woman 300 British pounds.

Shortly after the BBC aired the documentary in 1999, Marie almost committed suicide, standing on his balcony and threatening to jump. He couldn't bear the disgrace of the scandal. He received several death threats and was forced to move from his home. Marie's seventeen-year-old daughter was told that her father was a pimp, and even his parents were subjected to threats and abuse. Marie accused MacIntyre of entrapment and libel. He claimed that he had been provoked by MacIntyre into making the remarks on the hidden camera and that the footage had been carefully edited to make him look bad. He challenged MacIntyre to produce footage of him touching or even talking to a model. "I was drunk and he [MacIntyre] took advantage of it to make me look bad," Marie claimed. "I said things that I didn't mean."

Nonetheless, Marie admitted that he should have watched what he said. "I should not have said those things, even to a friend, even drunk," Marie told *Talk Magazine*. Marie blamed the models' parents for not keeping a closer eye on her. "All the underage girls [in the film] are English. All the drug girls are English. It's an Anglo-Saxon thing. . . . Call me an asshole, but those parents should look after their kids."

Marie's lawyers demanded that MacIntyre turn over his original footage so they could point out where it had been edited to make their client look bad. The BBC refused to release it. Marie managed to convince many that he had been set up. But he was under fire again a year later when he married nineteen-year-old Russian model Irina Bondarenko. "He's disgusting," said a former Elite model.

"First he tries to deny the BBC documentary, and now look what he does. He goes ahead and marries a model more than thirty years his junior. Ever since I met him more than ten years ago, he's always been up to the same stupid tricks. I don't think he'll ever grow up."

Marie's remarks and actions struck panic in the hearts of parents of teenage models all over the world. Many parents pulled their daughters out of model agencies, hoping to prevent them from victimization. "I was just about to let my daughter go to an Elite audition in New York," said mother Sheila Mason, whose twelve-year-old daughter Jade had been approached by several model scouts. "But after seeing the MacIntryre report, I decided not to let her go anywhere near those creeps. I'm surprised some of them weren't put in jail. It's wrong for these men to be allowed to carry on. It's dangerous."

On film, Xavier Moreau had bragged to MacIntyre about how he was going to have sex with finalists in the Elite Model Look contest, where the average age of contestants is fifteen. He also made several racist remarks, complaining about models of African descent. "These attitudes are simply unacceptable in any society," said international human-rights activist and Oxford scholar Charles Small. "I can't believe that men like this are allowed to control such a big industry. It's scary."

Carolyn Park, a twenty-one-year-old model who was interviewed for the exposé, told MacIntyre she had become addicted to drugs when she was sixteen. Park said she had needed drugs to cope with the daily grind of the modeling industry. She revealed that she had been given a regular supply of cocaine by a booker at Marilyn Models, her Paris agency. "With what I do, and how much I travel, and how unstable it is, there is no way I could come off drugs," Park said.

In the wake of the BBC documentary, Casablancas was forced to suspend four Elite staff members. But the world was far from convinced that the fashion industry was on the road to change. "Casablancas was just trying to cover his own ass," says model scout Johnny Oz. "He should have resigned the second all this came out. Anybody who knows anything about Casablancas knows that he's no saint himself. For Chrissake, Casablancas has dated so many young models himself over the years, it's amazing that he has been able to cover it all up for so long. He and his agency should have been exposed years ago."

Notorious Karin Models boss Jean-Luc Brunel didn't seem concerned by the bad publicity wrought by the "MacIntyre Undercover" story. Only a month after it aired, Brunel joined his colleagues in Rio for New Year's eve with his new sixteen-year-old girlfriend in tow. In Rio, Brunel boasted to Marie and Casablancas, both on their best behavior in light of the BBC scandal, about how he had flown in the baby-faced brunette from Moscow. After all his friends got mad at him, Brunel finally sent his girlfriend back home. One agency booker who was in Rio at the time reports that Brunel literally started a panic. "His timing was completely off," the booker says. "Casablancas was still trying to do damage control. The last thing he needed was Brunel to stir things up. If the press had gotten wind of it, the shit would have really hit the fan."

MacIntyre's work evoked a huge outcry for reform from people within the fashion industry. Former sixties fashion icon Twiggy called for a ban on the use of models under the age of sixteen. She demanded more protection for models from an industry she described as "much seedier" than it had been when she modeled. Twiggy said she would have killed the Elite executives if her daughter had been the subject of such abuse. "If I was the parent of one of those girls, I would have been on the plane and those guys would have been dead," she told British fashion journalist Nicole Martin. "I absolutely support a ban on young girls being professional models. No question. It's appalling that these awful people can do whatever they want to and have such control over them."

Twiggy, now in her early fifties, claimed that since she and Jean Shrimpton changed the face of the fashion industry with their miniskirts in the 1960s, sexual abuse of women has become an integral part of the business. "Anything that's worth the billions that the fashion industry is worth has to be corrupt," Twiggy told Nicole Martin. "Sadly, money breeds corruption."

Conversely, New York fashion marketing guru Dale Cox defends his industry. He says the Elite scandal merely represents an uncouth hidden element present in every society. Cox, who over the years has worked for many top agencies throughout the world, refuses to acknowledge that Elite was caught in the eye of the storm. "Nonsense, complete nonsense," Cox asserts. "The BBC reporter was seeking something to feed his fantasy and the agents at Elite graciously played along. If the agents were half as bad as the BBC made them out to be, then why would any parent in their right mind let their daughter model for Elite? I know many models at Elite and most of them are happy. Sure there's the odd incident, but that can happen in any work environment. It's not fair to single out one company."

Cox does agree, however, that the fashion industry should introduce its own code of ethics and blacklist agents who ignore the rules. Regardless, he acknowledges that commercial pressures make it hard to apply such an ideal to established agencies. "Many of these people are legit and they feel the bad publicity they've received is overstated because of a few bad apples," Cox says. "But the established agents should make it their duty to lead the way and set a good example. I do hope that, at least, they'll make it very clear that they don't knowingly and willingly condone abusive behavior."

After the BBC documentary aired, Donald MacIntyre feared for his life. That same year, he posed as a wealthy, established criminal in order to infiltrate a gang of English football hooligans known as the Chelsea Headhunters. He made a lot of enemies. After the model piece, MacIntyre received death threats and had to go into hiding. Speaking of MacIntyre's ordeal, model scout Johnny Oz remarks, "There are lots of powerful, criminal types involved in the modeling industry. There was an unofficial bounty out on MacIntyre's life. He took on some very powerful people. As a result, MacIntyre became the new Salman Rushdie of the U.K."

CHAPTER 26

• • •

Straight, No Chaser

Back in December 1988, CBS *60 Minutes* aired a shocking investigative report about the many models who had been drugged, raped, and sexually harassed by the world's top agency owners. Investigative reporter Craig Pyes portrayed the modeling industry as infested with agents who were notorious hustlers and playboys. Pyes concentrated on the biggest agencies.

Pyes's report revealed that both Euro-Planning's Claude Haddad and Paris-based agent Jean-Luc Brunel had been accused of sexual harassment by many models. Haddad's reputation for being nasty to his female models was already legendary. It's safe to say that, to this day, most models think Haddad is a total sleazeball. Haddad has made truckloads of money scheming and plotting against rival agents. Despite his infamous immorality, he has been more conspicuously successful than almost all others in this cutthroat industry.

In the early eighties, Haddad formed a joint venture with his archrival, Elite's John Casablancas. Haddad, like most other agents at the time, was determined to topple Casablancas from his pedestal. "Haddad was obsessed with Casablancas because Casablancas was the hottest young agent to rise to power and prominence," explained journalist Martin Smith. "Haddad knew that if he teamed up with Casablancas, it would be a win-win situation. Casablancas and Elite now yielded more power than any other agency in the world."

At one time Haddad had been one of the top agents in Europe, and this appealed to Casablancas, who had just set up Elite offices in New York. After Eileen Ford dissolved relations with Haddad, Casablancas seized the opportunity to cash in on Haddad's wealth of connections. Ford had been displeased by the way Haddad presented himself as a larger-than-life figure, mercilessly trying to seduce as many models as possible.

Casablancas quickly realized why Ford had severed ties with Haddad. After a brief association, Casablancas stopped working with Haddad in 1984. Casablancas was worried that Haddad's sleazy tactics would tarnish his own reputation. He disagreed with how Haddad tricked models into having sex with him.

According to author Michael Gross, Casablancas told a journalist that Haddad was guilty of sexual misconduct. "Claude Haddad has a devious way of trying to get into girls' pants," Casablancas said. "It's pathetic. I ended my relationship with him after I sent him a girl, and he just got into bed with her once he had her in his apartment. He never even made a pass at her, never tried to sweet-talk her or hold her hand. It was embarrassing for me as a man. Certain moments he doesn't think with his head—he thinks with his cock."

A former model who worked for Haddad in the mid-eighties accuses him of "gross sexual conduct." She charges that Haddad once threatened to have her blacklisted if she didn't agree to have anal sex with him. "He's the scum of the earth," the model says. "If you played his game, he was nice to you. But if you didn't do drugs, drink, and suck his cock, he became nasty. I was naive when I met him. I fell for his false charm. I had sex with him several times before I realized that he had at least another half dozen lovers. One night he wanted to give it to me from behind and I refused. We had already had sex several times that night and I was very tired and sore. When I refused, he threatened me and told me that if I didn't do what he wanted, he would make sure that my modeling career was over. So I had to do it."

Back when he worked with the Fords, Haddad met model Suzy Amis, a former winner of the popular Face of the Eighties contest. Haddad seemed to fall head over heals for Amis, showering her with gifts and promising that he would steer her career to the big time. Amis, then seventeen, fell for it. She became lovers with Haddad for two years before going back to New York in 1982. According to an agent who once represented Amis, Haddad left many unhealed scars. "Suzy was such a young, innocent girl before she met Haddad," the agent said. "He took advantage of her naïveté for his own personal and sexual gain. Those two years were very hard on Suzy. She had no idea what type of monster Haddad really was."

During a one-on-one interview, CBS *60 Minutes* journalist Diane

Sawyer raked Haddad over the coals. Sawyer asked Haddad about the accusations against him. Amazingly, Haddad acted as if he had done nothing wrong. At times, he even seemed proud of his sexual conquests. He bragged to Sawyer about how he was able to attract young, beautiful girls. When Sawyer asked him how he felt waking up each morning in an apartment full of models, Haddad gave a cocky grin. He called his models "flowers." "Just smell them," he said. "That's it, just smell the perfume." Sawyer, seemingly disgusted with Haddad, asked him if he had tried to make some of the flowers bloom. "When people say something, it's always a little truth," he replied. "I hugged them . . . I tried to flirt with them."

Haddad's answers angered both his colleagues and fashion fans. The heads of major modeling agencies, including John Casablancas, condemned him. Haddad had alienated his few remaining allies.

"I knew he was bad, but not that bad," said Quebec fashion journalist Eve Beaupre. "The CBS interview sunk him for good. Nobody would take him seriously again. Parents of young models now knew how bad he really was, and they wouldn't let their daughters go anywhere near him."

Diane Sawyer asked Hadded if he had ever resorted to rape or sexual blackmail. Haddad's response was evasive. He said he couldn't recall, but added, "it's possible" to his response. Everyone could read between the lines. Sawyer had finally nailed one of fashion's all-time sleazeballs.

Several years later, Haddad told bestselling author Michael Gross that he was still angry about the *60 Minutes* report. He called the report "the revenge of mediocre girls" who had never become top models. "I work with beautiful girls. Okay, I try to fuck them," Haddad told Gross. "It's not a crime. In France, you can fuck all the girls you want to." Haddad told Gross that he resented the way Diane Sawyer had handled the interview. "This girl who interviewed me, could she swear that she never fucked people to succeed? I hate American people. I want to kick the American girls out of the business because they are prostitutes, sex cash machines, and whores. You are the dirtiest people I've met in my life. I'm not bitter. It's a fact. The girls who fucked me, they fucked me maybe expecting something would happen. Maybe they love me. You never hear a big model complaining of being in bed with me."

The most powerful model agents at the time—Claude Haddad, John Casablancas, Gerald Marie, and Jean-Luc Brunel—were more alike than any of them cared to admit. All four were shrewd, ruth-

less, and flamboyant. All were more preoccupied with the accumula-
tion of power, money, and beautiful women than anything else. And
all four maintained a love-hate relationship with each other.

"At times they seemed like they were each other's best buddy,"
says journalist Martin Smith. "But they all did things behind each
other's backs. I think one of the big reasons they all got into the business was to have power over beautiful, young women. For a long
time they never talked publicly about one another because they knew
that they were guilty of the same practices the other one was doing.
All four agents were known to be playboys, and you would often see
them show up seven nights a week at clubs in New York and Paris
with seven different women. I once saw one of them making out with
one woman in a Paris club at around 11 P.M., another woman at
midnight, and yet another woman at around 2:30 [A.M.]. That's how
these guys operate. They need to fuck as many women as possible in
order to feed their big egos."

Jean-Luc Brunel has long been regarded as one of the most notorious of French playboys. Brunel has a reputation of perversity that
is consistent with his role as an agent and guardian to young models.
He is the dean of the model-dating beat. The Paris-based agent dated
hundreds of beautiful models and was once married to stunning
Swedish model Helen Hogberg. Hogberg divorced Brunel in 1979,
accusing him of infidelity and excessive drug abuse. Needless to say,
Hogberg didn't have any trouble getting her divorce. Brunel admitted that he hadn't been an exemplary husband, and sustained ir-
reparable damage to his reputation as a result. Brunel's prospects
didn't look good.

Depressed and broke, Brunel got a job as a booker with Karin
Mossberg's agency in Paris. Mossberg, a straightforward and plain-
spoken woman, knew Brunel through his ex-wife. She hired him to
compete with the other top agencies that had hired notorious business sharks and agents like Claude Haddad. Mossberg appreciated
Brunel's arrogance and recklessly aggressive demeanor, and was convinced that Brunel could propel Karins success.

Within two years, Brunel turned Karins upside down and became
its principal owner. Despite his business success, he was heavily criticized for improper moral practices. There was no disputing that he
was highly competent as an agent, but it seemed that most people
who worked with him hated his guts. He became known for running
afoul of the rules. At Karins, many models claimed that Brunel had
sexually exploited them. One former Karins model accused Brunel of

encouraging her to sleep with some of the most powerful people in the modeling industry. "He was the epitome of sleaze," the model said. "He tried to get his models to become cozy with his colleagues because he thought it would increase his business. Maybe it did, but a lot of innocent girls got hurt along the way."

John Casablancas told Michael Gross that Brunel was a disgrace to the modeling business. "I really despise Jean-Luc as a human being for the way he's cheapened the business," Casablancas said. "There is no justice. This is a guy who should be behind bars. There was a little group, Jean-Luc, [Brunel] Patrick [Gilles], and Varsano, [Serge] who were very well known in Paris for roaming the clubs. They would invite girls and put drugs in their drinks. Brunel would fly all the girls from Karins to St. Tropez to spend weekends with them. Everybody knew that they were creeps."

Journalist Martin Smith agrees with Casablancas's assessment. "I've seen many seedy characters in this business, but Brunel is at the top of the list," he says. "He wanted to put his cock in as many models as possible. I know many models, some of them barely into their teens, who have horror stories about how he gave them drugs and tried to have sex with them. Guys like him should have their balls cut off for causing so many women harm."

One former Karins model, who refused to be identified, said Brunel and a group of his friends invited more than a dozen models to a private party at one of their apartments. By the end of the night, seven of the women had been forced into having sex. "Most of the women felt they had been raped," she said. "But they were afraid to report it to the police because Brunel would ruin their careers. He got away with everything. He socialized with a lot of powerful people and paid them off by offering them dates with gorgeous women. In most other countries, he would have been regarded as a potentially dangerous man."

Not all of the models Brunel worked with have an unpleasant story to relate. Christy Turlington worked with Brunel and became one of his close friends. She regularly stayed at his Paris apartment. Turlington says she saw a sympathetic side to Brunel, very different from what so many other models have reported. Although he leveraged his position at Karins to get beautiful women, Turlington attests that Brunel made his moves in measured steps. "I'm sure some of the stories are over-exaggerated," she says. "In this business you never know what to believe. When I worked with Jean-Luc he was very ambitious, trying to work himself to the top. He worked long hours to build Karins into a top agency."

Craig Pyes's *60 Minutes* story, however, painted a portrait of Brunel as a sleazy man obsessed with sex and drugs. Brunel's blunders made for entertaining TV. One model told Pyes that Brunel had encouraged her to do drugs with him on several occasions. "He'd always give me a little vial of cocaine," the model explained. "He did that with all the girls."

Another ex-Brunel model, who also prefers to remain anonymous, says that she was not surprised by Pyse's investigation. She claims that Brunel came on to her several times while she worked for him, and that he forced her to have sex with him on her kitchen floor. "We got stoned and drunk one night and then Jean-Luc started taking advantage of me," she says. "He took off my clothes and started going inside me. I remember trying to figure out the next day if I should call the police and have him charged for rape."

After the CBS report aired, several powerful players in the modeling business, including Ford Models, severed relations with Brunel. Eileen Ford, who claimed she was unaware of what Brunel had been up to, told Brunel to take a hike several weeks after the televised report. Ford had always had a soft spot for Brunel, and had tried to convince models not to cooperate with Craig Pyes's investigation. After Pyes's report aired, Ford couldn't believe some of the accusations against Brunel. She decided to stop doing business with him.

"Deep down I think that Eileen knew what Jean-Luc was up to, but she wanted to ignore it because he was her right-hand-man in Europe," says journalist Martin Smith. "She was very disappointed after she saw the report. Being a woman who prided herself on high moral standards, she had no alternative but to sack Brunel. She was horrified by the reports of Brunel drugging several models in order to get them into bed. She called her staff to an emergency meeting and the consensus was unanimous in favor of ending relations with Brunel."

Although Jean-Luc Brunel tried to refute every aspect of Pyes's report, few people were willing to give him the benefit of the doubt. The day before *60 Minutes* broadcasted its shocking report, Brunel married his girlfriend of two years, model Roberta Chirko. Many people thought Brunel married Chirko in anticipation of the story. But he denied that it was a last minute attempt to clean up his image. He insisted that he was in love with Chirko and that the timing was coincidental. "Maybe the marriage had been planned, but I knew that it wouldn't last long," said a model and former lover of Brunel. "Jean-Luc isn't capable of making an emotional commitment. He can't keep himself from making passes at beautiful women. He doesn't care if he's married or if they're married. He'll fuck them no matter what."

Shortly after their marriage, Chirko heard rumors about her husband's extramarital affairs. Chirko was deeply in love with Brunel, and tried to ignore the gossip. She confronted Brunel several times and he denied being unfaithful. She asked a couple of her model friends at Karins who regularly partied with Brunel to report back to her, and the reports weren't good. Chirko found out for sure that Brunel had resumed his playboy antics. Heartbroken, she left Brunel and began divorce proceedings. She remained friends with Brunel and continued to work for Karins in New York. "I admire her so much because she must have gone through hell," says journalist Martin Smith. "Most people would sever ties completely, but I guess she needed to keep working."

Several people close to Brunel said that he regretted the way he treated Chirko. He claimed to have learned a hard lesson about how to treat people. "Anybody can say what they want about Jean-Luc, but I know for a fact that he wasn't proud of the way he treated his wife," said one Karins agent.

> He would have liked to save the marriage because he really cared about Roberta. He often told me how much he loved spending time alone with Roberta, away from all the chaos of this industry. Sure, he had a problem controlling himself around women, everybody knows that. But it caught up to him and it cost him his marriage. When his divorce with Roberta went through, you could tell how bad he felt. Deep down, he's really the type of man who would love to settle down and raise a family. But his ego gets in the way. He tries to get all the beautiful models to love him because he needs to impress people and use it as power over them. It's like a sickness. Maybe if he found another job he could straighten himself out. Once he deals with all the bullshit in his life, he might make everybody realize that he's not the bad guy most people make him out to be.

Brunel has complained to friends that the *60 Minutes* report was not well-balanced. He was disappointed that Craig Pyes didn't say more positive things. "It was an interesting report, and a lot of it is true," Brunel admitted. "But it only showed one side of the story.

There's another side to the story that was completely left out. I take my job very seriously and have worked hard to reach the point I'm at now. I just wish some of the good things I've done would have been pointed out."

Brunel wasn't alone in his opinion that the CBS report was biased. "I've known him for many years, and let me tell you, nobody has worked harder than Jean-Luc," says one of his former colleagues. "He does everything in his power to try to get his models the best jobs. CBS did a complete hatchet job on him. So what if he likes to sleep with gorgeous models? There are not many men out there who wouldn't do the same if they were in Jean-Luc's shoes. It's too bad the CBS reporter didn't dig deeper and find out who the real Jean-Luc is. Jean-Luc cares about his models and has helped many of them get through some tough times in their lives. He treats the people he works with like family and his door is always open to current and past models who have worked with him."

Still, many of Brunel's colleagues agreed with Pyes, and believed that Brunel was trying to weasel his way out of another dilemma. Brunel's behavior has been under scrutiny ever since he began in the modeling business. One of his former secretaries at Karins called him "not a man of commitment, but an opportunist."

In 1997 the president of Ford models, Joey Hunter, left his job at Ford to open the New York branch of Karin Models with Brunel. Despite the fact that in Paris Karin represented top models like Daniela Pestova and Rebecca Romijn, Brunel needed Hunter's good reputation to hide his own sleazy past in New York. But the honeymoon was short-lived for Hunter and Brunel. Brunel became upset with Hunter for his constant warnings about hitting on young models, and for not minding his own business. "I hired you as a partner, not as a watchdog," Brunel told Hunter.

In June 1999, Brunel decided that he had had enough. He took Hunter to lunch at New York's famous Balthazar eatery, and told him not to bother showing up to work anymore. At this point, Hunter was so tired of dealing with Brunel that he was more than happy to resign. Brunel and Hunter tried to agree on a severance package, but Brunel kept changing the terms. Finally, Hunter decided to get his lawyers involved. Hunter sued Brunel and Karin Models, demanding that the agency cease using his good name in their business dealings.

"My approach to doing business is very different from Jean-Luc's," Hunter said. "Jean-Luc used me because he needed someone who is credible. Without me, many people would have refused to do business with Jean-Luc because his reputation is terrible. We just have totally different views about how to do business."

CBS reporter Craig Pyes later told author Michael Gross that people like Jean-Luc Brunel and Claude Haddad try to cover their tracks by denying their wrongdoings. Pyes said that Brunel and Haddad rank among the sleaziest people in the fashion industry. "Hundreds of girls were not only harassed, but molested. We're talking about a conveyor belt, not a casting couch."

Many models in Pyes's report confirmed that they had been drugged and sexually abused by Brunel and his entourage. Pyes said that two of the models he interviewed had broken down and ended up in psychiatric hospitals after Brunel and his friends allegedly drugged and abused them.

Commenting on the aftershocks of the *60 Minutes* exposé, fashion consultant and former model Esther Reese remarks, "The CBS report shocked the entire fashion industry. Parents of young girls were outraged and became very reluctant to allow their daughters to pursue modeling careers. It's amazing that Brunel was able to keep his career going after the report. He should have been barred from the industry. Instead, he still continues to be a major player in the modeling business."

The minority of decent model agents feared that people would group them with Brunel. Many of these agents did everything they could to distance themselves from the CBS report. "My Paris agent was a very decent man who was devoted to his wife and three children," Esther Reese says. "After the *60 Minutes* report he was worried that every agent would be typecast as being a sleazebag. He went out of his way to be extra kind to the models he represented, and he showed copies of the *60 Minutes* report to the new models who were hoping to be represented by him. He wanted them to be aware of the dark side of the business. I have known models who had decent agents, and they said they felt the same way. Every agent suffered for a long time because of the way some of the big agents abused their power. It's important for young models to know that not every agent is a con. There are some very decent ones, you've just got to be choosy to find them."

Frances Grill, founder of the Click Agency, is one of the few fashion power brokers who is universally respected by models. Grill mortgaged her home and poured every penny she had into Click, named in tribute to the diligent fashion photographers she had worked with at another model agency, Ten. Grill felt that not enough men were being used as models. She is almost solely responsible for the rise of the male supermodel. She signed up several unusual models, such as the bald Jenny O. and transsexual Toye. "She was caring, daring, and innovative," recalls Talisa Soto, the Click model who became the first Hispanic supermodel. "But most of all she was fair. She wasn't concerned with all the glitz and phoniness of this business. She wanted to create art, to create something new. Every agent out there should take lessons from her."

Grill's alternative style and inspired choices built Click into a powerhouse among agencies. Click models were different—artistically speaking, a level above other models—and fashion photographers lined up to capture them on film. Not only did Grill set a trend in terms of look, she only worked with people who would treat her models fairly. "She was well aware of the horror stories that go on every day in this business," said one photographer. "She stood up for her models all the way, and made sure that the conditions for them were perfect. If something went wrong, she took responsibility. Fashion photographer Bruce Weber once told me that he looked forward to working with Click models more than any others, because he knew the shoot was guaranteed to be different than most of the boring stuff photographers normally shoot. It was tiring trying to make blonde bombshell models look sexy and provocative over and over. So many of them are so annoying to work with. With Click, it was exciting to shoot models who were bald, or who had mohawks and tattoos."

Click had used other unconventional models, like Buzzy Kerbox, the world's most famous surfer. Kerbox will never forget the favor Frances Grill did for him. In the early eighties, after being repeatedly rejected, Kerbox hooked up with Click and landed a major deal with Ralph Lauren. It completely changed his world, opening up more doors than ever before. He no longer had to worry about money, and he got loads of publicity. Wherever he went, people asked him for his autograph. Kerbox became a full-fledged celebrity.

Many of Grill's models, past and present, praise her for giving them the break no other agent would. In fact, Grill herself admits her secret is finding unique, far-out-looking models that other agents have no idea how to market. "She has always been ahead of her time," says former model Diane Parks. "I remember when I met her for the first time, back in the eighties. I had snake tattoos on my back. That's all she asked me about. She gave me her card and told me to call her."

Edward Garrett, a London fashion historian, says that if not for people like Grill, the modeling industry might have died years ago. "It has such a bad reputation because a lot of terrible things happen and so many of the people involved are crooked. There are definitely still some good people left, like Frances Grill, who bring credibility back to the industry. Eventually people will wake up and refuse to do business with the bad agents. Then things will become stable, and models won't have to fear for their lives."

PART FOUR

• • •

Beauty and Myth

CHAPTER 27

• • •

The New York Diet

I had mixed feelings about the fashion scene in New York. On the one hand, it was much more exciting and real than Los Angeles, with different fashion events happening every night of the week. I enjoyed going to old warehouses and lofts to watch New York's up-and-coming designers showcase their newest collections. The people in the industry were more progressive and avant-garde than those anywhere else I had been. Everyone I met was very forthcoming and cooperative. On the other hand, the sheer number of horror stories I uncovered in New York was overwhelming. It seemed that every model I met had some nightmarish experience to share. Or, perhaps it was that I had finally heard one too many stories of murder, rape, and drug overdose.

The thing that disgusted me most about the New York fashion scene was the number of models who had severe eating disorders. Their obsession with thinness was frightening. Despite the growing popularity of the voluptuous look, most models I met in New York shed more pounds than was healthy. In the next few chapters, I examine how the pressure of having to look a certain way—be a certain weight, skin color, or age—can destroy a model's career. Many suffer emotional breakdowns and end up in the hospital.

I bumped into supermodel Sophie Dahl while she was making the rounds at New York's trendiest nightspots with her new beau Mick Jagger. Proud of her work and her physical strength, Dahl has maintained her voluptuous look despite advice to slim down. Her inspirational attitude outlines the importance of being confident about one's natural appearance and health in an industry that's gone mad. "If I would have listened to everyone's advice, I would probably be thinner, but not as successful," Dahl said. "I'm a believer in trying to look the way you really are. If people can't accept your natural self, then it's their tough luck. You have to look at yourself every day in the mirror, not them. When I wake up, the thing that I want most is to feel good about myself, and comfortable in my own skin."

Very few models I met in New York shared Dahl's point of view. Everyone seemed to be more obsessed with thinness than with wellness or self-confidence. Calorie counting was the most popular game in town. With surprisingly advanced mathematic skills, models kept track of calories more diligently than they kept track of the money they spent. Yet models seemed oblivious to the health- and beauty-inhibiting side effects of calorie restricted diets, which include bloating, abdominal distention, constipation, depression, failure to produce collagen (the major protein of all connective tissues), headaches, lack of energy, hair loss, menstrual difficulties, sleep disruption, yeast infections, and water retention.

Model Gertrude Chambers presented a frightening account of a model's morbid obsession with dieting in order to further a fashion career. Born in 1984 in Wyoming, Gertrude is tall with long, dark hair. She started out, as models often do, doing catalogue ads for local stores. When she was thirteen, Gertrude was invited to go to New York to do some test shoots. Since Gertrude was an A-student with academic aspirations, her parents had reservations about letting her pursue modeling, a career that offered no guarantees.

Gertrude first ventured to the Big Apple with her mother Anne. When her mother was forced to return to Wyoming for work, Gertrude was repeatedly rejected for modeling jobs and fell into a deep depression. Equating extreme slimness with professional success, and convinced that her career was hindered by her weight, Gertrude began a starvation diet. She ate only one low calorie meal a day, with no snacks to sustain her. Gertrude's attempt to shed pounds turned into a curse—anorexia nervosa. Her weight dropped to ninety-two pounds, twenty-five pounds less than her normal weight. She sought psychological counseling and was told that due to her drastically reduced calorie intake, she was starving her body.

As soon as she started dieting, Gertrude took up smoking cigarettes. Most of the thinnest models she'd met in New York were also heavy smokers. The nicotine in cigarette smoke stimulates the release of noradrenalin in the body, a neurohormone that instructs brown fat cells to consume stored fat. Brown fat can burn between 200 and 400 calories a day, which can amount to a weight loss of a couple of pounds a month. One can only wonder why the weight loss advantages of smoking aren't advertised on cigarette packs.

Anyone who has noticed the fashion industry's obsession with rake-like thinness, exemplified by the string of skeletal models on the catwalks, can sympathize with Gertrude's motivations. Gertrude developed a fear of never being slim enough. No matter how much weight she lost, she had to lose more, as in her mind thinness was equated with success. With each pound she lost, she believed she was one pound closer to ultra-stardom. "I knew I was self-destructing, but there was nothing I could do about it," Gertrude says. "I was taken in by the pressures of the industry. I lost complete control of myself. I was in such bad shape, and the worst was yet to come."

Gertrude developed an acute heart disease common to anorexics. At first, her doctors were puzzled by this ailment and couldn't isolate the cause. Once they realized that Gertrude was anorexic, they put two and two together. Gertrude underwent months of treatment. She became extremely depressed and came close to death several times. "There were many times when I didn't think that I'd pull through," she says. "Things had gotten so bad. I was so tired and weak. I had given up."

To complicate matters more, Gertrude developed yet another side effect of anorexia, a plasma potassium level so low that it was potentially lethal to her already distressed heart. She became even more depressed because doctors were unable to tell her when she might recover. Her ability to concentrate dropped to about thirty minutes at a time, and she just about gave up hope of being cured.

Things finally took a turn for the better when Gertrude hooked up with a woman doctor in Manhattan who practiced natural medicine. Dr. Mia Kazner became Gertrude's spiritual healer, helping her to develop a more positive attitude. Dr. Kazner made Gertrude read natural health magazines and books about spirituality. One of the books that helped Gertrude was Deepak Chopra's *The Seven Spiritual Laws of Success*. Following the book's seven basic principles of spiritual wellness, concepts equally applicable to any physical or emotional challenge, Gertrude's health finally stabilized. She worked hard to regain her health, and within a year her weight was back to normal. Instead of quitting the business like so many models do after a major crisis, Gertrude decided to stay in New York and pursue her dream. She abandoned her hopes of being a runway model and just concentrated on being a working model. She also decided to finish her education and enrolled in a local high school.

"I went through some very tough times," Gertrude says. "But with the spiritual guidance of my doctor, I finally overcame it all. All I wanted to do was work as a model. I look at modeling as a true form of artistic expression. I hope to be in this business for many more years to come, but on my own terms. I learned that it's not worth it to try to keep up with everybody. You've got to look inside yourself first and then decide how to work in this business and still be happy at the end of the day."

CHAPTER 28

* * *

Steroid Relief

When American soccer star Brandi Chastain tore off her shirt after scoring the winning goal in the Women's World Cup in July 1999, she did a lot more than show the male world a black sports bra. With her biceps and abdominal muscles rippling in the sunlight, Chastain helped to redefine the fashion industry's notion of beauty. Endorsement deals poured in, and Chastain became the most sought after pinup of the year. For the first time in years, the heroin chic look was out and the healthy, strong, athletic look was in. Chastain left fashion editors clamoring for her services.

According to journalist Martin Smith, had Chastain exposed her black bra a few years earlier, at the height of heroin chic, she probably would have gone unnoticed by the fashion industry. Back then, Smith says, unless a girl was emaciated with her shoulder bones sticking out of her clothes, nobody would have been interested in her. "It's awful, because the fashion industry was practically promoting anorexia nervosa," Smith says. "Just go back and look closely at the models in the early nineties. They all had the same thin look. The pressure on them to stay skinny was so intense that a lot of them developed severe eating disorders. That's why so many models in the nineties did hard drugs. They were replacing their craving for food with drugs. I know a model who says that she did lots of cocaine to stay thin and would often eat barely a slice of bread a day because she had to stay thin."

Anorexia nervosa, which is a pathological obsession with dieting and thinness, affects more than one in every 100 female adolescents in the United States. A majority of these victims never fully recover.

About 20 percent eventually die. Many psychologists and researchers attribute the growing number of anorexics to the television and fashion industry's use of waiflike models in the nineties. "The media is responsible for hypnotizing young girls into believing that they should look like skin and bones," says Arthur Rudy, a journalist who has written extensively about teenage girls' eating disorders. "When young girls pick up a magazine or watch a TV ad and see somebody like Kate Moss as the featured model, they want to end up looking exactly like her. Most girls aren't as thin as a Kate Moss, and they start going on diets to try to [become] so. It becomes an obsession, and in the process, many of the girls become very sick."

Victims of anorexia and their families struggle to understand why what started out as a simple diet turned into an eating disorder. On the morning of April 15, 1997, Celine Sauve, the sixteen-year-old model daughter of French millionaire Theo Sauve, was admitted to a Paris hospital. She was near death from starvation. Celine had started her decline some time before, by excusing herself from the dinner table to vomit and get rid of the calories from her meal. She concealed her illness, pretended nothing was wrong, and watched as her weight continued to drop. In March 1996, her parents became increasingly concerned when they discovered diet pills in one of Celine's drawers. They thought that Celine, at 5 feet 6 inches and 103 pounds, was already too thin. Celine, who started modeling at age thirteen, was living in denial. Whenever somebody close to her brought up her weight, she became overly defensive. "C'est rien," Celine would reply. "It's nothing. It's part of my job to stay thin. That's how my agent wants me to look so I can compete with the other girls for jobs."

If Celine's life had been a simple downhill trajectory, her illness could have been seen as tragic but inevitable. During the first few years of her modeling career, however, Celine had been a healthy, athletic-looking 115 pounds. She liked to feast on French and Italian food after a day's work. But when her Paris agent told her that she had lost several jobs to thinner models, Celine started dieting. She never looked back. After months of watching Celine self-destruct, Theo Sauve eventually took the advice of a counselor and convinced his daughter to enter a pricey rehab clinic. It was then that he realized he was most persuasive not as a businessman, but as a grief-stricken father.

Celine's doctor says she would have probably died if she hadn't taken her father's advice. Today, Celine's weight is back to normal.

She has quit modeling and is studying computer graphics. Theo Sauve beseeches other parents of models to watch their children closely for signs of anorexia. "Because of Celine, I've been in contact with so many other parents of models who are concerned that their children have eating disorders," Sauve says. "It's unfortunate, because there's too much pressure put on trying to be thin in this business. I encourage most parents to try to get their children to quit modeling if there are signs that they have an eating disorder. It can become very dangerous if they don't act quickly, before it becomes too late to do anything."

Some model agencies, far from being vigilant about potential anorexia victims, thrive on recruiting painfully thin girls. According to an investigative report in *Company Magazine*, teenage girls who already suffer from eating disorders are often approached by model agencies seeking new "superwaifs." Some are told to lose even more weight, according to the magazine, and are put on excessively harsh diets by their model agencies. One former model agent admitted that "the look is thin and the thinner, the better."

Lucy Cope, fifteen, told *Company* that she had been pursued by two top agencies that thought she had the perfect look. When she was approached, Cope was anorexic, weighed less than 100 pounds, and was a patient at a hospital for eating disorders. Another girl, Lucy Stanley, who was five feet, eight inches and 125 pounds, was flatly refused by a number of agencies that told her she was too heavy. At the time she was suffering from anorexia and bulimia. "At one agency I was told, 'with a bum that size, you won't get anywhere.' Another said my hips were way too fat . . . I lost several pounds and I looked like a maniac. My cheeks were hollow, my eyes had sunk into my face, and my skin was terrible. How can that be considered beautiful?"

Most model agencies deny trying to recruit girls with eating disorders. But one agent admits that the heroin chic look is what most agents seek. "The industry wants pencil thin models because weight is such a big issue to teenage girls. I myself don't hire models unless they're very thin. I hate to do it, but I have no choice because that's what the magazines and advertisers who pay my salary want."

One of the agencies not mentioned in the *Company* article was Elite. Sam Thorburn, who headed the New Faces at Elite premiere, told British medical journalist Celia Hall, "If a girl comes to us who perhaps needs to lose a few inches off her hips, we'll send her to our nutritionist to make sure she gets a healthy diet. You don't have to starve to lose weight. You couldn't model if you were anorexic. You need an awful lot of energy and enthusiasm."

Not all fashion industry moguls are guilty of promoting heroin chic. Shortly before the 1997 *Company* article, Omega Watches withdrew its advertising from *Vogue* and other glossy fashion magazines in protest against the use of unusually thin models. Accurist Watches had spent almost $200,000 on a controversial ad featuring a model whose ribs were clearly visible under her sweater. She was so thin that she wore the watch around her upper arm instead of her wrist. The slogan was "Put some weight on." Accurist was attacked by the media and by eating disorder experts for exploiting emaciated models. But the company claimed it was only trying to make a point about the debate over thin models. A statement by Accurist said the ad campaign "confronts a current and much debated issue. . . . While being provocatively contentious, the idea does not seek to condone the vogue for anorexic models, but takes a fashion icon and uses it to emphasize the point of difference within the solid silver watch range—their weight." Wendy Stone, a representative of the advertising agency TBWA Simon Palmer, which created the controversial ad, said that they were trying to poke fun at the fashion industry. "We are absolutely not saying that it is right to be thin or anorexic," she said. "The model was chosen because she looks thin, not because she looks unwell. The way it is shot does make her look pale, but that is just the style the photographer is using at the moment. . . . We are making the contrast in a tongue-in-cheek way to make our point."

Accurist Watches was condemned by the Advertising Standards Authority (ASA) for its "glamorization of such a thin model, in conjunction with copy that played on her size, causing serious offense." The ASA received eighty-three complaints, many from people who had suffered from eating disorders themselves or knew friends who had. Although the ASA did not establish any regulations against the use of thin models in the future, it did issue a warning. "Advertisers need to be sensitive to the broader messages they are sending out when they use social issues to sell," the ASA said in a statement. "Playing on, or glamorizing, those who are obviously underweight may cause offense and be thought irresponsible when the complex issue of eating disorders is such a matter of social concern."

When British model Melissa Silver started modeling at sixteen, after being discovered by Beth Boldt, the same talent scout who discovered Naomi Campbell. Soon after, the six-foot, blond-haired beauty was diagnosed with Hodgkin's disease, a cancer of the lymphatic system. Silver was forced to put her career on hold for several years, undergoing chemotherapy and radiation treatment to fight the cancer. At one point, a priest read her her last rites because it didn't look like she would survive. Finally, Silver recovered and returned to modeling at age nineteen. She looked skeletal—She weighed less than 100 pounds and was all skin and bones. Still, Silver was a hit with the major fashion houses. She received countless offers for modeling jobs from the likes of Calvin Klein, Versace, Christian Dior, and Armani. Her waiflike look made her a highly valuable commodity.

Even after her cancer went into remission, Silver felt that she practically had to starve herself in order to remain desirable within the fashion world. She was right. Silver became one of the top models in New York, and was envied by models considered "overweight" in France because they weighed more than 100 pounds. Silver now faced a new health crisis—an eating disorder. She frequently battled with nausea and weakness. At the insistence of her father, Silver started eating properly again and put on a few pounds. Luckily, she was able to overcome another major threat to her health.

Today, Silver is well, and at measurements of 34-24-35, has cut back on her modeling activities to concentrate on acting. She has appeared in several major TV series, including *Sex and the City* and in such films as the James Bond flick *Golden Eye*, in which she played a Bond girl. "For the first time I feel totally content with myself and my life," Silver says. "Battling cancer wasn't easy, and being super skinny was also hard to overcome. I've beaten them both and now I can concentrate on just being who I am. If people in the industry don't like my look, that's fine, I'll just find someone else who appreciates me for my natural self."

The heroin chic craze has not only inspired a generation of weight obsessives, it has also lent an air of glamour and legitimacy to drug abuse. *British Vogue* editor Alexandra Shulman agrees, but only to a certain extent. She believes that heroin chic models can have a bad effect on readers who have serious drug problems. She admits that near-anorexic models often look like they're on drugs, which makes them appealing to users of hard drugs. Nonetheless, she doesn't think fashion magazines should be condemned for the photographs they use. She says that people need to be able to pick up a magazine and fantasize. "I don't believe that fashion images promote the use of drugs per se, any more than I believe that we encourage eating disorders per se," she says. "But I am pretty sure that it is possible that someone who is already vulnerable might find that vulnerability fed by something that we publish. . . . I am a magazine editor, and it is my job to create the most interesting magazine that I can possibly achieve."

Sociologist Andrew Clayman, who once taught a course called Society and Pop Culture at the University of London strongly disagrees with Shulman. The media, Clayman says, must act socially responsible and not encourage anything that might be harmful to the general public. "It's almost like saying that it's okay for the media to write racist things because it's only entertainment. I don't see any benefit in trying to create a fantasy world. Even if most people take it with a grain of salt, the few who take it seriously can hurt themselves and others. How can anybody justify using anorexic-looking models? So many people die from this disease. It's a very serious issue and should not be glamorized in any way."

American model Carla Jones developed anorexia shortly after she signed up with a New York agency in 1998. Carla, then fifteen, worked long hours to achieve success. A fellow model noticed dark pools under her eyes and contacted Carla's mother out of concern. Carla had lost a lot of weight in a short period of time. At five feet, ten inches, she weighed less than 100 pounds. Her mother Linda assumed responsibility for her daughter's illness. She felt guilty for having encouraged her daughter to become a model. "I should have discouraged her from pursuing a modeling career," Linda Jones says. "She was too young and wasn't ready to deal with the psychological pressures of the job. It was all my fault. If I had made Carla stay home and finish high school, none of this would have happened."

During the first several months of her illness, Carla became despondent and suicidal. She was afraid to eat, as if eating would have some immediately negative repercussions. Carla didn't want help. Finally, after weeks of desperate pleas, Linda convinced Carla to check into an eating disorder clinic. It was another eight months before her weight stabilized and the doctors said it was safe for her to return to a normal life. Carla spent the next year trying to put the pieces back together. "I couldn't cope with the life of a model," she says. "My agent put so much pressure on me to stay slim. It got to the point where I started to feel guilty every time I would eat something. And it drained me psychologically. The only reason why I got through this was because of the love and support my family gave me. Without it, I would probably be dead."

* * *

Fashion photographer Brian Smith predicts that the fashion industry's preoccupation with thinness will be replaced by healthier and somewhat more muscular models. Smith, however, is concerned that this will still lead teenage girls to unhealthy compulsions, like being fitter with larger muscles. "Most models who make it big go to some extreme to get the edge over everybody else," Smith says. "They do whatever it takes, whether it's drugs, sex, or starving themselves to be thin. I think that the heroin chic will give way to healthier looking models, and I'm sure the models will find creative ways to beef up their bodies with substances and anabolic steroids. It will be a kind of reverse anorexia."

Dr. Gary I. Wadler, a professor of clinical medicine at New York University School of Medicine, says that it's time people just accept each other for who they are and how they look. Until that day comes, Wadler believes, people will continue along a path of self-destruction. "We've gone from the overweight beauty of the Rubens women, to the thin rail of the Twiggy types, and now back to something in between, the lean but muscular type. These are people who are virtually addicted to the mirror. But they will never be satisfied with what they see, and this is now happening to teenage girls who want bigger muscles no matter how much bigger their muscles have become."

According to psychiatrist Dr. Michael Lee, many models show signs of an emotional disorder called body dysmorphism. An excessive preoccupation with a trait or traits of the body that the sufferer views as ugly or defective eventually alters the sufferer's perception of his reflection in the mirror. Victims of dysmorphism obsess over their body's image even when they are quite attractive. Lee attributes this problem among young models to the immense pressure that is put on them. "They become obsessed about every detail of their bodies and they lose control of themselves. The modeling business can be very cruel and young teenage girls should think very carefully before they head to New York to try to make it. It has cost many innocent girls their lives."

Nina Young, a model from a well-to-do Massachusetts family, believes that models would not develop eating disorders or abuse their bodies if more focus was put on better treatment. Young describes the fashion industry as "a meat factory." "Most models are good and interesting people," she says. "They're very innocent before they come to New York and Paris. But when they get there and start working, the pressure on them to remain successful is inhumane.

Everybody from the agents, designers, and photographers wants them to maintain a certain image. It's hard to do that in any walk of life. Things change and you must go with the flow. I've known so many young models who have completely gone over the edge because they couldn't keep up being a certain weight. It's so easy to fall apart in this business. One day you're successful and the next day you feel ugly and then the whole world starts to cave in."

Former seventies model Veruschka believes that models lose the ability to think logically when they become overly obsessed about their looks. They become irrational, argue with people who try to help, and throw temper tantrums. "I've known so many models who want to be the best looking, the thinnest, and the most popular," Veruschka says. "But so many of them become miserable in the process. They become too competitive and lose their sense to think clearly. It becomes an addiction and they often wind up paying for it dearly. The only way to survive is by knowing yourself and by being yourself. If people don't like it, then it's their problem, not yours."

CHAPTER 29

● ● ●

Cosmetic Hangover

For a model, whose livelihood depends on her pretty face, the endless struggle to enhance her beauty can be frustrating. It often leads to severe emotional problems. Every model must spend hours each day on personal care. Cosmetics, skin care, hair care, body care, and fragrances are a daily routine. Most models admit that looking their best is not easy after working all day and partying all night. They share hangover cures, from raw eggs to a teaspoonful of Vodka, to help each other through the morning after.

Models take the greatest of care with their faces. Many use disposable paper towels to dry their face for fear of touching bacteria lurking in regular cotton towels. Most sleep in the nude, to allow skin pores to "breathe" during the night. Hand and foot models sleep with socks slathered in petroleum jelly on their hands or feet to keep the skin looking soft. Other models often sleep with teeth-bleaching trays in their mouths on nights before a shoot, despite warnings from dentists that this can destroy the teeth, or even cause death. A New York prosthodontist (a dentist that specializes in dental implants) who has treated many well-known supermodels says that models can spend up to $100,000 trying to get the right smile. "About 90 percent of the top supermodels have had dental implants put in because they want to have a perfect smile," says the prosthodontist, who wishes to remain anonymous. "In many cases, they don't need them. But once they come in for a consultation and the prosthodontist smells how much money they have, in most cases [he] only tells them about the most expensive treatment plan. A good number of the models who are conned by the dentists end up with more complications to their mouth than ever. Most dentists I know, including myself, are businessmen first. When we smell a rich client sitting in the chair we won't hesitate to jack up the price as much as possible."

One Los Angeles plastic surgeon, who also declined to be named, admits that he has, in the past, removed the bottom rib from some models in order to create a slimmer appearance. "This is a hot, new, radical surgery," he says. "Women in the Victorian era did this routinely to get those tiny waists. It's not a surgery I even approve of, but for those clients who insist, I do it." The surgeon adds that most models he has as clients get cheek implants. "It's a simple procedure where we add a prosthetic cheek bone atop the real one. This enhances the beauty of a face, as we see beauty in North America and Europe."

One model who I'll call Brittany, says she enjoyed partying and doing drugs every night when she was working in New York between 1994 and 1998. She admits that she had to spend hours each morning covering eye circles and blemishes on her skin with foundation and concealer. "Every night I went to clubs and got wasted," Brittany says. "The next morning I would have to spend hours using fleshtone concealers and foundations to try to make my skin look fresh for that day's shoot. I . . . often had puffy eyes from coming home at five A.M. [and waking] up two hours later for work. We always kept used tea bags and a cucumber to use as cold compresses—those really make the puffiness go down."

Brittany's former roommate did hard drugs and would spend hours trying to cover up the track marks on her body from the heroin she injected. "Her agent used to come over every day and help her put on the makeup. She was a top model and her agent was worried that if the marks showed up, she would lose her high paying jobs." Many models interviewed for this book admit that it is common practice to shave off scabs and cover the open wounds with powder and foundation in order to look flawless for a photographer.

Gia Carangi, the heroin addicted covergirl who died of AIDS in 1986, was blacklisted from modeling because fashion editors discovered track marks on her body. Carangi, who once graced the covers of *Vogue*, *Elle*, and *Cosmopolitan*, was the top model of the late 1970s. She redefined the fashion industry's standard of beauty. Fashion editors decided not to use her anymore because of her turbulent lifestyle. Carangi was soon reduced to turning tricks on the streets of New York and Atlantic City. At twenty-six, she became one of the first women in America to die of AIDS. "Gia's handlers spent hours trying to help her cover up the track marks on her body," says Elyssa Stewart, a former lover. "The problem was that her people were more interested in hiding the marks than helping her personally. Gia was by far the most interesting and provocative model of her time. At first, fashion editors knew about all the drugs she was doing, but they didn't care. In fact, at one shoot for a major magazine one of the editors supplied Gia with a bag of cocaine and some heroin right on the set. It's only when word leaked out that she might be HIV-positive that the editors used her drug habit as an excuse to blackball her."

According to Stewart, Carangi is the reason why so many models today shoot heroin under their toenails or tongue, where track marks cannot be detected. Some have lost toenails to infection, some have blinded themselves by injecting heroin into their eye. "A lot of the agents, who care more about making a buck than anything else, warn their models that if they do heroin, they should inject it in careful places," Stewart says. "They tell the young models the stories about Gia and how she was blackballed. They warn them to be careful not to become the next Gia."

Carangi grew up in Philadelphia. She was a favorite model of top fashion photographers Arthur Elgort, Francesco Scavullo, and Helmut Newton. Carangi was renowned for dressing in men's clothes and wearing no makeup. Her rebellious "take no shit" attitude took the fashion industry by storm. "If Gia would have spent more time in the beginning using makeup to cover up the marks, nobody would have put up a fuss," Elyssa Stewart says. "But she hated makeup. She wanted to do things her way. In the end, when she allowed her handlers to use makeup to cover up her marks, it was too late. She was already considered untouchable."

According to journalist Martin Smith, about two thirds of the models we see in the big fashion magazines use makeup to hide traces of their debaucherous lifestyle. "Many of them are stoned during the shoot itself," Smith says.

The makeup today has become so sophisticated that no matter how much a model partied the night before, they could look as good as new for that day's shoot. It's unbelievable. About a year ago, I was at a party in London. The party ended way past three in the morning. Several well-known models were there and they were all partying with us. One of them, who had been smoking joints and drinking rum all night, told me she had a shoot for *British Vogue* the next morning. I asked her how it was possible for her to get up and look good after such a wild night. She replied, 'I do it all the time, it's normal. Nothing that a little makeup can't touch up.' I noticed her leaving with a man she was making out with all night at about 3:30 A.M. It's beyond me how somebody can wake up for work and look good the next day.

Models use makeup not only to hide drug use, but also to camouflage the stress and environmental factors that can leave their face resembling a war zone. Pimples, dehydrated skin, chapped lips, and tired-looking complexions must be revived to look dewy by the next day's shoot. "Time takes its toll," says aesthetician Nancy Harris. "No matter how beautiful a model is, it's important for them to have the right makeup for emergency situations. If a model is going through the menstruating period, it's necessary for them to use the proper liquids and makeup to get rid of glaring pimples. If the model goes to a photo shoot with chapped lips, they need to have a good lip balm handy. If they're not prepared, it could prove costly."

Harris says that the key ingredient for models is a foundation that is versatile and long lasting. "It's difficult standing under those hot lights all day. It's important to find a foundation that is light and natural looking and easy to control. For the last ten years many models have been using only natural products. It's much less rough on the skin and can prolong a model's career. It's important to check out which products are as natural as advertised. It's important to check the ingredients of the product. If there are lots of chemicals at the beginning of the list and the plant oils are at the end, that product isn't natural."

One of the makeup essentials for models is mascara. Finding a mascara that goes on smoothly without smears or globs can be difficult. "There's a lot of mascaras out there, but few can withstand the daily grind of a model's job." Harris says. "I've noticed so many times in fashion magazines how badly a model's mascara looked."

Models always start with very clean lashes, with no trace of cream or moisturizer to cause clinging. Most use the brush vertically to carefully coat each lash.

Most women and men who read the big fashion magazines envy the athletic or slim physiques of the featured models. But models spend thousands of dollars a year on diets, manicures, pedicures, carefully colored hair, and tanning beds in order to look glamourous. "Guys often fall for the obvious," supermodel Hedi Klum said in a

Cosmopolitan interview. "Taking time out to pamper yourself is a great way to feel special and get completely comfortable. It doesn't have to be elaborate—a quick-dry manicure and pedicure can take just a few minutes. Or you can spend hours treating yourself to hair, makeup, the works."

Professional makeup artist and fashion consultant Gabriella Santorini says that many people are sorely disappointed with the results when they try to copy the styles of their favorite models. Santorini knows of many people who've had nervous breakdowns because they were unsuccessful in trying to look like a Claudia Schiffer or Christy Turlington. "It's sad," she says. "Women and men watch a stupid infomercial and become convinced that they can look like a supermodel if they buy some new skin or hair product. What a bunch of crap. I've worked in this business for many years and the only way to do it is by being happy with who you are first. Then it's easy to start to look beautiful. Everybody has certain characteristics that are appealing and that can be brought out to make them look good, no matter how fat or thin they are. The best way to start is by looking at yourself in the mirror very carefully and being thankful for who you are."

Santorini has done makeup for many models over the years and believes that looking good is mostly spiritual. The proper frame of mind is essential. "It's important not to change your look in a rush," she says. "A makeover should be done gradually. One day you can work on your tan, the next day on the eyebrows, and another day on your lips. If you do it all at once, you may not like the new product and it'll be too late to change it for that evening's occasion."

According to Santorini, most good models use their natural beauty first and foremost. "False nails, false eyelashes, they're all obsolete," she insists. "Good models don't need any of that. If they color their hair, it's usually just a touch, giving it a more artistic and distinguished look."

Since 1997, Tracey Walker has been the most featured model on the Internet. Walker, who struggled for years trying to make a name for herself as a regular model, found a forum online. She promotes her career and shares beauty secrets and modeling tips. Now in her mid-thirties, Walker says that a natural diet is the key to staying young. On her website, Walker lists the ten most important steps for looking young and fit. All of her steps stress natural maintenance. "Drink lots of water . . . water helps to keep the moisture in your skin," Walker says. "Forget about tanning booths. As an avid beach bum in the summer, I use the highest SPF sunscreen I can find. In the winter months, I give my skin a rest. Minerals are important. Take natural mineral supplements daily."

Fashion makeover artist Autumn Wheeler agrees with Walker's recipe for good looks. "When you pick up fashion magazines, a lot of the times the models look awful. It's easy to tell when they're not using good, natural makeup. It takes a toll and it starts to show on their skin. Some models should take their jobs more seriously and cut down on the late night activity and replace it with exercise and good natural care. It will help them avoid appearing on the pages of *Vogue* and *Bazaar* not looking their best."

CHAPTER 30

• • •

Niki Taylor Tragedy

To the public, being a supermodel appears to be the ultimate life—fame, fortune, and invitations to the best parties. Incredibly, most of the models I met during the course of my investigation led lives defined by insecurity and bad habits. Once they become famous, it's not hard to become depressed and fall over the edge.

Supermodel Niki Taylor is a good example. Taylor once appeared in six different magazine covers in a single month. Now a spokeswoman for Cover Girl cosmetics, Taylor earns more than $5 million a year. Yet her road to superstardom has been fraught with challenge and tragedy. A paragon of patience and a devoted parent, Niki's nightmarish experiences have colored her reactions to everything and everyone around her, often driving her to severe anxiety. Skewed by paranoid perceptions of her friends' hidden motivations and a poor self-image, Taylor's stomach would often knot as she watched people close to her doing drugs and carrying on, certain that the end result would spell disaster. Despite vowing that fame would not disrupt her life, when she became well-known in the mid-nineties, her worst fears materialized. Her life became entangled in booze, tragedy, and deception.

For years, Taylor has struggled to come to terms with the tragic death of her younger sister Krissy, also a top supermodel, who died at age seventeen in 1995. Niki found Krissy lying unconscious on the floor of her home. Both the media and people close to Krissy suggested that drugs and alcohol had been involved. Yet doctors and the Taylor family insist to this day that Krissy died of asthma and an undetected heart condition. For Niki, things just kept going downhill after Krissy's untimely demise, culminating with a massive car crash that almost claimed her life as well.

In May 2001, Niki Taylor was in critical condition with internal injuries after being a passenger in a car that crashed into a utility pole in Atlanta. The car's driver had lost control on a curvy road. Taylor, who had been wearing a seat belt, was not thrown from the car but went into shock and developed unbearable stomach pains. Taylor underwent several hours of surgery and remained in critical condition for days, with severe liver and abdominal injuries. The car's driver, Chad Renegar, and another passenger suffered only minor injuries. Renegar insisted that no drugs or alcohol were involved. He said he looked down to answer his cell phone and ran off the road.

"For just a moment, I was distracted by something that was not part of what I should've been doing at the moment, which was driving," Renegar, twenty-seven, said in an ABC-TV interview. "The result of that has changed the lives of three people and their families. Think about things like that. There's nothing on that phone that can be nearly as important as what's going on in front of you."

Taylor, the mother of twin six-year-old boys, appeared on the cover of *Seventeen* magazine when she was only fourteen. She has been a regular in ads for Liz Claiborne fashions and Cover Girl cosmetics, and was featured in a *Sports Illustrated* swimsuit issue.

As her modeling career progressed, people close to Taylor sensed a real potential for trouble. Many of Niki's friends thought she had become too self-absorbed, and had allowed the men in her life too much latitude. Her ex-husband, football player Matt Martinez, was overly possessive of her and occasionally resorted to fisticuffs with men who tried to charm his gorgeous wife. "Matt's basically a great guy, but he's a jealous type," says one of Taylor's close friends. "It drove Niki nuts. In the end, she couldn't put up with it anymore. She couldn't go out in public without feeling that Matt was scrutinizing every move she made. It destroyed their marriage."

After Martinez, Taylor dated notorious nightclub impresario and alleged mobster Chris Paciello. Paciello, who owned the South Beach hotspot Liquid, started dating Taylor in 1996. He made romantic overtures to Taylor while she was still married to Martinez. Once the marriage ended, Paciello, considered one of Miami's most eligible bachelors, swept Taylor off her feet. He wined and dined her, giving her expensive presents and taking her on trips all over the world. Paciello, whose real name is Ludwigsen, was good pals with Madonna and has been linked romantically to Daisy Fuentes and Jennifer Lopez.

Paciello was never up front with Taylor or his other celebrity lovers about his murky past. Authorities later alleged that he participated in the murder of a Staten Island housewife during a botched 1993 robbery. Paciello was then a vital cog of the dangerous, bloody Bath Avenue Crew. On December 1, 1999, Paciello's cover was finally blown. He was incarcerated along with eight other alleged members of the notorious Bonanno crime family in a sweeping racketeering indictment. Prosecutors charged Paciello with laundering mob money through his Liquid nightclub. A month later, Taylor's name emerged in the Paciello scandal.

Prosecutors called upon Taylor to explain the $10,000 in cash Paciello had given her, money that she'd carried with her on a trip to New York. When Taylor found out that she would have to testify, she feared for both her personal safety and career. The last thing she needed was to be dragged into Paciello's slimy affairs. Afraid for her life, Taylor traveled to New York with bodyguards and under tight security provided by U.S. federal marshals. She agreed to testify voluntarily rather than under a court subpoena. "The whole thing turned Niki into a complete nervous wreck," says a friend. "I [have] never seen Niki so worried. It was almost as if she was being put on trial. She desperately tried to keep the whole thing quiet. She wasn't proud of her past association with Paciello. The first time I saw Niki with Paciello, I tried to tell her he was only trouble. But she wouldn't listen. She seemed to get off on the excitement of being with him because he was sexy and the most powerful nightclub owner in Miami. Niki told me that there was never a dull moment when she was with Paciello."

In New York, Taylor admitted to receiving the cash. She claimed that she spent at least $9,000 of it on a shopping spree at Barney's. She never suspected that the money might be dirty. She told prosecutors that she hadn't been with Paciello for more than two years and had lost contact with him.

Although Taylor managed to emerge from the Paciello scandal relatively unscathed, it seems that every time she rebounds from a tragedy and her star is again on the rise, something dramatic happens. Taylor's fellow models are stunned by what they perceive as her constant misfortune. "Even when her prospects look good, you don't know what will happen next in her life," says journalist Martin Smith. "I know many supermodels who say that they believe that

Taylor is cursed. At only twenty-six years old, she's already made many stunning comebacks. Sadly, one must wonder if her luck will one day run out. Perhaps the best thing for her to do would be to find something else to do in life, something that will fulfill her while keeping her and her twin boys safe. The worst thing that could happen would be for those boys to grow up without a mother. Niki's got to realize that and be more selective [about] who she hangs out with."

Despite her personal woes, Niki Taylor assumes a commendable role in fashion history. She is considered by many to be the heir to Cindy Crawford as America's most popular model. Yet it is still difficult, even for those who know her intimately, to apprehend the dark hole from which she repeatedly emerges. Moreover, every time Taylor puts another negative episode behind her, another one crops up. Taylor has tried everything from psychological counseling to various spiritual exercises, but unfortunately, the end result is always devastation.

"I pray every day that she will be able to live in peace," a friend of Taylor's says. "She's a great person. For the life of me, I can't figure out why so many bad things happen to her. It's not as if someone's out to get her and make her life bad. Everybody loves Niki. Maybe she should pack up and move from Florida to somewhere where she can make a fresh start. There are too many haunting memories for her in Florida. I don't think it's healthy for her and her boys to stay where so many sad things happened to her. Niki's still young, so she should try to do whatever she can to stabilize her life."

CHAPTER 31

• • •

Skin Deep

Like Niki Taylor, Naomi Campbell has also had a consistently turbulent career. Recently, Campbell has made more headlines for her erratic behavior than she has for her modeling. Campbell, however, is justified in blowing her top. Breaking the racial barrier in a lily white industry has been an uphill battle.

On one frustrating occasion, Campbell was waiting backstage at a Gianni Versace fashion show, reading an issue of *Vanity Fair* when suddenly her best friend, Kate Moss, breezed past, followed by crews from MTV and the *Today Show*. Both crews hung on Moss's every word, cameras focusing on her every move. Moss caught Campbell's crestfallen look and sprung into action. Apparently, the camera crews were not interested in Campbell that day because she had recently been featured on another network. But in the modeling business, it is pretty much an unwritten rule to give less attention to non-white models. After all, the majority of fashion magazines cater to an affluent, white demographic. Moss was disgusted with the attitudes of the cameramen and threatened never to cooperate with them again. "It's people like you who create tension in this world," Moss told the crews. "Get out of my face or I'll have security show you the way out."

From the day Naomi Campbell began modeling in her early teens, she has always tried not to be offended by the homogeniety of the white fashion world. She has dealt with the racism of the industry with strength, grace, and perseverance. She is bright, articulate, and charming. She is a black beauty in a white woman's world. There were times when her fellow models refused to sit with her on a plane or share a bedroom with her. Nonetheless, Campbell has maintained her composure and held her head high. She has rarely spoken publicly about the ignorance she's had to contend with every day of her career. "Naomi is the Jackie Robinson of modeling," legendary fashion designer Gianni Versace once said. "She's great at what she does, and always takes the knocks without fighting back so she can open the door for other black models. Any black model who has a job today should thank Naomi."

Campbell, born in 1970, grew up in Streatham, South London. She was raised by her mother Valerie, who was a well-respected model and dancer herself in the 1960s and 1970s. Valerie Campbell knew from the beginning that her stunning young daughter was destined to follow a career in showbiz. She worked hard to earn enough money to send Naomi to dance school and to the internationally acclaimed Italia Conti stage school. "Naomi was interested in the arts ever since she was a little girl," Valerie Campbell recalls. "She was enamored with the London theater scene and she dreamt of being an actress when she grew up. She had a lot of talent and drive, and as a parent I wanted to help her realize her dreams. The entertainment business is very tough, but if anybody was going to make it to the top, it was going to be Naomi. She has always remained very focused on achieving her dreams."

Campbell got her big break just by walking down the streets of London's Covent Garden, where she was discovered by Elite's Beth Boldt. As a teenager, Campbell often hung around the London theater district, trying to catch a glimpse of celebrities. She used to gaze at the marquees of the theaters and fantasize that her name would one day be up there. Elite model Beth Boldt says she knew that she had discovered a star the moment she first caught a glimpse of Campbell. "I was walking in the street and I saw this girl who had an amazing and unique look," Boldt recalls. "I followed her to see how she moved and walked and then I went up to her and asked her if she wanted to be a model. She said yes, and that was it. I was impressed not only by her looks, but because she was so polite and smart. As an agent you discover so many girls whose careers don't go too far. It's hard to predict who will be successful because it's such a cutthroat business. But I knew right away that Naomi was going to be a superstar."

In 1980, Campbell made history when she became the first black model to appear on the cover of *French Vogue*. At first, *Vogue*'s editorial staff was reluctant to put Campbell on the cover in fear that it might offend some of its loyal readers. After a huge debate, the editors decided to put Campbell on the cover, hoping it would create a stir and boost sales. "A lot of people were against having Naomi's face on the cover," said a *French Vogue* editor. "There was some pressure put on by the head office in New York, because they wanted it to be sort of a test run to see how the public would react. Finally, we decided to go with Naomi. It was one of the smartest moves ever. The issue dumped off the stands instantly. Naomi became the toast of the fashion world. If not for that historical cover, you probably wouldn't see as many black models out there as you do today. Naomi opened the door. Suddenly, blacks and other visible minorities were attracting interest in an industry that, up until that point, had been about 99.9 percent dominated by whites."

Soon after, every major fashion magazine came knocking on Campbell's door. In short order, Naomi appeared on the covers of *British Elle*, and *American Vogue*, and was photographed by legendary fashion photographer Steven Meisel. Campbell was widely regarded as the hottest commodity in the modeling business and considered to be one of the top three supermodels in the world. "It happened so fast," says fashion journalist Nelson Ethier. "Naomi went from rags to riches in such a short period of time. Sure there were a couple of black models before her who made some noise, like Iman, but none of them really broke through and created opportunity for other blacks the way Naomi did."

Naomi enjoyed the adulation and fan support usually only given to rock stars and royalty. She not only broke through racial barriers, but she wore some of the most daring and provocative outfits ever seen on the catwalk. Nobody in the twentieth century revolutionized modeling more than Naomi Campbell.

The media descended on Campbell's personal life shortly after she rose to fame. She became a favorite target of the tabloids. All kinds of wild stories about her private life emerged in print and on TV. The public craved every detail of her love affairs with famous men like ex-heavyweight champ Mike Tyson, actor Robert De Niro, and U2's Adam Clayton—and the media delivered. Cameramen kept 24-hour Naomi vigils in order to get the scoop. "Reporters would camp out on the street where she lived and wait for her to come out," says tabloid reporter Bert MacFarlane. "It was a media frenzy. Naomi didn't try to hide anything. She was very open about what she was up to. You would see guys like De Niro coming out of her flat at five in the morning. It was a tabloid reporter's dream. Naomi was great at playing up to the cameras. Even when she would be caught in embarrassing situations, she played up to the cameras. In the beginning of her career she was the delight of the media. Whenever reporters were assigned to cover her, we knew it wouldn't be difficult to get a story. Something was always going on with her."

Campbell plays the press like a virtuoso, making the kind of provocative statements that are certain to keep her in the public eye. But she usually avoids answering questions about the color of her skin. One of the most hotly debated topics has been whether Campbell likes to date white men. A reporter from the British tabloid *News of the World* once harped on that subject at a press conference in New York. Campbell's response brought down the house. "Have you ever slept with a black woman?" she asked the reporter, who happened to be a white male. "Who cares?" she continued, "We all come out of the same place."

Campbell reveled in the controversy. So long as the public and the press were debating the image she had so divinely crafted, she could only bask in the resulting publicity. "When I retire, people will respect me for all the abuse I've put up with," Campbell says. "Some of the greatest leaders, like Ghandi and Martin Luther King [Jr.], also put up with abuse and often had to hold their tongues. I'm fortunate 'cause at least I'm able to make a ton of cash while being abused."

Despite her tough exterior, Campbell is deeply shaken whenever she is kept off a magazine cover because of the color of her skin. She believes that she's lost millions of dollars in publicity because of the racist attitudes of editors at some of the world's leading fashion magazine's. "Most of them have never heard of the word 'integration,'" Campbell says. "You'd think that we were still living in the Deep South or in the old South Africa's apartheid."

In March 1998, Campbell came up with an idea for a *Harper's Bazaar* shoot in Cuba, and flew there with Kate Moss and photographer Patrick Demarchelier. The trip was a blast. The girls partied with Leonardo DiCaprio, a close friend of Moss, who showed up at the spur of the moment. DiCaprio treated the girls to expensive dinners and many bottles of champagne during his three-day stay.

According to Demarchelier, Campbell was assured that she would be on the cover of the magazine's May issue, and if not alone, then alongside Moss. A short time before the magazine hit the stands, Campbell found out otherwise. She was furious. "The pictures look great, and I'm always glad to see one of my close friends gracing the cover," Campbell said. "But after years in this business, I'd hoped to see more progress in ethnic diversity. Looking at the covers of most fashion magazines in the past year, I have to say that I'm disappointed in the limits of that progress. There are so many different types of beauty out there, and for all of people's good intentions, that doesn't always come across."

Unfortunately, this was not the first time Campbell was excluded from a cover because of her skin color. In 1996, the May issue of *Vogue* featured a gatefold double cover. Niki Taylor was featured on the front and Naomi was neatly tucked away inside. Originally, Campbell was supposed to be center stage, but one of the magazine's editors argued relentlessly that a Campbell cover would not sell as many copies because she's black.

Vogue editor-in-chief Anna Wintour spoke to the issue of discrimination in a Letter from the Editor in the July 1997 issue, which featured black model Kiara Kabukuru on the cover. Wintour, one of the most highly-profiled people in the business, admitted that racial barriers still exist in fashion. "The color of a cover model's skin (or hair for that matter) dramatically affects newsstand sales," she wrote. "Although it is rare for an issue of *Vogue* to go to the printer without one or more black models featured prominently inside, they appear less often than I, and many of you, would like on *Vogue*'s covers."

Naomi Campbell believes that the paucity of blacks on covers and runways is only the tip of the iceberg. Campbell learned from her close friend, legendary South African freedom fighter Nelson Mandela, that education and awareness are the keys to opening the door for disenfranchised minorities. "Oh, eventually they'll come around and start giving blacks and other visible minorities equal attention," Campbell says. "But the problem is much deeper. There are few black editors, designers, and agents. After our careers are over, we have nowhere to go, unlike white models who always manage to get work. They'll come around eventually," she whispers, transfixed, "don't let it be forgotten."

Still, many top magazine photographers and editors admit they would rather see a white model than a black model get a cover. "It only makes sense," says a former *Elle* magazine editor. "The people who are spending the big bucks that support the fashion industry are white. It's a fact. Blacks should create their own niche market by modeling exclusively in magazines set up for the black population, the way *Ebony* magazine became a voice for black artists. I'm not racist, but it's all a matter of economics. In life, it's not good to mix apples and oranges."

Attitudes like this have enraged academics from all over the world. "Until people drop the issue of the color of one's skin, we will always live in an unjust society," says South African sociologist Chengiah Ragaven. "In sports and entertainment, there is an underlying, subtle form of racism that needs to be addressed. They would rather have the faces of whites on posters and ads instead of blacks. That's only because they're not educated. Society needs faces of all origins to be represented. It's not fair to say that whites can relate to only whites and blacks to only blacks. Until these stereotypes are shattered, nothing will change. People will continue to deprive themselves of going forward."

Naomi Campbell's success paved the way for several other black supermodels, including Tyra Banks. Banks, who was discovered in Los Angeles as a skinny, leggy teenager, was immediately offered a one-year contract in Paris. She got into modeling to help support her family financially. Originally, Banks was turned down by five modeling agencies because they thought her walk was too awkward. "The sixth took me on," Banks says. "But said I could only do catwalk modeling because I wasn't pretty enough for photo shoots." Banks was scheduled to start college classes in film writing and directing when she got her big break. Her first gig was a magazine cover, and she went on to do twenty-five fashion shows that season, compared to the five or six that a lucky new model usually gets. "I was doing as many shows as the top girls," Banks says. "But they all had limos and I had to go everywhere on the Metro. I was exhausted. The only reason I carried on was that I didn't want my dad to bankrupt himself putting me through college."

Although she got more jobs than most other models, Banks says that she has always had to deal with the same recurring issue, the color of her skin. Banks learned right away that if she wanted to succeed at modeling, she would have to ignore the overt racism in the fashion business. "I might not get so many covers as a blond, blue-eyed girl would, but when I do get one, it is the equivalent of getting ten covers, because everyone notices."

The biggest challenge Banks has had to face throughout her career is the perpetual comparison drawn between her and Naomi Campbell. Wherever Banks goes, the media compares her to Campbell simply because they're both black. In July 1997, for example, Banks tripped and fell in New York while shooting an ad for Cover Girl cosmetics. Immediately, the media and fashion people exclaimed that "Tyra's done a Naomi," comparing Banks's fall to Campbell's famous gaffe when she toppled over on her high heels during a Vivienne Westwood fashion show. "If it was a white model who fell, nobody would have compared her to Naomi Campbell," says ethnic relations advisor Christopher Webster. "But because Tyra Banks is black, people couldn't resist drawing comparisons, even though they look completely different. Only uneducated people make this blunder. It's clear that people in the fashion industry are still very ignorant and should make an attempt to improve in the field of race relations. Many high profile areas in entertainment have made great strides over the years in race relations, including the film and music industries. But it's very clear that the fashion world still has a long way to go."

The constant media-inspired comparisons have created friction between the two supermodels. Campbell has gone out of her way to distance herself from Banks. She gets angry when magazine and newspaper articles compare them, or call Banks "a younger looking version of Naomi."

It was reported that Campbell once demanded that Banks be dropped from a Lagerfeld show because she didn't want the media to turn it into a competition between the two. Banks was outraged and fled Elite, the agency that both she and Campbell were under contract with. "Naomi has gotten very bitter when people start comparing Tyra Banks to her," says one of Campbell's former lovers. "She makes it a point to go out of her way to distance herself from Tyra. She feels it's so unjust, because the only reason they're being compared is because they're both black. I can't blame Naomi for feeling that way, especially because Tyra's still young and trying to become one of the top supermodels. There's no way she can be compared to Naomi at this point of her career. Naomi's a legend, one of the greatest supermodels ever."

Publicly, Banks refuses to comment on Campbell's notorious dislike of her. Privately, however, Banks is not thrilled about the way Campbell has treated her. According to a supermodel who has worked closely with her, Banks feels that Campbell has sometimes acted like a spoiled brat, bringing disrepute to the modeling industry. "Tyra is hurt by Naomi's attitude toward her," the supermodel says. "She can't figure out why Naomi has so much resentment. I can't blame her, because Tyra is not the type of person to piss people off. Everybody who has met her likes and respects her. Naomi is making a mistake by criticizing her. Maybe it's sour grapes because Tyra has crept up on her during the past few years and has been getting more prestigious shoots. Before, Naomi ruled. Now she has to make room for Tyra and other young black models."

Ever since the topic of race gave fashion editors something solid to fight about, minority members of the industry have united and built an ever-higher resistance to the white fashion machine. To understand the plight of visible minorities, it's essential to grasp how strongly some of the influential whites in the fashion business oppose integration. Like the members of most other elites, the people calling the shots in the modeling business are protective of their comfortable status. Until a recent illness curtailed his schedule, fashion designer Harold Taylor divided his time between London, Miami, and his $3 million mansion in southern California. Taylor is a designer of great scope and accomplishment, and is known as one of the most innovative independent designers in North America. Yet during his heyday in the mid-eighties, Taylor was not willing to employ non-white models. If model agents showed Taylor a composite card with the photo of a non-white model, he told them he wasn't interested. "I'm not racist, I'm just a businessman," Taylor explains. "I have many friends who are non-white. Anybody who is calling me racist is barking up the wrong tree. The fact is that my clothes cater to an upper scale white crowd. Why would I want to hire a black model? In any business you've got to know your market inside out. Why would I even consider using a black model when the people who buy my clothes are Caucasian? That's like advertising a soul food restaurant to a group of white businessman. It doesn't make any sense at all."

Sandra Boyd, a tall, black model from Florida, was once told by Taylor that she was "too lazy, like so many other colored people" after she tried to get him to hire her. Boyd threatened to sue for racial discrimination. "I didn't have enough money to launch a case. The lawyer's fees would have been too much. I wasn't making a lot of money then. I was devastated by what Mr. Taylor said. But I was used to being called much worse things. So many of the people in this industry are racist. They live as if it was still the 1800s."

Most shocking of all is that Taylor doesn't deny Boyd's story. "She was too persistent and wouldn't leave me alone," Taylor explains. "At first I politely told her that I wouldn't hire her. But she refused to take no for an answer. Then she got out of hand and started harassing me. I said some things that I regret saying, but I only said them because she wouldn't leave me alone and was becoming a big nuisance. But if she says I'm racist, that's slander, and I'll sue her because it's completely false. I might not hire black models, but I have so many black friends who can vouch that I'm anything but a racist."

The trend has begun to reverse to a certain extent, however, as new clothing lines like FUBU sportswear begin to span the racial divide. An insider at FUBU noted that the company owes its success to the fact that it has always positioned itself as a black company. They picked the name, an acronym of "For Us By Us," to make sure everyone knew that this was an enterprise created by and for members of the black community. Whites, Puerto Ricans, and people of other nationalities quickly caught on to the hiphop trend and launched FUBU's sales into the stratosphere. Soon after, the Willie Esco line, which also had its origins in a minority community—this time an Hispanic one—came to the fashion fore. Again, the innovative designs grabbed the attention of white America. Indeed, many minority groups, such as the Syrian Jewish community in the King's Highway area of Brooklyn, New York, are responsible for a large number of fashion enterprises throughout the world. Some people would be shocked to discover that the fashions they think originate with white Europeans and Americans really come from all these creative people in minority communities.

In the new millennium, fashion firms and advertising agencies should turn their attention toward minority models if they want to impact society, according to sociologist Edward Farr. "The concept of having to use a lily-white model is as dead as a doornail," Farr says. "This is one industry that has been slower than the rest of the world to integrate. But the trend is changing. People are finally taking notice of this and are boycotting the labels that continue to exclusively use white models. In the end, the people that are open to using models of all backgrounds will win, while the ones that try to remain white will eventually go out of business. Society is more educated today and [it's] not going to put up with these attitudes anymore."

CHAPTER 32

• • •

No Gettin' By

Supermodels deal with enormous pressure over the course of their careers—some handle it with poise, others with panic. In fact, many of the world's top supermodels have attempted suicide during the prime of their careers. According to psychologist Charles Braxton, it is common for almost 75 percent of the top supermodels to become chronically depressed and suicidal after the first few years of their careers. Braxton explains that this astonishing percentage stems from the fact that models' looks start to fade after a few years and they become worried about losing their jobs to younger models waiting in the wings. "The first couple of years of a supermodels' career is great," Braxton says. "They're treated like Hollywood royalty. But in the third and fourth years it starts to get difficult, because the magazines and designers start looking for fresh, young faces to replace them. This is not a business in which you can plan a lifetime career and expect to receive a gold watch for your service after twenty-five years. It's a business that forces you to wake up from the dream after only a few years and realize that you're too old to still be doing it. So many models have trouble dealing with this and wind up going over the edge."

Braxton says that a model's despair is heightened if she has done a lot of partying and philandering during her career. "If they've stayed out late every night and slept with all kinds of people, it makes it twice as hard for them," Braxton says.

Because one day, the models wake up to find that nobody wants to give them free cocaine anymore and that people don't look at them anymore as sex objects because they've earned a reputation as being cheap. I've seen it happen so many times. The models fall into a deep depression and often wind up . . . suicidal. The only way this will ever be prevented is if the models go into this business more prepared. They've got to be realistic and expect to last only three to four years if lucky. Then they should move on to other things in life like a new job or starting a family. Too many of them try to hang on at the end for their dear lives when in fact nobody wants to hire them anymore because they're too old. This is a young business. The designers want to hire people in their teens. Once you're in your mid-twenties, unless you're Cindy Crawford, it's all over. You've got to move on.

For Naomi Campbell, 1997 was a year of turmoil. While she was still one of the most successful supermodels, Campbell was sinking deeper and deeper into the heavy nightlife scene in New York, London, Paris, and Milan. She was depressed because she couldn't hold on to a man long enough to develop anything serious. Her string of lovers seemed interested only in having steamy, sexual relations with her. She drowned her disappointment in drinks and late night partying. It was around this time that Campbell fell out with many of the fashion people close to her, and earned a reputation for being a troublemaker. "Naomi has a lot of resentment because so many people have used her during her career," says one of Campbell's colleagues. "She didn't really know how to deal with it. So she rebelled and starting giving everybody attitude. By the mid-nineties it became very bad for her because she realized that wherever she went, men would try to con her into getting into bed with them. Naomi's always dreamt of meeting the right man. But she started to think that men were all bad and that her dream would never happen."

By the end of February of that year, Campbell had experienced the first of several mysterious illnesses that would afflict her. She was admitted to the Wellington Hospital in London after collapsing with what her spokesperson described as appendicitis. Campbell, then twenty-six, had been dining with her new boyfriend, Joaquin Cortes, the stunning Spanish flamenco dancer when she collapsed. Members of the media suggested Campbell was pregnant because she appeared to have gained several pounds during recent months. Campbell's illness forced her to miss several scheduled appearances, including London Fashion Week, a show in which she was supposed to have top billing. "Naomi was very distressed during this time," said one supermodel. "When I read the reports of her collapse being due to appendicitis, I knew it wasn't true and that there was much more to the story. I had seen her several days before and she looked terrible. She looked overweight, weak, and appeared to not have slept in a few days. I asked her if she felt alright and she hesitated to answer. I knew something was troubling her."

Campbell stayed out of the spotlight and rehabilitated for the next couple of months. According to several people close to her, she considered quitting the model business several times. "She was depressed and she needed to find some new meaning in her life," says a close friend. "I had never seen Naomi in such a bad state of mind. She seemed desperate." On June 15, 1997, the months of depression finally caught up to her. Campbell was vacationing with her boyfriend and some friends on the Canary Islands when, one day, friends noticed something was very wrong—Naomi was not waking up. She was rushed to a hospital, where doctors found a large quantity of barbiturates in her blood. Front-page headlines blared the news of what most perceived as a suicide attempt. After being discharged, Campbell left the hospital through a kitchen entrance to avoid being photographed by the dozens of photographers camped outside. She looked tired and extremely frail. A close friend of Naomi's recalls that she had never seen Naomi look as worried and disoriented. Naomi was driven to the airport, where a private jet flew her off the island and back to her London home.

A manager of the five-star Hotel Santa Catalina in Las Palmas, Spain, where Campbell and Cortes were staying, said that there had been a vicious argument between the couple in the hotel bar and that several of the other guests had complained. The Madrid daily *El Pais* reported that during the argument, Campbell lost control and threatened to kill herself. An Iberia Airlines pilot at the hotel, said he overheard Campbell saying she was going to kill herself. "They were arguing very loud," the hotel manager said. "Then they went up to Ms. Campbell's room and loud noises were heard. More complaints were phoned in to the front desk."

A doctor was called in the early hours of Sunday morning when somebody reported to the front desk that Campbell was "going to die if help didn't arrive soon." The doctor immediately called an ambulance, fearing that Campbell might have overdosed. The doctor confirmed that Campbell had indeed swallowed a large amount of barbiturates.

According to one of her close friends, Campbell had indeed threatened to commit suicide after an arguement with Cortes shortly before being rushed to the Nuestra Senora del Pino Hospital in Las

Palmas, Spain. Apparently Campbell had been deeply hurt several times during the previous month when Cortes made overt gestures toward other women. To make matters worse, a couple of weeks prior to the vacation, several magazines had run photos of Cortes getting cuddly with a voluptuous blonde in the southern Spanish resort town of Marbella. It was reported that he was having an affair with the woman. Finally, Cortes had infuriated Campbell earlier in the year after he was quoted in a newspaper saying that he dreamt of having twenty different children by twenty different women. "Naomi was head over heels in love with Joaquin," a close friend explained. "She had never been so fascinated by any man as she was by Joaquin. But the problem was that he didn't have the same feelings. He wanted his freedom and he wasn't willing to give up his lifestyle of having affairs with many beautiful women. Having Joaquin as a boyfriend was a woman's worst nightmare and I wasn't surprised how it devastated Naomi."

Campbell's handlers immediately tried to dispel the media's attempt to portray the incident as a suicide attempt. Johnathan Goldstein of Olswang, Campbell's solicitors in London, said shortly after the incident that reports of Campbell overdosing were completely untrue. He said that Campbell had suffered an allergic reaction to antibiotics. "Ms. Campbell is perfectly well and fully recovered and will be leaving [the] hospital later today," he said. "She wishes to make it clear that there is absolutely no foundation whatsoever to the story that she had taken an overdose."

Campbell, who said she took the holiday in the Canary Islands to "recuperate" before an assignment in Paris, issued a terse statement a couple of days later again denying that it was a suicide attempt. According to one of her close aides, she was pressured by her advisers to issue the denial. Naomi, however, admitted that she was severely depressed during this period and needed a break from modeling. "For several months before the accident in the Las Palmas, Naomi was in no condition to walk down the catwalk," explains entertainment author Esmond Choueke. "The people in her camp gave a lame excuse to try to cover it up. But by all accounts, there was much more to the situation. Her handlers did a poor job of ducking what really happened by saying it was an allergic reaction. The media's not stupid. We knew that the incident was drug related. Several people confirmed that Naomi might have been suicidal because she fell out with her boyfriend. Over the years I've seen many famous models try to cover up a bad incident. Some of them get away with it. But in Naomi's case it was obvious that there was so much more to the story. To this day, Naomi still tries to dodge [the question] when she's asked what happened that June night. Maybe we'll never find out, but I'll bet everything I own that it was more than an allergic reaction."

Joaquin Cortes refused to discuss the incident, but told a friend that he felt sorry about the situation because he had been leading Campbell on. "I'm responsible for this as much as anybody," Cortes said. "I've put Naomi through a lot recently and I shouldn't have done some of the things I did. I just wish it wouldn't have turned out like this."

Cortes visited Campbell in the hospital three hours after she was admitted. He was told to give her some time to calm down. He entered the hospital through a back door to avoid the hordes of paparazzi swarming around the main entrance. At Campbell's bedside, Cortes apologized to her profusely. He told her that he loved her and was extremely sorry for upsetting her.

Still, it had been a largely one-sided relationship since the couple met the previous year on a fashion shoot for *Elle* magazine. Campbell thought that Cortes was her prince charming, while Cortes still had a keen eye for other women. Shortly after she was released from the hospital Cortes ended the relationship. "Cortes was a big playboy and it was driving Naomi crazy," says journalist Peter Williamson. "After Naomi wound up in the hospital, he finally realized that it was time to be up front with her and break up. Naomi came close to dying that night, and if Cortes continued to lead her on, it might have killed her. He realized how fragile her feelings were and he didn't want to be responsible for what might happen to her if he continued to break her heart."

CHAPTER 33

● ● ●

Fashion Cafe Cataclysm

Models are constantly approached by overzealous entrepreneurs who want to cash in on their names in order to sell products. It can be very misleading. Models often get duped, promised remuneration they never receive because the projects they contribute to go belly-up. A good example is the Fashion Cafe. Originally intended to be fashion's answer to the Hard Rock Cafe, the Fashion Cafe is best remembered for being shut down due to a series of lawsuits.

Tensions between Christy Turlington and Fashion Cafe mogul Tomasso Buti had existed from the beginning. The two were brought together one night by troubles that befell Naomi Campbell. Campbell was to attend a Revlon opening at the Fashion Cafe, then schmooze with the 300 guests at the request of Buti. Although Buti was well aware of Campbell's depression and her battle with alcohol and drugs, he told the bartender to keep recharging her glass with double shots of Johnnie Walker whisky. Within an hour, Campbell was visibly drunk and barely able to stand. She stumbled into the tiny cloakroom just to the left of the cafe's entrance.

Turlington had agreed to lend her name to Buti's Fashion Cafe in 1995. Along with fellow models Claudia Schiffer, Naomi Campbell, and Elle Macpherson, she felt increasingly put off by Buti's way of doing business. Buti used his marriage to supermodel Daniela Pestova to help attract the top names in fashion to his business venture. Pestova was well respected by most people in the business. She had earned a reputation for being hardworking and unselfish. "Daniela Pestova is really a very sweet girl who cares a lot about other people," said a colleague. "It surprised everyone that she got involved with someone like Buti, who had a dubious reputation. But that's how it is in this business, gorgeous, innocent girls falling for seedy men who have money and power. Most of them end up regretting it."

Turlington, who was accompanied by a female friend, was planning to leave early. She had an early shoot the next morning for the Italian edition of *Vogue*. On her way out, she noticed Campbell bent over in the cloakroom, looking helpless. Turlington was heartsick at the site of her helpless colleague. Peter Svenson, a fashion marketing executive, was also getting his coat to leave. He helped Turlington comfort Campbell. The two stood to either side of Campbell. Turlington held back her friend's hair and spoke to her gently. Svenson stroked Campbell's back. He opened his coat with the other hand to shield them from view.

"This is all Buti's doing," Svenson told Turlington. "He tried to get Naomi smashed." It was common knowledge that Buti's favorite supermodel at the Fashion Cafe was Naomi Campbell. "I know that Buti likes to give models booze," Svenson said. "But this is the last straw."

This was yet another occasion for Turlington to defend a colleague, even if it meant jeopardizing her own career. Turlington's own life was peopled with playboys, hustlers, and socialites who had lured her into sex and drugs. She had barely recovered from her own brush with alcohol a year earlier. And a model friend of Turlington's had recently died of a drug overdose. Despite suspicions that an ex-boyfriend had deliberately tried to drug her friend, no charges were ever brought against him.

Several models approached Buti in front of stunned onlookers. One model grabbed his cigarette and put it out on his back. "I'm through with you and your enterprise, it ain't for me," she yelled, embarrassing Buti in front of his admiring clientele. "I'll make sure that everybody finds out the truth about you. I'm tired of pretending that everything is fine. This is one venture that I would like to forget. I'm going to go home and forget that I ever got involved in this whole thing."

Turlington was offended by the spin Buti put on her involvement in the Fashion Cafe. Buti lied to the media, claiming Turlington and the other three supermodels were major shareholders, while nothing could have been further from the truth. None of the supermodels owned any interest in the business. According to Turlington, the only money they had received were appearance fees for star-studded events and Fashion Cafe outlet openings all over the world.

"Christy never liked the way Buti constantly lied," revealed a close friend. "She thinks Buti is a total sleazebag. When she got involved in the project, she thought it was legit. But soon after, she regretted her decision. Christy is a woman of integrity, and she doesn't like to be around shady people. She had no idea what Buti was really like. She discovered that he was taking her and the other supermodels for fools. Even at the first press conference to promote the opening of the Fashion Cafe, Christy couldn't believe the words coming out of Buti's mouth. It was complete bull. He stood in front of dozens of reporters and lied to them about everything. After the press conference, Christy told me she wasn't sure about the whole thing anymore and thought Buti was a complete fraud."

Turlington, who became famous for her sexy Calvin Klein underwear ads, started to boycot Fashion Cafe openings after she realized that Buti was not being up front. After attending the Fashion Cafe opening in London, Turlington refused to appear at those in Jakarta and Barcelona.

Turlington's boyfriend, Jason Patric, was infuriated by the way Buti treated her. "It's so stupid to show up there and pretend that everything's alright," Patric told Turlington, according to a close friend of Turlington's. "The whole idea of the Fashion Cafe is ridiculous. It would have worked if somebody who knew what they were doing was in charge. But the way Buti and his people set it up is disastrous."

Jason Patric pressured Turlington to distance herself from Buti and the Fashion Cafe. When he finally convinced her to sever ties with Buti in 1998, Turlington wanted anything related to her removed from all of the Fashion Cafes, including all memorabilia. Turlington threatened legal action if Buti didn't comply. She demanded back the Calvin Klein bra and panties she had worn in an ad and donated to the Fashion Cafe's first location in New York's Rockefeller Center.

"Christy didn't want anything of hers in the Fashion Cafe anymore," says journalist Mark Stewart. "She was very upset by the way she was treated. Buti was afraid that Christy would expose him to the media if he didn't cooperate with her, so he didn't put up a fight. He gave her back everything with her name on it. If he hadn't, he knew he would have been sued, and if it ever went to court, he wouldn't have had a leg to stand on."

Shortly after Turlington broke away from the Fashion Cafe, two of the other supermodel "partners" followed suit. Claudia Schiffer and Naomi Campbell both bailed out after accusations of embezzlement and fraud surfaced around Buti. Campbell recalls the Fashion Cafe venture was one of her worst experiences. "I was used," she says. "In the future, I will be more selective about lending my name to new ventures."

Several lawsuits were launched against Buti for tax evasion, embezzlement, and the secret, unauthorized sale of Fashion Cafe shares to new investors. Buti's lawyers, from the prestigious firm of Pavia and Harcourt, had done all the legal work to get the Fashion Cafe concept off the ground. The firm was now suing Buti for not paying $413,000 in legal bills. Buti countered by saying that he wasn't satisfied with the firm's work and felt that he hadn't been adequately represented. "[Buti] always comes up with a new excuse to weasel his way out of paying his debts," said one of Buti's former advisers. "He's done a lot of harm to the fashion world by acting in such an unprofessional manner. People like him give this business a bad name."

To make matters worse for Buti, Rockefeller Center management started proceedings to evict the Fashion Cafe for neglecting to pay several months rent. A New York judge seized the Fashion Cafe's finances temporarily and appointed an independent monitor to assume complete control of the restaurant chain while the whole legal mess was being worked out. Buti hired well-known criminal lawyer Stanley Arkin to represent him. "Buti knew he was finished, but he hired Arkin because he wanted to avoid going to jail," says a person close to Buti. "There was no way he could get out of this one, even if he came up with the cash to pay off all the creditors. A lot of people wanted to see Buti get what he deserved because he had ripped off so many people in the past. There was no way they were going to let him get away with what he did."

The charges for embezzlement were the most serious. They were outlined in two separate lawsuits filed by investors against Buti, his brother Francesco, and the Fashion Cafe. The suits outlined charges that as much as ten million dollars had allegedly been siphoned from the Fashion Cafe chain. The lawsuits further charged that the money had been diverted into Swiss bank accounts. Luigi Palma filed one of the investors' suits against Buti. Palma claimed that Buti had embezzled millions to finance his expensive lifestyle, including a $25,000-a-month apartment in Manhattan's Olympic Towers, a luxury beach house in Southampton, New York, and a $2 million house in Miami. Buti's luxury cars, including two Porsches, a Ferrari, and three Mercedes Benzes, were worth more than $1.5 million combined.

An Irish investment group launched the other lawsuit against Buti. The Irish investors charged Buti with redirecting millions from the Fashion Cafes to other companies he controlled in order to fund his outlandish lifestyle.

According to Paul Tharp of the *New York Post*, Buti raised more than $15 million from numerous investors. Tharp claimed Buti got funds from Dublin-based investor group Tolsbury, Panama-based investment group Dilcomp, and from an investment group in Gibraltar, Rinwald Investments. Buti also received close to $5 million from private investors: Beverly Hills dentist Dr. Guido Brachetti, two prominent Roman businessmen, accountant Alfredo Chiarizia, construction executive Valerio Morabito, and of course, Florida investor Dr. Luigi Palma. The lawsuits claimed that Buti grossly exaggerated the Fashion Cafe profit projections with a promise that it would soon go public and be traded on Wall Street. Buti told the investors that the chain would soon be worth more than $120 million. Buti had the investors believing that they would each make between $14 million and $30 million profit in three years.

"Buti was such a good seller, it's surprising he didn't also try to sell them the George Washington Bridge," says Wall Street economic analyst Bert Hayward. "They must have been smoking something funny when they went for Buti's plan. How in the world can he have expected to show that much profit within the company's first three years? It just didn't add up. I have clients who are connected to the fashion industry. It takes time to make a buck, whether you're selling clothes or hamburgers. Something stank from the start and I'm surprised more people didn't catch on right away."

To understand the investors' naïveté at the beginning of the business venture, it's essential to consider the strength of Buti's business proposal. Many investors say they got involved in the Fashion Cafe only because Buti had put together a solid business plan that seemed destined for success. "I was doubtful, but his numbers added up," said one investor. "I never thought he was lying because he seemed so honest. I've been duped before but never this bad. He wined and dined us and presented figures that were irresistible. And there's no doubt that a lot of us, including myself, got involved because we started getting visions of all the gorgeous girls that would be around. Buti was married to a supermodel and he made it sound as if we could also be with a model if we got involved. In the end I was without a gorgeous girl and I lost a ton of cash which I'm still fighting to get back. I'll never do a deal again that quickly. It's my own fault."

The Fashion Cafe investors could have avoided being duped if they had done their homework. A notorious Italian playboy who claimed to be from a wealthy family, Buti was actually the son of a bottlecap manufacturer. According to *New York Magazine*, when Buti arrived in New York from his native Italy during the mid-1980s "he didn't have two pennies to rub together" and he had left behind more than fifty false checks that added up to more than 4 million lire, according to documents filed in Italian courts. He also left behind a reputation as an insatiable hustler. "He had a very shady past," says Italian journalist Pietro Gordini. "I was surprised to learn that he had raised so much money to start the Fashion Cafe. If he tried to do it in Italy, he wouldn't have raised nearly as much because his name was dirt and not many people wanted to do business with him."

Through a spokesperson, Buti denied to the *New York Post* that he had bounced checks. "Those were all paid, and that was ten years ago," he said. But a longtime friend says Buti was just trying to cover his tracks. "He bounced a lot of checks in Italy, I can guarantee you that," he says. "I still meet people when I go back home who want to cut off his head because they feel he took advantage of them. I'll always remain friends with him because we've been through so much together, but I would never trust him again, even if he comes clean. A guy like him can always turn back to his old tricks."

Giorgio Santambrogio, one of the owners of Next Modeling Agency who managed the career of Buti's wife Daniela Pestova, filed suit against Buti for stealing the Fashion Cafe name from his Milan restaurant that was established twenty years ago. Santambrogio said in federal court that Buti uses models to make money, and that models only appeared at the Fashion Cafe when they were paid to do so at high profile events. Santambrogio accused Buti of conducting business "with unclean hands . . . he lies, because he says models are there and nobody is there. . . . There are no models there."

Buti's lawyer didn't deny Samtambrogio's claims. "No one says that Claudia Schiffer eats a hamburger there every week," lawyer Judd Burstein told the *New York Post*'s Paul Tharp. "How many times do you see Arnold Schwarzenegger chowing down in Planet Hollywood, or Wayne Gretzky in All-Star Cafe? The models play a role in the business in terms of concept." Burstein told Tharp that it would be impossible to find out whether or not Santambrogio's story was true because "he committed suicide two weeks ago." But when Tharp contacted Santambrogio's lawyer David Jaroslawicz and asked him if the suicide story was true, Jaroslawicz replied, "Nonsense. I just talked to him yesterday, and unless that was an imposter, Giorgio is alive and well. He'd never commit suicide."

The flurry of lawsuits didn't seem to hinder Buti's lavish lifestyle. For his thirty-first birthday, Buti threw himself a star-studded party at the exclusive New York nightclub Nell's. The party, which was attended by supermodels Eva Herzigova, Naomi Campbell, and Ivana Trump, cost Buti more than $20,000. Many of his creditors were furious after details of the party were reported the next day in several New York papers. "I had spoken to him a few days before the party and he was begging for more time to repay me, claiming he was flat broke," says one Fashion Cafe creditor. "Then, a few days later, I find myself reading about how much money he was throwing around at his birthday party. It made me sick. I immediately phoned my lawyer and told him to start legal proceedings."

The Fashion Cafe's creditors look back at the entire experience as the worst investment they ever made. One major creditor admits that he still hasn't recovered financially. "There's a lot of things that I could have done with my money," he says. "When I invested in the Fashion Cafe, it was like kissing it goodbye. If I had any idea that was going to happen, I would have preferred just giving it to a homeless shelter or to some underprivileged group. I have learned one big lesson about the fashion industry—most of the people are phonies who are more interested in getting laid than getting paid. Before I got involved, one of my daughters wanted to become a model. I was trying to help her hook up with an agency. Since then I've convinced her to go to college and get a proper education. I've seen so many young models end up with nothing after a few years in the business. It's terrible."

The hundreds of disgruntled Fashion Cafe creditors ran the gamut of companies, and included G.A.F. Feelig, the company that supplied Fashion Cafe with milk. G.A.F. Feelig claimed that they hadn't been paid in months and that Buti owed them more than $8,700. The company's lawyer Michael Shanker confirmed that G.A.F. Feelig stopped delivering milk because of the unpaid bills. "We're pursuing them for collection," Shanker said. "The milk well has run dry." A staff member at Fashion Cafe says that by early 1998, many of the restaurant's suppliers stopped delivering. When word got out that

Buti had racked up hundreds of thousands of dollars of debts, few suppliers continued doing business with him.

Meanwhile, Buti's marriage to supermodel Daniela Pestova was on the rocks. Pestova was furious with Buti for not telling her about the true state of his finances. Journalist Johanna Berkman of *New York Magazine* reported that Buti made loan payments of $480,000 to Pestova in the name of the Fashion Cafe and another $700,000 to Daniela Pestova Entertainment, a company Buti set up as a front. Berkman found out that Pestova had no knowledge about the deals. While interviewing Pestova and Buti, Berkman seized an opportunity to ask Pestova about the transactions while Buti was called away from the table for a phone call. "What loans?" Pestova said, with shock written all over her face. "I didn't know about that. It's interesting you say that."

A week later Buti and Pestova announced their separation. Pestova told a friend that if it weren't for their young son, she would have sought a divorce. "Daniela's a very family-oriented person and she wanted her son to grow up around his father," the friend said. "But there's no doubt that she was having second thoughts. Some of the stunts her husband pulled disgusted her, and made her consider leaving him on many occasions."

Fashion Cafe creditors decided the only way to save the restaurant was to force Buti to resign. After much legal wrangling, and at the urging of a New York judge, Buti agreed. "Once Buti was out, there was a whole new push to save the cafe," said a Fashion Cafe floor manager. "Everybody from the waiters to the person who washes the floor had a new sense of hope. Getting rid of Buti was the only way we had of surviving. If he had stayed on, the Fashion Cafe would be doomed."

Even Buti's casual acquaintances didn't believe that he had the right stuff to become a success in the fashion industry. More than a dozen people close to Buti agreed to be interviewed for this book. They all agreed that Buti had been far more interested in associating with beautiful women and partying than in running a successful enterprise. "The idea of the Fashion Cafe was brilliant, but you had the wrong person in charge," said a close colleague. If Tommaso [Buti] had taken more pride in the actual business and been more honest with people, he would have succeeded. But he went into the whole thing with the idea that he would mislead people and hope to make it up to them when the cafe was successful. He was dreaming. Word quickly spread that he was crooked. It cost him his reputation. He basically killed himself."

Even New York billionaire Donald Trump managed to be bamboozled by Tommaso Buti. In December 1998, Trump announced the formation of the Trump Management Group, with Buti as his partner. Trump and Buti snatched Elite's former top agent Annie Veltry to run the agency's day-to-day operations, a move that infuriated Elite boss John Casablancas. Buti elicited Trump's support by promising to steal top supermodels like his wife Daniela Pestova, Eva Herzigova, Stephanie Seymour, and many others away from other big agencies. When New York State Attorney General Eliot Spitzer subpoenaed Buti amid allegations of embezzlement, Trump terminated their relationship. "Unfortunately, Tommaso will not be involved with the Trump Management Group or Trump Models, Inc.," Trump told Jared Paul Stern of the *New York Post*. "Annie Veltry is the president of the company in formation." Buti quickly issued a statement saying that he volunteered his resignation: "In light of my recent problems, I have resigned from the agency. I sold my stock back to Donald. I wish he and Annie luck, and I'm sure they're going to do a great job."

The decision forced Trump to find a new location for his agency. Originally, he had planned to headquarter the agency next to Buti's office in a renovated warehouse that had once housed Andy Warhol's factory. "Donald was afraid of the consequences of working with Buti," says entertainment journalist Bert MacFarlane. "It was a smart move for Trump. Buti had burned all his bridges. Anybody who embarked on a new project with him was asking for trouble because Buti's time was mostly going to be spent fighting old lawsuits."

Harvey Broomberg is a bouncer-sized New Yorker in his late forties with a background in sales of high priced ladies garments. Over the years, Broomberg has crossed paths with many of the leading players in the fashion industry, including Ralph Lauren and Bill Blass. Broomberg's wife Katie was once a model scout for several top agencies. This plugged-in couple says that ventures like the Fashion Cafe that generate bad publicity leave a dark cloud over the entire fashion industry. The Broombergs admit that the few people with high moral standards and ethics who remain in fashion suffer the consequences of the actions of unscrupulous people like Tomasso Buti. "I've never seen a business in which there are so many liars and crooked people," Harvey Broomberg says. "People like Tomasso

Buti make it hard for the few honest people in this business to make a buck. It's reached the stage where if you're not crooked, it's almost impossible to be successful."

Harvey Broomberg claims that many people in fashion resort to false publicity, misleading the general public and basically robbing them blind. He says the only way things will change is if the media and public stand up and refuse to let fashion moguls get away with it. "Look at Buti," Broomberg says.

> He constantly stood in front of TV cameras and lied about how Naomi Campbell and the other three supermodels were part owners of his Fashion Cafe. People then went and spent lots of money there under false pretenses. The same is done in a more subtle way by fashion designers. I've met people who will model clothes for certain big name designers but admit privately that they wouldn't be caught wearing those clothes unless they were being paid huge sums to do so. To me, that's false advertising. It would be like paying Bill Clinton to do anti-sexual harassment ads when we all know what he does behind the scenes. The public deserves better, and shouldn't be subjected to so much deceit. It's reached the point where we don't know what to believe because so much of it out there is a load of crap.

Throughout a fashion career that has lasted many years, Katie Broomberg has often heard agents lie about a model's background. Details such as age, height, and weight are often altered to match the specifications sought for an assignment. "I knew one agent in New York who used to lie all the time," Broomberg says. "He would do anything to ensure that one of his models got hired for a job. He would arrange for them to shoot new photos that made them look heavier, thinner, taller, or smaller depending on the specifications of the assignment. A lot of these photos were digitally enhanced to make the model fit the exact specifications. Several times after this agent's models were hired, their employers would get enraged because the model who showed up at the studio looked vastly different in person from what they were promised. But there was nothing they could do. By that time it was already too late. It would cost too much to send everyone home and search for another model."

Harvey Broomberg blames the "sleazy people" in the fashion industry for being too impatient to earn an honest buck. He says that, like in any other industry, it takes time to build a solid business and handsome cash flow. "People get into the business on a shoestring budget and after a couple of months they start to panic," Broomberg says. "Then they're forced to resort to sleazy tactics in order to save themselves from drowning. Many of them begin to churn out big bucks and from then on they never turn back. But their lies and illegal activities usually come at the expense of a lot of innocent people." Broomberg tells the story of one perfume manufacturer who claimed his new fragrance was filled only with natural flowers from Holland. The scent of flowers was in fact the scent of chemicals from a factory in California, many of which were potentially harmful. The businessman sold a lot of perfume at the expense of many innocent people who bought it under false pretenses.

Some people in the fashion industry, however, refuse to take part in the crooked tactics of their colleagues, sometimes with less than favorable results. Fashion salesman Bill Lockwood's commitment to honesty has failed to win him any praise from his own bosses, and has gone unnoticed in the industry. According to Lockwood, even his own employer, Trust Designs, occasionally misleads retail stores to boost sales. For that reason, Lockwood refused to accept a position as vice president of Trust's West Coast division that was offered to him years ago. "I couldn't take it because I would have had to do some things that I strongly disagree with," Lockwood says. "By remaining in sales, I'm able to keep things clean. In sales your boss doesn't care how ethical you are, just as long as you make and exceed your quotas. My formula for success is to be up front with my customers. I don't care how many stories there are about people in this business who are crooked and make millions of dollars. The bottom line is that you've got to go home every night, look yourself in the mirror, and try to be happy with who you are. If you're dishonest, it becomes very difficult to live with yourself."

To avoid being associated with false advertising or negative publicity, many models are now beginning to be selective about who they work with and for. By taking a stand, and choosing to work only for ethical companies that share their values, the models themselves have begun to influence the entire industry. In recent years, several models refused contracts worth hundreds of thousands of dollars to endorse fur products, unhealthy foods, or products that are made by companies that run sweatshops. One model turned down a lucrative Nike swimwear contract after hearing reports that the company was operating sweatshops in third world countries. "I couldn't live with myself if I did that," she says. "How could anybody feel good about themselves making all that cash at the expense of thousands of exploited workers? It's immoral. I would rather make much less money modeling something that is more politically correct. At least then I could feel proud of what I was wearing."

CHAPTER 34

• • •

California Dreaming

Brenda Carmen is an ambitious woman. Starting out as a model in the late sixties, she now works as a model scout in California. Carmen maintains a long track record of finding new talent, yet she knows perfectly well that it would be easier for her to recruit young, beautiful faces if she made false promises to them the way her competitors do. Yet it has always been important to Carmen to be up front with everyone she deals with, no matter how much it affects her profit margins. "Making money is not difficult in any business," Carmen says, "but making money honestly is harder. In the end I'm able to live with myself better than people who are crooks. I have two young daughters and I want to be a role model for them. It's difficult to do that sometimes because I work in such a shady industry. I admit that the vast majority of people in this business are crooks. But the few who are honest keep integrity alive for the whole fashion industry. We don't make as much money as the other 90 percent, but our careers certainly last longer. The dishonest ones drop off like flies after only a few years. I like to remember that many of them wind up in jail or leave the business because they've built such a bad name that nobody wants to deal with them anymore."

While many of Carmen's colleagues resent her for speaking out against the sleaze, many of them appreciate her high moral standards. "If more people were like her, there wouldn't be such a large problem," says a top Paris designer. "I respect her for trying to make an honest living." The problem is that there are so many corrupt people in the fashion business, the best way to compete is to follow in their footsteps. Most of the time, it's the only way to compete for the high priced contracts.

Most models have grown tired of being used as pawns by the powerbrokers of the entertainment industry. In July 1999, just thirty minutes before supermodel Magali was to board a flight to Vancouver to start filming *Head Over Heels* with Shalom Harlow and Sara O'Hare, Magali decided the project wasn't for her and returned home. Although she had been hired to play the role of one of four model roommates to Monica Potter's art-restorer character, she suspected that she hadn't been hired for her acting skills and rejected the many bedroom scenes in the script. "She bailed out because there was no doubt that the producers were just trying to make money off the models' good looks. They weren't at all hired for their creative skills," said a member of the film crew. "Magali wanted to become a good actress and she realized that if she took this role people might not have taken her seriously as an actress in the future."

Film critic Juan Bernardo applauds Magali's decision. He points out that many models in the latter part of the nineties tried to make it in Hollywood and were unsuccessful. "They sell out their looks and it damages them in the long run," Bernardo says. "Look at people like Cindy Crawford and Claudia Schiffer. They've both appeared in several films and have received terrible reviews. They always play the same character. Their performances have been terrible. They make it difficult for models like Magali who are serious about acting and want to break into the business. I respect Magali's decision to quit *Head Over Heels*. She showed us that there are still some people left in the business who care more about artistic integrity than they do about prostituting themselves to make money."

Many models are encouraged to engage in dishonest activity from the earliest days of their careers. Shanna Shank, a *Glamour* magazine covergirl and star of a Comme des Garcons ad campaign, left Company Management for ID Models without any notice. Shortly thereafter, thirteen-year-old Megan Morris decided to abandon Elite Models without any advance warning. After being flown in by Elite for the finals of their Look of the Year contest, Morris stunned everybody at Elite by announcing she had signed with ID Models. "Nobody in our office could believe what had happened," says one Elite agent. "Morris shows up, is wined and dined like royalty, appears in the contest, and then announces that she's signed with the competition. Years ago, betrayals like this just didn't happen. Everybody stayed loyal to their agency for years, sometimes even for their entire career. It's become a vicious free-for-all today, and sadly, nobody wins in the end. We all wind up miserable and paranoid. That's the unfortunate state of the fashion industry today. People seem more interested in destroying its reputation than giving it a good name. In the end, everyone loses and many people end up bitter and jobless."

CHAPTER 35

• • •

Bad and Ugly

Jill Edwards was a model in the nineties who somehow managed to avoid falling into the drugs and alcohol trap of the fashion world. Nonetheless, Edwards did become a victim of her refusal to participate in the sexual escapades that were proposed to her by her agent. A stunning black 5 foot 11 inch tall Californian, should have had no trouble getting a job. But by the time she turned nineteen nobody wanted her anymore. Before long, Edwards was feeling like the world had caved in on her. One February day in 1998 she stood on top of the roof of her nine story apartment building and put a gun to her head. She would have pulled the trigger but the building's superintendent chose that moment to check out a tenant's complaint about footsteps on the roof. "There was nothing left worth living for," Edwards says.

I got blacklisted for standing up for my rights and I was left without a job. Nobody wanted to touch me. Word got out that I wasn't cooperative like the other models who did drugs and slept their way to the top. I got into this business for all the wrong reasons. I respected modeling as an art and I wanted to be the best model possible. I'd go home every night and study the nuances of some of the more famous models and I would stand in front of the mirror for hours trying to imitate them. But I quickly got a dose of reality. On my first modeling job when I was fifteen, the photographer tried to get me to do cocaine and one of the lighting assistants kept making passes at me. I went home crying that night. During the next few years I experienced dozens of similar incidents that were much worse. Men who work in the business have tried to rape me, slip drugs into my drinks and food, and offer me lots of money to have sex. Being a model has been the biggest nightmare one could ever imagine. I believe that half of the people in the business are rapists, drug dealers, and criminals. The things that go on in this business are unbelievable.

Toward the beginning of 1999, Edwards sought psychiatric help. Since then she has enrolled in a community college to study economics and says that she is starting to love life again. "The emotional scars of what I've accumulated might never go away," Edwards says. "But I no longer feel desperate and suicidal. As long as I stay away from modeling, I think I can lead a normal life. I've had a lot of hard experiences at such a young age, but I'm determined to put them behind me and go forward with my life. I know it won't be easy because it was just a short time ago that I almost blew my brains out on the roof of my apartment building. I advise any girl or guy models who feel the same way I did to leave the business immediately and to seek professional help. Otherwise, they'll probably wind up dead."

Edwards believes that the only way the modeling business will change is if people start to speak out about what's going on behind the scenes. Until supermodel Jenny Shimizu piped up about the problems in an interview in 1998 in *Giant Robot Magazine,* Edwards says she felt isolated from other models. "I've never been afraid to speak my mind," Edwards says. "Most of the models know what really goes on, but they act as if nothing ever happened. I was brought up to speak the truth. I approached a couple of fashion editors at newspapers with my story but they weren't interested at all. A lot of these people are good friends with the people who run the modeling business. The last thing they want to do is ruffle any feathers. I felt a sense of relief after Jenny Shimizu spoke up. She is one of the most credible supermodels. After she spoke up I started to get calls to talk about what happened in my career. Finally, people started to take notice of what the model business is really like."

Raised in Santa Maria, California, Jenny Shimizu was working as a motorcycle mechanic when she was discovered in a Los Angeles nightclub by a casting agent. Shimizu, who is of Japanese origin, wears a ring in her navel, has a tattoo on her right arm, and is the total opposite of the archetypal glamorous supermodel. Her modeling career took off quickly. In a matter of months she went from making just above minimum wage as a mechanic to making thousands of dollars in one day. Shimizu has been featured in leading fashion magazines, including *Vogue, Harper's Bazaar,* and *Elle.* She has also appeared on the catwalk in the latest fashion shows of the most well-known designers, including Versace and Jean-Paul Gaultier. But most of all, Shimizu gained publicity for being spotted in the company of several of Hollywood's leading stars, including Madonna. "Jenny Shimizu is a cinderella-type story," says fashion writer Terrance Young. "She went from rags to riches in a very short time. Her story is remarkable. She went from hanging around with greasy mechanics to being friends with Madonna. Soon after making it big, however, she realized that the modeling business was not what she thought it would be."

Shimizu is not one to boast about her career. Every model, she says, has a moment of truth and the only way they can rise to supremacy is by making lots of sacrifices. Each time she made loads of cash, Shimizu says it disappeared as fast as she made it. Shimizu says she's been cheated out of thousands of dollars by the people who handled her career. A string of bad experiences in New York made Shimizu realize that modeling wasn't right for her. In 1998, she quit the business, moved back to California, and started up a video production company called Pandemonium Productions. Shimizu recalls her last big shoot, when she was chosen to model for a Pirelli calendar. "I was paid $20,000 a day. It's a lot of money, and then a lot of money is taken from you by your agency. Especially when they are thieves. They still owe me. Don't let your daughters grow up to be models!"

From the time of her first photo shoot, Shimizu had doubts about being a supermodel. She was amazed at how much drugs and alcohol the models consumed before a fashion show. "Everybody gets real drunk, but the cocaine takes the edge off," Shimizu says. "There's a lot of fiasco. But it is amazing how girls can turn it on for that five minute appearance they're doing, and come back when the show's over and be just. . . . Like I said, the cocaine takes the edge off."

Shimizu was fortunate enough to live high off the hog in New York in a massive, two-story renovated loft with a big fireplace on Greenwich Street that overlooked the Hudson River. Most models who go to New York aren't as fortunate and often live in very cramped quarters. "I met a couple of girls in New York that had to live in those model apartments and it's just gross," Shimizu says. "First of all, they're paying extremely high rent because the agencies own the apartments. They have one phone, so they're fighting over it. It's really gross. It's not right to have so much self-obsession in one apartment. Five models and one mirror. Can you imagine? Cat fights. . . . Modeling is fun and all, but how many times can you talk about who's cute and how much cocaine you did that night? Basically all you need to say is, 'Johnny Depp, three grams, Johnny Depp, three grams, Johnny Depp, three grams,' for the rest of your life if you [are] modeling." Indeed, most nights models in these group apartments just sit around if they're not out partying. They put up each other's hair, try out new makeup, and rub creams and lotions into their skin. According to a resident of one such apartment, not much reading or intelligent conversation goes on.

After a couple of intense years in New York Shimizu decided to move back to the West Coast. She could no longer bear the crooked modeling world and wanted to live a more normal life. Shimizu claims she was ripped off by a mother and daughter con team that she met through modeling. "They robbed me," she says. "I kissed that goodbye. It was just to keep that bad energy out of my life. It was worth it, a small price to pay." She was also greatly disturbed by the constant pressure from her modeling agency to lose weight. She says it forced her to turn to drugs. "A special diet," Shimizu explains. "It's called being very unhappy and doing very unhappy things to yourself. You don't eat a lot when you're snorting. There was definitely a lot of partying."

Shimizu's departure was a big loss to the fashion world. She had become one of the most popular supermodels of the nineties because of her unique, masculine look. As 1998 drew to a close, modeling agencies posted their lowest profits in a decade. At the end of the first three quarter, profits were down more than 50 percent from the previous year. In large measure, it was due to the departure of well-known models like Jenny Shimizu and the longtime queen of the catwalk Christy Turlington, who decided to go back to school.

"These are two of the best models ever," remarks a New York supermodel. "They both got fed up with what goes on in this business and quit to do something more meaningful. I can't blame them. It sure put a dent into the whole concept of the supermodel. Things slowed down in the business immensely. Models weren't getting the exorbitant fees they once got. Agencies were folding and girls were forced to find jobs as waitresses while their agents tried to get them work. I think that all the bad things that have gone on . . . have finally caught up with some of the evil people in this business. I applaud girls like Jenny Shimizu for speaking up. Right now her harsh statements may have contributed to slowing down the business, but in the long run things will pick up again and people will be more aware of how to improve things because models like Shimizu weren't afraid to speak out."

CHAPTER 36

• • •

Selling Out

In a recent and bizarre trend, many models are becoming nothing more than highly paid hostesses. Outlandish sums are waved before the noses of young women and the agencies that represent them by wealthy Arab sheiks who invite the models, actresses, and wannabes to work as "hostesses" at their many gala events. The answer is ususally yes. And romantic relationships are not a deterrent—when the husbands and boyfriends of these women find out that their partners can make as much as $100,000 or more in one week, they often allow them to accept these indecent proposals.

According to one top model agent in New York, many of the modeling agencies are paid off to convince the girls to entertain the sheiks. The agency's commission can be up to ten times the amount the girls earn on a regular photo shoot. The agent says that during a single year he receives up to fifty requests for the services of his top models. He only considers the offers that are higher than six figures. I once earned a $40,000 commission, cash in my hand, for sending our top supermodel over," the agent admits.

If I would tell you who it was, you would be shocked because she's one of the most famous supermodels in the world. She received $120,000 cash in her hand for entertaining a wealthy Arab oil sheik for one week. She said it was the wildest experience she ever had and she admitted to me that she had sex with the sheik every night she was there. Several months later, after she had appeared in magazines like *Vogue* and *Harper's Bazaar,* she went back and was paid even more. . . . I've had wealthy businessmen from all over the world call me to try to engage the services of some of the models I represent. I check them out. I make sure they're legit and that they really have the cash before I even consider asking the model to go. I don't consider offers that are less than $100,000 up front. It's too risky and it's also a waste of time. I know so many agents who have been screwed because after they send the models the people who brought them there refuse to pay the full amount. I make sure that 50 percent of the money is handed over in cash up front and the other 50 percent is handed to the model when she arrives at the airport in the country she's visiting.

Once the models arrive the scene is often quite different from what they were told to expect. The women say they're never told that full sexual relations will be a part of their duties during their stay. They quickly learn the truth. Once their plane lands in the foreign country, they're taken to the most luxurious suites in the world. Hotel staff wait on them hand and foot. They're provided with hairdressers, manicurists, aestheticians, and masseurs who spoil them beyond their wildest dreams. They're also given fabulous clothing to wear. All during these first few days, most of the models think they have landed in heaven. But the fantasy is quickly exposed.

Next comes the unexpected "health inspection." In a humiliating visit to a gynecologist's office, the models are carefully examined for any signs of sexually transmitted diseases. This gives them an inkling as to what the following weeks will really hold. If they ever had any doubt that they were going to be used for sexual gratification, those doubts are soon vanquished.

Some of the women who've experienced this say they had panic-induced tremors as they waited for what they knew would unfold in the upcoming day or two. What had seemed like a joyful lark just a few weeks before now took on a terrifying seriousness. These women lie awake at night, isolated in a foreign country with nowhere to turn and nowhere to go, wondering about the boyfriends and husbands waiting for them in America. Some of them have never slept with another man; from time to time virgins are even sent on these trips as an added "prize."

As one supermodel reported upon her return from a hostessing job, "There were some girls who were giddy, excited, and happy about being there, and they didn't even care about the fact that they were going to have to service strange men. However, the bulk of us just felt sick about it. They had taken our passports and we weren't fooled. We knew there was no way we would be able to come and go as we pleased. We made a bargain with the devil and it was a bargain we were obliged to fulfill."

During their stay these women were given liberal amounts of alcohol and driven around in fancy limos to luxurious discos every night. Well-dressed men spent most of the night talking to each other, perusing the stock of women from time to time until they had decided which ones they wanted for the evening. Either an aide or the special guest himself approached the chosen woman and let her know who her partner would be that night. The discos were decorated with plush furniture, pristinely clean bars, mirrors, and fancy lighting fixtures—almost a parody of the fancy discos from the *Saturday Night Fever* era. The women recruits were dolled up to look beautiful, and the dresses they were given were low cut and styled to show off their voluptuous figures. Their makeup, hair, and nails were all done up to perfection. They sat around tables with each other trying to drink a little more than usual in order to hide their nervousness and anxiety. "In a strange, sick sense they wanted to be liked even though they knew they were just being bought," said one model.

The women smiled and talked to one another in an attempt to look as if they were enjoying themselves. To a stranger it might have looked like some upscale, high-class party in a European or American five star hotel. In fact, that was what everyone pretended it was. The deejay spun the discs, the booze flowed, and all the "real" action happened far away from curious eyes.

Occasionally the new couple would talk or dance for a few hours in order to get to know each other before being whisked off in a limousine to a fancy hotel suite where, in a gentle fashion, sex would begin. On occasion, some of the men were violent and bruised the women, who were then asked to stay an extra week to make sure the marks had vanished before they returned home. But, on the whole, the men just enjoyed having intercourse with the beautiful women they had recruited for their pleasure. The luckier women became the steady date of only one man during the course of a one- or two-week stay, providing that the man really liked her. "We knew that if we succeeded in pleasing that one man, he would likely bestow jewelry and other gifts on us and would treat us well during our stay," says model Greta Voelkner, who was recruited to visit Saudi Arabia on two occasions in 1997. "The women who were brighter played along with the game and pretended they really liked the man in return. But most of the women were simply passed around and ended up having intercourse with . . . three to six men during their stay—none of whom bestowed any gifts whatsoever."

The saddest stories involve the women who go to all these lengths to please their hosts and are never paid the money they were promised. Instead of receiving as much as $100,000 for a week of so-called partying, they might get cheated and receive an envelope with only $10,000 in it. Of course, there was no one to complain to. And even if there were, the women were too ashamed to admit what they had done.

"Many marriages fall apart back in America when the couples realize they can no longer look each other in the eye after this incident," according to one model. "Suddenly, the handfuls of money the women have acquired [becomes] worthless in the face of lost trust and lost intimacy. The reality is a nightmare, not a dream come true."

Model Jade Tarlowe could easily afford to go anywhere in the world. The nineteen-year-old model from Pennsylvania earns more than $100,000 a year doing photo shoots in America and abroad. When she was approached by her agent in April of 1999 to go on a cruise organized by a friend of the Sultan of Brunei, she couldn't refuse. Tarlowe had heard many ugly stories from other models about being rented by wealthy aristocrats, but she couldn't resist the $75,000 fee that was attached to the visit. Although her agent tried everything to keep Tarlowe from the same fate that befalls so many other models during similar excursions, when the ship set sail for the Mediterranean it became a one-week cruise to hell.

Tarlowe says she was put through a thorough health exam when she arrived on the ship and was forced to crop her pubic hair because it was deemed too long. She says that the Arab sheik who bought her services got her drunk the first night at the ship's bar, slipped a tranquilizer in her drink, and forced her to have sex with him and two other women. "I woke up the next day naked in his bed with a strange woman lying right beside me," Tarlowe recalls. "I had no recollection of the previous night. I realized what had happened and I felt like calling the police, but there was nothing I could do. I felt so disgusted that I considered jumping off the ship and drowning myself."

Tarlowe says that when she tried to confront the Arab sheik the next day, he didn't show any remorse. "He told me that I was naive to think that I came here just for a vacation," Tarlowe says. "He was a very smooth talker. He tried to convince me that it was an accident and that everything got out of hand because we were all drunk. For a few hours I believed him until he pulled the same trick the next night and dragged me to bed with him again. From then on I decided to just play his game and give him what he wanted because I wanted to get paid."

At the end of the trip Tarlowe says she was paid the full amount for her services. When she returned home she couldn't look her boyfriend in the eye. A couple of days later they broke up. "He didn't say anything, but it was easy to tell that he knew exactly what had happened," Tarlowe says. "Looking back, it was the weirdest experience I ever had. I don't regret it because it opened my mind up to the ridiculous extremes some people resort to in order to have sex with beautiful girls." Tarlowe says that if another opportunity comes up, she will seriously consider it. "I learned a lot [about] how to deal with these people and now I know how to read them," she explains. "I would only do it again if I was single at the time and if the money was over $100,000. Where else can you make this kind of money tax free in just a week?"

According to former London model agent Charles Lobo, there is a ready supply of female models—sweet, young teens as well as seasoned twenty-something beauties—who are more than willing to do whatever the wealthy Arab sheiks want. For the sheiks, Lobo says, nothing is quite as satisfying as sleeping with beautiful Western women who are the lovers of famous actors and rock stars. "They want these girls to be their sex slaves for the full week," Lobo says.

They'll pay any price you demand as long as the women are willing to play ball. I once sent three models to the exclusive summer retreat of one oil billionaire. They were all given over $50,000 cash for their services. When I approached them none of them had second thoughts. In fact, two of them left my office and went to Harrod's to buy the most expensive lingerie to make sure that they wouldn't let the wealthy oilman down. When they got there the girls had group sex with him and did everything he could ever dream of. They returned with no shame and lots of cash. Now I send three different girls four times a year to entertain the same man. He can't get enough of it, and I make more money off this contract than I would off any photo shoot for *Vogue* or *Elle*. In fact, this contract is worth over 60 percent of my business for the entire year. Not every story you hear about these trips to Arab countries is filled with horror. As long as the girls have an agent who knows what he's doing they'll be well protected. But any girl who goes there on the premise that it's just a fun vacation is out of their mind. Nobody pays anybody that kind of money to just go sit by the pool in a bikini and sip margaritas.

The exorbitant fees models receive to entertain wealthy Arabs has triggered a scramble among model agents all over the world. Charles Lobo was one of the first agents to rent out his supermodels when the trend became popular in 1985. Lobo says that when it all started, the fees ranged from $2,000 to $10,000.

It was a lot cheaper because it was a new thing to do and it happened at a time before all the big supemodels like Claudia Schiffer and Cindy Crawford arrived on the scene. It was tough for models to get work then and when they did it was not for anywhere near the kind of money they receive today. Models were desperate and had to find other jobs. Lots of them worked as strippers and hookers. So when the opportunity came up to make this kind of money and travel, very few girls passed it up. One model who was one of the first to go over to Saudi Arabia ended up making a career out of it. She quit my agency and made it her job to go there three to five times a year. She made way more cash doing that than she ever made walking down a runway. It's unbelievable how much the stakes have gone up. Some of the sheiks' representatives have offered me perks like expensive cars and luxurious trips if I supply them with my most beautiful models. It's become quite a racket.

In 1998, Renee Gore was an aspiring model in Paris who lived in a ten-dollar-a-day room and took a variety of jobs to help make ends meet and pay for her haut monde lifestyle. That was before a wealthy Arab businessman chose her picture out of a magazine. He liked her looks so he contacted her agent and offered her $40,000 to visit him for a week. It was an offer Gore couldn't refuse. Although she was engaged to her agent, who was many yaers her senior, she didn't refuse to sleep with the wealthy businessman who paid her to go to Saudi Arabia. "When I got back from the trip the engagement was off," Gore said. "I wanted my freedom because I wanted to go back to Saudi Arabia and make more money. My fiance wasn't angry because he was also my agent and he was happy with the commission I was bringing in. He represented top models who worked all the big fashion shows, but [I was] his top money earner . . . because of the arrangement I had in Saudi Arabia. I admit that it was a high level escort job or even prostitution if you choose to call it that, but after all those years of struggling to make a buck I didn't care . . . I was so happy because I was finally making the kind of money I've always dreamt of. When I have enough I'll return to being a model. But this time I'll be able to afford to pick and choose what jobs I take."

PART FIVE

• • •

Final Undercover

CHAPTER 37

● ● ●

Manhattan Mayflower

After my undercover investigation in L.A. came to a screeching halt—I sensed it was time to leave before I got found out—I flew to the world's most extraordinary fashion hotchpotch, New York City. New York lends a surreal aspect to fashion, and I reveled in the strangeness and excitement of the city. Having no particular place to be during the first two days, I wandered around the city aimlessly, as if in a dream. By the third day, things were starting to take shape.

It took several phone calls before I finally got through to well-known fashion photographer Roberto Dutesco. Dutesco, whose work has appeared in *Details, Vanity Fair,* and *Vogue,* specializes in lingerie and fashion photography. He had little to say about the fashion industry's underbelly. I told him I was a young model who wanted his expert opinion about the state of the fashion business. He didn't want to analyze or add to the surge of model stereotyping, considering how much bad publicity had already resulted from the controversial BBC exposé. Dutesco emphasized that a few bad apples could ruin the reputation of everyone else in the industry. "I don't think it's fair to prejudge others because of the ignorance of a few bad people," he said. "A lot of bad things . . . have happened for sure, but there's also a lot of great things going on. I prefer to focus on the positive."

Another photographer, Robert Lee, who does models' portfolios and headshots, agreed to meet with me at the piano bar of the elegant Mayflower Hotel on Central Park West. I told Lee that I was a model from Canada looking for work in New York. I asked him to meet me for drinks to discuss doing some photos and to get his opinion on the New York scene. Like Dutesco, Lee was tight-lipped. He refused to elaborate on the sleazy side of modeling. He told me that it was not in his best interest to do so. "If I speak out, it will be tough to get work with the agencies," Lee explained. "There's an unwritten rule in this business for photographers—not to talk about the bad things. I could tell you all kinds of crazy experiences I've had with famous models, but it would only give me a bad name."

Before he left, Lee did describe one very memorable experience. Behind the stage of a major 1999 New York fashion show, he witnessed two of the top models he had recently photographed hurling racial slurs at a Japanese model just minutes after strolling down the catwalk. They were angry because the Japanese model had refused to wear an outfit that she thought was too revealing. According to Lee, one of the models yelled out, "You dumb, prude, Jap shit." "For the first time in my career I felt like quitting," Lee said. "I felt betrayed because I had worked with these models and thought that they were decent people. They had no right to treat someone like that. The Japanese model didn't want to wear a certain piece of clothing because it wasn't her style. She's entitled to do that. Models have no right to mouth off like that no matter how famous they are."

After my meeting with Lee, I spent most of my time in the company of John Gavin, a former New York talent agent who didn't seem to mind befriending the models he had met during his fifteen year career. The forty-five-year-old Gavin, dressed in brown slacks and a red T-shirt, shared many stories about his wild experiences in the modeling business over beers at the Mayflower. "I've seen Naomi [Campbell] and Linda [Evangelista] at parties drunk as skunks," Gavin said. "I've seen older men cheat on their wives with models young enough to be their granddaughters. It's a wild and crazy business. I wouldn't let my daughters go anywhere near it."

Gavin blamed a lot of the sleaze associated with modeling on fashion designers. He described them as young people who live peripatetic lives and design everything to suit the needs of their generation, with no sense of moral accountability. "The best designers try to stay free of conventional expectations," Gavin said. "But often they get too carried away. So many of the clothes they design are just meant to shock and create controversy. It's gotten to the point of becoming offensive. The designers have to wake up and realize that the clothes they create can influence a whole new generation. They have to create with moral responsibility."

While Gavin may have made his name by being an agent with a code of ethics—he even carries around the Ten Commandments in his wallet—he regrets how often he's had to contend with disreputable agents and designers during his career. "I can count the good guys in this business on one hand," he said. "So many people I've dealt with over the years had some sort of hidden agenda. It's rare to meet people in this business who are completely up front. There's a fine line in this business between recklessness and responsibility."

Gavin claimed that the stories behind the modeling industry have all the elements of a Hollywood blockbuster. He predicted that unless things change soon, the modeling industry won't have much of a future. "Eventually someone will take the initiative, come in here and try to shut it all down," he said. "There are not many other businesses out there that have such crap going on. I think it's time to clean things up. Too many innocent people have been hurt."

Gavin gave me the names and numbers of several important contacts in the industry, including his close friend Jeremy Abitol, a retired fashion designer who is a walking encyclopedia of modeling. Abitol knows everything and everyone in the business. His added value is his knack for probing beneath the surface and trivialities. He considers his adventures akin to a fable of disintegration, appealing to the uninitiated because they reiterate a very deep cry for help. We met for dinner at New York's famous Carnegie Deli on Seventh Avenue at Fifty-fifth Street. Above the din of the dinner-theater crowd, Abitol described the changes that have rocked the modeling business during the past thirty years. His stories appeal to the uniniated who have no clue what really awaits them. "My experiences aren't of value to people who are already in the business," Abitol said. "They're of value to new models who entertain grandiose delusions. I've seen it all. This is a rough business. Over the years, I've seen so many people end up hurt and broke. When you pick up magazines like *Vogue* everything seems great. But that's just the small minority. The majority of people struggle in this business."

Abitol passionately promoted his opinions about the fashion industry. He complained about the way the business has changed. "In the sixties and seventies it was more artistic, more fun," he said. "Today, it's become totally commercial, totally insane. I used to like meeting people like Veruschka, Iman, and Cheryl Tiegs. They had lots of class and were intelligent people. It was easy to have a good conversation with them. The models out there today are way too young. They haven't experienced enough in life yet. It's ridiculous to watch a fifteen-year-old walk down the runway. They look lost and disoriented. Most of them don't even know why they're up there. This has got to stop before the public loses interest and the business goes kaput."

Abitol told me stories about his deceased wife, Ellen, a sexy and savvy Polish model he'd met after World War II. According to Abitol, Ellen cleverly manipulated the system by educating young models about the industry's evildoers. Abitol said that his wife quickly tired of the fashion world's backward attitudes toward women. "Ellen was a true pioneer, a true fighter for women's rights," Abitol said. "She devised a plan to make models aware of some of the perils of the business. She was like a mother to them. In those days, models were more accessible. They weren't bribed with drugs and money for sex. Sure, a lot of the men wanted to have sex with them, but they were a lot more casual about it. Today, many of the people running the industry behave like criminals. They do bad things to the models. The most shocking part of all is that these guilty people wake up each day without a care in the world while the young, innocent models wake up in terror."

Abitol said that if Ellen were alive today, she would be appalled by the way the industry has evolved. He described how vulgar and violent many modern models are when not overwhelmed by frustration or confronted by their own mortality. Abitol said today's models are a motley crew of screwed up teenage misfits. He was no kinder to model agents, saying that their stupid misdeeds make them thin, papery, and disposable. "Years ago models had class," Abitol said. "Today, they act like a bunch of animals. They party like there's no tomorrow. They make fools of themselves. Unfortunately, they have no choice but to act that way. The people running the business want them to behave like that. It's gone completely out of control."

Abitol, who designed clothes for Jacqueline Kennedy on at least three occasions, has devised a plot to turn the modeling business around. He wants agents to be required to get state licenses before they're allowed to operate. This will enable the government to throw the book at those who are corrupt. "It's the only way to return things to a bit of normalcy," Abitol said. "The government has got to step in and take action. Too many young people have gotten hurt, both mentally and physically. In order to give credibility back to the industry, rules have to be adhered to. The parents of the models desperately need something like this. Otherwise, they'll stop allowing their daughters to pursue modeling careers and the whole industry could go belly up."

CHAPTER 38

• • •

The Washington Square Beauty

I was sitting on a bench in Washington Square Park when model Kelly Davis—all six feet and 110 pounds of her—pulled up beside me. Davis had agreed to meet me at the urging of a mutual friend, John Decker, a freelance journalist who used to live in Davis's Greenwich Village apartment building. Davis was one of the most interesting models I met during my investigation. In 1998, she ended up homeless for close to six months after catapulting into a deep depression.

"It was sheer hell," Davis recalled. "I got completely fed up with the business. I was tired of all the parties, drugs, and one-night stands. I needed to escape, so I ended up becoming a street bum. It was the most important lesson of my life. It was also the most peaceful time I'd had in years. People don't realize how intelligent some of the street bums are. Many of them used to be rich and successful, and just fell out of sync with society." Davis told me how much she loves Washington Square, which is near the historic East Village neighborhood where Andy Warhol and Lou Reed brought hippiedom to the Electric Circus on St. Marks Place, and Jimi Hendrix's Electric Lady sound studio made its home. "Some of America's most brilliant minds and artists hung out here," Davis said. "Every time I come here I feel a certain special feeling. It's so relaxing and inspirational."

After lighting a cigarette, Davis began to describe her regrets about beginning a career in modeling. The idealistic Davis argues that if agents were forced to obtain state licenses, the abuse of models would end. Agents, she said, should be forced to register and pass

262

a qualifying test with their respective state. If there are complaints, the state should be able to intervene and decide on what action is necessary to take, such as suspending an agent's license. In fact, no one really knows what impact regulation would have on the welfare of models. In her opinion, it is not enough just to clamp down. "There are people who are still active in the industry who should be put behind bars," Davis said. "Until someone is singled out and charged, even the strictest regulations won't put an end to the abuse."

Davis, who now works as a waitress in Manhattan, painted a lurid portrait of the drug abuse so prevalent in the modeling industry. She admitted that she found herself in a whirlwind of drugs during the height of her career. "I spent a couple of crazy years in Milan before coming back to New York," Davis said. "I'd be lying to say that I was sober more than I was straight. In fact, I'd be surprised if I was sober more than 5 percent of the time. I was completely crazy. I did lots of cocaine, heroin, and drank scotch all day. I'm surprised I'm even alive."

In describing her wild drug use, Davis failed to disclose that she had attempted suicide several times. She also neglected to mention that she had once fainted on the catwalk during a Milan fashion show. Our mutual friend John Decker filled me in. He warned me that Davis would probably not want to reveal all the gory details. "Whatever Kelly tells you is true, but she'll probably leave out a few details," Decker said. "She's been through hell. She'll give you good stories about the modeling scene. Don't press her unless she feels like talking."

Davis recalled how she first got involved in modeling back in the mid-nineties. She described how, as a nice but rebellious fifteen-year-old from Long Island, New York, she wanted something cataclysmic to happen in her life. She had been approached by three separate agencies, all claiming that she had the "right look." At the time, she was anorexic, weighed ninety-eight pounds, and was receiving treatment at a center for eating disorders. "Looking back, I can't believe that so many people were interested in me," Davis said. "I was a complete mess, a total basket case. Instead of getting a model agent, I should have gone to a psychiatrist."

One of Davis's brightest memories was meeting supermodel Krissy Taylor back in 1994, a year before she was found dead on the floor of her Florida home by her sister, model Niki Taylor. Like Davis, Krissy Taylor began her modeling career at a young age.

When she died in July 1995 of a rare heart condition called right ventricular dysplasia, she was only seventeen. "I spotted her one afternoon on the terrace of a Greenwich Village cafe," Davis recalled. "I went up to her and started asking her for advice on the business. She told me that the key thing was to try and have fun and not take yourself too seriously. Her advice stuck. Krissy seemed more special than anyone I had ever met. She was very positive and down to earth. When she died a year later, I broke down and cried. All that I could think was how nice she was to me that day. Her death was a great loss to the world."

A year later in 1996, Davis hooked up with former New York agent Dan Bonifore. Shortly after they met, they became lovers and moved to Manhattan together. Bonifore was not the most reputable person in modeling. In 1988, he was arrested for beating up his ex-wife. By 1990, he was tens of thousands of dollars in debt and had to declare personal bankruptcy. "The combination of Dan's sexuality and intense intellect was hard to resist," Davis explained. "He was twenty years older than me, so I was able to draw from his experience. He was my sugar daddy. Dan made sure I always had cash and wore the most expensive clothes."

But shortly after their affair began, Davis lost her idealism about being involved with an older man. Bonifore was often verbally abusive, and frequently stayed out all night partying with other models. "He called me a slut and a whore," Davis said. "He tried to intimidate me so he would have complete power and control over me."

Acting on impulse, Davis packed her bags and headed to the airport, where she purchased a one-way ticket to Milan. "If I wouldn't have done that, I probably would not be alive today," Davis said. "I needed a change. In Milan I was able to start over. Nobody knew me there. At first I kept a very low profile. I was all business. I passed my portfolio around hoping to get work. But within a few weeks, I got caught up in the whole Milan scene and started hanging out in the bars. In many ways, Milan was much worse than New York. Everyone I met there seemed to be strung out on something. It was one big twenty-four-hour party over there. Dan Bonifore was a mouse compared to some of the sleazebags walking around Milan. If you don't play the game in Milan, nobody will work with you. You've got to go there under the assumption that you're going to party your ass off."

The one thing about Milan that bothered Davis more than anything else was how models seemed to go to any extreme to get work.

And she wasn't just referring to sex and drugs. Davis recounted a horrifying story about Martine, a fourteen-year-old model she befriended in Milan. Shortly after Martine's arrival, her agent told her that unless she trimmed down, she would not find work in Milan. Within a year, Martine had overdosed several times and had been admitted to the hospital four times. At one point, she was fighting for her life, receiving nourishment through an I.V. drip. According to Davis, Martine had become a dangerously emaciated young woman, which brought back memories of Davis's own bout with anorexia. "Her situation was worse than anything I've ever seen," Davis said. "Because she tried to lose weight, she ended up anorexic. The last time I saw her she looked like a skeleton. It was the scariest thing. I had been through a similar experience, but nowhere near as bad. I wasn't in denial. I was able to help myself. No matter what Martine tried, things just seemed to get worse."

Davis continued, saying that Martine was flown back to the U.S. by air ambulance for treatment and support from her family in South Carolina, and she hasn't been heard from since. "I hope she's still alive," Davis said. "I still get shivers down my spine every time I think of how she looked when I last saw her. It was frightening. Martine was my wake-up call. I knew that I would have to get out of the business soon. I had just seen too many crazy things."

Over the next few years, Davis's life did not improve much. Although she managed to get some work in Milan doing sports calendars, she could not seem to break into the major fashion magazines. She once embarrassed herself by fainting on the catwalk during a fashion show given by a designer friend. "I was drunk and high," Davis admitted. "It was an experience that I probably deserved. I was living it up a tad too much. I thought I was on top of the world."

That incident forced Davis to rethink her modeling career. Eager for a fresh start, she returned to New York. Since ex-boyfriend Bonifore had died in a car crash a year earlier, she no longer feared being abused by him.

Davis's first year back in the United States was not much easier than her Milan experience had been. She had trouble finding an apartment on her tight budget. Then, due to a minor recession that had hit the fashion industry, she had trouble finding modeling work at all. Nobody was hiring new models. "It was then that I completely lost myself," Davis said indignantly. "I felt worthless and just let myself go. I used to think that I'd always be able to find work, no matter what [happened]. It was a nightmare. I couldn't make a dime. I was like, 'Oh my god, how will I get money to buy bread and water?'"

Being unable to pay the rent and having to live on the street was a big eye-opener for Davis. She spent one bone chilling winter sleeping on benches in Central Park where she had plenty of time to think. "I was down-and-out," she recalled. "I learned a valuable lesson. Never get too cocky. One day you can be on top of the world, but the next you could be begging for your supper. If I could turn back time, I would do a few things differently. I would have had someone protecting my interests. I worked hard as a model but wound up with nothing in the end because I used my money to party instead of investing it properly."

After a jarring signal from her pager, Davis left to meet a friend. Our meeting had lasted more than two hours. At this point in my journey, I decided to abandon posing undercover to concentrate on getting the story-behind-the-story of the New York modeling scene. Davis's tale propelled my journalistic instinct. She told me to check out some of the city's trendiest clubs. "You'll always find models in the VIP sections of these clubs," she said. "If you go there, you'll witness all the sex and drugs firsthand."

CHAPTER 39

. . .

New York Club Chaos

Sitting in a roped-off VIP area, drinking champagne, and laughing with a group of young models sounds like a sweet way to relax on a Friday night. Yet this is not the case in New York's trendy nightclubs, where owners turn a blind eye to drugs, prostitution, and corruption.

I was sitting in the most exclusive area of Chaos, the popular East Houston Street nightclub frequented by many celebrities and wealthy trendsetters such as Madonna, Leonardo DiCaprio, and Gisele Bundchen. I was with a model friend, Hilary, who also works as a high class $500-an-hour prostitute to help make ends meet. Hilary—a 5-foot 10-inch blonde with a body that turns heads, knew the hulking bouncer, who looked like a cross between Shaquille O'Neal and Hulk Hogan. Hilary used her connections at Chaos to buy an eight ball—3.5 grams of cocaine—before turning on her pager in order to receive calls for her services. "Before I go meet someone at a hotel I like to be high," she told me. "It helps me get through the night. I spend about $150 a night on coke, not bad considering I earn about $3,000 a night. I come to Chaos before work because it's the place I'm most comfortable in."

Hilary introduced me to her dealer, a skinny white man around twenty-two who handed Hilary a tightly rolled foil package and a small lump of white powder to taste in full view of everyone on the VIP balcony. "It's pure stuff, the best," the dealer said as Hilary handed him $150. "You're one of my best customers. I give my good customers only the best."

Sitting at Chaos, one would never know that New York nightclubs have been the recent subjects of heavy crackdowns on drug use. Chaos seems to have weathered the setback—it was business as usual. The club owners did not seem to have learned a single lesson from all the negative publicity—except perhaps, that the drug trade is a good way to attract a clientele with deep pockets. In fact, I have never before seen as much coke and $100 bills passed around as openly in a nightclub as I did that night.

As I met more of Hilary's model friends, I became overwhelmed by the severity of the drug abuse problem associated with the profession. Sarah, a self-described model-stripper-prostitute, was surrounded by ten lanky models, all getting high. According to Hilary, Sarah hangs out at Chaos in order to recruit young models. "Her escort agency gives her a kickback for every beautiful model she brings in," Hilary said. "Escort agencies are starved for gorgeous, young faces in New York. Sarah makes good cash steering new blood into this lucrative business. I, for one, can say that I've made way more cash turning tricks than I ever made modeling."

According to one former club owner, the drug trade prevails in New York's high-end nightclubs because profits are ultimately dependent on it. Models and people in the fashion industry, he said, buy more drugs at clubs than any other group. "When you sit down and do the numbers, it's amazing what you come up with," said this former owner of a well-known Manhattan nightspot. "Cocaine, ecstasy, and other designer drugs bring in clientele. . . . Many of the biggest models have come in here to buy these drugs. They spend thousands and thousands of dollars. . . . People want to have access to drugs and feel comfortable. If you don't allow drugs then you might as well forget about getting the right clientele who can afford to buy $10 drinks."

Tony Theodore, one of Chaos's owners, was livid after *New York Post* undercover reporters saw Chaos management and security guards turn a blind eye as coke changed hands under their noses in the club's VIP section. The *Post* also reported that Chaos frequently turns away customers lacking celebrity connections, while the elite who were granted entry were never checked for drugs. "The policy of the club is absolute zero tolerance for any drug use or sale," Theodore told *Post* reporter Jessica Graham. "We have some very, very sharp-eyed managers in there."

For years, many a New York mayor has promised to completely eradicate drug use in nightclubs. Yet due to the allure and profit of cocaine, not one has been able to persuade club owners to keep dealers away. One-eyed nightclub boy wonder Peter Gatien has been the subject of more controversy than any other club owner. Gatien's Tunnel Club at Twelfth Avenue and Twenty-seventh Street has been the scene of countless drug-related incidents, illegal alcohol sales, and overdoses. Gatien—who also owns Limelight, another popular model hangout that is overrun by drugs—received even more bad publicity when sixteen-year-old Terrance Davis was stabbed to death during a fight that started inside Tunnel and spilled out onto the street. Davis's death was reminiscent of another tragedy that had occurred at Tunnel in 1999, the fatal overdose of Long Island teenager Jimmy Lyons.

Margaret Lyons's son Jimmy overdosed on a lethal mix of ecstasy and Ketamine that he consumed while celebrating his eighteenth birthday with friends at Tunnel in January of 1999. Lyons argues that the city of New York should shut Tunnel down, and she has since filed a $5 million civil racketeering, wrongful death, and negligence suit against Tunnel owner Peter Gatien. "How many more innocent people have to die before the city wakes up and shuts down these dangerous clubs?" Lyons said. "Every time I read about another victim at these clubs my wounds are reopened."

City officials and neighborhood activists have fought for years to put Gatien out of business. Over the years, however, Gatien has successfully defended himself in court against repeated charges of bribing police officials, receiving kickbacks from drug dealers who operate in his clubs, and participating in the murder of drug dealers and key people who might testify against him. In 1999, Gatien pleaded guilty to cheating on state taxes and served a ninety-day jail sentence. Steven Lewis, forty-seven, Gatien's longtime aide, was found guilty of conspiracy to distribute narcotics as well as aiding and abetting drug dealers at Gatien's clubs. He now faces up to twenty years in a federal prison, a long way from the glamorous lifestyle he enjoyed while working for Gatien.

Lewis admitted that Gatien earned much of his money from drugs. His confession about the origin of Gatien's profits was substantiated by Limelight techno promoter Lord Michael, who said, "I give Peter more money from drug sales than he makes at the door." Yet at Gatien's trial, Lord Michael denied having given Gatien any drug money. Regardless, Lewis stuck by his story and claimed that everyone working for Gatien is well aware that his clubs are a mecca of drugs.

New York clubland denizen Paul Kent accused Gatien of using

high profile models to bring big male spenders into his clubs. Kent said that he'd seen the likes of Naomi Campbell, Kate Moss, and Gisele Bundchen dance under the strobe lights at Gatien's clubs. "That's the best way to attract the elite," Kent said. "When word spreads that Naomi is going to show up, every rich man in New York rushes to get in the door. Although they know that their chances of getting close to Naomi are slim, it's guaranteed that Naomi will attract hordes of other hot, young models. One night at Limelight, I saw a stocky, bald businessman in a suit arrive single and leave at 3 A.M. with a gorgeous teenage model on each arm."

Kent claimed that drug dealers at Gatien's clubs openly work the dance floor and bathrooms armed with a seemingly endless supply of pills and powders, including ecstasy, acid, speed, cocaine, and Ketamine. "Some dealers I know make more than $15,000 a week working the clubs," he said. "Many of their clients are models who use drugs to stay thin. One dealer I know told me he's sold cocaine to many of the big supermodels. Drug use in New York nightclubs has reached epidemic proportions. It's easier to get drugs than a glass of water."

Before my friend Hilary left to respond to a client's page, she introduced me to an assistant model agent who confided that part of his job involves taking young models to clubs for sex and drugs. "Modeling is just one part of their jobs," said the agent, who introduced himself as Charles. "When I sign a girl up, I make sure to take them out to a club the first night, get them drunk and fuck them as soon as possible. Once you fuck them, the party begins. They get hooked on drugs and just want to party like animals. I'm able to bypass the lineup at all the big clubs because the bouncers know that I bring in beautiful girls who will entertain the people in the VIP section. Most of the models I bring are between fifteen and eighteen years old."

When I met him, Charles was with three young models, all dressed in skimpy tops and mini skirts. "You want some coke?" Charles asked me. After I declined, Charles drew a lush line of powder for his girls and presented them with a $20 bill. Mandy was the first to put the bill up to her nose and inhale. The other two models quickly followed suit as the bouncer watched with a smile. "This is paradise," Charles said. "I feel better here than I do in Club Med."

As the night wore on, the crowd began to thin out. Before I left, Charles offered me the services of one of his models. "She's all for you tonight," he said, putting his arm around my shoulder. "She's willing and able. All for you." After I declined his offer, I began to make my way toward the exit. On my way out, a dealer approached me and tried to sell me an eight ball. I refused but asked him how his night went. "Not bad," he replied. "Every beautiful bitch in the joint is high on my shit. I can't ask for anything more. I feel like the king."

CHAPTER 40

• • •

Behind the Catwalk

New York Fashion Week 2000 was the perfect way to see firsthand what goes on before a fashion show. The Chaiken show was a tribute to creative inspiration. Everyone backstage was an artist of some sort—model, jewelry designer, hair stylist, and make-up artist—each contributing their special flair to the show's theme. Clearly this is more of a visual than a verbal culture, although most of the models backstage didn't mind saying a few words. Amy, a striking seventeen-year-old model, was sitting next to supermodel Bridget Hall. "This is so much fun," Amy exclaimed. "I think we're going to put on a great show tonight."

Chaiken epitomizes the finest blend of class and cutting edge design. It is one of the most anticipated shows of the week, and lures a bevy of TV and print journalists from all over the world. In this crowd, TV star Joy Behar from ABC's *The View* caused a commotion by asking supermodel Frankie Rayder if her mother had given her that name because she wanted a boy. Rayder, a tall brunette whose sister Missy was also modeling at the Chaiken show, lashed out at Behar. "Fucking idiot," Raydar snapped to MAC makeup artist Gordon Espinet. "What is she, Joan Rivers on crack?"

Raydar doesn't like to take crap from anybody. She has worked hard for several years, to make it as a supermodel. She hit it big internationally in May 2000, when both she and her sister Missy appeared on a *Harper's Bazaar* cover, scantily clad in string bikinis.

"I don't think that Joy Behar meant any harm," said one of the Chaiken event's organizers. "But her timing was off. The last thing the girls need minutes before a show is to be insulted. It's a big distraction because they're so busy preparing a million things for the show."

After the show, I attended a party at a loft where the guests included numerous models and fashion dignitaries. Joints were passed around like candy while conversation was frequently interrupted by the loud popping sound of champagne bottles opening. Spirits were high and the mood was festive.

That night, everyone gossiped about how Gisele Bundchen had opted out of modeling for Carolina Herrera's show after the designer refused to pay her the $50,000 appearance fee she demanded. Gisele tried to downplay the incident by saying; "I'm only doing the biggies this year—Oscar [De La Renta], Michael Kors, Calvin [Klein], Donna [Karan]."

"Gisele is starting to think she's bigger than life," said one photographer. "It's about time she wakes up and realizes that money's not everything. There's no room for greed during important events like New York Fashion Week."

In this crowd, the name Gisele is more likely to conjure up the image of a hustler than a model. Makeup assistant Kim Freedman claimed that Gisele uses her outsized self-confidence to make her peers resentful. "I don't think she should steal headlines here with stupid stuff like how much money she wants to be paid," Freedman said. "This is not the place for that. Here, it's all about art, all about how to shine on the runway."

Meeting Freedman, one can see that she tries hard to be hip in a crowd that is considered society's trendiest. She was wearing a see-through T-shirt and a diamond nose ring. She said that she loves New York Fashion Week because it brings out the essence, spirit, and timelessness of true fashion that is seemingly absent from many designs that are so popular of late. "When you have Chaiken, Badgley Mischka, and Betsey Johnson showcasing their finest new creations in the same week, there's nothing more in fashion you can ask for," Freedman said. "Most of the outfits you'll see this week will blow your mind. It's so refreshing to see because the fashion industry has become so over-saturated with junk in recent years."

At the party, I met a stunning Swedish model named Paulina who was perched elegantly on an antique sofa. I sat down beside her and started talking. Paulina was schmoozing her way through New York City in an attempt to find a good agent. Although the striking blonde already had an agent in Sweden, she had ambitions of advancing her career by blazing a trail through New York. Paulina was the most philosophical of the models I met. Aside from the fact that she does yoga daily and is a big fan of Leonard Cohen, I discovered that Paulina was obsessed with spiritual growth and naturalism. She differed from all the other models I had met in that she didn't take drugs and possessed a talent for shrewd observation. "I'm not here to be famous or to try and sleep my way to the top like so many of the girls try to do," she said. "I'm here to learn and draw inspiration from the world's most incredible designers. I'm here to focus on my own growth, because when I grow, everything and everyone around me doesn't wither, they grow, too."

One of the highlights of Paulina's stay in New York was having access to the city's secondhand stores where she scoured the racks for bargains. Paulina, who has a keen eye for color, showed off the yellow handbag she bought at a thrift shop for four dollars. "Pretty funky style, eh," she says. "I bet that if a model would use this in a show thousands of people would go out and buy it. You see, you don't have to wear only Gucci or Calvin Klein to make a statement. I'm sure some of the best designers go to cool thrift shops for inspiration. Where else can you find such unique stuff?"

Paulina said she hoped to hook up with the right people so that she could model at next year's fashion week. "It's my dream to be part of this," she said. "It's different from anything else I've seen. I don't care much about Milan or Paris. New York's the place to be. I get a natural high just being here and experiencing the crazy energy. And the people are more down to earth and real than anywhere else I've been. I've been to fashion events in other cities and all that goes on is men trying to screw the young models. Not here. It's relaxed. Women can be women without feeling fear."

Reports on New York Fashion Week 2000 were overwhelmingly positive, highlighting a refreshing transition from the shocking designs of years past. "This could be a good sign of things to come," journalist Esmond Choueke said. "There was some real character and quality to the shows this week. Before this week, I was one who started believing that perhaps fashion is a dying industry, like so many articles in the media have insinuated. But if the designers in the industry stick to respecting fashion as an art and not as a means to shock people, I think that there's hope after all to keep supermodels showing off cool designs on the catwalk for years to come."

CHAPTER 41

• • •

On to South Beach

Winter, Miami Beach: my final stop on this wild odyssey. Every year thousands of models from all over the world who are seeking work flock to Florida's beautiful South Beach. Tourists walking along the trendy Ocean Drive strip cannot miss seeing a camera crew shooting ads with models at almost any hour of the day. For example, my first night in town I went to the News Cafe at around 11:30 P.M. I noticed a crew sitting on the patio shooting an ad for beer. In any other city a shoot like this would attract a crowd of onlookers, at least out of curiosity. In South Beach, however, it's routine. Nobody at the News Cafe seemed to care. Nobody crowded around the cameras or models. In South Beach, seeing a modeling shoot is as novel as seeing a car go by.

The next morning I hooked up with two models I knew from my hometown of Montreal. Elise and Valerie were sipping champagne and smoking a joint in their rented one-and-a-half-room apartment at the corner of 11th Street and Washington Avenue, which is in one of South Beach's seedier neighborhoods. Outside, it's common to see street hustlers rubbing elbows with fashion photographers, models, and golden agers. It was 9:30 A.M. The two Montreal models were getting ready for a hard day's work. Elise, eighteen, had a photo shoot for a Spanish lifestyle magazine. Valerie, twenty-two, whose last job in Montreal was strutting her stuff at the popular strip club Chez Paree, was doing a test shoot for a soft porn magazine. As they listened to the sounds of Bjork blaring out of an old, beat-up ghetto-blaster, they seem strangely detached, as though the memories drifting through their minds were scenes from someone else's life.

"It's all fuckin' bullshit here, but it beats being in the freezing cold in Montreal," Elise said. "The only good thing is the night life. When I first came here I discovered clubs that make clubs in Montreal look like nursery schools. They're so wild. In some of them you can buy cocaine and ecstasy at the bar. But here people are so ugly, so fake. They all think they're above everyone else. The men in the modeling business are gross, they just want to fuck you. The women are bitches. One day they're your best friend, the next day they're telling everyone how fucked up you are because they're afraid you might be chosen for a job they want. You can't trust anybody here."

Elise and Valerie are among several hundred Canadian models who flock each year to Miami's South Beach, hoping to become fashion's next pretty face. South Beach, a bustling area of topless beaches, historic architecture, crime, and nightlife, has become one of America's fashion meccas. Ever since the 1980s, when *Miami Vice* brought South Beach international exposure with its violent but stylish portrayal of an area steeped in crime and clad in Don Johnson's sockless loafers, fashion moguls from all over the world have set up shop here.

"It's a crazy world here," said Elise, her low-cut, tight-fitting blue lace dress revealing more than a touch of cleavage. "You're at the mercy of the men who run the industry. And if you don't play the game you won't get work. It's that simple. You got to eat with them, drink with them and sleep with them. If you don't, you'll lose out to the next girl who will do all that. The competition here is crazy. Everybody is out for themself."

Valerie admitted that she enjoys partying and doing drugs almost every night. She spends hours each morning covering eye circles and blemishes on her skin with foundation and concealer. "Every night I go to clubs and get wasted," she said. "The next morning I have to spend hours applying makeup to try to make my skin look fresh for that day's shoot." This morning, Valerie had puffy eyes from coming home at 6:00 A.M. and waking up two hours later for work. She applied cold towels to make the puffiness go down. "It better go down soon," she said. "I don't want to lose this job. It's expensive here. I need the cash." When Valerie's short of cash, she moonlights at a downtown Miami strip club. "I'm lucky 'cause I have other ways of making money," she said. "I hate doing it but I'll never go hungry. I just wish that I could get enough work as a model. I don't want to have to dance nude my whole life. It's a tough life."

Both Elise and Valerie have applied to the biggest model agencies in South Beach, including Boss Models and Next Management. "We've hooked up with smaller agents 'cause it's too competitive to get into the big agencies." Valerie said. "There's too much competition in the big agencies. It's better to find somebody smaller who will spend more time trying to find work for you."

According to model scout Vincent Lopiccola, Quebec models rank among the most popular in South Beach. "Everyone in the business here loves to hook up with French girls from Quebec," Lopiccola says. "They have a reputation for being so hot. Hotter than the Swedes and the Latinos. Loads of fun. The agents love them because most of them will do anything, and I mean anything, to get hired. One well-known agent brags to me about how he's never hired a girl from Montreal who didn't give him head the same day he hired her."

Elise and Valerie admitted that they'd learned every trick in the book about how models hide traces of their drug injections from the night before. Elise said she knows models who shoot up heroin under their toenails, under their tongue, or between toes to hide any track marks. "Before a shoot I have seen models cover up needle marks with body foundation. It's a crazy world here. But I'm strong. I won't leave until I finish doing my business here. I want to go back to Montreal with a lot of American dollars in my pocket. And I'm willing to do whatever it takes to realize my dream."

EPILOGUE

• • •

Last Call—The Death of a Legend

Before ending this book, I feel it is important to examine the life and death of fashion's most famous designer and personality, the great Gianni Versace. Without Versace, no book on modeling or fashion would be complete. Versace was brilliant, ruthless—an inspiration to anyone interested in success.

It was not until Gianni Versace was found dead outside his art deco mansion in Miami's South Beach area that his killer, Andrew Cunanan, captured international headlines. Immediately after Versace was murdered on July 15, 1997, Cunanan's mug shot was plastered across news broadcasts and wanted posters in bars and cafes. Versace was shot shortly before 9 A.M. on the front steps of his home as he returned from buying magazines at the News Cafe three blocks away. He was pronounced dead at 9:15 A.M. at Jackson Memorial Hospital's Ryder Trauma Center in Miami. Cunanan had shot Versace twice in the back of the head.

After he killed Versace, Cunanan had more than a thousand law enforcement agents on his trail, setting off one of the biggest manhunts in recent history. Cunanan was also suspected of murdering four other people. He began his killing spree in late April 1997. At the time he was in serious financial trouble. He owed a total of $46,000 to Neiman Marcus and three other stores. He had charged $21,000 on one American Express account alone. When Cunanan's body was discovered in a houseboat a few miles from where he had gunned down Versace, a .40 caliber gun—the same type used in the killing of Versace and two other victims—was found near his body. Cunanan had commited suicide with the same gun by shooting himself in the mouth. The houseboat's owner, Torsten Reineck, a German businessman who owned a gay health spa in Las Vegas, was wanted on fraud charges in Germany. Although Reineck had not been in the boat for several months, police said it was possible that Reineck used the boat as home base.

Investigators did not rule out the possibility that Cunanan might have once known Versace. Cunanan knew several of the other people he murdered, including his ex-lover Jeffrey Trail, who was found on April 29, 1997, rolled up in a carpet in the Minneapolis apartment of architect David Madson. Subsequently, Cunanan was suspected of killing Madson, who was also a former lover. Although no motive has ever been determined by police for Cunanan's murder spree, it's clear that he had been infatuated with both Versace and Trail. Trail's sister Lisa, who had had dinner with her brother and Cunanan a couple of years before the murders, told a *New York Times* reporter that Cunanan idolized her brother. "When Jeff got a haircut, Andrew had to have the exact same haircut," Lisa said. "When Jeff went to San Francisco and got a certain style of baseball cap, Andrew had to go to San Francisco and get the very same cap. When Jeff grew a goatee, Andrew grew a goatee."

In light of the circumstances surrounding Trail's murder, many people speculated that Versace once knew Cunanan. People close to Versace tried to dismiss this claim as nonsense, saying that Versace was just the victim of a deranged killer. But in the weeks after Versace's murder, it became clear that Versace and Cunanan had met on at least several occasions. A former roommate of Cunanan's told John Quinones of ABC News that Cunanan knew Versace. "They had met previously. Very, very briefly," Erik Greenman told Quinones. "Just over a few cocktails and stuff like that. That was the extent of what I know from that, but he did meet Versace and some of the models at the time." Quinones asked Greenman if Cunanan bragged about meeting Versace. "It wasn't a brag at all," Greenman replied. "He didn't particularly like Versace. You know, didn't like his designs either. He thought they were pretty hideous, actually. The thing he liked about Versace was he was an older gay man that had power and wealth and admiration, which is everything that Andrew wanted. . . . Because Andrew couldn't have that. Couldn't have what Versace had . . . I mean, that's what Andrew lived for."

Another young man, a former lover of Cunanan, charged that perhaps Cunanan wanted revenge against Versace for snubbing him as a model. "Andrew approached Versace about doing some modeling and Versace didn't seem to be too interested. It must have happened around the early nineties. Several days after it happened I spoke to Andrew on the phone and he was calling Versace all kinds of nasty names. He told me that he wished that something bad would happen to Versace because he was too arrogant. It really seemed like he had a vengeance for Versace."

Some people speculated that Versace and Cunanan might have been lovers once. A volunteer at a nonprofit San Diego coffeehouse said that Cunanan told him that he would seek revenge on whoever had given him AIDS. "He was mentioning some of the things he had done sexually," Mike Dudley said. "I explained the things were sort of in the gray area and he should take greater precautions." Dudley said that Cunanan became enraged, kicking a wall and vowing to get even with whoever had infected him. But Cunanan's reaction was only based on an assumption about the repercussions of his promiscuous past. He had never told anyone that he had tested positive for HIV. In fact, the autopsy on Cunanan revealed that he was not HIV-positive. "Andrew was just paranoid because he had had so many lovers," says Robbie Garrett, a former lover of Cunanan's. "He didn't want to take an HIV test because he was afraid of getting bad news. But he seemed convinced that he had AIDS."

Versace himself had not been tested for HIV before he died. He certainly had many affairs with men young enough to be his sons. "It seemed as if Gianni had a different toyboy each week," recalls an ex-lover. "It didn't surprise me when I heard that he got shot. He led an extremely flamboyant lifestyle. The first thing I thought was that Cunanan must be an ex-lover trying to get revenge."

A former associate of Versace, who wishes to remain anonymous, believes it may be possible that Versace and Cunanan were once lovers. But there is no way, the associate insists, that Versace would have done anything to make Cunanan want to kill him. "Gianni was promiscuous. He liked to have young male lovers, but he was good to all of them. He treated them with respect and wouldn't do anything to harm them. It's possible Cunanan might have been involved with him at one point, although no one will ever know for sure. But it's clear that Gianni didn't do anything to warrant being murdered. Cunanan was clearly out of control. Until his body was found, every gay man in the world lived in fear of becoming his next victim."

Gianni Versace was fifty years old when he was gunned down by Cunanan. He was one of the most respected designers ever. Versace had revolutionized the presentation of fashion. He filled the front row seats at his fashion shows with celebrity faces. He then used those celebrities in high-profile ad campaigns. He hired top fashion photographers such as Bruce Weber, Helmut Newton, Herb Ritts, and Richard Avedon. Courtney Love, Madonna, Jon Bon Jovi, Elton John, Patricia Arquette and Prince were all Versace models at one time or another. "He was the most warm, caring, sensitive family man," Jon Bon Jovi said.

A week after Versace's death, more than 2,000 people gathered in Milan's gothic cathedral to honor him. Before the memorial service, many of Versace's close friends paid their final respects in the courtyard garden of Versace's downtown palazzo, where the urn containing his ashes sat on a simple altar. The mourners included Carolyn Bessette-Kennedy, Naomi Campbell, Eva Herzigova, Anna Wintour, Sting, and Diana, Princess of Wales, who was to die tragically one month later. Diana wore a black dress set off by a single string of pearls. "He was the best friend I had," Diana said. "He had a golden touch. His instincts rarely failed him. His memory will live on forever." Elton John and Sting performed a solemn rendition of Psalm 23, "The Lord is my shepherd" that brought the attendants to tears. "Gianni and I were like brothers," Elton John said. "We were very similar. We had the same taste. He taught me about art, and I taught him about music. He was someone on my level of thinking. We were continually trying to improve our creativity. You never left him without being stimulated about some aspect of fashion or art or life. There was no fear with Gianni. Sometimes he was right, and sometimes he was wrong. Every artist is like that."

Many of Versace's rival designers attended the memorial service as well, including Karl Lagerfeld, Gianfranco Ferre, Carla Fendi, and Giorgio Armani. "Today the shocking tragedy of what happened is overwhelming, and I can't believe he is no longer among us," Valentino Garavani said the day Versace was killed. Garavani was close friends with Versace. "I saw him a few days ago and he was laughing, enjoying life and the beautiful things that surrounded him and that were part of him. . . . I can't believe anybody would want to do this to him."

Born in the town of Reggio Calabria in the south of Italy, Gianni Versace grew up watching his mother, Franca, run a successful clothing boutique. Franca Versace, a talented dressmaker herself, employed more than forty seamstresses on her staff. After finishing high school, Gianni joined his mother's business. From that point on, he only wanted to be a successful designer. "Designing came to me," he once said. "I didn't have to move. . . . When you are born in a place such as Calabria, and there is beauty all around—a Roman bath, a Greek remain—you cannot help but be influenced by the classical past."

In 1972, Gianni was recruited by several Italian fashion houses in Milan to create collections. His gift for design was remarkable. Versace joined Italy's elite group of fanciful designers such as Armani, Valentino, and Benetton. His spectacular designs challenged French dominance, and placed Milan on par with London, Paris, and New York as a mecca of design. "He was the most innovative designer ever," says a colleague. "He had a flair for creating patterns that were original pieces of art. He was a student of history and he tried to combine the past and present in his designs like nobody else. He was to fashion . . . what Louis Armstrong was to music—an innovator."

The head office of the Versace fashion house, founded in 1978, is in Milan. It is run and owned by family members. Versace's brother Santo is president of the company, and his sister Donatella is creative director. In 1993, Versace battled a rare cancer of the inner ear. Versace vowed to overcome his health problems. "There were a lot of tests and scans and treatments that were hard," Versace said. "But as I said, I'm very optimistic. I never fall down. I always fight."

Since Gianni's death, it hasn't been easy for the Versaces to maintain the reputation their brother worked so hard to create. Donatella Versace fell out with several of Gianni's close associates as she tried to reshape the Versace empire. Antonio D'Amico, Gianni Versace's companion of many years, publicly criticized Donatella's changes to the fashion house. Donatella dismissed D'Amico's claims. "My relationship with Antonio is exactly as it was when Gianni was alive," she said. "I respected him as the boyfriend of my brother, but I never liked him as a person. So the relationship stayed the same."

The surviving Versace siblings have spent millions to protect themselves from bad publicity. In May 1999, the Versaces managed to cease the publication of a highly controversial biography of their brother that would have revealed many negative things about their own lifestyles. *Undressed: The Life and Times of Gianni Versace*, by Christopher Mason, depicted the Versaces as being unfair to their employees and having a flair for overspending. Author Mason said that while he was researching his book, the Versaces went to great lengths to make his job unpleasant. According to Mason, the Versaces contacted the people he'd interviewed and tried to convince them to retract their statements. Mason said the Versaces offered the sources legal documents for them to sign and contacted other potential sources, trying to persuade them not to cooperate.

A spokesperson for Mason's publisher, Little, Brown and Co., said the book was scrapped because of legalities. "In mid-March, we received letters [from the Versace attorneys] threatening legal action. . . . We agreed with Christopher Mason that it could not be published in its present form, and he withdrew it."

Little, Brown and Co. had announced the book deal with Mason the day Gianni Versace died. The grieving Versaces were upset that Mason was being portrayed as a close friend of Gianni, when in fact they had met on only a few occasions in 1997. The Versaces considered Mason an opportunist. They claim he accepted a six-figure advance from Little, Brown and Co. for what one family member called "cashing in on our family's tragedy, the death of Gianni."

Ed Filapowski, the Versaces' New York press agent, said the Versaces were pleased with the final outcome. "It's apparent that Little, Brown and Co. lost confidence in this manuscript. It was full of inaccuracies and misrepresentations and clearly could not be salvaged. We did what anyone else would do under the circumstances, which is to defend ourselves and our name."

Still, Christopher Mason maintains that his facts were accurate. "I felt completely confident about my reporting, and I had substantial documentation," Mason told *New York Times* journalist Cathy Horyn. "I felt, sure, we were having problems, but they could be easily surmounted. . . . I certainly got the feeling that a lot of people were intimidated by the implications of talking to me for this book."

This was not the first time that the Versaces successfully took on the media. They have sued several British publications for libel, either winning in court or settling for damages and an apology. According to entertainment journalist Martin Smith, the Versace family is endangering freedom of the press by intimidating publishers with high-priced lawyers. "I can understand the family's concerns, but it can set an ugly precedent," Smith says. "The public has a right to decide whether or not an article or book is true. Nobody should be able to stop publication. If people think that they have been libeled after the book comes out, then they have the right to sue for damages. But not before."

A close friend of Donatella Versace admits that the Versace family often tries to control what's printed about them. "Sometimes I can't blame them, because the media has written so many disparaging things about them," the friend says. "But I don't think anybody has a right to stop a book from coming out, no matter what it's about. I do sympathize, however, with the Versaces, because they've been through so much. They just want to be left alone to tend to their business."

Six months after Gianni Versace's death, his family filed a lawsuit to block the release of his autopsy photos as police closed the case. Versace's family had dropped earlier objections to the release of any family financial information in the files, but remained determined to prevent the public from seeing the autopsy photos. "We're just asking for respect for a guy who was a murder victim," Versace family spokesperson Lou Colasuonno said. "Gianni Versace was the victim of a maniacal serial killer. And we should treat him like a victim—with respect."

Index